DIVINE MADNESS

Having recently sailed down from Long Island, the *Pleasure Dome* had unofficially been open for gambling, first up north, and now down south, for months.

In a sense these sudden demands were a blessing, allowing Harlan surcease from the pain of thinking about Laina and his growing awareness of the uncomfortably close situation. In fact, his greatest strain came from the burgeoning guilt he tried to deny, of which he was growing ever more conscious. He had realized his enormous treachery in regard to everyone surrounding him—Alex, Matthew, Vivian, and particularly Laina. He had often fancied that he would have his fill of her; that would finally dispel the urgency, the pain of wanting. But as the weeks passed, he was astonished to discover the powerful physical urge, the drive in him to be with her. In the midst of all the chaos, he found himself inventing ways and means to be with her more regularly. He even considered personally supervising the remodeling of the rooms at the Broadbeach Club just to be near her in Long Island. He knew none of this made sense; he was thinking wildly, irrationally, and wondering if obsession might be a form of madness. . . .

EXCITING BESTSELLERS FROM ZEBRA

HERITAGE (1100, $3.75)
by Lewis Orde
Beautiful innocent Leah and her two brothers were forced by the holocaust to flee their parent's home. A courageous immigrant family, each battled for love, power and their very lifeline—their HERITAGE.

FOUR SISTERS (1048, $3.75)
by James Fritzhand
From the ghettos of Moscow to the glamor and glitter of the Winter Palace, four elegant beauties are torn between love and sorrow, danger and desire—but will forever be bound together as FOUR SISTERS.

BYGONES (1030, $3.75)
by Frank Wilkinson
Once the extraordinary Gwyneth set eyes on the handsome aristocrat Benjamin Whisten, she was determined to foster the illicit love affair that would shape three generations—and win a remarkable woman an unforgettable dynasty!

A TIME FOR ROSES (946, $3.50)
by Agatha Della Anastasi
A family saga of riveting power and passion! Fiery Magdalena places her marriage vows above all else—until her husband wants her to make an impossible choice. She has always loved and honored—but now she can't obey!

THE LION'S WAY (900, $3.75)
by Lewis Orde
An all-consuming saga that spans four generations in the life of troubled and talented David, who struggles to rise above his immigrant heritage and rise to a world of glamour, fame and success!

A WOMAN OF THE DAWN (1066, $3.75)
by Antonia Van-Loon
From the excitement and joy of the turn-of-the-century, to the tragedy and triumph of World War I, beautiful Tracy Sullivan created a mighty empire—and cherished a secret love!

Available wherever paperbacks are sold, or order direct from the Publisher. Send cover price plus 50¢ per copy for mailing and handling to Zebra Books, 475 Park Avenue South, New York, N.Y. 10016. DO NOT SEND CASH.

THE PLEASURE DOME

BY
JUDITH LIEDERMAN

**ZEBRA BOOKS
KENSINGTON PUBLISHING CORP.**

ZEBRA BOOKS

are published by

KENSINGTON PUBLISHING CORP.
475 Park Avenue South
New York, N.Y. 10016

Copyright © 1981 by Judith Liederman
Reprinted by arrangement with Arbor House Publishing
Company. All rights reserved.

All rights reserved. No part of this book may be reproduced in any form or by any means without the prior written consent of the Publisher, excepting brief quotes used in reviews.

Printed in the United States of America

For my daughters
Melissa and Madeleine—
with much love.

In Xanadu did Kubla Khan
  A stately pleasure-dome decree:
Where Alph the sacred river ran
Through caverns measureless to man
  Down to a sunless sea.

> SAMUEL TAYLOR COLERIDGE
> "Kubla Khan"

I.
DISPERSAL
1941-1942

CHAPTER 1

Looking back, if Laina Eastman were to remember only one particular day in all of her childhood it would probably be the day it ceased—when childhood abruptly came to an end and she entered that fragile, bittersweet, and much misunderstood world of women. Not that she recognized the absolute finality of that transition then, but there was no doubt that the summer of 1941 was a turning point in her life, just as it was in the lives of millions of others throughout the world.

Everywhere she went the talk was of war and the London Blitz. She could escape it for a while at an Andy Hardy movie, or dreaming over a Glenn Miller broadcast, and there was always the Hit Parade to look forward to on Saturday night. The rich flocked to their American clubs and resorts to while away that oppressive summer, their European playgrounds being closed for the duration. No one seemed even dimly aware that this might be the last of those slow, shimmering, bandstand summers.

She had walked alone, as far up the beach as it was possible to go. It was about five o'clock, the time of day when the sun and sea wash an almost painfully clear light over everything. She felt adventuresome, free, satisfied with being fifteen—a child really—until that day. As this was her second summer at the Broadbeach, she could not in all honesty equate herself with the "Broadbeach brats," a title of dubious distinction granted only to those teenagers who had grown up at the famous seaside resort. Their families had spent the summers and winters of their lives here at the Goldmarks' hotel or at the other one in Miami Beach, the Hibiscus Gardens.

Laina had almost reached the last cabana court at the end of the two-mile strip of beach. No Man's Land, they called it then, the less expensive cabanas that nobody who was anybody wanted. It was deserted as she approached, strangely quiet, with only the occasional rasp of a seagull as it dipped and swooped upwards again from the foam-scalloped shore.

And then she saw them. The woman was not easy to miss with her lion's mane of sun-drenched hair and her smoothly bronzed body. But it was not she on whom the young girl focused at first, it was *him*. That face—handsome and familiar, so familiar to her. She stopped, momentarily stunned, collecting her thoughts . . . Could it be? Yes, it surely was Manny Gaynes, the famous comic, movie star and vaudevillian, there in the flesh, kissing Mrs. Goldmark, the resort owner's wife. Mrs. Matthew Goldmark. Laina stood half-hidden by the wall of the cabana.

Manny Gaynes was the star act appearing at the hotel for the weekend. Every week a different star attraction was featured in their beautiful Twilight Room. Last week it was Harry Richmond and his top hat, next weekend it would be Sophie Tucker resplendent in her beads.

As Laina watched, unable to leave the scene, Faye Goldmark lay limply in his lap, a leaf of wilted lettuce. He stroked her hair, and now and then he kissed her. He seemed different now, very different from his movie roles.

Faye Goldmark, famous for her long legs and short shorts, was wearing a very brief two-piece bathing suit.

THE PLEASURE DOME

The top half had become undone somehow. In one quick motion, Manny Gaynes tossed it into the sand and pulled the elasticized satin bottoms below her knees. Laina, cowering in her corner, was rooted to the spot. She had never seen anything that even hinted of sex except in movies—certainly not in her own home. Her parents had been separated for years and her mother, a Catholic, had given the impression of being celibate until she died two years ago. Sometimes Laina wondered if that was at the root of the problem between her parents—the mixed marriage.

She ran all the way home and locked herself in her room. The cooling, louvered windows of the old French chateau-style house were open and she could hear the occasional whoosh of blowing reeds and rushes. She thought about her father then, wondering what he would say if he knew. But she realized she could never tell him such a thing.

Alex Eastman, Laina's father, was one of the richest men at the Broadbeach. But he was in no way favored by the management, although he knew Matthew Goldmark and even his father, Jessie. They had locked horns in one "deal" or another, then retreated quietly to their separate corners. Throughout the years, their businesses occasionally touched. Alex owned a vast string of ballrooms on the Eastern seaboard and while he didn't feature the name stars that the Goldmarks did, he had at one time or another hired every big band of the day. He was not allowed many hotel privileges nor was he even invited to the Goldmarks' table during showtimes. There was little doubt that Alex was considered a most eligible bachelor. He was rich and enormously attractive, with his compact, disciplined body and sentient blue eyes. He had always been wooed by women and his susceptibility to them was probably closer to the root of his marital problems than he cared to admit.

When he first married Inez Brian he considered her someone quite special. To Alex, who had never even had a friend who wasn't Jewish, she was the essential *shiksa*. He was enthralled by her gentile eyes (to him that meant a certain placidity of expression), her auburn hair and her doll-like figure. Her nervous intellect excited him. He had met her while working as a bouncer in a dime-a-dance palace. She was the bookkeeper in the back room, often working late nights like himself, shy and disapproving of what took place out front. He responded to her romantic, virtuous nature and married her before the onset of the depression. It was a period of optimism, and he was bursting with plans for his future.

Inez had promised to bring up the children in her husband's faith but no sooner had she given birth to their first child, a son, than she regretted her hasty and emotional decision. She resented Alex's eager, romantic friends from the lower east side of New York. She misunderstood their urgent idealism, their bleeding hearts, branding them either anarchists or socialists. In fact as he remembered it now, the only thing they ever agreed upon was Franklin Roosevelt's vigorous pragmatic liberalism, as an answer to the nation's growing despair.

It was of course no answer to her own. His work, the hours he kept, his burning ambition combined to make her feel excluded from his life; her own insecurities, together with what she felt she had given up for him, caused her to feel gnawing dissatisfaction. Without the solace of the church, she slowly began to disintegrate.

Alex gradually found religion. He kept all the Jewish

holidays, donated large sums of money to Jewish charities, and planned his son's Bar Mitzvah almost from the moment he was born. He told Inez that this renewed discovery of God was due to the terrible events taking place in Europe—but even as he said it he felt somehow culpable, as if he were not telling her the whole truth. Somewhere inside he sensed his own rebellion against what he considered his big mistake, marriage to the wrong woman. He decided, belatedly, that he was not cut out for marriage in general.

Nowadays, he enjoyed a sort of fraternal rivalry with the Goldmarks, warily watching each other's moves. He was considered something of a maverick because he didn't avail himself of the Broadbeach Hotel's luxurious facilities, most of which cost extra. He had joined because it was simply a pleasant beach facility near his home, a place to take the children during the summer—a place where a growing girl might make the right friends, *contacts*. Most of all there were the indoor and outdoor swimming pools that he and his son were so addicted to. They loved to rush into the icy ocean early in the morning and finish off in the indoor pool, race feverishly, then race home for a huge breakfast.

CHAPTER 2

At six o'clock the sun was playing reckless games with the July evening, one minute potent, the next remote. The Mediterranean pink stucco of Clara Goldmark's dressing room in the Broadbeach Hotel was illuminated by fickle rays that seemed alive with particles of dust. From below she could hear the band playing Latin music for cocktail dancing, a woman's seductive laugh. In the distance, she heard the soft ping of tennis balls, a *goyish* sound. Her ear was still not attuned to the music of affluence.

Infused among her senses was the sound of the sea—the complex yet monotonous cadence of her life for more than a decade. Clara tended to think of her life in terms of decades, crystalline chunks of life, like rock candy—which made it seem sweeter but shorter—more essential. Not that she was complaining; she was not. She had savored life, enjoyed it thoroughly from the time she met Jessie Goldmark in the Williamsburg section of Brooklyn.

The baby of the family, she was eighteen when they had come over from Frankfurt, where her family was considered affluent. In Brooklyn, they were hardly more than another immigrant family, treated unceremoniously. She was disappointed in America, and while Williamsburg was far from elegant, it was *alive*.

Her father had set up a little millinery business in downtown Brooklyn. But Clara was lonely. Her sister Mia was engaged to marry a young man from an orthodox family, and because he refused to leave Germany, she had remained there with him. Clara's brother had migrated to Austria earlier and was prospering in millinery there.

Clara rarely thought about that—about the early beginnings—the old country—the old ways. She had buried it long ago when she married Jessie Goldmark. But sometimes she ached to hear the *Mamaloshen,* that dark secret language that her parents had sometimes spoken, the soul of a people. When she first met him, she thought he had almost forgotten his heritage. Born into an educated German-Jewish family, he seemed as ignorant of his Jewishness as he was unaware of anti-Semitism.

She stood before her mirror, picked up her pearls from the dressing table, South Sea pearls like plovers' eggs. She bent her head and lifted her arms to clasp them around her still smooth throat, as she had done almost every evening for the last ten years. Jessie liked her to look regal. Then suddenly she dropped them heavily on the table. She felt guilty wearing an elegant Mainbocher gown while her sister or brother might be at this moment prisoners of the Nazis. The news from Germany on the condition there was scant; but the situation did not look good at all. Mia's son-in-law had already been taken to a camp for "resettlement" according to the last terrified letter she had received from her sister, almost a year ago.

A letter lay open on her dressing table where she had dropped it down with sadness that morning. It was from a cousin in Warsaw. The news was not good. No one had had any news of her sister Mia, or her married daughter, in over five months now. As for her brother, she hadn't heard from him since the war in Europe began.

Beneath her window the dying strains of the popular

song "These Foolish Things" drifted, swayed, then settled down to haunt her. She was overcome with a nostalgia, not so much for what had been, as for what could never be again. Clara Goldmark was approaching those peckish years when nothing seemed quite right today, and almost everything was better yesterday.

She really didn't care for the resort hotel business, didn't take to it like her daughter-in-law, Faye. Faye was cut out for it, and if she sometimes appeared a little wanton, it was only because her childlike nature—her unaffected appreciation of the pleasure principle, enabled her to escape from the numbing boredom of this business. Men buzzed around her like flies. She had a way with men. Clara wished a little of it would rub off on her daughter Vivian.

But Clara rarely complained to her husband about the business lest he somehow blame their son Matthew. After all, it was Matthew who had really conceived it, fallen in love with it from the start. Perhaps he had thought that was what Faye wanted. He had never really accepted his father's leather goods business and, she thought with a sharp stab of pain, Jessie had never really accepted it either.

She heard the familiar click of ice cubes that heralded Jessie's entrance into a room. He usually carried a glass of limeade or lemonade to assuage an unquenchable thirst, a condition brought on, he said, by advancing age and hotel cooking. Jessie Goldmark was tall and heavyset with warm, dark eyes. While he was far from handsome, his florid complexion and white hair were arresting. He didn't look like anyone else in the world.

Jessie fell into the big chair in the living room, glass in hand. The stucco walls kept the heat out, and the ocean kept the room blessedly cool. At times even he, like his son, was amused by the contradiction of this pink Mediterranean palazzo of a hotel being situated at the eastern tip of Long Island. But there was no doubt in his mind that their hotel had turned the small, craggy fishing village of Broadbeach into one of the most successful summer resorts in the east.

"So, Clara, are you almost ready?" His words carried only the slightest trace of a German accent. She came into the living room now, and she could see by his face that he thought she looked beautiful.

"I must shower and change," he said, "but first sit down for a moment, please." He laid his head on the back of the deep, comfortable chair and looked directly at her. Jessie had also received a letter today.

"I want to talk to you. About the war—this place," he said, making a wide arc with his hands to indicate the hotel. "You've never really liked it here, have you?" he asked, looking into her eyes. "You have tolerated it for me—for Matthew."

"Oh, I don't know—it has its moments," she smiled.

"The life is artificial and burdensome, isn't it?" He seemed to be feeding her the lines, as if that was what he wanted to hear.

"A little like living in a glass house perhaps." She wanted to please him. "Jessie, what are you trying to say?"

"Well, we may have to give up this place, for the duration anyway. With war imminent the navy wants to take it over for a naval training base. It will make a wonderful training base, what with the beachfront."

"Will they rent it or buy it? What sort of money are we talking about?" she said, suddenly the pragmatist.

"I may donate the property," he said, sipping at his drink.

"Can we afford such a grand gesture?"

Jessie put the glass down. "Well, frankly no. But it is what I'd *like* to do. We haven't discussed finances yet."

"Perhaps it would be the best thing for Vivian. After all, here she's almost a fixture. We're *old* parents for her, Jessie, and if anything happens to us, I want her to be married, settled down—looked after."

"My, my. We are not *that* old."

"Still, I would feel better seeing Vivian married to a nice boy—like a lawyer."

"No sooner does a boy enter law school than he is automatically cleansed of sin and pronounced 'nice boy' by you. I wonder what happened to the bad lawyers, the shysters. Ach, Jewish mothers," Jessie said, shaking his head and smiling. "They only want to marry off their daughters and keep their sons at home—for themselves."

"Did I do that?"

"No. No, but you would have liked to, admit it."

"Nonsense," Clara snapped, "I'm glad Matthew is married."

"To Faye?" He sat up straight in his chair.

"Happily, I might add," she said emphatically.

"Well, I suppose Matthew wouldn't be happy unless someone gave him a hard time. He is a bit spoiled."

Clara rose, annoyed, and moved gracefully around the room. "You are too hard on him, Jessie, you always were. You wanted him to tear the world apart, and yet you handed it to him ready-made, all pink and shining by he sea."

"He could have never made it in the leather business."

"Then you could have let him sink or swim. It builds character."

"You never would have permitted that," Jessie sighed. It was a tired subject. "I am anxious to tell Matthew the news about the hotel. He doesn't adjust to change too well."

He rose, came over to the mirror where Clara stood absently patting her hair. He clasped the pearls around her neck. "Without them it would be like going down to dinner naked," he whispered intimately. "Tradition," he said, "tradition is very important in this business."

"Tradition stifles progress," she replied with a half-smile as he closed the door of the shower. Clara removed the pearls and carefully dropped them onto the dressing table. They weighed a ton tonight.

CHAPTER 3

Matthew Goldmark, shaggily handsome and rich, had considered himself a loser until he met Faye Eisman. To the gentle Matthew, Faye was well named—she was pure fey—an imp, a beautiful toy. She taught him what fun was. He had had very little in his life until then. He could not believe his good fortune when she accepted a date with him, then later, another. Soon he was coming down from his parents' home in Habersville, New York every weekend and staying at her elegant Park Avenue apartment with the approval of her family and his. It seemed to him that Fay's personality was an open and direct rebellion to her staid and correct family, with their liveried servants and their six-course meals served in the oak-paneled dining room with its subdued lighting. To Matthew it never seemed bright enough to see what he was eating or, more importantly, to see Faye's extraordinary hair, which ranged in colors from honey brown to golden blonde and which she wore long and heavy around her small face. He would not have known what he was eating, in any case—he was that much in love.

Matthew had asked himself, why? Why would she fall in love with him when there must have been a hundred more romantic suitors to choose from?

The truth was that there were not a hundred "suitors," in fact not more than one or two, and they did not appear to be serious. Perhaps the young men were afraid of her. Afraid of her enormous appreciation of beautiful things, of the way she smoothed her expensive leather purse with the heel of her hand, or the way she whipped up the back of her sheared beaver coat smartly before she sat down so as not to damage the "puch" and whenever possible flicked the chair daintily with a handkerchief.

Faye at eighteen was a freshman at Finch College a sort of girls' finishing school in those years, and she didn't get to meet many boys. It was mostly through her older sister's boyfriend, Owen, that she met any at all. No, she considered herself quite fortunate to have found such an eligible suitor so early in the mating game. She basked in the sunshine of his obvious adoration and fell in love with his loving her. Most of all she yearned to get away from her family. And nobody any better had come along—not even as good. Matthew was charming and refined, with his quiet smile and serene expression. He was bright, educated, and of German-Jewish background like herself. And he came from a wealthy family.

He met her at a reunion of his prep school at the Waldorf Astoria. Although he had attended prep school in New England, and graduated from Yale University, he rarely left Habersville and he didn't get down to Manhattan as often as he would have liked. He had considered the city a wonderland of cultural beauty and intellectual excitement. New York, New York—the very rhythm of the name was a staccato zing like the city itself—and like Faye.

As a child, Matthew adored his father as no one else. He loved Jessie still, but nothing he did seemed to please him. Vivian, his sister, who appeared cool-headed and shrewd, pleased her father, but Matthew was too fine, too soft spoken, too self-effacing, his pale gray eyes too melancholy to please Jessie Goldmark. Now and then Jessie saw flashes of business acumen in him. Nevertheless, Jessie feared for his son's financial future. The Goldmarks never knew what poverty was. Jessie had made sure of *that* . . . He had maneuvered his way through the Great Depression relatively unscathed, keeping his money out of the market and in shoes instead. People would always need shoes, he would say. He had come to America poor but determined . . . Even now, Matthew still regarded his father as martinet and benefactor.

When Faye and Matthew began planning their honeymoon, they chose the Breakers in Palm Beach. Although they requested their reservation some three months in advance, they received a reply saying sorry, but there were no vacancies and that first consideration was always given to their "old clientele." Matthew was shocked, never considering his Jewishness as being anything extraordinary. He did not consider it an asset, as did some of the more liberal and romantically idealistic Jews of Eastern Europe (who had very little else to hold onto); or a deterrent, as did some of the nouveau riche of his acquaintance who made painful and almost comical adjustments to accommodate the white Protestant ethic and hide their guilty secret. No, the Goldmarks thought of themselves simply as American Jews who made their contribution to American commerce. Matthew knew the facts of life, but when personally confronted by it, he was somehow shocked. He couldn't quite believe it, so he sent out two letters, one requesting another date, the other signed by a well-placed and elegant gentile friend of the family's. His own was turned down. But Gary Dutton's request was immediately granted. Matthew was stunned. He had heard about these restrictions, but hadn't

THE PLEASURE DOME

actually believed it. Some dim stubborn corner of his brain insisted that if they existed at all, they did so for other Jews, but not for *him* or *his*. Matthew, in a curious state of disillusioned enlightenment, canceled all plans for an American honeymoon and to Faye's delight decided on a European trip instead. Europe, he insisted, was far more tolerant and liberal than "the land of the free and home of the brave."

They decided to tour romantic Italy. On a balmy May day in 1924 they boarded the *Ile de France* in New York, surrounded by friends and family, three steamer trunks, and ten pieces of luggage containing Faye's trousseau.

The first stop after Paris was the beautiful Villa d'Este, a resort hotel on Lake Como in northern Italy. In more prosperous times it had been the gorgeous private estate of the noble and wealthy Este family. But it was the grand old Lido in Venice that most impressed Matthew. It sat like a mighty jewel on the small rocky cushion of Lido Isle. The serpentine lines of its graceful stone and stucco edifice spread itself for miles along the turquoise Adriatic. Its Moorish arches and secret coves of biscuit pink brought to mind throbbing tales from the Arabian Nights and perfumed temples of delight. Matthew, although a diffident man, was not immune to beauty.

Espresso in tiny Cappi de Monte cups arrived every morning at nine with pannetone, a sweet fruited bread, warmed and fragrant, brought by a black page in eighteenth century Venetian-style costume complete with feathered turban and satin doublet. The world outside might be sinking into a great depression, heading for extinction, but as long as Venice itself did not sink into the sea, fascism, racism, anarchy could storm its gates, but they could not enter here.

JUDITH LIEDERMAN

Neither Matthew nor Faye was exactly an innocent abroad. Faye had been to Europe before, and Matthew at least to the finest resort hotels in America, including the more elegant Jewish family hotels in the Catskills. Still, the Lido in Venice was a far cry from anything he had ever experienced. It made a lasting impression on him.

When they returned home, Matthew had made the second independent decision of his lifetime. The first had been to marry Faye, the second was to buy a resort hotel. He wasn't at all sure if his parents would go along, but, he reasoned, they were in the market for real estate. He knew they were looking for a business they could be active in.

Faye was breathless with excitement. She had only begun to take stock of her new situation. She hadn't realized until now what life might be like buried in upstate New York as the wife of a leather goods manufacturer. New York City, at best, might become a monthly excursion—unless she could talk Matt into keeping a pied-à-terre in New York, but that seemed unlikely.

What good was it, all the elegant accoutrements of her life, the Porthault linens, the Tiffany silver, the antique Spode china, the Mainbocher gowns and lingerie from Léron? What good if no one was to see them? That is, no one she cared about, no one who could appreciate her exquisite taste and even envy her a little.

At first she thought the whole idea of the hotel business ridiculous, demeaning. "What would we be?" she asked, "but glorified innkeepers, endlessly involved with servants and staff, laundries, purveyors, butchers, butter and egg men?" But then Matthew made her see what a showplace this could be for her. She would be the resort's

THE PLEASURE DOME

first lady, he had said, her charms and talents on constant display.

She became his staunchest supporter, his cleverest advocate—and finally, his most dissatisfied guest. In the end it was not difficult, because Matthew sold his father on the emotional level, dwelling on the restrictions against Jews at the better resorts.

"Look, Dad, even though we are in the midst of a depression, there are very few hotels that will take our business. They'd prefer to starve first or close down," Matthew had argued plaintively. "We can open our doors to our own people, and cater to those who have had other doors closed in their face." Matthew's pale face took on a warm glow.

Jessie nodded, smiling a little philosophic smile, and asked, "But what do we know about the hotel business?"

"What we don't know we can learn, and what we can't learn we can hire. The best—we'll hire the very best."

"And what makes you think that the best, as you call it, will come to work for us, a Jewish family with little or no experience in this business?"

"For enough money they'll come," Matthew said.

Clara certainly didn't care much about it all. She seemed to take the whole business with a grain of salt, as if it was an expensive hobby. It was Matthew who cared.

Sometime in 1928, the old Broadbeach Hotel and Country Club was up for sale. A broker brought it to their attention. The De Frees family, who had owned and operated it for years and kept it rigidly restricted to Jews, now sold it gratefully and at a tidy profit. There was something about its Moorish arches and oceanfront grandeur that reminded Matt of the Lido hotel in Venice. In the end the depression nearly wiped them out. But

25

with borrowed money they bounced back and bought, at a distress price, another resort hotel in Miami Beach, the Hibiscus Gardens.

And it caught on not miraculously, but by dint of hard work and Matthew's dread of failure—his passion to impress his father—and his bride, the mother of his son. A year after the marriage, at little more than nineteen, Faye was ill-prepared for the responsibility of motherhood and promptly set about engaging a series of solid German nurses to take over her duties, but somehow she never felt young again, no matter how hard she tried.

In the beginning they made few physical changes. The most dramatic change, of course, was the clientele. But little by little word leaked out as to the change in management. The elegant arbiters of the powerful Christian world began to desert their old stamping grounds, and were replaced by those Jews still left with enough money to spend it lavishly at the Goldmark Hotels.

Jessie, who had reluctantly sold the leather goods business, kept the books and stayed in the background. Matthew envied him this anonymity. He himself did not much like being thrust out front, dealing directly with the guests, but someone had to do it. His father had grown suddenly old and self-conscious about his accent. They hired urbane, charming, gentile managers but they didn't last, and the steady guests could not identify with constantly changing personnel. More than anything, the Goldmarks wanted the reputation of a family hotel, a discreet holiday haven for all the family. "We must present a solid family picture," Jessie would caution his son.

Jessie was a shrewd man. He knew that success lay in knowing every aspect of this business inside and out. He knew that Matthew could handle the inside, but the business really hinged on establishing a good one-to-one relationship with the guests, keeping them somewhat in awe of management, so that there remained a certain mystique. The guest must always consider himself fortunate to be one of their privileged clientele.

Matthew's natural diffidence was often mistaken for hauteur. Jessie liked that. And if Matthew did not translate enough glamour and mystique to the guests, Faye more than compensated for it.

CHAPTER 4

Harlan Steven Chase lay on his back in bed and stared hard at the white stucco ceiling. He liked to luxuriate in bed. It was only eight o'clock on Sunday morning but getting up for Mass was no problem; he was an early riser. It was just that he wasn't in the mood for devotions today, or any day for that matter. His mind of late was focused on subjects like lust and money. Wasn't that why he worked at the Broadbeach Hotel the last few summers? As long as he made the most money he could with the least possible discomfort, he was satisfied, though not necessarily happy.

He had until nine-thirty to be in church, and after that he had to be at work. He felt certain that the Lord would forgive him this trespass—working on Sundays, because it was a practical necessity. They were a large family and his father, now in his fifties, would soon be retired from the bank where he had worked as a guard for the last twenty-five years. He hadn't put aside much money but was inordinately proud of having sent four children through parochial school. In the end it was only Harlan who went on to college. Two of his sisters were married and although Janine, the youngest, worked as a teller at the bank, she contributed very little to the straining budget. Harlan didn't like to think about it because he really didn't contribute much either. He was nearly thirty and had nothing to show for it but a college degree

THE PLEASURE DOME

and a handful of AAU swimming medals. He did not even, until recently, see anything strange about living at home at his age. Going to Mass occasionally was a concession to his mother that he strongly resented. His father, he knew, had given up on him long ago. The fact that he was the only son in a family of four adoring females only served to make him more complacent.

He lay there and wondered sheepishly what he was doing with his life down at a swimming pool, flexing his muscles and titillating the repressed Jewish girls. He preferred thinking of himself as a gifted failure, with his robust and independent mind and his mighty physique. He also had a knack for making friends among the people of all faiths and classes—particularly the wealthy.

He thought about the war in Europe and knew that he would be drafted anytime. That was fine with him because he felt that he had reached an impasse in his life. He would welcome the hiatus—if the goddamn Germans didn't get him first.

There was a gentle knocking and his mother entered the room. "Oh, I'm glad you're awake, Harlan. I've just made some lovely pancakes and—"

"Ugh, Mother, that's barbaric—pancakes—so early?" For years he had been trying to get the family to have Sunday breakfast after church. "Juice and coffee will do just fine," he said wearily.

"Well, that may be just fine for you, but don't expect the rest of us to face God on an empty stomach." She gave the mirror a quick wipe with a tissue, and the dust from it danced in the beam of summer sunshine that slanted across the room.

He stretched, yawned and jumped out of bed with one stride that took him easily to where his mother stood by the dresser in the small room. He enveloped her from behind in a bear hug. "Mmm," he said, kissing the back of her neck with a loud sucking noise.

"Aw, go on, you big ape," she said, pushing him away, but laughing and rosy from it. "Tsk—God, boy, put some clothes on. You're enough to make the devil blush."

He laughed and stared down the length of his smooth muscular body. "I'm wearing shorts, mom, what do you want, it's summer."

"I know, I know," she murmured, an appreciation of what she had created, mingled with a strange irritation.

His sister Janine was already seated at the table neatly dressed for church. Janine, the youngest and his favorite, was almost finished and sat dreaming over her coffee.

"Good morning, your holiness," he said, rumpling her hair affectionately. His father, at the head of the table, pursed his lips in disapproval, cleared his throat as if to speak, and said nothing. James Chase was big, big as his son, and handsome, too, in much the same way, but his own confident masculinity not as blatant, toned down by hard work and the constant siring of female offspring.

"Hey, it's okay, Pop, as long as the church gets one of us, you ought to be satisfied," he winked at his sister playfully. Janine was planning to become a nun, but it was obvious that they thought it a poor translation of their hopes for Harlan.

James Chase looked at his son with an air of distaste. "And what would the priesthood be doing with the likes of you?"

Everything Harlan did at home was met with indifference and criticism from his father.

Marge sat down now, sipped her coffee thoughtfully. "Son, would you like to join us for dinner at your sister Evelyn's tonight? Or are you going to Anya's?"

"Oh yeah, probably, Mother," he answered absently,

THE PLEASURE DOME

"but thanks anyway and give her my love, haven't seen Evelyn for a while."

"She's busy, you know, the babies and all and—" his mother stopped suddenly and shifted her conversation midstream. "What about Anya, Steve?" She called him by his middle name as a term of endearment. She had given him her family name, but sometimes thought it sounded too formal, harsh to her ears, and she called him by the saint's name she loved.

"What about her, Mother?" he said, throwing down the last of his juice and pulling his car keys from his pocket.

"Well, with you going off to war and all, I just thought . . ."

"You worry too much, Mom," he said and patted her head on the way out. He wondered why his family was so intent on marrying him off to Anya Morgan. Certainly she was not the first girl he had gone with—there had always been some girl or other. It was almost two years now and he really had been quite faithful. He thought very highly of Anya but now he realized he was tiring of her. Her hoydenish ways no longer seemed so provocative and the ease with which he had seduced her had at first surprised, and now annoyed him. He knew he did not love her, that she loved him helplessly, and that he needed help to get out of Broadbeach . . .

Harlan drove with Janine in his own car, a shiny black roadster. He would go directly from the church to the club. His parents followed in their old La Salle, gone colorless and rust-freckled with the years. He looked at the flat, uninteresting landscape and felt equally flat, shriveled by the endless sand and salt of this colorless place—so many summers and winters of his life.

Broadbeach, Long Island was several miles from Montauk on the eastern tip. It was so named because of its unusual expanses of broad white beaches. It became a different sort of town in summers and Harlan, who hated it in the winter, hated it only a little less when the sophisticated and well-heeled summer residents arrived. Although no longer as socially prominent as it had been in the late twenties, it still carried with it a certain aura. In the course of events it was left, for the most part, to the elegant German-Jewish families, captains of industry who rented for the summers. They had little choice other than the Catskills, which they considered crass and beneath their dignity and not within commuting distance of their businesses. The Broadbeach was unique and bore little resemblance to the family hotels in the mountains. The great hotel complex was the hub to which all the spokes of the town connected. Most of the small businesses supplied it with goods and services and were sustained by it. In their publicity brochures the Goldmarks called it "a completely American, thoroughly democratic environment."

Janine was silent, as she so often was lately. Calm resignation seemed to have settled onto her gentle pretty face.

"Janine, what's up? Out with it."

"What—?" She looked genuinely perplexed.

"I'm going away in the fall sometime, and before I go I want to know what your plans are—I—well, I'm liable to be gone for an indefinite time—a long time."

She was silent for another moment and then she said matter-of-factly, "I know. I've had the feeling that this autumn would be—important for us both."

"Well, I'm not sure yet how important it will be for me—all I know is I've stayed around here years longer than I should have."

"Don't you know," she cried, suddenly interrupting, "that I'm going to the Sisters of St. Joseph in September—to novitiate—?"

There was a stony silence and then he said, "You're so young, barely nineteen, you've plenty of time to make such a decision."

"It's what I want to do, Harlan—and the folks have got their hearts set on it."

"The folks, as you call them, are ignorant bigots. It's *you* who would be giving up and walking out on life—you've never been a quitter," he said, looking at her now instead of the road ahead. Blotches of color seeped through his tan. "What is it *you* want, Janine?"

"Giving myself to God is not exactly giving up, is it?"

"Yes, yes it is, it's the easy way out—"

She looked amazed. "I don't know," she said, skeptically, "I just don't know."

"Well, for God's sake until you know, do nothing," he said without a trace of his usual detachment.

"I'll have three years before my first vows," she argued. "If I find it's wrong for me, that I'm not cut out for it—I'll know it in time. Of course, I'll get home now and then—I could be home for the wedding—that is, if you and Anya are—"

He cut her off impatiently. "Honey, we're going to be at war before long—nobody knows if they're coming or going right now—"

"Is that what you tell Anya?"

"Look, Jan, how do I know what I will want when and if this thing is over, or even if I'm coming back at all? You can see it wouldn't be fair to any woman."

"Don't you love her?" she persisted.

"Love is a luxury for the rich."

Janine seemed to consider this for a moment. "If you

really mean that, then I'm sure I'm doing the right thing. I couldn't live my life without love." She said this with such fervor that Harlan studied her curiously for a moment.

"And in the church you are loved by Christ? Girl, where's your spunk?" Harlan seemed perplexed. This was a side of her character he was not familiar with.

He realized now he hadn't seen Marc Anselmo around for a while—Janine and Marc had been fond of one another since she was fourteen. His family belonged to the same parish. Harlan's father, James, didn't approve of Italians. "They're all heathens, the lot of them. Besides that, they're *gangsters,*" he would often say.

The funny thing about it was that there *were* some rumors about the Anselmo family and Mafia connections, something about Marc's uncle who lived in Jersey. Harlan had given it little credence through the years—Marc was a handsome and charming kid—now he began to wonder.

He began to slow the car for the left turn into the Church of the Immaculate Heart. He saw the familiar solid working-class people of the community standing in eager, sociable clusters, the early arrivals, for whom Mass was the high point of their week.

CHAPTER 5

Mondays were always quiet down at the swimming pool, just a handful of teenagers swimming and fooling around, mostly boys. Laina Eastman rarely went there but stayed around the cabana, usually alone, reading or occasionally chatting with Caroline—when her mother would let her out of her sight, which wasn't too often. Mrs. Segall was more dependent on Caroline than Caroline was on her; at least she felt confident that she could manipulate Caroline, something she could not do with her cardplaying contemporaries.

Laina knew knew where to find her brother Seth. He was half man, half sea-animal. He was always in the pool or sloshing around its aqua blue perimeters. Now he stood melting into his own puddles, and tall as he was for his nearly seventeen years, he was overshadowed by the towering and dramatic figure of Harlan Chase, the swimming coach, whom she had met a couple of times before. Her brother had introduced him with a certain amount of awe and pride of possession.

Seth was the coach's favorite, and he was in a constant state of excitement over Harlan Chase. Laina understood why, but for quite different reasons. Every muscle was in exactly the right place, and there were plenty of them. He seemed more deeply suntanned than usual, but then the last time she had seen him was near the beginning of the summer. She waved and went over to where they stood near the diving board. For a moment she envied her brother's ability to be so completely immersed in a project.

"Hi there, sis," but it was not her brother who called to her. It was Harlan.

"Hey, how's he coming along?" she asked, trying to sound like an older sister.

"He's getting there." Harlan looked at Seth approvingly.

Seth wiped his dripping nose with his hand and, still panting, said, "You want to time this one for me, Chase?" and took off in a dive.

Chase didn't even look at his watch; he looked at Laina. She noted the green-flecked eyes in a sunbronzed handsome face, an Irish face, though not typical because of its strong aquiline nose, a face already seamed by years of sun and water, and the telltale signs of living. Laina was impressed by age. She made a mental note to ask Seth how old this man was.

"Haven't seen you around these parts much lately," he said. "Where've you been?" What he said seemed perfectly natural but the way he looked at her made her feel awkward and schoolgirlish even though she was already fifteen years old.

"Up the beach," she murmured, pointing uncertainly in that direction.

"Now, why would a pretty young lady like you do such an unsociable thing all summer long?" he said, one eye on the pool where a few children were slogging each other with water-filled bathing caps.

"Young lady" was patronizing, she thought. "A thing like what?" she asked.

THE PLEASURE DOME

"Like reading, alone on the beach," he said smoothly.

"Oh that, well there really isn't much else for me to do."

"Have you tried anything else?"

A moment's confused silence and then she answered simply, "I really love to read."

He was chastened by her seriousness. "Well, you ought to try taking long walks along the beach. Next to swimming it's the best thing for the figure, although that doesn't seem to be your problem," he said, his eyes resting languidly on her breasts.

Laina wished that her two-piece bathing suit was a more discreet one-piece, but she felt deliciously mature.

"Where's your boyfriend?" he asked in a throwaway line, with one eye still on the action in the pool.

"What boyfriend?"

He laughed then, a warm, unself-conscious laugh.

She noticed his hair—rich and chestnut streaked by the sun, or was it the beginnings of gray? Thrown into confusion, and laughing and blushing, she said, "I don't have a special boyfriend—yet."

"What's the matter with these guys, don't they have eyes? You're the prettiest girl around here."

She felt a little dizzy and wished her brother would emerge from the depths. When he did, they stood around close in a ring, talking and laughing. A breeze blew up, rippling the surface of the pool. She tasted salt in her mouth and felt the raised goose bumps along her arms and thighs.

Suddenly she wanted to go home.

Her brother didn't look even the least interested in leaving. Reluctantly he gave in.

"What's the hurry?" Seth asked, obviously annoyed.

"It's getting late," she mumbled awkwardly, "and Ginger'll be angry if we're late, she's always in a hurry to get dinner done with—you never want to tear yourself away from that ape," she said with a rush of hostility.

"He's okay," Seth said warmly. "You know how many medals he's got at home? He's a big man with the AAU—and the ladies too—"

"Big deal," she murmured half-aloud. "Well he's *big* anyway—"

"Well what's wrong with him? You don't even *know* him." Seth was growing red in the face as he spoke.

"How could I know him, he's not *my* coach, and who said I had anything against him?" She paused. "How old is he, anyway?"

"Oh, twenty-seven or twenty-eight, something like that. I know he swam for his college, and he's been out of school for a long time."

"Oh" was all she said, but her mouth remained a large round open void for a moment longer. They trudged along the crunchy terrain in silence.

"So what does he do in the winter, go to the Goldmarks' hotel in Florida, I suppose?" she said deprecatingly.

"No, he's with the Manhattan A.C. Teaches there I guess. He's asked me to his house for dinner tonight and then one night soon I want him to come to our house for dinner." He pushed his fair hair back from his eyes. It was still wet from the pool.

They passed alongside the ninth hole. A handful of golfers were finishing up their game, gauging and measuring distances cannily with squinted eyes.

Laina snatched at a tall reed from the open lot where the rushes grew wild. She thought briefly and guiltily

THE PLEASURE DOME

about what she had seen a few days ago and felt her nipples grow hard. She shivered a little as if a cool breeze had just come up, but it had not.

So one Sunday evening in late summer, Seth brought his idol Harlan Chase home to dinner. Harlan seemed strained, uncomfortable in slacks, a shirt and neatly knitted tie, and a sports jacket. Overly formal for the occasion, Laina thought. He looked around him, seemingly fascinated by the luscious carpeting and elegant furnishings throughout the large, high-ceilinged old house. It was in no uncertain terms the summer residence. He was not overly startled by their informal elegance here. He had been in and out of the homes of the rich since he had gotten out of college and began teaching at their clubs.

Through the open casements, the smoke from the charcoal fires mingled with the sea air. Sunday was barbecue night at the seashore and Laina felt awkward sitting rigidly at the dining room table, being served formally by the maid Ginger, while her father presided rather stiffly over the proceedings. Harlan was the very essence of good manners. Even cavalier, pulling out the chair, waiting to begin until Alex lifted his own spoon, answering his sometimes condescending questions in a quiet, respectful voice.

They talked earnestly about sports and the war, about Harlan's induction into the marines and Seth's draft status—he would be seventeen at summer's end, and still had another year of high school to complete.

"Well, you certainly look like a marine, kid," Alex said, his acute blue eyes resting for a moment on Harlan's handsome face. "I suppose you'll have all the girls flocking around you in your uniform."

Alex's forthright statement was somehow painful to Laina. At fifteen she was aware of a vulnerability so intense as to be humiliating.

"Sure as hell, you probably have more than you know what to do with right now—huh, kid?" Alex was in his forties, and had a tendency to refer to anyone his junior as a kid, as if no one younger would ever have his vast experience.

Laina looked at Harlan carefully and thought that he could hardly be called a kid.

Harlan laughed diplomatically and said nothing—nothing about Anya, or his engagement.

"Tell me, Chase, how did you escape the draft this long? They started taking them almost a year ago," Alex said.

"Well, for one thing I was teaching swimming over at the Marine Naval Base in Atlantic Beach nights and weekends until this summer—"

"Do you think they'll send you overseas right off?" Alex interrupted.

"I think so," he said quietly. "I expect right after the boot training." Harlan was eager to get him back on the subject of business, a subject on which Alex was far more eloquent. "What do you think will happen to the hotel in the event of war?"

"Ah, I don't think it will be affected much; in fact, it should be good for business in general. People spend more money in wartime—psychological, I guess," he mused, "and then too there should be more clientele—the European resorts will be off-limits now, if not closed entirely—"

"I guess you've heard the rumor that the Broadbeach is closing down," Harlan said, looking at his plate of food. "Or rather it's being closed and bought by the navy for a

THE PLEASURE DOME

training base—its location right on the ocean makes it a natural—"

"Yes, sure, I've heard those rumors—but that's all they are, just rumors. The whole thing's crazy, makes no sense—" but Alex did not explain further.

"You seem very familiar with the business."

"My own is closely allied," he said. "Entertainment businesses all touch on one another—I've known Jessie Goldmark for years, and of course the kids too—"

Harlan smiled dubiously. Laina longed to touch his lips with her fingers.

"I see you're smiling. I suppose Matthew and Vivian are hardly kids. They must be quite forbidding to work for," he ventured.

Laina thought she saw a muscle tighten in Harlan's cheek.

"Oh, I really have very little to do with them," he said smoothly. "I'm way down at the other end of the business, you might say." He said this with a rueful smile and a lifted brow. Laina had a sudden feeling that he was laughing at them all, tolerating her father, the Goldmarks, the resort—that he was glad that he was leaving, leaving it all behind to the foolish, the rich—

"The business is a tough one, Chase," Alex said. "Running a resort hotel that size is no easy matter, I assure you. One has to have the knack for it—the personality—"

"And the Goldmarks have it?" Harlan asked.

"No, not really, they're cold fish—most of them, except the old man—and it's he who built the business. Took much of the steady Jewish clientele away from the Quisisana in Capri, the Du'Cap in Antibes, and Lido in Venice. It does manage to hold on to a certain old world, European aura."

"Unfortunately, that world is on its way out," Harlan said with an unusual amount of assurance.

"You are probably right, but who knows—we are in a curious state of suspension right now, nobody really knows anything for sure—and there will always be a need for resort and recreational facilities, and if indeed we do get into the war, which is inevitable, I foresee it coming back twice as strong afterwards." Alex leaned back in his chair and suddenly shifted the thrust of his conversation. "What was your major in college, anything in particular besides swimming?" he asked.

"Yes, as a matter of fact—psychology," Harlan said with a certain amount of relish.

Alex seemed taken aback—this was out of keeping with the image he had created for the boy.

After dinner the conversation became stilted as they shifted onto the deep overstuffed sofas. Finally the snores from Alex's chair rudely proclaimed the evening at an end.

CHAPTER 6

Laina found herself spending more and more time around the pool, although she rarely went swimming. She mostly stood around in a very tight satin lastex swimsuit, one moment standing erect, the next hiding her heavy breasts with her arms, feigning cold.

Harlan was usually busy and rarely took any notice of her during the day, but she thought she caught him looking at her surreptitiously from time to time.

Sometimes when the crowd thinned out around five in the afternoon they'd walk down the beach together, she talking earnestly, he bantering, amused. He was well aware of, and even flattered by, her childlike innocent worship. She seemed mesmerized by the fact that he was a Catholic. The little she knew of Catholicism, she had learned from her maternal grandmother, who seemed to have a working relationship with the saints and who frequently warned her that her mother was already in purgatory for defecting from the faith. The rest she learned from the Christmas pageant, in which she once succeeded in securing a part, and then only as one of the three wise men.

It was almost six o'clock in the evening and the late summer sun was devoid now of its earlier broiling anger. Laina lay on a blanket on the sand in front of her cabana, soaking up the last rays of the sun. The Krimans, who occupied the choice corner cabana, were just picking up the baby's gear, and their three-year-old was toddling up the boardwalk with the nurse. It would be quiet now—completely quiet. She would have the beach all to herself—to drift and dream—and she turned up her radio a little louder and rolled over on her back. Jimmy Dorsey's "Blue Champagne" was playing. She felt restless with the almost complete freedom she had at fifteen. She had never abused her father's *trust*—but was it trust or *disinterest?* The question sometimes pained her—she did not like to think about it.

She thought about walking up to the front beach to talk to Caroline, who was rarely allowed to leave her mother's side, even during her eternal card games, not so much due to maternal concern as to the fact that Mrs. Segall never knew when she'd need her to fetch this or that, her glasses from the room—or simply when there'd be a hiatus and she might find herself completely alone. Mrs. Segall was always hedging against loneliness.

Laina quickly rejected the idea. She couldn't manage to look at Mrs. Segall now, in fact she was even a little uncomfortable with Caroline since she learned last week that Mrs. Segall made Caroline wait outside in the hall while she entertained men in their suite. She wondered casually where her brother was and decided he was probably at the pool. She'd been down there entirely too much lately, she decided, and didn't want to go near it. At low tide the ocean was hypnotic. She was drawn in by its gentle ebb and flow, its insistent, perfect rhythm.

At first she saw only his enormous shadow loom up against the whiteness of the sand and then the great bulk of him perpendicular to it. He was walking along the water's edge, having just finished his daily swim in the ocean. She saw him looking in the direction of her cabana. She was going to look away quickly, but then reflexively waved wildly to him, and he came jogging up the beach toward her.

"What are you doing here so late?" he asked.

"Oh, just watching the ocean." She was not certain how to address this man who stood looming above her. She was afraid to look up at the bulging, wet trunks that clung to the base of his body. His smile was insinuating—teasing, as if he were enjoying her confusion.

He fell down beside her easily, in the sand. For a moment neither spoke. She sifted sand through her long tapering fingers. He leaned over and she could almost taste the salt on him. He lifted her chin and said softly, "Hey, what's that I see in your eyes now, is it a speck of dust or some handsome six-foot lad by the name of Alan, or is it David? Now let me guess." She looked away quickly, afraid that he might read her thoughts, which she was sure were transparent, spilling out of her own golden-green eyes.

"Never mind me, I'm just a child," she said bravely, "what about you? You should be married or at least thinking about it at your age."

He raised his eyebrows quizzically and bellowed with laughter. "Why?" he asked.

"Why? For one thing it's your duty to the church to raise a great Catholic family, isn't it?"

"How come you know all that?"

"My mother was a Catholic."

He studied her more intently.

"Are you a believer, Harlan?"

"In what?" he asked ingenuously.

"Oh come on, you know, in your religion, in Catholicism?"

"I'm what you call a lapsed Catholic"—he laughed—"no, a failed Catholic. But I got the love of Jesus right here in my pretty green eyes," he said, putting his face close to hers, his eyes dancing, his mouth suddenly fierce.

Warm color flooded her cheeks. He had a way of talking that she liked. His words had foreign cadences. She seemed compelled to complete the strange catechism. "Why have you 'failed'?"

"Why?" he said and was silent a moment. "Sooner or later we wind up in the same place, so what's the difference on what terms we go? My sisters are pious enough to atone for my sins." He laughed again and clenched his white teeth.

She relaxed, feeling that he had somehow narrowed the breach between them with his irreverence. She rolled onto her back and said, as if it were a revelation, "Then I suppose Jesus was a failed Jew."

"Amen," he said in a sepulchral voice. "Have you nothing newer than that to share with the world?"

"Is it that hard to be a good Catholic?" Laina asked, dreamily drawing her fingers along the sand. "The church makes it easy for you—after all, you can absolve yourself of sin merely by confessing it to a priest."

"Listen, if you are thinking of converting, I'll talk to my sister Janine for you, she's *almost* a nun."

Laina wondered if he was angry with her, perhaps she had gone too far, presumed too much.

He was accustomed to quiet girls like his sister, girls bred in the Catholic School System, who did not ask too many questions. Laina's lively curiosity both annoyed and attracted him. Most girls were fairly transparent. Their feelings easily discernible, their sexual ones anyway. He sensed something almost subliminal about this child, this girl, that unsettled him. She was different. She looked like a woman, but was still childlike; she was a

THE PLEASURE DOME

Catholic-Jew, a fact that he found exotic; she had a very rich father, a beautiful body—and she was far too young. Harlan clearly wished to change the subject.

"Are you coming to the big swim meet Sunday night? You'll want to see your brother swim, I know—and there will be a beach party afterwards, bonfires and marshmallows and weiner roasts."

"I don't know," she said cautiously. "It will be a late evening and—"

"What's the matter, baby, afraid of the dark?" he asked, brushing his suntanned face close to her lips.

When he called her "baby" in that succulent way she felt like a woman. She felt a twinge somewhere near her stomach. He pulled her roughly to her feet and unwrapped the damp towel from around his neck and, laughing slightly, flicked it across her buttocks and said, "You'll be there," then ran off down the beach toward the exit. She wondered why she hadn't thought to ask him for a ride home—or, better yet, why he hadn't offered her one.

CHAPTER 7

The swim meet had been a glorious success, and a triumph for Harlan. Almost all of the five hundred guests and members had turned out. They sat in parade stand seats set up in tiers around the Olympic-size swimming pool, and applauded wildly with each victory. It was clearly Harlan's night and he loved the attention.

Laina was there with Caroline, surprisingly unaccompanied by her mother who obviously didn't need her tonight. Babs Singer was there, in white dimity, looking strangely demure and sophisticated at the same time, as if she had just stepped out of a Hattie Carnegie window. Of course, Faye Goldmark was there too, her hair an aurora borealis about her face.

Laina caught a glimpse of David Goldmark, who was talking and laughing pleasantly with Babs and a couple of other girls. He was somewhat delicate looking and vulnerable, with small features except for the large Goldmark nose. His entire face looked unfinished, as if a sculptor had begun it and lost interest in the project before he had refined it. The large horn-rimmed glasses he wore were interesting.

Laina hadn't seen Harlan for a week, and she decided that he was avoiding her.

Seth Eastman had walked off with the fifteen-to-seventeen-year-olds honors, winning first prize in every category, breaststroke, backstroke and crawl. Harlan and

THE PLEASURE DOME

he were inseparable that evening, the classic romantic portrait of master and protegé. Their bodies, wet under the kleig lights, glistened when they walked.

Alex Eastman would have been proud. He hadn't wanted to miss the event, but he did miss it. Alex was always missing out on the special events of his life. He had to work that night.

Laina felt sad inside, disappointed for Seth. He knew in advance that his father wouldn't be there, but still he kept looking up at the stands as if expecting a miracle.

Tonight Laina begged Caroline to stay with her. She wanted to wait around for her brother. But he was standing around, showing no signs of going into the locker room to change, jumping about—agitated, sparring and jabbing with Harlan and a couple of other boys.

As the crowd began thinning out, Laina became absorbed in watching Vivian Goldmark talk earnestly to Harlan. With his hands on his hips he was looking deep into her eyes with great interest, hanging on her every word. Her tiny, flat-chested frame quivered with laughter now and again, and she gesticulated gracefully with her hands for greater emphasis.

"C'mon, Lainie," Caroline said anxiously, "I've really got to go now. I'll meet you at the beach party."

"No, no, wait please," she said. "I'm coming with you." The thought of being the last person there alone and obviously waiting for him was humiliating, particularly since he had said, "You'll be there."

People were milling about on the glass-enclosed terrace, spilling down onto the beach. The glass window walls were open in places and an amplifier was sending out onto the beach the throbbing sounds of "Perfidia."

Laina's eye caught Caroline's parents in a discreet corner of the terrace, enmeshed in that peculiar solid silence of theirs. They were obviously waiting for their daughter to come along and release them from their mutual imprisonment. Mr. Segall jumped up immediately when he spotted the girls and asked Laina to join them, but Tash, who regarded any female younger than herself as a potential rival, was barely civil.

David Goldmark came over to their table. He was entering his senior year at prep school in the fall.

David made no secret of his admiration for Laina. He asked her to dance. Tash pursed her lips disapprovingly. Laina couldn't decide if the look was because she would have preferred he ask Caroline to dance—or herself.

He held her very close.

"When are you going back to school, Dave?"

"Mmm?" he murmured happily in her hair. "Oh, probably in September. Haven't seen much of you this summer. Where have you been keeping yourself?"

"Oh, around mostly—just around," she said. "If you had wanted to find me, I'm sure you could have."

Duly chastened, David laughed and said with enormous candor, "You're right Laina, but what in hell was I going to do with a fifteen-year-old virgin?" So it boiled down to that again, she thought with disappointment. Is that *all* it's about?

Over David's shoulder Laina could see the party area begin to fill up. Many couples were dancing on the terrace now and some had taken off their shoes and were dancing on the sand. A small wooden bandstand was festooned with gaily colored crepe paper. Its lanterns gave off a greasy yellow glow. Faye Goldmark was dancing a slow rhumba with the South American dance teacher. Her brown eyes were dilated and glazed by the alcohol and music. Down along the beach, clutches of guests gathered around the bonfires, newly lit by the hotel staff. Waiters carried trays of marshmallows in their pristine blue-and-white boxes, and bright pink frankfurters looked rubbery in their uncooked innocence. Mounds of raw hamburger (all kosher meat), were carried high on trays toward the bonfires to their eventual demise—death by burning and cannibalism. Long buffet tables, covered with paper cloths and scotch-taped against the ocean breezes, held platters of picnic fare, jeweled salads and gelatin molds that danced and quivered like houri out of an Arabian night. At stategic points on the beach, portable bars dispensed the finest wines and liquor. The air smelled sweetly smoky and faintly fishy.

Harlan Chase sauntered over to the activity. He had carelessly covered his bathing trunks with a white terry cloth jacket that he left unzipped, displaying his brown, almost hairless chest and a large silver St. Christopher's medal. He was still with Vivian Goldmark, who smiled happily and occasionally inclined her head graciously like a queen to this or that familiar guest. He caught Laina's eye and treated her to his insolent and infectious grin. Laina ignored him with enormous intensity.

"Let's sit down, Dave," Laina said, "I'm—sort of tired."

"Tired? You didn't do any of the swimming tonight, which reminds me, where is Seth? I'd like to congratulate him. He was terrific," he said, steering her toward the beach. "He ought to sign up for the navy."

"He's signed up for college, Dave," she said sharply. "He's going to Brown in the fall. He's still so young, so please don't go giving him any crazy ideas."

"I'm no recruiting officer. Hiding behind these spectacles are a pair of lewd and lascivious eyes, blind to everything but pleasure," he said, feigning a wolf slather and playfully nuzzling her neck.

She pulled away, alarmed.

"You know what your trouble is," he said, pushing her silky hair back from her face, "you worry too much for a kid."

They sat down on the sand without benefit of towels or blanket. It felt cold beneath her buttocks. She shuddered slightly.

She noticed Harlan was standing in a group around one of the campfires. Vivian was close beside him, discreetly clad in a white sweater and slacks. Babs Singer was there too, touching his arm, playing the great beauty, playing it rather well, Laina thought enviously. Harlan did not flick a glance in her direction. They could have easily drifted over there and joined the group but instead she got up and said quite suddenly, "Dave, I think I'd like to go home, it's getting late." He jumped up, surprised.

"Oh, stick around a while, Lainie, we're just getting into gear," he said with a debonair wave of his hand.

"No really, I ought to be going—my father—well—he worries about me when I'm late," she trailed off lamely.

"Well, frankly," David said, "I'd really like to hang around a bit longer. So, will Seth take you home? Where's he been anyway? Let's ask Chase over there. He'll probably know."

"No, no, please," but before she finished protesting he had bounded away.

Without looking behind her she hurried back to the enclosed terrace, skirted the dance floor and headed out of the lobby toward the exit. She felt overcome with embarrassment and an awful sense of superfluity—a

THE PLEASURE DOME

floating appendage. She was suddenly very cold in her shorts and halter. She dreaded the walk home alone, but she didn't want to annoy Seth on his big night.

The lobby was deserted, but hummed with the residual sounds of the festivities beyond. She began walking rapidly toward the lobby to the front exit. She heard a man's swift determined stride behind her and quickened her pace. She felt suddenly breathless and weak but she did not dare to look behind her, although she heard him call her name softly. At the front door she breathed deeply and steadied herself a moment.

"Well, well, if it isn't Laina Eastman and in a fine hurry too," he said with the exaggerated brogue he used when he was feeling pleased with himself. His face was flushed. She could smell beer on his breath. He barred her way so that she could not get down the steps. "What's your hurry, girl? You're running like a scared rabbit."

She thought he looked foolish standing in the formal lobby of the hotel in his trunks.

"Your young man tells me you're leaving all of a sudden. Why? The night is young and full of stars—"

"He's *not* my young man and I was bored," she said, quietly looking away from the lime-green scrutiny of his eyes.

"With young David the hotel heir? Impossible."

"I didn't mean David. He's very nice."

"So nice that he doesn't even offer to take you home? Well, we'll just make sure you're bored no longer. Let's go back to the party—"

"Oh no, thanks, it's late and I've got to walk home—"

"Walk home? Girl, you can't walk home alone at midnight. The banshees and werewolves will surely eat you alive," he said in an urgent whisper. They were standing on the front steps now. "It's a gorgeous night. We can walk part of the way along the beach."

Instead of leading her back to the party, he propelled her down the front path of the hotel. "We'll bypass the main beach and have the whole world to ourselves." He put his arm around her shoulder protectively and kept up a sort of running patter as he guided her along the driveway and out to the darkened beach behind the hotel. The vastness, the endless black stretched out into shafts of moonlight, as if tossed into the sky like spears.

They did not walk along the water's scalloped edge, but on the walk that ran along the sand. She bent briefly to remove her sandals. He took off his beach jacket and placed it around her shoulders. "Don't want you to catch a cold and keep you out of school now, do we?" The reference to school embarrassed her.

They came to the area where the slatted walk ended at the barbed wire. They walked back out to the driveway in order to get around the boundary. The area here belonged to the city. It was unweeded and had been allowed to run wild with clumps of ragweed and thistle. Fireflies and mosquitoes nipped at their bare legs.

"Let's go for a swim in the ocean," he said. "Have you ever been for a midnight swim?"

"No, never," she answered honestly. "I—I'm not much of a swimmer, Harlan."

"Well, let's see if we can't give you a few lessons—now's a good time, it's moontide, not too many waves." He took her hand, urging her along, laughing and running.

She followed him hypnotically, but as they neared the water's edge she pulled back a little. "It looks rough out there and sort of wild."

THE PLEASURE DOME

But he did not relent and continued pulling her until the first icy splash took her breath away. He held her hand tightly and pulled her over the waves. Soon they were beyond the breakers in deeper water, black and slightly puckering, with the light breezes. He took her on his shoulders and gave her a ride, then threw her off, making a great whoosh on the silent water. Roughhousing. She was laughing between chattering teeth. He pulled her on his lap facing him, or perhaps she had floated there light as air. She wasn't sure—she wrapped her strong young legs around his waist and playfully pulled his hair—her own streaming down wet and wild, robbed of color by the neon white of the moon.

He caught her suddenly on the mouth and kissed her. Her first impulse was to pull away, but he held her very tightly, and there was really nowhere to go in the vast expanse—and so she found herself kissing him back fiercely—tasting the beer and fresh sea salt on his lips. She felt his body through the thin silk of his trunks, bulky and hard against her thighs, but as she did not understand its precise signal, it gave her the general, satisfying resistance of muscle.

He took his arm from around her waist and let his fingertips drift across her breasts beneath the water. The sensation was new and wonderful and her reaction was to intensify the kiss. He untied the thin strings of her halter top and it came down in a spasm, exposing the full torrent of her large firm breasts, the nipples pulled in tight by the cold. He stared appreciatively at them—garish in the moonlight—and bent to kiss them.

She felt a sharp tightening in her lower belly and between her legs.

"Touch me," he begged, gently urging her hand downward.

JUDITH LIEDERMAN

She tore her hand away and swam, half-stumbling, and then breaking into a muddled dog paddle, away from him toward the shore. Her heart was beating so fast that she felt sure it would suffocate her.

"What's the matter with you, for God's sake?" he called after her, half-amused. "I didn't do anything so terrible. I didn't hurt you, did I? Anyway, it felt good, didn't it?" Still half-teasing and half in fright, she kept swimming away from him. She thought she saw him turn his back in disgust—walk away in the shallow water—like a disappointed child. Then he turned around and saw how far she had gone out, or else been pulled out by the undertow.

"Come back, come back," he called, "there's a tow out there," but she only heard the echo of "there" and she thought, terrified now, that she was swimming toward the shore. But she began to realize dimly that she was being pulled in the other direction, strong and sure by a force mightier than she understood. She knew she could no longer battle it. She was running out of breath. Her lungs felt as if they would burst with her efforts. Huge black waves tossed her forward, the tow dragged her back again, pulling at her as if she were on a rack. Desperately she tried to catch sight of Harlan but could hardly see through the haze of spume and elliptical shadows. He reached out for her, but a wave obliterated her. He swam powerfully against the next wave and snatched at her thin white arms that were stretching upward as if in final supplication. He caught hold of her finally across the shoulders, slightly above her bared breasts, and smashed downward through the waves. The return was easier with the ocean helping them back. He made sounds of reassurance—"Just relax, go loose, Laina, go loose, don't fight it, we're almost there—almost there," until the last wavelet washed them up on the beach. They lay there together for a moment, white and spent and panting, biting the air in gulps. He rolled her over on her back immediately and covered her mouth with his, lightly pinching her nostrils, breathing, then removing his mouth to listen for an outward rush of air and then again and again. He realized that she had very little if any water in her lungs. He picked her up in his arms and carried her to the cabana where it was warm. He placed her gently on the padded chaise inside the bath house. With a towel he massaged her trembling half-naked body, restoring a faint color to her face and lips. He asked if there was any liquor in the cabana and she pointed in the direction of the narrow closet. She sat up slightly and sipped at the scotch he poured into a paper cup. She became conscious of her bare breasts, and color flooded into her cheeks. She felt warm and a little woozy. She snatched weakly at a towel nearby.

He shook his head and clucked his tongue. "After everything, that's all you're worried about?"

"Thank you," she said weakly and lay down with the towel around her.

"Seems to me you could do with a few swimming lessons," he said smiling and took a gulp of scotch from the bottle. He sat in a chair nearby and kept pulling on the bottle. She noticed how bloodshot his eyes were.

"I did a stupid thing, I'm sorry," she said.

He went inside of the little dressing cubicle and came out with a towel. He dropped it casually over her waterlogged shorts. "Take them off," he commanded. "You'll catch your death."

Hypnotically she pulled at her shorts, clutching the towel with one hand, but she was too weak. "Here, I'll help," he said and pulled them down, pushing up the towel with his efforts; the golden brown triangle of hair was momentarily exposed to him, and she lay back weak with shame—and a strange euphoria. She thought dazedly that he was removing his trunks also. He sat at the edge of the chair naked and terrifying and rubbed her feet, "to bring up the blood," he said. He let his fingers play along her thighs. She moaned and made a hopeless gesture at tightening the towel across her thighs. He let his fingers stray up into the outer boundaries of her secret places where the hair grew springy and honey-colored. He touched her gingerly. Her body was an unsprung coil.

"Relax," he whispered, which seemed to reinforce her sense of helplessness. She closed her eyes in a sort of trance. In a moment he was kneeling above her, pushing her thighs apart—trying to insert himself, large and swollen, into her reluctant body. She pushed at his face, scratching it until she drew blood from his chest, his shoulder. She pulled free with sudden strength but he pinioned her hips with his hands. Her body recoiled with the unexpected intrusion. His St. Christopher medal lay like a circlet of ice between her breasts, then became with vigorous movement a weapon that seared her flesh. He drove hard into her, unable to control himself. She felt a burning and a tearing sensation, as if her soul were coming apart. She wrestled with him slightly but it was useless under the weight of him, and her movements only seemed to excite him further. He drew back slightly for a moment, only to prepare for another onslaught. He seemed powerless to stop. She cried out in pain, which he took to mean pleasure, and began murmuring, telling her how much he had been wanting her and for how long. But she felt only an overpowering shame for her sudden openness, her terrible vulnerability.

"I had to have you, I had to," his words were as urgent as his movements—he seemed to have lost his mind somewhere inside her body. He was not making any sense, she thought crazily.

She was silent throughout as if watching an act in slow motion from a long distance away. All she could think of at this moment was that he was ruining her life.

He took the shortcut across the inside pool and out through the chauffeur's room toward the exit and garage. It was well past midnight and he was thankful that none of the usual crowd of black-clad chauffeurs was there now. Normally they congregated there between trips awaiting their next assignments, playing pinochle and poker, drinking soft drinks and gossiping about their employers.

Harlan, wearing only a towel around his wet suit, his feet still bare, carried Laina in his arms. She was wrapped in a blanket he had found in the cabana. Beneath the blanket Laina still wore the damp clothes she had started out the evening in—and his terry cloth jacket—hers had been abandoned somewhere on the sand. At first he thought she had fallen asleep, then he decided she had fainted—her pulse was so weak—but he knew now, she was in a state of mild shock. For the first time that he could remember in his haphazard life, he was *scared*. He would tell her father about the near accident, the narrow escape, but what if she told about the rest, or if when the doctor examined her he—he—no, no, he pushed that aside, it was too far-fetched. Alex Eastman would never believe such a thing connected with his young daughter and she certainly wouldn't tell him.

He was glad this summer was over. It had been a

travesty. He was glad that he was going into the service—going to war—war seemed to level all things.

Her father had just returned and looked suspicious even before anyone spoke. She was relieved that he was there, but she felt the sharp edge of anger. He was always just a little too late. Ginger was awake, bustling around efficiently in the kitchen. Through a veil she heard him tell Alex in the smooth officious voice he donned for swim meets, "There was night swimming at the party, she went a little too far out. You know kids," he said indulgently. "A good night's sleep is all she needs." Laina, sitting woodenly at the kitchen table while Ginger fussed with a "good hot drink," listened as if he were talking about someone she did not know. Her father's deep voice cut through her cottony stupor.

"Thanks, Harlan," Alex said, slapping him on the shoulder fraternally. "Needless to say, I'm in your debt."

"Only doing my duty," he answered inaudibly. Alex mistook his quietness for the humility he liked in everyone else but himself. Laina was suddenly very much awake, every fiber in her body tingling with revulsion. Vomit rose thick and sour in her throat, but she fought it down and rushed from the room. Brushing past her father, she noticed the faint residual odor of perfume on his clothes and was immediately inundated by a wave of loneliness colder and blacker than the ones from which she had just escaped.

Later that night she woke with a sob that struggled up from someplace deep inside. At first she remembered nothing. She was disappointed to find that it was still dark—except for a luminous glow from her dressing table, an unfamiliar soft smudge of light . . . Memory flowed back bringing with it the pain of other years . . . a memorial candle that marked the second year of her mother's death. Alex had dutifully reminded her to buy it. She wanted to get up, to cup her hands around its warmth but she could not move. She thought with a new understanding of Hans Christian Andersen's "Little Mermaid" and feared that every step she took would be like walking on knives, that her secret insides would spill out of her . . . She felt the pain between her legs but would not acknowledge it. She wanted to touch herself there, but did not dare to.

She stared at the light transfixed. Her mother's flame danced in the glass, a modest reminder that she had lived—and her life hadn't been much. Even that memory flickered on the edge of extinction.

For what seemed like hours, Laina lay in the darkness, wondering how she would face the rest of her childhood—the girls at school, with their purity and their aspirations.

CHAPTER 8

A few weeks after the club's official Labor Day weekend closing, the Goldmarks threw a staff party, a sort of farewell party for executive staff members—housekeepers, maitre d's, dining room captains and the athletic department. Some hundred and fifty people in all.

Harlan had made up his mind not to attend. He had seen enough of this place to last a lifetime—yet he felt compelled to go. He had a few drinks at home alone, then telephoned Anya and asked her to go with him. Anya made him feel substantial. So once again and for the last time, he thought, he found himself on the enclosed terrace overlooking the ocean.

Anya Morgan had reddish hair, which she wore short and boyish, freckles and an expression of consternation. She was slender and delicate like Vivian Goldmark. When she stood next to Harlan Chase, she disappeared, she was so small. She hung on his arm now with a faintly proprietary air that clearly bespoke the tenuous nature of their relationship. Harlan stirred a drink with his index finger and listened to the conversation of Jessie Goldmark and Derek Fielder, the golf pro.

"But Fielder, don't tell me you're going to enlist. Aren't you a little out of your prime?"

"Well, an athlete is always some five years younger than the ordinary guy, right, Chase?" he said, winking at

THE PLEASURE DOME

Harlan as if to bolster his point. "No, I doubt that they'll have me unless it's a desk job."

Jessie did not look impressed. He had become somewhat disenchanted with the golf pro since he had been named corespondent in a recent divorce case involving one of the resort's most prestigious families. Jessie and Matthew were great sticklers for keeping the place free of gossip. After all, this was a family hotel. "Well now, you can't compare the exercise of a golf game to swimming," Jessie said. "That really puts you in shape. Just look at that guy," he said nodding in Harlan's direction.

Matthew wandered over to them, drink in hand, and seemed to hover like a ghost above the proceedings. "Chase, have I met your young lady?" Matthew said pompously.

"This is Anya Morgan," Harlan said smiling, "Matthew Goldmark, our strength and our redeemer."

"Well, what do you make of our hero?" he said, reaching up to put an arm across Harlan's shoulder.

"A hero? I don't think I understand." Anya seemed annoyed.

"Well, er, he's going into the marines next month, isn't that right?"

"Yes, but after all he *is* twenty-eight years old and they've been drafting for a year now."

Harlan gave Anya a curious look.

Matthew looked down at his feet as if trying to think of a reply. "You know we'll be host here to the navy for the duration, and who knows how long afterwards," he said only half-aloud. Then he turned to the golf pro. "Did you know that they're going to tear up your golf course, Fielder, and build Quonset huts all over them? How are you going to feel about that?"

"Frankly, Matt, I don't give a damn." Anya seemed pleased by his answer and now it was her turn to laugh, only intensifying the shocked look on Matthew's face.

"A Robert Trent Jones course, three-quarters of a million dollars sunk into those greens and he doesn't give a damn, tch, such loyalty is truly touching, Fielder."

Jessie Goldmark was looking in the direction of Faye, who was quite drunk and leaning languidly on the dance teacher. Matthew's eyes immediately followed his father's. He knew his family disapproved of her behavior, considered her ostentatious. His mother, Clara, who was in poor health, rarely came to staff functions anymore. But she would hear everything. She always did. Jessie told her everything.

"Well, what's the prognosis, Chase? Do you think we'll go in there and fight for the British?" Jessie asked.

"I think we've got to get into it. Of course, we won't be fighting for the British, we will all be fighting for our own skins," he said.

"How long do you think it will last and what are our chances?" Jessie asked.

It seemed ironic to Harlan that now at summer's end important people were suddenly interested in his opinions on something besides the aquatic progress of their sons and daughters. "I believe we'll win it. Of course, Mother Russia will be the problem—"

"She usually is," Jessie commented dryly.

Matthew interrupted with unfamiliar hostility. "How do you Irish here feel about fighting for the British?"

Harlan eyed him coolly for a moment—"I'm an American, Mr. Goldmark, just like yourself and if *we* go to war I'll be fighting for *my* country, not the British."

"It is difficult for me to relate the Germany I remember as a boy to what it is today—or has become,"

THE PLEASURE DOME

Jessie said slowly, with only a faint trace of an accent.

"I wonder if it really has changed that much," Matthew said. "Perhaps it is only we who have changed, and our perspective of the German people."

"How can *you* know this, Matt?" the father said now. "You have never even been there. It was a different world then—a center of music and the arts. Goebbels and Goethe just don't seem to mix."

But Matt said sharply, "Yes, but the people, Father, the people were always like this, insecure and suspicious of change—a hard people."

As they talked, Harlan felt breathless with the urgency of making plans. He wasn't quite sure where to begin. Already he saw how war changed lives, postponed living.

The group around Harlan and Anya had diminished considerably and Vivian Goldmark could be seen hesitating on the fringe. At first Harlan barely noticed her and then he felt her steady quiet gaze with such compelling force that he lost his usual calm and interrupted Matthew in the middle of describing plans for rebuilding the Broadbeach *after* the war.

Anya nodded coolly to Vivian. They had met before. Vivian's sharp wit and barbed tongue belied her rather calm exterior and usually put Anya on her guard. She noticed the rapt attention she always paid to Harlan when he spoke, digesting his every word as if they were gourmet delights. He responded to this by inclining his head intimately to her ear. It pleased Vivian immensely and infuriated Anya.

After a while when the group broke up into segments, he was surprised to find himself cornered between the two women. They seemed to be chipping at each other with small talk. Vivian asked if Anya had any fall plans.

"Oh, I don't have any special plans yet," she said,

casting an oblique glance at Harlan, "except to try to spend as much time as possible with Harlan before he leaves," she said, pressing his arm intimately. "I work for my dad you know, he's a contractor here on the beach and of course that keeps me very busy," Anya prattled on. Harlan was clearly annoyed.

"Yes, I guess you'd say I do the same thing, work for my father, that is," quipped Vivian.

"What will you do, now that the hotel is closing—" Anya indicated the terrace and ocean with a wide sweep of her arm.

"Oh, who knows, maybe have more time to get into trouble," Vivian said smiling devilishly into Harlan's eyes. "There is the hotel in Florida. I could always go down there."

"That doesn't sound very challenging," Harlan said rather dispassionately.

"Challenges can be a pain in the ass," Vivian said. Harlan laughed richly and agreed. Anya did neither.

Later, driving home, in the dense silence of painful indecision, Anya said, "Why do you allow them to patronize you like that, why? It's not you, you are someone else entirely, when you are with them—"

"Anya," he said, "I get what I want. Right now I don't want anything from them, but when and if I do—well—" He left the sentence unfinished.

She finished it for him. "When and if you do, I will not be here, I promise you that—"

"Nor might I," he said, crinkles creeping into the corners of his eyes, the ones that welcomed that old teasing smile.

"No, Harlan," she said, "I mean it this time—what with your going away and all, it's time—" she trailed off unsure of her ground. Then she turned to him and said softly, "What do you say, do we get married or not, before you leave?"

He saw the pleading in her eyes and was embarrassed for her. He thought sadly how Anya, like most Catholic girls, was consumed with guilt—about sexual relationships, the sins of the flesh. The guilt fed the desire and the desire created more guilt. Round and round it went in a vicious circle.

"What? And make you a war widow? Not over my dead body," he said and tried to pinch her cheek.

She pushed him furiously and said, "Ach, that charm is wearing thin at your age. It's good-bye then, is it?" When she was upset she often dropped into dialect.

"Perhaps it is better, Anya. Now is not the time to make life decisions."

He had stopped the car in front of her house but she sat there for a moment, sodden with misery. "It would be if you loved me. If you loved me, it would be the rightest time of all." She jumped out of the car and ran stumbling in the dark. He made no motion to follow her but sat quietly for a moment, and then drove off.

CHAPTER 9

Harlan received his induction notice sometime in mid-September as expected. Then he did a strange thing, something he had not really expected to do. He telephoned Vivian Goldmark and asked her to have dinner with him in New York. War was in the air, and although he was not a hero, he was about to become a warrior. He lost no opportunity to capitalize on it.

He did not suggest calling for her at Fifth Avenue. Instead he asked her to meet him at the Roosevelt Hotel. He had had a couple of swim meets there and knew it better than any of the places uptown.

When he hung up he thought to himself that he had done a good thing, had made a positive move, although he wasn't quite sure why. Perhaps it was her tone of voice, he thought he could hear her heart beating wildly through the telephone wires.

She arrived a little late and out of breath but looking fresh with the startled look of a young doe about her—very much on her guard. He had driven in from the island and had already fortified himself with a couple of bourbons.

He jumped up from the bar and asked the captain for the table he had reserved, then he led her protectively to the table, his arm draped casually across her narrow sloping shoulders. Seated opposite her, he took her hands

THE PLEASURE DOME

in his immediately and said, "Vivian, I'm glad you could come."

"Did you think I wouldn't or couldn't?" she asked, holding back a smile.

"Oh, I don't really know what I thought," he said. "I—"

"Harlan, we're really not strangers to each other. You've been down at our place for two summers now—so let's not go through all those painful formalities of what is generally referred to I think as a 'first date.' That would be utter nonsense for us, wouldn't it?"

He laughed heartily, stretched out his long legs under the table and relaxed. He was prepared to enjoy this evening after all. Vivian had a quick mind and a sharp intellect. She tried hard to compensate for what she thought she lacked in sex appeal by developing a rather unusual if sometimes caustic sense of humor.

Having delivered her little speech and observed the positive results, she too seemed to relax somewhat. "Let's order a drink, shall we? I see I have some catching up to do," she said, observing his flushed face. For a moment Harlan had forgotten that Vivian Goldmark was no stranger to nightlife and the incumbent drinking. He realized that almost half of her twenty-five years thus far had been spent hanging around hotels and their readily accessible bars. In her own way she was almost the beach bum he was. The drinks came. They drank them gratefully in silence.

At nine o'clock Guy Lombardo took over from the small Latin trio. All around them couples got up to dance to the opening number, "Stars Fell on Alabama."

"Would you trust me on the dance floor?"

"Why not, Harlan, I'd trust you anywhere." She said

this with such earnest confidence that it took him off guard a little.

"Girl, you're a fool to be such a trusting soul—you don't *really* know me that well. You've never been alone with me, have you now?" He leaned forward, frowning darkly and feigning mystery.

She knew the brogue was for her benefit, an attention-getting device of sorts, a tool that was sure to generate excitement of one kind or another.

"Oh, come now, Mr. Chase, you can speak standard English perfectly well."

"I thought I was," he said innocently.

"Yes, but now and then it becomes quite inflected—your brogue comes and goes, seemingly dependent on whether or not your glass needs refilling."

"Ah ha, so the jig is up, eh? And speaking of jigs—shall we?" he asked, indicating the dance floor, which was packed with servicemen. She laughed happily. They got up to dance and he had the sensation of standing alone on the dance floor. She was so light, so ephemeral, that she seemed hardly there. Her body was so small and taut, that he could barely press against it and feel the yield of flesh.

They moved light as air across the floor. Harlan was a graceful dancer, good at all things physical. Usually when he danced close to a woman he became sexually aroused, if only induced by proximity and the warmth of flesh, but that was not the case now, and it worried him a little. The music grew slower and sweeter. Close by, a pretty sinuous blonde was dancing wrapped around her partner. He thought of Laina Eastman and he felt the throb of an erection tighten his pants. He was conscious of a growing obsession for this girl—a mere child, he thought. He feared the night with her would come back to haunt him, but felt quite sure that he had nothing to feel guilty

THE PLEASURE DOME

about. It wasn't as if she didn't *want* him—right along she had wanted him. Perspiration formed on his upper lip like buckshot.

Vivian moved away from him a little and he noticed with some amusement that she was perspiring also, although it was not unduly warm in the room. It seemed momentarily strange to him that someone so small could even perspire.

Vivian was a traditional girl brought up with the best and worst of traditional Jewish values. To have agreed to meet him clandestinely like this was in itself a breach of faith; to flirt with and encourage him at all was playing with fire. She knew she was acting contrary to her upbringing, even to what she herself believed in—but she had no wish to stop, she was having too good a time, for once.

The liquor, the intimacy of the last few minutes on the dance floor had made her reckless. They had just sat down again when she said, "I've been brought up to believe that Catholic boys are only interested in whiskey and women. Tell me, is it true?"

"Well," he said slowly, as if deliberating, "I can't speak for all the others, but as for myself—basically, that's about it."

She blushed and frowned a little, but her eyes shone.

He leaned forward, cupped her face in his hands and asked, "Why are you frowning?" He dropped his voice to a stage whisper. "I thought that's what you wanted to hear."

She pulled away and said stiffly, "Oh, come now, Harlan, are you really *all* that pleased with yourself? Somehow I just don't think so."

"You think I'm really some sort of a Pagliacci, who's laughing while his heart is breaking, eh?"

She assessed him carefully, gave him a level look with her alert brown eyes and said, "I just don't know—I'm not sure—from the little I know of you I would say you are a rebel of sorts . . . You hate the very thing you're drawn to."

"You sound like a psychiatrist. What, may I ask, are your credentials?"

"The best ever," she answered quickly, "—the hotels. I see a new drama every day, and every season the cast changes—down south, it changes weekly. . . ."

"*And* within your own family," he added dryly.

"Yes—that too, of course."

There was a pause. He fooled with the matchbook cover and then flipped it negligently into the ashtray. "What do you intend to do with your life now that the hotel has closed?"

"Oh, I don't know, lie around in the sun at the Hibiscus, help out in the office now and then. Last year I was 'social hostess,' but since I didn't find an eligible husband, dad demoted me. Evidently, I'd failed in my duties."

Harlan roared. "So now what?"

"Oh, they're trying to get me to open a chic little dress shop in the lobby—a boutique—cocktail clothes and accessories—you know . . ."

"Yes, I think I do, they're trying to turn you into the professional spinster sister. If you're not married and pregnant by the time you're twenty-one, they just assume you're unmarketable and relegate you to shopkeeper or the like. It's the same with a Catholic girl, except instead of a shop it's a nunnery," he said acrimoniously.

He leaned forward earnestly and folded her hands in his. He noticed that she seemed momentarily transfixed by his hands that were large and tanned and slender. His long graceful fingers curled around her little ones.

"We won't let that happen to you, will we?" he said.

They began to see each other at least twice a week in that month before Harlan went off to boot training, meeting usually at the Roosevelt Hotel on Forty-seventh and Madison Avenue. The clandestine nature of the relationship appealed to Vivian. For once in her life, she felt mysterious and beautiful. He had counted on that. He also counted on presenting himself to her family after, and only *after*, he had succeeded in taking her to bed, which he didn't think would be too difficult.

Vivian at twenty-five was, if anything, embarrassed by the burden of her virginity. She had dreamed so long over its ultimate disposal that relinquishing it to Harlan Chase was no particular sacrifice. It was in fact the ultimate consummation of those dreams. A tall handsome man with lime-green eyes had swept down from out of nowhere, and invaded her body like some wild-eyed avenging angel. His attentions, the violent nature of his lovemaking, flattered her beyond any shadow of her doubts—of which there had been many.

It began the Saturday night he had decided to stay in town, rather than drive back to the Island, as was his habit. The weather played right into his hands. A persistent downpour alternated with gale force winds, the residue of hurricane Gilda off the Florida coast. On the morning of the day they were to meet, she telephoned Harlan and told him that he would have to come by and pick her up at the apartment, because it would be impossible to get taxis or any other means of transportation in such weather and on a Saturday night. "Since you'll be coming by, why don't you come up and say hello to my parents? I know they'd enjoy seeing you again." This she knew was not entirely sincere. Jessie and Clara Goldmark would not have exactly welcomed Harlan Chase as a suitor for their only daughter. They had barely exchanged three sentences and a few polite smiles during the summer months.

Harlan thought a moment and then simply said, "Okay."

But when he pulled up in front of her apartment building on Fifth Avenue, the wind was howling viciously, and the rain had caused the traffic to be backed up for miles because of double parking and the necessity to drive slowly. He asked the doorman to ring the apartment and tell her to come down—there was obviously no way he could park tonight. The umbrella that the doorman carried to protect Vivian against the elements had blown inside out, and by the time she got into the car her carefully combed hair was in disarray and she seemed upset. She said nothing.

"You see, it is impossible to park tonight, and anyway you know, Viv, I don't have too much time left. I'll be leaving in a week or so. I think I'd like to keep you all to myself for a while longer, sort of our *thing*," he said intimately, "but I promise I'll see them before I leave, how's that?"

He hadn't even asked if they knew about him, or what they thought about his not coming up to the apartment. Perhaps, he thought, they really didn't care—that they were too settled to become irate.

They drove silently for a while, both deep in their own dreams, and then he said, "Viv, I've really missed you this week. I'm growing used to having you in my life.

Leaving will be very much more difficult than I thought."

"You'll be at Fort Monmouth for a couple of months anyway, won't you? Well, that's not so far, we'll still be able to see each other—I mean, I can always come out there to see you . . . can't I?" she trailed off uncertainly.

"Of course. It's just that who knows what kind of time—or privacy—we'd have there." There was a strained silence and the rain beat mercilessly against the windshield. Automobiles were weaving and skidding drunkenly, buffeted by the powerful winds.

"I think the only thing we can do tonight is go back to the hotel. I'm staying in town tonight because there's no way I could drive back—and anyway . . . I want to be with you," he said abstrusely.

She looked at him squarely now and said, "Harlan, why don't—you realize that you've never been inside of my house." She said this as if being inside her home was some sort of natural prerequisite for being inside her body.

"Perhaps next time, Viv. You haven't made it a condition of our relationship, and I didn't realize how important it was to you until now."

"It wasn't—really—until now."

They had dinner in the lovely old dining room of the hotel. They couldn't run around in this weather and this way the hotel would take his car. She didn't argue the point.

After dinner he said, "It's getting late. Perhaps I'd better get the car out to take you home."

"You sound like you have a late date," she said defensively. He looked at her and felt momentarily saddened. He knew that she loved him. It was there in her eyes. He wanted desperately to love her back. He was attracted to her candor and intelligence.

He cleared his throat, leaned forward and took her hands, braiding her small fingers like winter twigs with his great elegant ones and said softly, "Will you come up to my room? It's nothing very special but it has a sterile sort of charm, I suppose."

"Well . . . perhaps until the rain subsides a bit," she said cautiously.

All during dinner he thought of ways to seduce her. Up until now, sex had always been for him a completely easy, natural and intensely satisfying release, without involving the usual plotting or scheming undertaken by the other bachelors he knew.

The small room with its cell-like window was some twenty-five floors above the slick sounds of rain and traffic and smelled of Camay soap and irradiated heat. The wind whipped about the upper towers in a hushed frenzy.

She looked sad and frightened and distracted by indecision, dispelling any erotic feelings he may have been able to summon. He sat down suddenly on the bed and said quietly, "Look, Vivian this is silly, I feel like a goddamn overgrown adolescent," he said, falling down heavily on the bed, his arm flung carelessly across his eyes as if to blot out a painful image. This particular gesture made her falter momentarily, and she moved toward him with a sudden tender gesture of remorse, then straightened up, stood for a moment on the threshold as if waiting for him to coax her.

Slowly she began to unbutton her dress. She stared at him, her lip trembling. She laughed nervously. With that he lost no time. He began to undress her slowly, murmuring his pleasure as each of her finely made garments dropped to the floor and revealed her childlike body. She trembled and he pulled her to him. "Christ, do you have to look so damned scared?" he said, close to her ear.

"I'm sorry."

"It's time you began to live, in fact it's overdue," he said and carried her to the bed. Her slight body barely made an indentation on the mattress. As he covered her body with his, she made small choking sounds. He thought perhaps she would suffocate beneath him, or somehow come apart at the seams, but instead he found her responding with a passion unequal to her frail body, whispering shy endearments. Suddenly the face of Laina Eastman enveloped his senses. She was laughing, he was stroking her breasts in the water, garish in the moonlight, her long taffy-colored hair spread out on the surface of the water. . . .

Vivian moaned beneath him, and he surrendered himself to her—and to the moment.

Afterwards, he lay beside her absently stroking her hair and looking somewhere far away. She pulled herself up on her shoulder and drew his face toward her and smiled at him. There was a certain sureness, a lovely clarity about her then, and in that moment he thought perhaps he loved her.

CHAPTER 10

War was declared. The hotel was closed down and a sign went up that said "Government Building, No Trespassing, Naval Property—Do not go beyond this point."

Matthew Goldmark had no choice, he had to lease the Broadbeach to the navy for the duration of the war. It was prime oceanfront footage—five miles of beachfront property and some one hundred acres, including the golf course. Soon the virgin territory would sprout barracks and Quonset huts. They would teach the boys the secrets of the sea, launch the mighty ships that would sink the enemy and win the war. He did manage to salvage a little personal satisfaction from it. He had made a sizable contribution to the war effort. He was grateful that he didn't have to contribute a sixteen-year-old-son. It was obvious to him that this would be a grand opportunity to make money. That the war would make him the millionaire everyone thought he was. During a war recreation businesses prospered. No, he would take the million dollars in cash, and some four hundred thousand dollars in notes payable, and wait out the war by running between his apartment in New York and the Hibiscus, their remaining hotel in Miami Beach.

At the tail end of the depression he had been offered almost twice that by a private group. But who was certain of anything then? Besides, Faye hadn't wanted him to sell. The resort was her stage, her domain. She was "too young to be buried in obscurity," she said.

Matthew really had very little to do now. He could sit on the money or invest it if he wished, but there was no telling how the war would go at this point and he was afraid to make any commitments so early. He planned to put it away for afterwards, to reinvest it in the hotel after the war. No matter how much they compensated him, it would hardly be enough, and who knew how long this war would last? And with inflation, who knew how much his dollars would be worth in the final analysis? He would buy war bonds—he believed in his country.

After the bombing of Pearl Harbor, Harlan's outfit received their orders to go overseas. He was afraid he would not get a leave before shipping out, for they were being canceled left and right. However, he was granted a two-week pass before leaving for California and then, who knew for where, probably the Pacific, he thought.

There were two important matters he had to attend to before he left, his sister Janine and Vivian Goldmark. Women, he thought, why was his life bounded by women? In a way, it was a relief to be in the all-male confines of the marine training camp. The rigorous maneuvers were a welcome catharsis for him.

His sister Janine had written to him from Fields of Grace, the convent where she was novitiating. It was in Patchogue, Long Island, not too far from the family.

It was ten-thirty in the morning when he arrived home. He was relieved to find only his mother there. Somehow he did not feel ready to face his father's cold disdain, his general holier-than-thou attitude. He needed to be admired today, pampered even. His mother was good at it.

His mother had always been a good cook and she had prepared a homecoming feast with loving care. He assessed her carefully now, taking her hand to his cheek. "You look lovely, Mom. You grow lovelier every year."

The color came up to her cheeks. She smiled her appreciation. "You're thinner," she said. "Your appetite seems to have shrunk in the bargain."

Harlan sensed a slight tension. He wondered if they had heard about Vivian. He knew his father would disapprove, he had always been suspicious of his Jewish associations. Harlan himself didn't really know what he felt about Jews. As a boy he never heard of them, as a man he didn't understand them.

"Mom, I've got to use the car this afternoon."

"Where are you going? You've only just gotten here. To see Anya?"

"No, you *know* I am not going to see Anya. I'm going to Janine. How far is the damned convent from here anyhow?"

His mother colored at the blasphemous adjective.

"Why didn't you ever mention it in your letters?"

"She said that she'd prefer to write to you herself, which she did do, I see."

"I wrote to her but she never answered my letters."

"Perhaps she was just afraid of further displeasing you, she knew what your reaction would be."

"Mother, how could you let her do it?" he cried.

His mother seemed stunned by his anger. "But we should be so proud!"

"Proud—proud of what? Of running away to hide? I can't talk to you on this subject, I can't talk to you. I could never talk to Dad either," he said. "I never could talk to him at all," he said.

"Listen please, son, for a woman, almost anything is

better than marriage, with the endless childbearing and constant housework. There is at least some respect in being a nun." She said all this as if there were only two possible choices facing a Catholic girl. Was it her life she hated so, his father, or both? Harlan wondered as he strode out the back door to the garage.

He thought as he drove east toward Patchogue, how this too was in some way his fault—his sister's life. He felt responsible. As if she were going to be his stand-in with the Almighty. It was the *priest thing*. They had counted on him becoming a priest. Janine was really only second best and he knew it. But still his parents were mollified. He wondered if the church would consider her a fair exchange.

Patchogue was even more desolate than Broadbeach— he thought, the atmosphere plaintive and saline.

As he approached the grounds of the convent, the building seemed smaller than he had imagined it. Religious retreats seemed to have shrunk since his childhood. A nun opened the heavy oak door to him, and when he asked for his sister by name, she went to call the reverend mother. He waited in the parlor, remembering his last confession, the venial sins of his boyhood. His own thoughts made him feel guilty. He had sat here only moments and already he was feeling contrite. But it was foolishness—the only sin he had ever acknowledged short of murder was to allow a good woman to go to waste.

He studied the walls lined with holy pictures, pictures of the Virgin draped in varying shades of holy and regal blue, and wished to get this over with as quickly as possible. He had no patience for the fine-honed amenities of the church.

A moment later he heard the clicking of beads, followed by the gentle swish of a long skirt, and the mother superior appeared before him like a great night breeze.

"So you have come to see Sister Mary?" she said, inclining her head deferentially to Harlan.

"No," he said. "I am waiting to see my sister, Janine Chase."

"Sergeant Chase," she said, stifling a smile, "surely you know that when your sister came here to us she gave up her own identity and took the name of a saint we, or she, thought most suitable. What better than Mary? She has all of the outer beauty of the Virgin and perhaps some of the inner beauty too."

Everything that is good comes through Mary. He remembered these words of his boyhood. Under the assault of so much goodness he felt impotent. "May I see my sister please?" he said brusquely, rising from his seat, risking rudeness.

"Yes, certainly you may, but she is in the chapel at devotions now. It is down the long hall to your left." Her voice was cool and crisply instructive, the way he remembered the voices of the nuns at school.

He strode down the hall feeling somehow compromised. Nuns in twosomes sailed by. He speculated about their sex lives, but their faces were illegible, set in masks of goodness. Vacant dwellings in God's country, he thought. He pushed open the doors of the chapel and was surprised by its spaciousness, height and depth. He stood for a moment trying to accustom his eyes to the darkness. He marched down the aisle, squinting into the empty pews. The chapel seemed completely empty. As he reached the altar and crucifix he genuflected and crossed himself mechanically, a learned reflex. He rose quickly and looked about him. A thin beam of sunlight slanted in from the tall stained-glass window in the far corner, alive with specks of dust and prisms of color. Across the aisle he thought he saw a small, solitary figure.

"Janine," he called as he approached, so as not to startle her.

He stood, towering beside the kneeling figure. She seemed not to notice him at first, or even to hear him, so intense was her devotion to her prayers.

"Janine."

She looked at him and seemed to sway slightly—he pulled her arms and forced her almost roughly to her feet.

"Harlan," she whispered, "so it's you, you've come, I was afraid you would go off without seeing me."

"Did you think I could leave you behind?"

She smiled indulgently, "But Harlan, you don't understand. You never have."

"Now is the time to get out—now," he pressed.

"Harlan, this is what I want," she said quietly.

"You are afraid to live and grow, isn't that so?"

"Yes, perhaps I am, Harlan. This is a better life than poverty and too many children, like my sisters, like mother," she said. His mother's words bounced back at him.

"You have let yourself be brainwashed by mother. Don't listen to her, she's only an ignorant woman. She sees herself in your black habit, but I notice *she* didn't do it herself!"

"Please, Harlan, stop it. This is a church, they will hear you."

"You are young and beautiful and have your whole life ahead of you," he said. "Don't you want children someday? What of Marc Anselmo?" he asked in desperation. "Why don't you speak of him anymore?"

She placed her hand on his arm. "Sh, sh," she said. "No one can have it *all*, Harlan." She reached up to kiss his cheek and then an instant later he saw the last of her black robes disappear through the side door of the vestry.

"Coward!" he cried after her to the empty chapel.

He arrived at the Goldmark apartment, resplendent in his marine officer's uniform, a *ninety-day wonder*. He handed his peaked hat and white gloves to the Negro butler at the door. The maid who served their drinks with tiny caviar and sour cream crepes was a Father Divine girl. Vivian had been brought up by a series of Father Divine girls. When one got sick or angry or quit, another miraculously materialized to take her place, sent by one of the agencies owned by Father Divine, one of his vast business enterprises. It was part of the religion. One girl was supposed to be just like any other; it was the faith that counted, not the individual body that housed the spirit.

The Goldmarks were cordial, nothing more, nothing less. Jessie treated Harlan the same way he had when he first interviewed him for the coaching job, two years ago. Then, Harlan was only out to conquer the pool; now, he was in deep water, perhaps over his head. Chase wanted his only daughter. Against his will and better judgment, Jessie recognized that he was fighting a losing battle. And so with extreme embarrassment and a sheepish uncertainty, he asked Harlan his intentions while Vivian and Clara had gone to the kitchen to see about the hors d'oeuvres.

Harlan was taken off guard at first. Then he looked into Jessie's eyes ingenuously and said, "Why, I plan to marry her, sir, and steal every last quarter you have!"

THE PLEASURE DOME

Jessie looked alternately confused and angry, then broke out in rich guffaws. He distrusted him only a little less from then on.

Sometime during the second week of his leave he eloped with Vivian to Greenwich, Connecticut. It was "just spontaneous," Vivian later told her parents. However, that did little to ameliorate their feelings of having been misled. Jessie could only see her ultimate perdition in this act of what he considered momentary frivolity. But Vivian did not hear his doomsday prophesies; she was too happy, too overcome with a careless joy.

Unlike her sister-in-law Faye, she did not believe her life was charmed, that everything was coming to her, dues owed a fairy princess. She fully appreciated the gift of Harlan's name—and body.

Harlan would be a good husband, he made up his mind to that. In any case, he had a hundred years to think about it. He would be shipping out in a week.

Sometimes he wished that her breasts were larger, or that he wouldn't think about Laina Eastman anymore whenever he thought about sex, which was often, but he had buried his past with his St. Christopher medal. And now Vivian would be his stake in the future.

CHAPTER 11

The summer of 1942 was the first summer after the Broadbeach Club had closed and Alex Eastman didn't know what to do with Laina and Seth. They begged him to let them go out to the beach house and just sort of lie around, reading and loafing and swimming in the ocean. But Alex was conscience-riddden over their lack of supervision, terrified of a repeat of Laina's fearful accident, of infantile paralysis, of bombs dropping on New York City. No, he could not permit an aimless, unstructured summer. What had he considered summers at the Broadbeach? Laina wondered.

Joe Salzman owned the health club in one of Alex's dance hall buildings. In summers he ran Camp Choctaw. It was not nestled in the Poconos or discreetly tucked into the pine endowed forests of Maine, as was generally considered socially acceptable for a summer camp in those years. Instead the small coed camp made its home in the mosquito-riden marshes of Lake Ronkonkoma, New York. Alex had never seen the camp but assumed if Joe Salzman owned it it must be okay. Alex assumed that anyone who paid him a hefty rent was pretty much *okay*.

Joe arranged for Laina to become a junior counselor. He was doing Alex a favor because Laina was too young to be a counselor and too old, she said, to be a camper. At sixteen she was the "juniorest" of all the counselors and

THE PLEASURE DOME

was immediately assigned to a group of six-year-olds, the toughest age group at camp, she was told, the one nobody else wanted.

The senior counselor of her cabin, Syd Hirsh, was twenty-two with waist-length hair dyed a whitish blonde and a good body. During the day she wore eyeglasses and pulled her hair into a tight bun and looked deceptively unyielding. The evenings were quite another matter. She let her hair down in a dramatic shower of platinum, wore makeup and, to Laina, appeared decidedly yielding.

Caroline Segall had wrested a summer from the possessive clutches of her mother, and was somewhere between junior and senior counselor at Camp Choctaw. Caroline, who referred to herself as a war casualty due to the demise of the Broadbeach, arrived only to scoff at the rules and regulations set down for counselors as well as campers, and the unsophisticated and inelegant boys who comprised the male staff. She chattered obsessively about them, calling them by nicknames.

It seemed to Laina that Syd spent most of her time in front of the mirror examining her almost poreless skin and complaining about invisible blemishes. Sometimes Laina got a chance at the narrow slab of mirror in the bunk and she practiced rolling her shorts up like Syd, until they exposed the early curve of buttock. But she smoothed them discreetly down again before going out. Syd called her a prude and teased her mercilessly about her detachment from boys. Syd said, "You'll be very pretty when you grow up. Guys will like you. You look fuckable."

Laina considered Syd crude and guessed, somewhat enviously, that she even enjoyed sex. Syd said that she was engaged back home, but she also appeared to be engaged in a hot summer romance with a handsome counselor a few years younger than herself.

Laina's tight body had the oddly erotic quality of being both narrow and full. She saw the way men looked at her and thought she must be pretty, with her honey-blonde hair and greenish-yellow eyes, but it only frightened her. She wore large sunglasses and loose, shapeless shirts, but her full breasts shook visibly when she walked quickly or ran with the children, despite the constraining brassieres she wore.

She was careful to avoid the boys' side of camp whenever possible, though often she was certain that Syd purposely led the campers to the baseball and volleyball fields to be closer to them.

Caroline almost immediately took up with a group of senior counselors that included Syd Hirsh. One of the counselors, Judd Epstein, had taken up with Syd, after being rejected by Laina for reasons unclear even to herself. Not that she cared. The trouble was she didn't seem to care about anything and that worried her. Laina felt curiously separated from her own sex. Caroline said she was just a "CT" and would get a reputation if she didn't watch out. So Laina stayed in the bunk with the children most nights, so that Syd could sneak up to the hill with the handsome Judd. She lay on her cot in the dark while the sleeping children called out for their mothers or cried and wet their beds. Laina felt sorry for them and wondered sadly why anyone would send a six-year-old to camp.

She loved Friday nights, which were the high point of the week. In pristine Shabbas whites Laina tried hard to look chaste. She stood alongside her small charges at the outdoor services and their young hopeful voices soared and arced to the setting sun while mosquitoes nipped at their bare legs.

THE PLEASURE DOME

"Hear, O, Israel: The Lord our God. The Lord is One." The young rabbi who looked old and wise was also the music counselor, his wife was the dietitian. He wore thin wire-framed glasses and a white satin yarmulke as for a wedding. Laina thought he looked pensive and moody. When he chanted the ancient Hebrew words *"Sh'ma Yisroel Adonoy Elohenu Adonoy echod,"* the girls buzzed and giggled but Laina was glad she was a Jew and thought of her father with a sudden nostalgia, and wondered if he would come up to camp to visit her.

After services they all trooped into the mess hall. They sang the plaintive "Hatikvah," and finally amidst giggles, sighs and the scraping of chairs they were seated. *"Baruch ato Adonoy Elohenu . . ."* —they said the prayer over the bread and then the counselors whisked the food onto their own plates with lightning speed. Joe Salzman knew that Jewish parents felt less guilty about sending the children away to camp if the food was plentiful.

Cabin Six, the older girls' table, sang, "Two, four, six, eight, who do we appreciate. Aunt Toni, yeah!"

Syd murmured, "Ass kissers." Toni was the head counselor, a handsome woman in her late thirties, a retired ballroom dancer. Syd said the only qualification she had for being head counselor was probably that she gave good head. Laina didn't know what that meant but guessed it was something darkly funny, from the way Caroline roared with laughter.

Just before dessert the waiters vanished mysteriously only to reappear at the front of the room for the waiter's chant:

> Peas, beans, borscht and potatoes
> Shabbas is here
> Tip, tip the waiters!

They jumped high in the air—"yeah"—everyone in the room applauded warmly. The visiting parents looked on self-consciously. "What should I give?" they whispered, embarrassed by the scrupulous reminder, fearful that they might not *give* enough, and *their* child wouldn't get as much to eat as the wealthier children.

Laina's cabin didn't have any visitors this weekend. It was still early in the season. She looked around the mess hall and saw the sprinkling of parents, faded replicas of Broadbeach parents. Not as affluent or trendy, or rich, they seemed earnest, bewildered. She wondered if money and privilege gave people certainty, undid the confusion. It had not helped *her* much. She wondered if it had helped her father. When a parent did come up to visit and gave her money, she burned with shame. She looked at these people and realized that her father would say he could "buy and sell them." But then again Alex said that about almost everyone.

Caroline and Syd were always bending the rules and getting into trouble with the head counselor. They were all irresponsible, she said, and that included Laina. As a result they were constantly on OD (on duty), a punishment detail similar to night guard in military service. They persisted in sneaking up to the hill with their boyfriends after general lights out, leaving their "OD's" to Laina, who volunteered cheerfully. Anything was better than winding up on the hill with Caroline's cliquish and carefully coupled friends. So at nights, amid the thick electric whir of crickets, she haunted the small campus with her flashlight, listening for a child's cry, and tried to decide why she was old before she was ever young.

"Why don't you go out at nights with us?" Caroline inquired peevishly one day. They sat on a blanket, during rest hour, eating summer cherries, with their faint inky flavor. Caroline was polishing her nails. When Laina didn't answer Caroline shook her hard and said, "You're not even half as much fun as you used to be, I'm sorry I ever came here with you." A mysterious covey of planes roared overhead in formation—nowadays a lone plane was cause for concern. Caroline, in a surge of patriotism, waved wildly and threw kisses high up into the air. Laina watched the neat pattern, two dipped their wings on the left, then two on the right. She felt relieved, practice maneuvers, she thought. With every new phalanx of planes she feared an air raid, worse yet, Invasion. Terrified that the Nazis would invade her country—her body—They would tear her limb from limb. Some Catholics were going to the Concentration Camps too. Ah double jeopardy! If ever *we* did not win the war she was certainly doomed. She tried to pull her mind away from such thoughts.

Joel Persky walked over to them and kicked the blanket awkwardly with the toe of his sneaker, raising a cloud of dust—"God," Caroline said, "Is that your idea of charm? Ugh!" but he took no notice of Caroline. He was watching Laina.

"Your lips are purple," he scoffed. "Have some cherries." she said. Joel took this for an invitation and flopped down negligently onto the blanket. "Your mouth looks like one of those cherries," he said, and then whispered in her ear, "and I'll bet it tastes just as sweet." Caroline looked annoyed and rolled over on her back pretending to sunbathe but kept an ear cocked in their direction. "Will you meet me at the Rec. Hall tonight?" Laina knew that the staff hung out there most evenings after taps, but she had yet to make an appearance there, and she had been dismissed by now as a "loner," "peculiar," "a cold cookie." Caroline nudged her and whispered that if she said no again, she wouldn't talk to her for the rest of the summer.

Laina was torn between the terror of enforced isolation, and the cold fear of losing her autonomy—of having to do things she had no wish to do, with people she did not care about.

Joel Persky was okay for a boy of eighteen, though not nearly as adult as her brother, she decided. He wasn't particularly attractive, but at least he didn't have any pimples.

"How come you're so unfriendly, huh, Laina?" Joel said nudging her gently.

"How come you're so skinny?" Caroline put in uncharitably. Joel colored and said, "Careful, Caroline, or you won't get any seconds."

"Hmmf, with what they've got to eat here, I could do nicely without *firsts*."

"I'll remember that."

Joel got up to leave reluctantly. "So listen Kid, I'll see you in the Rec. Hall tonight after lights out, or are you "O.D." again?" he said pointedly. "Oh won't you tell me when you're not O.D. again—Sunday, Monday, or always" he trilled, in parody of the latest Perry Como hit tune.

"No, no, I'll see you there Joel" Laina's voice trailed off, it was barely audible. "Well let's try at least to sound cheerful about it shall we," he said, "I'm not exactly asking you to a funeral." But he walked away whistling.

It was pebbly and steep walking up the hill. It was studded with clover blossoms and moss. Caroline and Bill were laughing and teasing with the easy familiarity of old lovers. Syd Hirsh was nowhere in sight. She rarely came to the Rec. Hall either. Probably because "their affair was getting out of hand" Caroline said.

Once they reached the knoll at the top of the hill Caroline and Bill disappeared. Joel kissed her a few times and did not seem surprised by her lack of ardor. He kept poking his fingers inside the elastic of her snug fitting underpants, but she pushed him away. "Oh please Laina" he begged. "Just let me take them down a little—I only want to look for a minute—please let me have a look." She tried to sit up. "Please," he said. "Just for a minute, nothing can happen by just looking." He deftly rolled her underpants down to her knees. She was grateful for the numbing darkness. He could not believe his good fortune. He groped for the flashlight, found it, and directed its cruel beam toward her thighs, illuminating her guilty secret. Somewhere in the brush nearby she heard Caroline's gusty laugh. "Please let me touch you, just a little," he whined close to her ear. "Just a little." She hated his whining, and pleading. He directed her hand to his groin. She felt his penis large and hard. Her heart was beating in her temples, in her throat. She began to tremble visibly. He took it to mean excitement. He dropped the flashlight and began to touch her, to put his fingers in the secret places of her soul. His head was close to hers and she remembered the crisp chlorine smell of Harlan's hair. Her hand closed around the heavy flashlight on the ground between them. She pushed Joel away slightly and brought it down on his skull—three, four, five,—she did not know how many times. There was a stunned silence. She thought perhaps she had killed him, perhaps he was dead. But she heard him bellow in pain, "dirty c.t." as she ran down the hill—running, running helter-skelter in the blackness.

Joel had to spend a week in the infirmary for a mild concussion and for the balance of that long hot summer she was considered pretty much of a pariah. Joel had his table changed. The new waiter gave her dirty looks. Evidently some of the story had drifted back to Toni, the head counsellor. She called Laina into her office one afternoon during the week that followed for a "little talk." Toni sat back in her desk chair and tried to look at once motherly and authoritative. But Laina thought she only managed to look tough, with her high cheekbones and winged eyebrows and her sly smile.

"Seems to me that you have been acting very strange all summer long. I haven't called you in here before because frankly the children seem well cared for—but your personal conduct is quite another matter."

Laina shrugged her shoulders dispassionately.

"You don't seem to have any interest in anything, yet I am convinced that you're intelligent," she said. "Very intelligent. It's as if you wore a veil. Yes, that's it, you are hidden by a veil of some sort." Laina stared at her, but still did not speak.

"You know this is basically a coed camp. There are male staff members living side by side with us—or haven't you noticed?" she asked curiously. "You can't expect to go around here dressed in that inflammatory style without inviting trouble."

"What is inflammatory about me?" Laina asked, hurt and surprised.

"Oh I think you know—tight shirts, short shorts, blouses tied up tightly, no bra, et cetera."

"But I do wear a bra," Laina was indignant at the rank injustice. "Always, and all the girls tie up their blouses and roll their shorts, only I hardly ever do."

Toni interrupted her sharply. "I don't care what the

other girls do. *Your* general manner is attention provoking."

Laina felt the sharp salt taste of tears in her nostrils but she held them back. She looked small and delicate sitting before this muscular athletic woman. Toni leaned toward her intimately. She could smell the heavy perfume. There was something lush, Latin about her. She reminded her somehow of Faye Goldmark. Laina drew back instinctively.

"Tell me, Laina," Toni dropped her voice, once again confidential, "do you have a boyfriend in the service perhaps?"

There was a brief fragile silence, then Laina replied clearly, almost eagerly, "Yes, he's in the marines." Laina seemed alarmed by her own answer, as if a ventriloquist had projected for her. Her cheeks flamed feverishly.

Toni sat back almost triumphantly. "Oh, so that's it! Aren't you a little young to be so deeply involved with a boy? How old is he anyway?"

"I, I don't know," she said, "maybe twenty-five, or—I don't know." Her eyes looked as if they were seeking refuge—a small forest animal cornered.

"Twenty-five! Why, he is a man, not a boy, and you, you are only a child, a child really, parading around as a woman." She said these last words softly. Laina was glad she hadn't told the truth. "Are you going to tell me that you are still a virgin? You are not going to tell me that, are you?"

Laina, stunned, did not know what to answer, or if she was expected to, or even why she was being asked such a question. She wondered if Toni quizzed the other junior counselors in this manner. Why were people forever plumbing her body and soul for secrets? She said in one great breath, "I am only sixteen, what do you expect?

Yes, of course I am, and anyway, why should it matter so much to you?"

Toni seemed defeated. She ended the interrogation abruptly as if she had suddenly grown bored with the subject matter. She put her on bunk duty again for the balance of the summer, of which some three weeks remained. Laina was secretly pleased. It put an end to decisions and choices and provided a legitimate excuse for her remoteness.

So she and Caroline were back patrolling the bunks again. Armed with flashlights they roamed the mosquito-laden, citronella-scented night, and wailed into the moonlight, "Oh, won't you tell us when we're not OD again, Sunday, Monday, and always."

Sometimes Caroline met Bill behind the bunks, where grew an anarchy of weeds, and Laina covered for her, while they whispered and huddled there among the salamanders and other summer night-things.

One afternoon Seth came to visit. They sat at an outdoor table under an umbrella on the visitors' grounds and talked for a while, skirting the subject of their father. Laina kept taking his hands in hers, dropping them, and taking them up again.

"You seem agitated." He looked around him. "You haven't liked it here." It was not so much a question as a statement. "Not that I blame you. Hasn't been much of a summer for either one of us, I guess." Seth had hung around mostly alone all of that long hot summer. He hadn't really known what to do with himself until college started in the fall. Many of his friends had already enlisted, the rest had joined the ROTC at their colleges.

THE PLEASURE DOME

Alex wouldn't hear of it. "Officers were the first to go and the first into battle," he said.

They talked for a while and then she said, "How come dad didn't come up with you?"

"Oh Laina, you're not really surprised, are you? You ought to know him by now."

"Yes, I suppose so, but still."

"He can't change. He runs himself ragged." Laina thought Seth's defense of Alex was pretty weak.

"For what reason?" she asked.

"I think it's what keeps him from thinking, about things, about mother," he said.

"Do you miss her, Seth?"

"Yes, don't you?"

"Particularly when the parents come up on visiting days, or when the little kids in my bunk cry out at night. Oh, I don't know. I guess it's always there just beneath the surface."

"He telephones, doesn't he?"

"Yes, every week. The last time was when you got on the phone."

She was disappointed that he was not staying overnight. Shortly before he left, during twilight when everyone else had retired to relax before dinner, he told her the news. "Laina, I have something to tell you. I've enlisted in the marines. I'll be leaving next week for boot training in San Diego."

She was stunned. "But college, what about college? Seth, you promised dad. What does he say?"

"I haven't told him yet. I've put it off as long as possible. I'll tell him tonight, if I see him, or tomorrow."

"But why Seth? You are only eighteen, and why the marines?"

"Why not? My swimming training should come in handy there, and who knows, maybe I'll meet up with Chase. That would be great fun. Maybe he'll even be in charge of my outfit. Besides, I like the uniforms." He laughed, but his laughter lacked warmth or merriment.

Her lips began to tremble. "Seth," she said, "you can't let anything happen to you, you're all I have."

He took her in his arms then and held her tightly, and said, "It isn't home I'll miss, Lainie. We've never really had a home. It's you. You've been home and friend and family, well—all of that to me."

The children clung together. She buried her head in his hair and was embarrassed to realize that this was the first flood of warmth, of human feeling she had experienced in a year—a sleepwalker rudely awakened from a disturbing dream.

That summer ended with Color War, flamboyant enough to suit even the jaded Caroline. The counselors were assigned teams and asked to compose songs and cheers for the big sing that would end Color War and close the camp season officially. It would be time-consuming, involving much of their leisure hours. Rabbi Dinitz, the music counselor, would collaborate, but made it quite clear that he would not have the time to devote to it officially. As it turned out he had none. To Laina and Caroline this seemed a heaven-sent opportunity. It would be better than patrolling the bunks at night. Both girls loved music and Laina had been writing poetry furtively for years. They each volunteered to head up a team and to collaborate on the lyrics. Caroline was a glib conversationalist and could put her talents to positive use, for a change.

THE PLEASURE DOME

Toni del Falco looked skeptical. It was obvious that she simply didn't trust Laina or Caroline.

"I have never before put the biggest event of the camp season into the hands of junior counselors." Toni delivered a lecture on the merits of responsibility and then reluctantly gave permission for Laina to head the White Team's sing, while Caroline would lead the Blue. She had been cornered by lack of options.

Their first job was to choose the music to which they would adapt the appropriate lyrics. They finally agreed upon the music of the Grieg Concerto for the Blue Team and the music of the Russian composer Borodin—strong handsome music, for the White Team.

Caroline with her sharp tongue and irreverent heart came up with clever and sardonic lyrics. Laina's were crisp and sweet. All day long Laina's head buzzed with catchy phrases and rhymes. She no longer heard the children. At night in her bed, she dreamed the lyrics over and over. They became tangled in her old dreams. She saw her father dodging bombs on the streets of New York—her mother in the dress she wore for Seth's Bar Mitzvah—her brother's body, shattered into bloody fragments. Sometimes she dreamed that she was embraced by a handsome officer, whom she dismembered with an ax.

But the days were joyful. She had created something. She was no longer bored. She was worthy. It no longer mattered which team won the sing, for all the songs were theirs. Caroline led her team into the gymnasium with such style and panache that her team won by a small margin. But everyone was astounded at the professionalism of the songs. The whole presentation, in fact, was a shining success.

* * *

It was late in January when the telegram announcing Seth's death came from the war office. Alex went into his bedroom and shut the door for two terrible days. Laina was more alone than ever in the apartment on Central Park West. She leaned against the door and heard his dry wracking sobs. She tried to imagine her father crying tears that were wet and warmer than rain, like her own, but she could not. She sat huddled in a corner thinking how unworthy she was, how she deserved these rude shocks. Why else had her mother, and now her brother, abandoned her? And her father too, hadn't he always shut her out? And even Harlan Chase must loathe her too. Why else would he have assaulted her so cruelly?

In the days that followed she sometimes sleepwalked through the apartment, went into Seth's room and lay down on his bed and slept there until morning—until Alex or Ginger found her.

On one of these mornings, arising early, exhausted from a fitful sleep, she went to the window and saw the children playing after a rain. They seemed sharply defined against the fresh-washed air, uncomplicated, one-dimensional as paper dolls. Two girls crossed the street. They walked jauntily, their hair blowing behind them in the wind, cradling their schoolbooks against their beginning breasts, as if savoring their youth and innocence. One boy kept throwing a ball up over the awning and letting it roll down again, the same way Seth used to do when he was nervous or worried about something. It made a dull, soft sound—whoosh, whoosh.

"At the going down of the sun, and in the morning we will remember them. . . ."

Alex stayed up nights rereading the letters from his son by the light of a dim bulb, as if the stingy light might in some way atone for his sin of being safely out of harm's way. For a full week he stayed away from his business and neither showered nor shaved.

Until now, Laina and Alex had spent their lives remote from one another, but when he finally emerged from his room, fresh and clean shaven, he took his daughter in his arms. "I've been selfish," he said, playfully slapping her buttocks. "But from now on it's you and me against the world, kid!" he said, and he meant it with all his heart.

Laina tried to remember when he had last put his arm around her. But later on, looking back, she would not forget that morning, the morning when she first "met" her father—or so it seemed to her. He had always worked long hours, mostly nights, and her mother had somehow managed to keep the children away from him—as if to keep the stain from spreading.

"Put on some coffee, Laina," he said, "and we'll have breakfast together, just the two of us. What do you say?"

"I don't even know what you eat for breakfast," she said gently.

II.
REUNION:
1946-1949

CHAPTER 12

It was the late fall of 1946 and the very last thing that Clara Goldmark had said to her grieving family before she died was that she was grateful that God had spared her to see the outcome of the war, to see the victory. She would have preferred to linger a while longer, if only to see the reopening of the Broadbeach Club, but she was not a demanding woman, and she died as she had lived, with an absence of melodrama. If sometimes she had appeared to outsiders a bit supercilious and stiff-necked, it was not due to an overly formal education but rather to one that was highly empirical.

At ten o'clock that evening the family sat around the sprawling oak-paneled den of the Fifth Avenue residence, feeling drained. The air was still thick with the homey odor of stale pickles and rye bread. They had just completed the last day of the *shivah* and had fed some two hundred mourners in the last four days. They came in waves, a sea of faces moving around the apartment, fingers greasy with fat delicatessen sandwiches, lipstick slightly smeared. The *shivah*, Matt thought gloomily, was no better than an Irish wake. Vivian was helping in the kitchen. He was pleased that she had made it to their mother's bedside before she died, and that she had the good taste to leave Harlan behind in Broxton, Massachusetts, or wherever it was they had settled. He had always felt uncomfortable around him, and now that Harlan had a wounded leg and medals, Matthew felt somehow diminished, particularly in Jessie's presence. He wondered how long the coaching job at the university would last, now that Harlan was unable to participate actively.

Jessie Goldmark squinted at the celebrity pictures facing him on the far wall. There he was, a younger Jessie, drinking convivially with an assortment of celebrities—Flo Ziegfeld, George Gershwin, Russ Columbo. He threw his hands in the air in a gesture of helpless fury. "They're all gone, damn it, all of 'em—all gone. Like one great sneeze," he said, his eyes half-closed. The death of a contemporary threw him into a fury at his own mortality, and the death of his wife only reminded him of the urgent need to get his house in order.

Matthew moved to his father's chair like a gust of wind. "I know how lost you must feel at this moment, Father."

"I will miss her. She was a great help to me."

"I'll help you. You know you can count on me," Matthew said passionately.

Jessie appeared to look through him. "There is no question that I will need help, but I doubt that I will find the sort of help I need within these walls."

There was a brief mournful silence. "What we will need is money, my dear Matthew—plenty of it," he said, sighing deeply.

Matthew winced. He did not wish to talk about money now—with his mother barely cold in her grave. He missed her already. She had always been his ally, his only friend.

"The Broadbeach," Faye said knowledgeably, "how much is it going to cost to put Humpty Dumpty together again?"

"Ah, a couple of million might do," Jessie said, his eyes half-closed, his fingers forming a triangle beneath his chin.

"Do we need it?" Vivian said as she entered the room.

"What—the two million dollars?" he asked.

"No, the Broadbeach." She circled the room, hampered somewhat by advancing pregnancy. "What do we really need it for? Let them keep it. It's no good to us as it is. Just a huge financial burden that will beat us down." She lowered herself carefully onto the sofa next to Matt. Heavy with pregnancy, her belly protruded ostentatiously from her narrow frame, the outline of her navel pushing up proudly.

Faye eyed her with distaste and said, "Tell me, Viv, is it you or Harlan that insists upon embracing the lyrical rhythm method? It's not too reliable, you know, dear. That's why there are so many Catholics."

"Steven is almost four. Don't you consider that a decent interval?" Vivian replied banteringly.

"Depends on what the interval is *from*."

"Faye, please," Jessie said wearily.

"The point is that *I* want to take it back," Matthew interrupted. "First of all, our summer people have been deluging us with requests and second of all, I think it will pay in the long run—and pay big."

Faye smiled her satisfaction. She clearly wanted her summers back at the Broadbeach Club. "So then what's the problem?"

"The problem is we haven't got it. Oh, we've got the million dollars to buy back the property. Between what is in the bank and what we can raise on the Hibiscus, we can buy it back," Matthew said with assurance. "But it will take almost twice that to return it to any semblance of order, much less elegance. The place looks like an abandoned WPA project right now! Every cent we made during the war we poured into the Hibiscus and we've just about broken even there."

While Matthew spoke, Jessie pursed his lips as if sucking on a lemon.

"Well, Father, isn't it true? Have I said anything that is even in the least bit exaggerated?" He felt suddenly vulnerable, with no one to stand between him and his father.

"No, you haven't exaggerated, but you have left out some major points, while stressing some minor ones. The money we need we can probably borrow from a bank."

"At scandalous rates," Matthew put in defensively.

"Or from some other source," his father continued, ignoring his outburst. "But it is management that troubles me. Steady, experienced management. Personnel, a staff that does not change from year to year, one that our regular guests can readily identify with. That has been the biggest problem right along. There's nobody around who gives a damn!"

Matthew jumped up from his seat. "Father, that simply is not fair. I care, I care very much. You know I've always considered the hotels my special province. After all, it was Faye and I who implemented the whole thing."

"Yes, and still I'm not convinced that you're really cut out for it, Matthew."

Matthew was trembling. He particularly disliked being criticized in the presence of his wife. "I'm sorry that you don't approve of my business methods, Father."

"Do I have to approve of your business methods too? No, I don't approve of them."

There was a strange uncomfortable silence. Matthew felt as if he were awaiting the executioner's blow. He prayed the ax wouldn't fall now, not in front of Faye and

THE PLEASURE DOME

Vivian. Vivian understood Jessie. That was why she left home the first chance she got and buried herself in the cranberry bogs of Massachusetts with her goy.

"Oh, calm yourself, Matthew. I wasn't casting aspersions, merely taking stock of a serious situation. I simply don't wish to be active in management anymore. I'm too old. Once we take back the Broadbeach, it will be too much for any one man to handle."

To Matthew's sensitized ears the words inherent in that phrase were *much less, someone like yourself.*

"Vivvy, you were always good with ideas. Have you any suggestions?"

Everyone fell silent.

"Well, I'm sure *you've* called the Cornell Hotel School already," Matthew said, hurrying to answer for his sister.

"Any young man with anything at all to offer would have spent the last four years in service," Jessie announced.

Matthew winced.

"That's utterly ridiculous," Faye said. "Enough of this flagwaving, let's get back to the subject of financing." She seemed anxious to abandon the issue of personnel. "What about some of our friends? The guests, the regulars like Rosensweig or Segall, or Alex Eastman? I understand he made an absolute fortune during the war. He is a good businessman, or so I've heard."

Matthew shook his shaggy head. "No," he said. "No, this is ours. It has always been a family business—catering to families, a place where the generations can return. We don't want, don't need any outside investors." He seemed offended by Faye's pragmatism.

"You know, Matthew," his father said, "I wonder if we can afford the luxury of so much sentiment now. The

109

whole world has had to twist and bend a little in these last few years. Nothing stays the same. Shouldn't we too roll a little with the times?"

Matthew wanted the credit for carrying them through the war years in the black—for keeping the Hibiscus Gardens almost up to its prewar luxury standards. It had been a full-time job just trying to get produce, meat and poultry, keeping an eye on ever-changing bartenders, and watching out that the steward didn't run a little black market business on the side with the sugar and coffee. All the while trying to smooth disgruntled guests' ruffled feathers.

"Well, Vivian," Jessie bellowed suddenly as if to include her in the general conversation, "when are we going to see that son of yours again? Sooner or later he'll have to surface. We'll need all the male heirs we can get to help us run the place. Which reminds me, Matthew, where's David? Seems to me I saw him earlier."

Matthew tensed visibly. "He was here, but I don't know where he's gone now."

"Perhaps you should," Jessie said pointedly. "Might do to keep an eye on him. That fancy boarding school and Ivy League college," he remonstrated. "did him more harm than good if you ask me."

Matthew gave his father a pleading look, but if Jessie noticed, he deflected it.

"And that's another thing, Matthew, get that boy out of that goddamn sissy music or acting school. Let's start teaching him *this* business. He's done enough studying. You'd think he'd have learned something at Yale besides buggering!"

There was an awful silence. Matthew looked as if someone had struck him in the face. He thought they'd agreed never to mention it, even among themselves. He was sorry now that he had ever taken him into his confidence. In an effort to force a closer relationship with his father, Matthew confided personal things and invariably was sorry. This time the old man had wormed it out of him. Matthew glanced over at Vivian. Her face was strangely impassive. He hoped she would not tell Harlan.

Faye fought back tears. "Father, how could you? You haven't even tried to understand!"

It was even impossible for Matthew to comprehend that his son had been expelled from Yale, his own alma mater, shortly before he was to graduate. The charge was "immoral behavior, lewd and lascivious conduct unbecoming a gentleman." That was the only statement the school was prepared to make. Other boys were involved, but for some reason David was the only one expelled. They would not explain—they did not wish to discuss it further, they said, when Faye went up to the school to plead his case.

Faye had dismissed it as adolescent hijinks. How dare they withhold his degree when he had earned most of it already, and with good grades? Finally, she succeeded in convincing them to grant his degree as long as he finished his senior year at an accredited school—somewhere else. So he chose the Juilliard School of Music. David wanted to be a composer.

"It will be nice to have David back home again," Faye said thoughtfully.

Matthew knew why his wife seemed to capitulate so easily. She could have him as her steady companion everywhere. Fuss and fiddle and rhumba with him. Drag him to her fittings and have him kibitz her card and Mah-Jongg games. He could hear her lacquered fingernails clicking against the ivory tiles now. David would lie there in bathing trunks, his smooth upper body slicked with coconut oil, browning in the tropical sunshine. All the reasons that Matthew had sent him away in the first place.

He wondered why he was in eternal combat with his father whom he loved more than he cared to admit, why he had allowed his own son, whom he loved less than he cared to admit, to drift free while he concentrated on winning his father's approval.

Matthew rose heavily from the deep armchair he had taken refuge in. He went to the closet and got the coats. "I think we'd better be going home." He helped Faye on with her coat. They kept a small apartment on Park Avenue, but used it only out of season like now, because of the hotels.

"Just a moment, Matthew. I want you and Vivian to drive out with me to the beach tomorrow, to look at the place, to talk it over—on the premises," Jessie said. "Vivian here hasn't even seen it lately and she's leaving in a day or so."

Matthew sighed heavily. He prayed that he would get a good night's sleep. He'd need to have his mind clear and sharp tomorrow.

Father and daughter sat quietly for a moment. Through the large windows they watched the lights of the city.

"I'm sorry in a way that he didn't come along with you this time, Vivian." Jessie seemed unable to dignify Harlan by using his given name and usually wound up referring to him as "he."

"I am, too, but there wasn't time. Between collecting the baby's paraphernalia and readjusting Harlan's classes, it just didn't seem worthwhile."

THE PLEASURE DOME

Jessie seemed deep in thought. "With another baby on the way you really couldn't survive up there without the extra money I've been sending, could you?"

"That's probably true, Father, but after all, it *is* my money."

Jessie went on smoothly, "It's yours because I chose to give it to you when I divided up the stock between you, your brother and your mother. Now your mother's share will be equally divided between the two of you. You and Matthew together are fifty percent partners with me." He said this as if it were a commemorative event.

"It's very generous—really—"

He interrupted her blandly, "One hundred percent will belong to you and Matt when I die, and by then who knows, there may be more hotels. Much depends on you and Matthew," he added with a certain reticence. "Let's talk candidly and carefully," he continued. "There are decisions to be faced and at the moment it may be necessary to regroup our assets and call on our reserves."

Vivian smiled at what she considered his Prussian military terminology.

"Vivian, I am not joking. We are in a stage of siege. You will see what I mean tomorrow, when you see the hotel. We need help—all we can get now. I'm certain I can even find something for that great guy of yours to do, too."

Her brown eyes opened wide. She smiled ruefully. "You mean you would put Harlan to work at the Goldmark Hotels? Christ, things must be blacker than I realized."

"Why?" Jessie's face was a mask. "He's worked with us before, hasn't he? Been around our places . . . has a way with people." He seemed to be convincing himself while he talked. "I understand he's going for his master's. What the hell is he studying, anyway?"

"Business administration."

There was an uneasy pause while he narrowly assessed his daughter. "Exactly what sort of business is he planning to administrate?"

"Oh, I don't know, Dad. I'm sure it's as obvious to him as it is to you that a man with a wounded leg can't continue to teach swimming forever."

"Precisely," said Jessie. "So what does he intend doing about it?"

She leaned her head against the back of the sofa. "We've been happy up there, Dad. There're some awfully nice people—lots of other young instructors and their wives."

"He's getting on a bit, isn't he? I'm sure they're all considerably younger than your husband."

"Yes, but I don't think that matters. They're all veterans. They have a common bond. They're all relearning the politics of living—they're enormously fond of Harlan, you know." There was a pause. "I love him," she said in a barely audible whisper.

"Well then, speak up, girl. That's something to shout about, not to whisper like some awestruck kid. How about him? Does he love you?"

"Yes, I think he does," she said carefully.

Jessie tried not to look embarrassed.

"I'll talk to him, Dad. I'll talk to him. I have the feeling that he may soon become disenchanted with Broxton. He gets claustrophobic in small towns. That might be part of the problem. I don't know if he'd want to return to Broadbeach. He would suffocate there. He was brought up in that town. It's a part of his life he'd just as soon forget."

"It would only be in summers. In winter we'd be down

south, or who knows where else. It's not at all bad down there in Florida."

Vivian smiled. "Bribery is absolutely unnecessary, Father. Actually, I've given it a good deal of thought."

Jessie was not surprised. "Well, I'm glad we understand each other, Viv," he said. "You need the money. I need the help. The rest is really quite simple."

"Good night, Father," she said. "I'm really awfully tired. All those people milling about—some guests I haven't seen since before the war. It was good to see so many familiar faces." She raised herself heavily from the sofa. "Just one more thing, Father. What does Matthew have to say about all this?"

"About all what?"

"Oh, come now, Father. About Harlan working with him."

"*For* him," Jessie corrected, and smiled his secret smile. He began to shake his head ruefully. "Tsk, tsk. I only said we'd find your husband a job, not *give* him the place."

The relationship between Matthew and Jessie had not improved during the war; if anything it had deteriorated. Jessie held Matthew responsible for negotiating the contract for the Broadbeach that, upon recent reexamination, appeared to be "pure suicide," he said, "with a little fratricide and patricide thrown in."

They had just walked the length and breadth of the property and now, after having revisited the scene of the destruction, they felt the desolation that hung on the wet salt air like cobwebs. Matthew looked at what remained of his once plush office and felt squeezed by life. Through the window Jessie caught sight of the barbed wire fence that now surrounded the entire property, which was overgrown with weeds. He thought of the concentration camps he saw in the newsreels. He did not know where to begin. He looked at his father and realized that for the first time in his life, he too was defeated. He saw Jessie cover his face with his hands, and wipe them across it as if to erase the memory of what he had just seen.

"Oh, Father," Vivian said, "you shouldn't have come back here now, it's too soon after mama. I—I could have seen it another time."

He shook his head. Then he said firmly, "No, I'm glad you saw it. I wanted you to see it. Looks like they fought the whole goddamn war right here," he said, making a forlorn attempt at levity. "I don't understand," he kept repeating, "I simply don't understand. How could you have left out the clause for reparations?"

"Look, Father, there *is* such a clause, they have to pay us for the golf course and put everything back physically as it was before."

"But that is only superficial—the hidden damage, the almost gratuitous destruction is apparent everywhere you look. I thought we had agreed on taking inventory and making them responsible for everything."

"They—they wouldn't b-buy it. We had j-j-just gone to war. How could I have in-in-insisted on burdening the U.S. government at that time with s-s-such matters when the main concern was survival?" Matthew's boyhood stutter returned only in combat sessions with his father. He continued uncertainly. "Could anyone know when or if the government would be in a position to pay? After all, I didn't want them to accuse us of profiteering," he added in a voice barely audible.

"You sold us down the river so you could play Mr. Nice Guy!" Jessie said wearily. "You are a perfect idiot."

Matthew, perspiring profusely, asked, "Why didn't *you* check the contract yourself, Father?"

"I thought I could leave that much up to you."

"Why not take your attorney to account instead of me?" Matthew replied. "We were supposedly represented by counsel."

"I relied on a businessman to close the deal, not a lawyer. Irv Maslow is only a lawyer, nothing more and nothing less."

"Oh, Father, why can't you just say you didn't foresee the future either? Why can't you admit we've made an awful mistake and let it go at that? Why do you always have to lay everything at my doorstep?" Matthew's hair stood out at the temples. The beseeching tone in his voice only seemed to incense the old man further.

Jessie clapped his hands over his ears.

"What did they say, Matthew? The navy—what did they say when you discussed these things?" Vivian asked softly.

"They said that restoring a Jewish country club to its former glory is not high on its list of priorities," Matthew barked.

They fell silent momentarily.

"We must exercise our option," Matthew said calmly. "It will be a challenge."

One that we *may* not be able to rise to," Jessie said, slumped in his chair. "What the hell are we going to do with some two hundred acres of rubble and confusion?"

"We can rebuild little by little."

"And who will help us to begin with this 'little by little'?"

"We will work it out."

They had five months left in which to buy back the property at their special option price of one million dollars; otherwise the government would put it up for general sale at double that figure. Matthew wanted to reclaim the Broadbeach desperately. He imagined it falling into disreputable hands, to tract builders, postwar land speculators, or back into the hands of anti-Semitic hotel people.

"Get some solid backing, that's all I can tell you," Jessie said. "*I* won't go to a man like Marvin Segall or Alex Eastman for help. But *you* may have to."

Matthew looked down at his hands and said nothing. He hated when his father said a man "like" this one or that one—it shrivelled the very life of a man. How would they be able to work with an invisible partner? he wondered. He could not imagine Alex Eastman being invisible.

Matthew rose with a sigh and kissed his sister tenderly, then nodded a farewell to Jessie. As he was going out Jessie called after him, "And I want your sister here *and* her husband to participate, do you hear me? It is hers, too."

When Matthew closed the door his head was ringing and his heart felt as if it would burst. He was glad Faye was not here.

Matthew did not object to having Vivian back. In fact, it would be pleasant to have her around. He was very fond of her. As for that big Irishman of hers, perhaps he could put him in charge of recreation or something. *Aquatic Director*. He tried it out loud for sound appeal. No, perhaps *Athletic Director* would seem more fittng. Perhaps he would create a new division, a new title. He wanted to maintain the dignity of the Goldmark reputation.

Matthew assumed that Harlan had married his sister for her money and wouldn't have to do anything the rest of his life but stay married to her. But he was wrong. He had underestimated his brother-in-law. Harlan did not want to receive something for nothing. What Matthew did not know was that subtle changes had taken place within the impressive framework of the man. If impending war brought on the first stirrings of introspection, the war itself had completed the process. When Harlan Chase went to war he forgot his fear of failure, so enmeshed had he become in the politics of survival. Because death lived with him every day for almost four years, he no longer feared it, he knew he could conquer it. He became a hero, the proud possessor of the Silver Star for bravery. He had been scraped, strafed, nicked and finally wounded severely in the knee at Tarawa in the Gilberts in '43. They patched him up and sent him back in for the duration. He was left with a slight limp, but he had lived, and now he intended to make the most of his victory over death.

He also became a father. Early in the war he received the news. For once, Harlan was happy, even in the midst of the carnage. Perhaps there was truth in the recruiting slogan that the Marine Corps builds body, mind and spirit. He had taken on a new faith, he believed in himself now.

The war had been the singularly sobering and most dramatic event in his life thus far. He feared that the rest of his life would only seem an anticlimax, unless he forced himself to utilize his every talent. Harlan began reading the *Wall Street Journal*, almost as soon as he returned from overseas.

CHAPTER 13

Matthew's life was coming apart at the seams. He was hurting financially. His portfolio was a shambles, his bank credit was exhausted and he was considering putting up the Hibiscus Gardens as collateral for the million needed to remodel the Broadbeach. He doubted seriously that a million would cover it. He was hurting emotionally too. He was disappointed in his son. Since the business at Yale, Matthew and Faye rarely talked about it privately or otherwise. Furthermore, Matthew feared that David might be a constant source of gossip among the staff and the guests. The hotel atmosphere would only bring out the worst in him.

He had spent the last month breaking Harlan Chase in, and while he needed the help, he had misgivings about the arrangement and about his brother-in-law. Matthew, whose well-ordered life had no room in it for revision, suddenly found himself suffering under the burden of enormous change.

He felt humiliated now to have to go to Alex Eastman. He really did not want to let in outsiders. This had always been a family business. Goldmarks didn't *schnorr*, certainly not from people like Alex Eastman.

But finally in desperation Matthew approached him. He had already contacted Marvin Segall and Irv Rosensweig, who had been noncommittal, unsympathetic. He had saved Alex for last; psychologically he wanted to

THE PLEASURE DOME

keep him as his great white hope. He felt he had a good chance with Alex, that the offer would appeal to his ego, but he had doubts about getting involved with him.

Now, sitting at a table in a corner of the immense and fragrant tropical garden of their Miami hotel, Matthew waited for Alex Eastman. He surveyed his domain and felt strong. Waiters darted up and down the slatted walkway, the famous peacock walk, on the periphery of the garden, carrying trays of drinks. In a corner a group played Cuban love songs. Everything was the same, he thought with a measure of pride. He had managed to bring everything back to normal here, to prewar standards, when it was a distinguished playground of gentile society. He had even brought the peacocks back, the hotel's symbol of elegance. He should be grateful; every other hotel in this town had been commandeered by the air force during the war; only the Hibiscus Gardens had been allowed to remain open for civilian use—a token gesture by the war department to compensate for what they had done to the Broadbeach.

He sipped his drink thoughtfully. His five o'clock scotch had slipped to four o'clock, and tasted better every day. Two had become three or four—or more.

He nodded his head graciously to a couple of familiar guests passing by, pleased by their recognition. He looked at his watch. Eastman was already twenty minutes late. He was about to signal the waiter for another drink, then looked up suddenly into the canny blue eyes of Alex Eastman.

"So, Professor, how goes it?" Alex said, slapping him lightly on the back.

Matthew struggled to his feet, ever conscious of the amenities. He didn't know exactly why Alex persisted in calling him "Professor." He suspected it was either a euphemism, or that he never remembered his name. "Having a good time here?" Matthew asked after they were seated.

"Well, I just arrived a couple of days ago. The weather's great—I'm lucky to miss the January blizzards. What could be bad?" The implied diminution of the hotel itself irritated Matthew momentarily. Alex had spoken these words with such a paucity of feeling that Matthew looked up in alarm. A dapper, handsome man, Matthew thought. He was struck by the deep-set blue eyes, and the lines that had appeared around his mouth in the last few years. Then he remembered that he had lost his only son early in the war. He wondered if he should mention it, but didn't know where or how to begin.

"We've had to change managers here almost as often as the sheets. I'm the only stabilizing force around here, I'm afraid." Matthew flirted with the subject. Alex pinned him with his incisive gaze, as if he could see into his soul, but the next instant he looked away. He seemed reluctant to discuss business. Matt cleared his throat to commence, but Alex did it for him.

"So when's the club going to reopen? I miss it, damn it!"

Matthew was delighted and jumped in confidently. He told him the whole story, much of which Alex had heard via the grapevine, and some of which he hadn't heard.

"But why weren't you adequately covered?" Alex asked. Matthew, the color rising to his cheeks, explained weakly, shouldering the burden of blame. Alex asked him what percentage each relative owned, and when Matthew mentioned his sister, he seemed surprised. "Oh, yeah, how is she? Is she married yet?" he asked.

"Yes, certainly, didn't you know? In fact, she has two kids already—sons: a four-year-old and a new baby." Before Matthew could continue, he saw Harlan Chase approaching the table with his small son Steven on his shoulders. "Speak of the devil," was on his tongue, but he quickly changed gears and said, "Vivvy's family! Here they come now." Matthew was clearly disconcerted by the interruption but wished to appear cool and gracious.

He looked perplexed, then by turn surprised and finally pleased.

"Why, for Chrissake, that's—er—that's . . ." He was grinning broadly by the time Harlan came over to the table, and thrust his hand out to him the moment he had lowered his child to the sand. "Won't you join us?" Alex asked pleasantly.

"Well, just for a moment; Steven here has a very wet bathing suit and his mother will shoot me if I don't get him upstairs pretty soon."

Matthew made the introduction and Alex waved it away impatiently. "Geeze, it seems a long time, whole civilizations have come and gone since I last saw you, kid."

"Yes, Mr. Eastman, but you don't look a day older, still fit as ever, I see." There was an expectant silence and then Harlan quietly spoke. "May I offer my condolences, belated I know. I mean about . . . I still can't believe it. I heard—I don't know exactly."

Matthew looked uncomfortable. *He comes out and says simply what I should have said immediately.*

Alex did not answer for a moment, and then said softly, "Some of them lived and some of them died. My son wasn't among the lucky ones—he was killed in the Philippines." Alex looked down at his carefully manicured nails. "But what about you?"

"I wish he'd been in my outfit—maybe I—but I'm surprised I didn't run across Seth sometime."

"You wouldn't have had much time; he was one of the first to get it in '43." The sudden silence was pierced by a woman's laugh from a table nearby. "So you married the boss's daughter, eh? When did all this happen?" Alex asked above the noise.

"Oh, a long time ago, at the very beginning of the war," he said and pointed to his son. "My son here is a grown man of four."

"What are you doing with yourself nowadays?" Alex inquired. "Still swimming?"

Matthew began to explain Harlan's position at the hotel.

"Well, for Chrissake, you shouldn't waste his time or his talents; a bright guy, as I remember it, and well educated too. Isn't that so, Chase?" he said affably. "I'll bet you have a fine war record too."

There was a stony silence, and Matthew said without great conviction, "Oh yes, Captain Chase here holds the Silver Star *and* the Purple Heart."

Harlan seemed uneasy, Matthew thought, fidgeting first with the bowl of potato chips on the table, soggy from the humidity (he must make note of that, to tell the dining room steward), then chewing intensely on a toothpick.

The little boy, who had been sitting on his father's lap, began to fidget. He played with a lock of his father's dark hair—lovingly he wrapped his small arms around his neck.

"Daddy, c'mon, let's go, I'm cold. Let's go," he said in his sharp clear treble. Harlan smiled and tousled the child's rich dark hair, the little boy's arms encircled his neck.

"Yes, I really must go now, but it is a wonderful surprise to see you again after all these years. Sooner or later everyone ends up back at the Goldmarks'."

"Ain't it the truth," Alex said and shook his hand warmly. "Be seeing you, kid."

THE PLEASURE DOME

That "kid" business annoyed Matthew. After all, Harlan Chase was almost in his mid-thirties. The sun had etched permanent lines along his eyes and around his mouth, but Matthew was conscious of the fact that every woman's eyes followed him as he rose from the table and walked toward the main building of the hotel.

He saw Alex glance at his watch. He must get him back on the track, quickly too, damn the intrusion—

"Nice boy," he said, "helluva good-looking kid," Alex chuckled.

Matthew was not to be deflected. "Well, in any case, Eastman, we are reopening this summer with or without the frills—no matter what. Our old guests will go along with our problems."

"Yes, yes, that'll be fine, that's what you should do." He seemed a million miles away. He turned to Matthew and said carefully, "You complain about changing managers every month, and that you can't do it all yourself. Well, there's your boy, for Chrissake, you ought to make *him* general manager instead of keeping him chained up on the outside like a dog," Alex spat out waspishly.

Matthew recoiled. Alex's Eastern European Jewishness embarrassed him. True, he was rich, and at this moment he needed his money, but as far as Matthew was concerned, he was an *embarrassement de richesse*.

"Give us a chance, he's only been here a short time. He's learning the business."

"Nonsense, he can't learn anything running around in a pair of bathing trunks. Besides, you're wasting talent; that's poor management."

"I had no idea you knew him that well," Matthew commented dryly.

"Oh yes, he was my son's swimming coach. He saved my daughter's life."

It was almost six o'clock. Tropical birds chirped at the

dying sun and a dusk violent with color descended upon the city.

Matthew ran briskly up the steps that led from the garden to the Spanish-style lobby designed by Dorothy Draper in the early thirties. He walked up to the reception desk anxiously. The night man, Lyle Bottiner, a fussy stringy man, had just come on duty and was stuffing mailboxes with phone messages. A handful of elegantly dressed women in "garden party hats," Faye called them, were drifting through the lobby like assorted flowers. Otherwise it was quiet. Everyone else was either upstairs dressing or undressing.

"Who is expected this evening, Bottiner?" he asked, looking over the reservation sheet.

"Oh well, there should be at least ten check-ins this evening, and of course you know Nathan Gabrilove should be arriving tonight sometime. I understand the train is late." Matthew's face showed fresh signs of strain.

"Oh, God, that's right," he said. "I had forgotten. Did you make all the proper arrangements, Bottiner?" he asked in a voice heavy with expectation. He knew the answer in advance.

As he expected, Bottiner drew himself up to his full height and said, "Really, Mr. Goldmark, I am *only* the night desk clerk here." When it served his purpose he was only the night desk clerk, other times he would have died rather than be referred to in that deprecatory manner.

"Yes, yes, well I'd better check with housekeeping right away." Nathan Gabrilove was the department store king—an *established* millionaire whose family dated back to the robber barons at the turn of the century. When

THE PLEASURE DOME

Nathan Gabrilove came to the Goldmarks', he came *en famille*—his wife, his two married daughters and their children, and from time to time his son and daughter-in-law. He also came fully attended by his staff—chauffeur, butler, maids and nursemaids. They occupied an entire floor. In the old days before the war, particularly at the summer resorts like the Willows in New Hampshire (which the Goldmarks owned for a few years in the thirties) and then later on at the Broadbeach, special decorations and remodeling of their rooms were demanded and generously paid for.

Matthew had wanted to put a stop to the "traveling road show" as he called it privately to his father—or bar the Gabrilove family entirely. The confusion and disruptions it caused were hardly compensated for.

Jessie wouldn't hear of it. "It would be disloyal to our old clientele, and hardly sound business." They needed all their solid and reliable paying guests now, in the hopes that they would return to the Broadbeach in the summer.

Matthew grabbed the desk phone and dialed the housekeeper's office. An endless wait—and no reply. He jiggled the cradle impatiently. "I've told her many times that someone should be in the office from five to seven o'clock," he murmured to no one in particular.

Bottiner was squinting myopically toward the far end of the lobby, looking uncomfortable, then downright pained. There was a shrill whistle, and then from the rear of the lobby there followed a strange cacophony.

Was that band music Matthew was hearing? He could not exactly make it out, certainly it was a bass drum and the sound of marching feet. A parade through the lobby? He did not permit conventions at the hotel.

With great bravura and in excellent marching order

the bellhops, some forty of them, apparently the day and night shifts, were being led in a smart drill by young Craig Rosensweig.

"About-face!" he commanded and blew the whistle shrilly. Like the Rockettes they turned smartly left, in unison, around the bend of the lobby and then with "eyes front" facing Matthew and the reception desk, in the center hall—directly in front of the elevators. Rosensweig had no intention of being missed.

"What in hell . . . ?" was all Matthew could manage for the moment as outrage began to seep through the dismay. Harlan had come in to check on something behind the desk. He looked amused. Matthew grew red and furious. He turned to Bottiner. "Just exactly *what* is the meaning of this?"

"Oh, sir, didn't you know? I felt sure you knew. It's 'The Changing of the Guard.' *Always* draws a crowd."

Matthew had a sudden urge to punch him. "Who told you that?" he asked, making an enormous effort to keep his voice low against the racket beyond the desk.

"Why, the bell captain, and well, just about everyone who works here—once a week on Monday nights when the shifts change." Bottiner's nasal voice was drowned out now by a sort of roll call.

As each bellhop's name was called he stepped out and Rosensweig shook his hand, placing in it a crisp bill. This was followed by a polite touching of the hat with the finger in imitation of a military salute and a hearty "Thank you." When an almost equal number stood out in front, Rosensweig called an "about-face" and they marched off somewhere into the recesses of the serpentine lobby. The remaining men received their tips and Craig Rosensweig called for dismissal in a confident, rolling basso.

THE PLEASURE DOME

Matthew stared in disbelief. Harlan grabbed his arm to slow him down, but he shook himself free. Fury propelled him to where Rosensweig stood whistling jauntily and waiting for the elevators.

"Mr. Rosensweig," he said in a voice not much above a whisper, "how long has this been going on?"

"Oh, Mr. Goldmark, good evening."

For once Matthew was not much interested in the amenities. "Come into my office please," he said, steering him perhaps a little too firmly by the upper arm.

A moment later he sat at his desk, facing the dark, handsome heir to the Pilgrim Mills, the biggest textile firm in the east. He remembered that the Rosensweigs and their four sons had passed the last twenty summers and winters of their lives with the Goldmarks, spending considerable amounts of money on elaborate private parties. The liquor bills alone had been staggering. The boys had grown into profligate spenders.

But Matthew felt out of control. He wondered if it was the liquor. He was white and trembling. "How dare you use my hotel for your own personal parade grounds—*and*—and my staff," he whispered hoarsely. "Is there anything you brats will not stoop to, to attract attention?"

Craig tried joking about it in an offhand manner, only inflaming Matthew further. "Well, really, Mr Goldmark, since no one ever said anything in all this time I simply assumed no one minded my having a little innocent fun!"

"Innocent?" Matthew cried. "Openly bribing my staff to behave in this outrageous fashion, before everyone in the hotel! Well, I want you out of this hotel by check-out time tomorrow, that's all I know. I will, of course, talk to your father. I don't care to discuss this with you any further." Matthew realized that he had boxed himself into a corner and wasn't exactly sure how he would get out. He was not anxious to confront the glacial Irv Rosensweig. And even then, what punishment could he mete out that would not involve the entire family? Matthew stood up suddenly, signaling an end to the brief and strangely aborted encounter. He needed time to think. He might discuss this with Jessie. He wished he had done that *before* he had blurted out the orders. Craig rose and strode angrily from the room without uttering another word.

Matthew leaned forward and opened the cabinet beneath his desk and took out a bottle of Chivas Regal. There was a bar setup on a rolling cart nearby, always ready with ice and mixers, but he sloshed the liquor into a shot glass and drank it neat. Perhaps he was growing tired of the business, the life, the guests with their endless squabbles over tables, their senseless competing for status. He suddenly wished he could retire, get away from it all, just be alone with Faye somewhere. But he knew he could not afford it, and that Faye would not leave. Somehow he felt certain that Faye and this business came as a package. He thought of Faye now. He needed her so much at this moment that his stomach felt tied in a knot.

CHAPTER 14

Matthew opened the door of his apartment and the scent of Faye's perfume immediately assailed his nostrils. He wondered if it meant she was going somewhere again, running, running, she was always on the run, breathless, frenetic. Lately they only made contact going or coming—touching fingers as in a relay race. He hoped desperately that she was not going out. He needed her tonight. His heart pounded in anticipation.

He glanced surreptitiously at Roosevelt, the Negro butler, to see if he too had heard it. Roosevelt murmured a gentle "Good evening Mr. Goldmark" and asked if he would care for a drink, or did he say "another drink"? Oh, well, it didn't matter, he'd have another. Just one more—he needed it after that session with Eastman and his brother-in-law. Sitting between those two men he had felt strangely trapped—as if they were somehow in cahoots against him. He knew it was ridiculous. Alex had barely even recognized Chase when he first saw him— but there was a certain cocky self-assurance that emanated from these two men that automatically set him on guard. And then this ridiculous business with Rosensweig, it was too much.

Drink in hand, he roamed through the giant rooms of the apartment Faye had specially designed out of three corner suites. For once the ocean view was intrusive. Seething and yearning and crashing back again, alive with the whole gamut of human emotions. It looked ominous, steel gray in the dusky light.

He opened the door of their bedroom without knocking and saw her emerge from the dressing room wearing only a filmy negligee. He could see every line of her body beneath it. She was already forty, and her body was even better than when he had married her twenty-two years ago. Twenty-two years of absolute fidelity. He could not remember ever wanting another woman.

He felt that familiar surge of excitement. "Faye," his voice was husky, "you look terrific, where are you rushing to? Can't we at least have dinner together for a change?"

"Yes, of course we can, darling—whyever not?"

He was disarmed by her acquiesence. He realized that he hadn't made love to her in months; he had been tense, tired all the time. He fell deep dead asleep beside her every night—that is, when she was there. Often she was not. "Dancing until dawn," she had said, usually with one or another of the young Latin American dance teachers or kibitzing with the entertainers. "You know I love show business." Always he looked away, aware that he was neglecting her, that the hotels had become more than family, friendship, love for him. It was foolish, innocent amusement, he told himself. Of course, he did not know where she was or what she did every minute of the day or night. He wasn't sure he wanted to. Not knowing was what excited him. He was ashamed of his weakness, his meanness of spirit, his vulnerability.

"Well, what happened today with Alex?" she asked as she moved about the room, her gown billowing as she pirouetted here and there busily engaged in her toilette.

Matthew approached her and she looked up, somewhat

THE PLEASURE DOME

amused. "I don't want to talk about that now," he said, "I just want to make love to you."

"Oh, Matt, please, I'm dressing. I've just had my bath."

"I don't care about that. I need you now," he said.

"You must have had a lot to drink," she said softly, intimately.

He bent to kiss her half-exposed breast; he knew how susceptible she was there. He hoped that it was to his advances only, but he could never really be sure. He locked the door and pushed Faye down on the bed.

"Matt," she said weakly, "you are acting crazy."

He tore her dressing gown. She wore no undergarments. Still dressed in his slacks and shirt he held her in his arms. He took her nipple in his mouth and caressed it slowly with his tongue. He let his lips slide down her body to her belly. He kissed her navel, her inner thighs, she moaned and parted her thighs. He moved his lips down and lightly inserted his tongue into the soft cushiony place between her legs. She moaned and stroked his head, guiding it firmly downward harder, harder, each time. When she began to cry louder, he unzipped his trousers and entered her, fully clothed. It did not matter, nothing seemed to matter now but to be inside her body, that warm, familiar, completely satisfying haven. He moved slowly at first and she murmured, "Yes, oh, yes, darling." He was ready to burst and thought he could wait no longer, and forced his mind to other thoughts. He must satisfy her, he must—and it was not until Faye urged him to climax that he relaxed and gave into complete soul-wrenching release. They lay in each other's arms. Then Faye reached for a cigarette on the night table.

Matthew had been very happy with Faye during the two decades of their marriage. She had always seemed a little mysterious to him, but they were compatible because they rarely questioned each other's motives. He trusted in the fact that they were in love and that they had always enjoyed a full and satisfying sexual relationship. That they each had come to the marriage bed a virgin and without prior experience, he considered a romantic asset. Faye did not. She was hungry for experience. Living as she did in a microcosmic prison, she feared life was passing her by.

"Tell me about this Alex thing, please, Matt," she said when she had inhaled the first drag from her cigarette.

"Oh, there's nothing much to tell, he was noncommittal—said he'd give it some thought. There's no immediate hurry. We are reopening this summer with or without the extra money." There was another silence. "Did you know he lost his only son in the war?" Matt said into the darkness.

"I heard something about it but I wasn't sure—how awful," she said. "And his daughter—he has a daughter, I think. Where is she now?"

"College, yes, I believe he said Barnard. We really spoke very little about anything personal, but just before he left, Harlan stopped by and—"

"Harlan?"

"Yes. Seems they know each other from before the war. Eastman's very fond of our brother-in-law. Saved his daughter's life once," he said. "A drowning accident or something."

Faye was silent for a moment. "Well, that's what a lifeguard's supposed to do, isn't it?" she said.

"Faye, why do you resent Chase so much?"

"Don't be silly—I don't."

THE PLEASURE DOME

"It is because he's so attractive and doesn't give you a tumble?"

"Rubbish," she said petulantly.

"What's rubbish? That he's so attractive—or that he doesn't give you a tumble?"

"Both statements," she said, "are rubbish."

"Ooh, then he *does* give you a tumble, ah ha. Where has he tumbled you, pray tell, my love?" Matthew said in one of his rare playful moments. Although the thought had never seriously occurred to him, it suddenly seemed feasible. "Actually he appears to have eyes only for my sister," he said, serious now.

"That's more rubbish," she said complacently. "But 'appears' is the right word—he's a slick article that one—I don't think there's a female guest under fifty who hasn't been caught up in his charm."

"He has a gift for women," Matthew admitted grudgingly, "and that's not all bad; it will keep them coming back—the single women, the rich widows, perhaps Alex wasn't so outrageous after all. He said that Harlan ought to be made general manager here."

"He said that?" She seemed taken aback. "What else did he say? Will Alex go for it, Matt, will he do it?" She was referring to the loan.

"I don't know yet, he's an oddball and a tough businessman."

"Did you try to sell him on it?"

"No, no, not really."

"Why?"

"Because I'm not absolutely sure that it's necessary or even that it's the right way to go—to let in outsiders, I mean. This has always been a family business. I don't know."

"Matthew," Faye moved closer to him, "by family you

mean *you—you* would do it all. After Jessie dies it would be only you, let's face it. There *is* no family."

Matthew was silent.

"To enrich this business, to grow with the times, we could use an injection of money, and yes, even fresh ideas."

"*Et tu Brute.*" Matthew looked stung.

"Darling, I just don't want you to work so hard, that's all." She kissed his bare chest where the shirt had come open, rumpled his thick graying hair and jumped out of bed. "I'll go order us something to eat and we'll have it here in bed."

When Faye returned with the tray, Matthew was asleep in the same position as when she had left him.

Sometime later Matthew half-awoke from a dream and groped for Faye. She was not there. He allowed himself reluctantly to drift back into a sleep that would be fitful for the balance of the night.

There was a full house in the subterranean glass-enclosed garden room of the hotel. Glittering personalities like Russell Drake were unusual here, especially during and since the war. "Russ" came down to the Gardens now and then for vacation and, as a special favor to Matthew Goldmark, appeared nightly in The Nest. All during that week Faye appeared nightly too, her eyes glazed and riveted on the interesting if not handsome face of the young crooner.

Faye made her way to her regular table that was directly in the rear but afforded a good view of the postage-size dance-floor-turned-stage. The regulars, a smattering of flunkies and special guests, were already seated and waiting for her. On rare occasions Vivian would join her, but Harlan never came down to the shows. He couldn't sit still that long.

Russell Drake was seated there waiting for her. He was chain-smoking and seemed agitated and nervous. Faye deftly took the cigarette from between his fingers and ground it out.

"You know, you'd better stop that," she said, indicating the cigarette Russell was lighting with an elaborate gold lighter she had given him, his lashes dangerously close to the flame. "The voice, the voice," she said tapping her own throat.

Irv Maslow, the attorney for the hotel said, "Listen Russ, we may not be paying guests but we're still expecting a top performance."

Russ ignored him. He leaned back in his seat and slid his arm along the banquette. He twisted a strand of her hair in his fingers.

"Where've you been so late?" he asked in an intimate voice.

"Just administering a little TLC to my husband," she said, laughing and fixing her long hair so that it came over one eye, Veronica Lake fashion. "You don't mind, do you?" she said with a hint of irony.

A waiter placed a couple of straight scotches before them on the table and Russ drank his down neat, then bounced up from the table, and with his young dancer-like stride, made his way to the microphone. Faye said no one could carry a tuxedo quite like Russell Drake.

Russell Drake had a beautiful, piercing voice. "Clear as a mountain spring," Earl Wilson had said in his Broadway column. He had studied to be a cantor, but he wound up paying homage to beautiful women, rather than to the glory of God. Russell was just coming into his stride shortly before the war. His career had been launched by

Matthew Goldmark who took a chance on a skinny Jewish kid from Brownsville with a protruding Adam's apple and kinky black hair. When he opened his mouth to sing, "heaven poured out," the female guests would say. When the war started he was able to maintain his civilian status, getting by on an entertainment deferment, and appeared at the big name spots like the Copacabana in New York, the Chez Paree in Chicago and the Coconut Grove in Boston. Then he was drafted and spent the next two years entertaining the troops. Not that he objected, especially when newsreels all over America showed pictures of him singing to swooning nurses, even if they were on little known islands in the Pacific. In the two short years since the war ended, he had, if anything, improved his star status.

At thirty, Russell Drake had already married and divorced two movie stars, and suffered two paternity suits, which Matthew insisted were dredged up by a misguided publicity agent. Now he was dreaming of doing a Broadway musical. So far it was just a dream—there were no bites, not even a nibble.

When the show ended, Russ sat down and received the applause gracefully by running his fingers through his hair deftly so as not to spoil the part and waves. "Listen, excuse me, folks," he said, "but I gotta do a recording tomorrow so I'm gonna cut out now. I'm all tuckered out. You know how it is."

"Yes, we know how it is," Irv Maslow said lasciviously and leaned back and puffed vigorously on his Cuban cigar. A discreet fifteen minutes later Faye excused herself, saying simply, "Good-night."

At the side entrance parked under a large coconut palm Drake waited in his white Cadillac convertible. She slipped in lightly beside him and said, "Where shall we go?"

"Well, I had kind of hoped to my place."

"Your place?" she laughed merrily. "Your place is *our* place. You're staying here this week, aren't you?"

"Yes, of course," he said. She was amused by his matter-of-fact "of course." Show business people were famous for their frugality.

"So it's your place or yours."

"Well," he said laughing a little, "I guess that's that," and turned on the ignition key. "Of course, there's always the car, you've got to admit this is as luxurious as some of your lower priced rooms." Faye didn't laugh. "C'mon doll, smile. I tell you what, we'll go up to the Seventy-ninth Street Causeway. How about the Harbor Lounge? It's dark and sexy and they play a lot of my records up there."

They turned up Collins Avenue and drove past the rows of white hotels moored like ships along the ocean, beyond where Indian Creek widened to form a dark satin ribbon of water and swung onto the handsome Seventy-ninth Street Causeway. Johnny Raye was crying a love song on the radio. Russ changed stations. They drove a few minutes in silence. They had taken a detour along Indian Creek Drive. He slowed down along the canal and stopped beneath a cathedral of palm trees. The scent of honeysuckle and wisteria wafted through the open windows.

"Faye," he said, "what's the matter, honey?" He took her in his arms and kissed her passionately. At first she hardly responded but he touched her throat and breasts and soon she returned his ardor with hot kisses, like a schoolgirl. Having been raised in a time of furtive sex and having had none until she was safely married, necking in the front seat of a car made her feel intensely young, especially with a celebrated crooner. "Faye, let's go into the back seat." She didn't answer but pulled away slightly. "You are being coy, c'mon Faye," his voice was wheedling.

"No," she said evenly. "Bad as I am, I couldn't go from one bed to another in the same night." From the sacred to the profane, she thought ironically. Strangely enough, she considered her relationship with Matthew sacred. He had never confronted her once in all these years—not made even a single scene. Well, she had been discreet. Perhaps he really never knew, or couldn't face knowing. She wanted to believe the latter. He had been so preoccupied in the last few years between pulling the hotel back into the black, dealing with his father, and resisting the influence of his brother-in-law, Harlan Chase—they had barely touched in passing. Except for sex, she didn't seem to matter, there was so little that she was needed for anymore.

Russell gave a long breathy whistle and stared at her for a moment intently. "I see, so that's how it is," he said, "you are letting me know how it is with you and Matt."

"Yes." But she was also trying to keep her lover aroused, in an endless quest to indemnify herself against neglect.

"Let's go home, baby," he said.

"What about the coffee?"

"I think we'll pass tonight," he said as he wheeled the car around sharply. "I'll have to get my own place next time, this is just no good." That was not at all what Faye had in mind. She longed for adolescent assurances.

CHAPTER 15

Matthew knew that Alex was planning to leave in a few days. He hurried to make one more appointment with him, just to see if he could get him to invest some money in the Broadbeach. Alex turned him down but mentioned that he planned to invite Harlan to the prizefights. There was a good heavyweight bout in Miami, he said. Matthew was somewhat disconcerted by the rejection but discarded any petty emotions for the sake of the greater good. Besides, everyone knew that Alex Eastman was a bit of an oddball.

It was steamy hot, even in Alex's expensive box seats. Air conditioning had not yet been installed at the old Downtown Stadium, and open doors and a series of large overhead fans were the only source of relief. This was only a preliminary fight, but it promised to be almost as exciting as the upcoming championship bout in New York. The arena was jammed.

Alex kept dabbing at his face with a handkerchief. Harlan appeared cool in his open shirt and white linen slacks. His appearance belied his feelings. If he was pleased by the sudden surge of importance he was enjoying, he was also vaguely uneasy and had considered refusing Alex's invitation, but his father-in-law had urged him to go. Harlan had become great friends with his father-in-law.

"Why not go?" Jessie had said. "Tickets are scarce as

gold; besides, he seems quite fond of you and perhaps you can even get him to come up with the loan, or some of it, anyway."

Harlan felt as if he were walking into the lion's den. Alex was an unpredictable man. As for encouraging him to enter the hotel business as a partner, he strongly doubted that he would take to such an unlikely union.

The heat was intolerable, and combined with the heavy odors of cologne and sweat; Harlan felt himself wilting.

The gong sounded for round five, and the eager, moist faces all around him leaned forward tensely toward the ring. The fighters, one black and one Cuban, were hitting one another mercilessly. "A good fight," Alex declared. The Cuban was a potential heavyweight contender.

During the intermission they pushed their way to the cold drink stand and took their drinks back up to the privacy of the box.

"So how much longer are you staying?" Harlan inquired casually.

"Oh hell, I've been here almost three weeks already—and I've got to get back home—I've got a business to run. Besides, I want to be there when my daughter comes home on break next week. I always try to be there when she is, nowadays. You know how it is now—*you're* a father. She's all I've got left and I'm all she's got. *You* remember my daughter."

Harlan nodded his head in agreement and gazed intensely into the bottom of his drink container. He remembered Laina's slim body, every nuance, pale gold and silky to the touch. He closed his eyes for a moment.

"Funny how life is," Alex said. "In a way, if it hadn't been for you I'd have had no one at all now—I'd have been completely wiped out. First my wife, then my daughter, and then of course my son—Seth—yeah, it's funny how things happen."

Harlan did not answer.

"You happy in this business, Chase?" Alex asked paternally.

"Oh, it's alright, I guess. I'd like to see some changes, some improvements. They're pretty set in their ways—they need someone like you in there to guide them, to keep them moving with the times."

Alex was clearly pleased by the flattery and responded in kind. "What about you?"

"I haven't got the money," he answered.

Alex assessed him carefully. "Listen, Chase, I've got to concentrate on my own business. I'm convinced that there are even greater fortunes to be made there, potential that I haven't even begun to tap, like the land it's on—I'd like to start buying up all of the property."

"The big bands are on the way out, Alex," Harlan said. "You hardly ever hear about them anymore and record production has dropped to about half of what it was before the war."

Alex interrupted. "But the Latin dance craze is moving in."

Harlan leaned back on the legs of his chair. "Still, it may never be as universally accepted as American dance music—anyway, it seems to me that it would be smart to diversify your interests or even consolidate."

Alex looked confused. "What do you mean by that?"

"Oh, I don't know, just groping," he said enigmatically, a toothpick wobbled dizzily between his front teeth. He flicked it across the arena. Harlan looked at him for a long moment. There was no trace of a smile. Then they both began to laugh. The gong sounded again and the fight resumed.

Silently Alex followed every punch with his eyes. The black boy was taking a brutal beating. "Why don't they stop the fight, for Chrissake," Alex whispered breathlessly, never removing his eyes from the ring. Sweat fell from his forehead down into the back of his shirt. "Ugh," he said, "I can't take it anymore, let's get out of here."

Harlan did not reply. His eyes were glued to the ring, a strange, almost rapt expression on his face. Realizing that he was being watched, he turned toward Alex. Alex turned away quickly from the hard green gaze, those strange eyes.

After the fight they waited in their box for some of the crowd to thin out.

"One helluva fight," Alex said and wiped his forehead. "A helluva fight. Hey, you can take it—you're tough. You don't get flustered by all that violence, huh?" As they rose to go, Alex slapped him on the back. "We're alike," he said. "You and me. The Goldmarks. They're different from us, soft and sweet like a rotten apple."

Harlan conceded to himself that Matthew was full of upperclass self-pity, but he carefully refrained from any criticism. That he was an outsider here—and middle-class—did not help his self-esteem, but he was conscious of the opportunity this meeting afforded him. He had to prove himself, to prove at all costs that he could outdistance their money, their background, their experience. He liked flirting openly, wildly with his outrageous luck. He placed his arm around Alex's broad shoulders. "Yes," he said, "we probably are alike in many ways, Alex. I wish you'd consider coming in with us so that we could work together. I'd like to learn from you. I know you could teach me a helluva lot."

Alex smiled warmly as they descended the stairs amid the smoky, steaming crowd. He knew what Harlan wanted. He'd known it for a long time. "I'll put up the dough," he said, "providing they make you general

THE PLEASURE DOME

manager. How would you like that, son?" Before Harlan could answer, Alex pressed his arm and pointed out a famous movie star close by in the exodus, whose face was legend, as was his reputation with women. Alex greeted him warmly and made a brief introduction. Alex knew everybody.

Outside in the torpid night Alex said, "Can you imagine, a goddamn pervert like him—screwing teenage girls. Why they oughta had him jailed for statutory rape—they should've thrown the book at him!" Harlan felt the blood rush to his face. He jammed his hands in his pockets to stop them from trembling.

Jessie allowed for a certain amount of discussion before making Harlan general manager, most of it with Matthew.

"Look at the way you handled the issue with Rosensweig—you became emotional. If Chase had been in there, he simply wouldn't have cared so much, he'd have thought only about the money they spend. He's not as emotionally involved in the business as you are. You could have saved your energies for more important matters."

Matthew suspected that his father was still angry over the loss of the Rosensweig family business, particularly since they were regulars. But Matthew seemed compelled to pursue the subject of his brother-in-law. "Do you really think Chase is polished enough for this sort of work?"

"Polish is not as necessary as charm is. Everyone seems to find him very charming."

"Do you, Father?" Matthew asked.

"Yes, yes, I do in a way. In the new, more modern ways. We will give him a big publicity buildup. You know, stressing his war record, his athletic record."

Matthew couldn't see what his war record or athletic ability had to do with managerial duties, but refrained from saying anything at the moment.

Jessie sat at their regular table in a discreet corner of the dining room. He ate a late lunch so as not to take any of the attention away from the guests at the height of the lunch hour.

"Then too," Matthew said, "how will our guests react to a gentile running *our* hotels?"

"As a matter of fact, I think he'll help us to diversify our clientele, bring in some non-Jews. We can't afford the luxury of segregation forever."

Matthew looked sullen. "Why not? Gentiles do."

"*They* can afford to," Jessie said smiling. "There are many more of them."

Jessie had never really been convinced like Matthew that it was a good idea to run his hotels only for his own people. Yet in the past he had bowed to the times. Otherwise, he would have had no steady clientele. "Those people stay with their own kind," he often said.

"But the war has changed much of that," Jessie said. "The bitterness, the hatred, has been brought out in the open. There is the climate of brotherhood in the air, a benign quality to life right now."

"But at such a price. The millions who were in the camps," Matthew said, shaking his head. "And who knows how long it will last?"

Jessie shrugged his shoulders. These were not his concerns. He would not be around to see the outcome.

"How are the children to be raised?" Matthew asked, somewhat out of context.

THE PLEASURE DOME

"What children?"

"Vivvy's, of course."

Jessie looked at Matthew over the rim of his coffee cup. "How was your son raised?" Matthew colored visibly. The irony did not escape him.

The Goldmarks were reform Jews. They rarely went to temple for anything more than the obligatory Bar Mitzvahs, weddings, and funerals, or the High Holy Days. They took what they wanted from their faith, the sensual pleasure—the comforts—and did not even feel guilty about it. Matthew suffered from pangs of guilt for his father, who considered himself a cut above the rest because he was a German Jew, and some guilt of his own because he secretly considered all Jews a cut above everyone else.

"Look," Jessie said, putting his cup down slowly, "when Vivvy came home and told us she was pregnant that day, five years ago, I told her one thing: 'Remember, Vivian, he is a born Catholic. He is taught from the cradle on that all Jews are Christ killers. There cannot help but be hidden resentments.' I told her this to prepare her, but now I consider her husband to be far too practical to be vindictive—and I am convinced they love each other."

"His sister is a nun, do you know that?"

"Yes, I do," Jessie said, "and that has only served to turn him further from his faith—"

"So he is a heretic in his own church. Faithless all around," Matthew persisted.

Jessie ignored the interruption. "The war, I think, did the rest."

"Yes, and even that was an act of selfishness, going off and marrying Vivvy on the run, then immediately filling her up with a child, never knowing if he'd return."

"I think he knew," Jessie said quietly.

Matthew was silent for a moment. He felt strangely bereft. There didn't seem to be anything he could tell his father about this man.

"He seems rather detached from it all, if you ask me."

"It's that very detachment that I think we need here. Besides, they tend to keep their feelings hidden more than we do; I'm afraid."

"Will he be out front at the club too?"

"I suppose so, it would give us and the guests a sense of continuity. For God's sake," Jessie said irritably, "why don't you give in with good grace, there's more than enough to go around."

Matthew was silent. He really didn't know why he was resisting. His sister was his rightful partner; her husband was simply representing her interests while she was busy being wife and mother. Somehow, if he reasoned this way, he felt better.

CHAPTER 16

The Broadbeach Club reopened with fanfare and enthusiasm. The guests were thrilled. The other summer resorts simply had not measured up, and they had suffered them with patience.

Most of the old clientele returned, even some they had lost to Europe before the war. A handsome group of new members, composed mostly of affluent young "marrieds," took cabanas, young couples who had married in haste during the war, marriages dependent on other marriages for survival. Matthew was a marriage broker of sorts. His hotels had in the past served as a kind of adhesive that held together many a fragile marriage, perhaps because the resorts offered enough diversion from which to escape marital tedium.

Harlan, in his impeccable white Palm Beach suit sharp against his suntan, dazzled the women and charmed the men. With flattering sincerity, he gazed respectfully into their eyes when they complained about the food, the plumbing, the accommodations, carefully gauging the right approach. Sometimes he would disarm them with a wink saying, "Well, the Goldmarks are pretty tight, that's the way they run a hotel, what can I do?" The guests, taken off guard both by the candor and treachery, were silenced and slouched back to their rooms. He raised the rates with a brio that left Matthew breathless and disapproving. Harlan said, "They'll love paying it. After the privations of wartime, it gives them a feeling of luxury." Jessie seemed enormously pleased. It was a necessity. Their operating costs had risen sharply.

Laina asked no questions about the hotel. It was as if it had never existed. Alex thought it was disinterest, but secretly she dreaded the summer. In the end she couldn't avoid the pleading look in her father's eyes. She couldn't cause him pain. He had sustained enough pain. All his relationships had gone sour, and he wasn't really a bad man, just an insensitive one.

Laina had spent the last four years locked up with her father. Before the war, before Seth's death, Alex had been a singularly detached parent. Never a temperate man, he had done a complete reversal after his son's death. He had become the guardian and protector of his daughter's innocence, a sort of personal keeper of the flame, frequently lecturing to her on the necessity of remaining chaste.

He took her with him everywhere he went. He was ambivalent about her appearance, at once proud of her appeal, and quick to subdue it, as if, were he to allow it to blossom—to take hold—she might come to great harm. Alex was preconditioned by a dime-a-dance psychology, and tended to see women as nefarious, skittish, and rather déclassé.

He thought she brooded a great deal, but attributed it to the successive deaths of her mother and brother. Alex had a tendency to oversimplify. He could not know her shame kept her quiet, her self-disgust caused depression. Even her college experience was not immune to his scrutiny. He insisted that she attend a local school where he could keep an eye on her, he said candidly, proudly, savoring his full responsibility as a father. So Laina remained in New York and reluctantly entered Barnard. All of her high school friends had been dispatched to ivy-covered colleges and universities throughout the country, and she felt the restriction keenly.

Even Alex's dates with female companions appeared to have dwindled to an occasional evening with some eligible woman or other, leaving Laina with the comforting if mistaken impression of her father's celibacy. Under his dominion, she wore a cap of many colors like a court jester, sometimes child, sometimes sweetheart, sometimes friend. Alex had few friends in his life. He always said he didn't have the time.

He had sold the big summer house at the beach, now that it was just the two of them, and took a large suite at the hotel, for which he paid a fraction of the going rate. He was an insider now and he liked it. Laina suspected that the real reason was that it gave her greater "exposure," an expression of her father's that invariably made her wince. She missed the old house with its louvered windows on the sea, but Alex attached little sentimentality to houses. He was the kind of man who could live in a place for years and never know what it looked like, or which street it was on.

Harlan had decreed that opening night would be celebrated by a gala masquerade ball, which in itself was a daring reversal of tradition. Matthew was offended. The masquerade ball was always left for the closing weekend, the Saturday night before the Sunday beach party. But the theatrical vein in Harlan's nature prevailed. It would be a provocative way to bring old and new guests together again, keep them guessing—playing who's who, who's here. It could only lend importance to the upcoming season, he had argued with his brother-in-law. By now he was fairly certain that almost every innovation of his would be met with resistance by his brother-in-law and with amused tolerance by his father-in-law. Matthew, like most insecure people, bitterly resisted change. But Harlan was not thin-skinned, he did not wound easily.

On opening night the Moonlight Room was full. Five hundred people jammed into a room suited for three hundred. The room was set up so that as the guests entered they were in full view of those already seated. None was permitted entry without a mask.

Laina wore a long medieval costume of layered, apricot chiffon complete with a train, her wheat-colored hair bound beneath a wimple of the same color. The dress was cut high, in the style of that period, emphasizing her breasts and the long graceful lines of her body. As she approached the entrance on the arm of her father, who bowed to the event by wearing a tuxedo, all eyes turned in their direction.

At the entrance she pulled back reflexively. The cavernous ballroom seemed to have taken on a life of its own. She was assailed by memories that had lain like a stubborn layer of dust on the periphery of her mind.

The lighting was lambent against the orchestra's metallic instruments, shooting prisms of light in all directions. Perhaps she had only dreamed this place. Yet nothing really had changed, except the outward appearances of the guests. In a corner a fox was dancing with a penguin, Marie Antoinette with her executioner, and a pair of Zulus danced the rhumba in war paint and ankle ruffs . . . Laina herself moved like a myth through the overwhelming reality.

They sat alone at a small table, where she felt embarrassed by their isolation, in spite of the fact that it was her choice. Everyone else was at large boisterous tables. But Alex was at home amidst the uproar. It was like this every night at his ballrooms, although the clientele there were considerably less disciplined. He had bowed to her wish not to be seated with the Goldmark family, although they had insisted. He had begged off on the grounds of his daughter expecting guests. In fact her one guest had been Caroline Segall, and at the last minute Caroline had deserted them for a better offer from Craig Rosensweig. She was seeing Craig on and off again, in between the times he was trying to forget Babs Singer. The war had done little or nothing to mellow or democratize the elder Rosensweigs, and they still sorely disapproved of Babs. Laina fidgeted with the card on the table that admonished the removal of masks.

"Darling, why don't you take off your mask?" Alex said, impervious to protocol. He patted her arm gently. Now that she was in her last semester of college, he didn't exactly know what to do with her. Marriage seemed the safest and most likely refuge. It was as if he felt the sanctity of marriage would absolve him from responsibility, would seal up her sexuality forever.

Laina had no intention of removing her mask. She disliked calling attention to her eyes. Even though they were large, feline and golden, she rarely wore eye makeup, even though it was fashionable then. She believed eyes were truly the mirror of the soul and she feared drawing attention to them, as if someone might look into her soul and see how rotten she was. Alex cleared his throat uncomfortably.

"Do you see anyone you know here?"

"Only Caroline," she said archly.

"Well, I see David Goldmark over there, an old friend of yours."

A breathless Caroline rushed over to them. Laina

wasn't sure if she was dressed as a dance hall queen or a cancan dancer, but decided they were one and the same, separated only by a continent. She sat down and was prompt to point out that she had won "C.R." for the evening. She began to guess everyone's identity, which she did with apparent ease. "Hmm, haven't you noticed how the costumes reflect their secret selves?"

Laina wondered how Caroline managed to know everybody's secrets. She looked down at her own attire and was quickly enlightened. Alex looked annoyed. Psychological probings always annoyed him. He suffered the pained intolerance of the insensitive for the sensitive.

"Mmm," Caroline said, "there's the gorgeous new general manager . . . the son-in-law. You know him, Laina." Caroline nudged her conspiratorially. "He was the swim coach here before the war." Her voice droned on. "It was due to *his* intervention that the Rosensweigs came back at all this summer."

Laina, numbed and passionless, felt suddenly drunk with fatigue. Caroline kept crossing and uncrossing her legs and showing her black lace thighs from beneath a froth of petticoats whenever any of the young men passed by the table. Laina assessed her friend secretly and decided that she hadn't really changed much through the years. Caroline was considered brilliant, she knew, and she had recently graduated from Skidmore with honors. She was talking about a career in advertising but she really wanted to be a writer, a novelist. People said she had a way with words. Maybe at twenty-two she *had* already seen enough of life to write about it. Still, she knew that Caroline wanted to get married. She could *not* imagine why, when she thought of the Segalls' marriage. Still it was the thing to do. The boys had just gotten home from the war, lonely and rootless. They wanted to marry and settle down, raise a family. For many girls it seemed the easiest way out. There were few decent jobs around for educated women. Besides, Laina and her generation, who were raised on the love songs of the day, with their extravagant sentiments, and the movies with their saccharine-sweet heroines, found the concept beguiling.

Alex looked nervous, his eyes straining toward the Goldmarks. He was still impressed by the Goldmarks. After all, he had a sizable investment in the hotel now and didn't want to miss any top-level executive gatherings, even social ones, not as long as he was only a few yards away.

"Will you be alright if I leave you for a moment?" He excused himself before she could object, and headed for the Goldmarks' table. Everyone there was dressed in formal attire, bowing to their own edicts by way of the small black masks. The family must never share the banality of their guests, was Matthew's credo.

Caroline looked around restlessly, murmured some excuse and disappeared from the table, leaving Laina alone.

She stared hard at the Goldmark table, though it was obscured by the pocket of action that surrounded it. She recognized them all, they were easily identifiable. Only Vivian's appearance was much changed. She was no longer a paper doll, but fuller and riper with a new dimension. She wore her smart gown with an air of assurance.

The dance floor was packed, the room ached with the heavy odors of perfume, perspiration and costume rental camphor. Waiters were darting everywhere with the frantic look they invariably wore for important evenings.

The music stopped suddenly and Matthew stepped up to the microphone to announce that the next dance would be a *guest guesser* or a mixer of sorts, where guests were to try to find old friends. "No dancing with anyone from your own table," he cautioned.

Dear old Matty, Laina thought. A confused silence followed the announcement and her eyes strayed toward her father. It was typical of him to leave her sitting there alone while he conducted business. She thought she saw the back of his head beyond the bobbing and weaving crowd. She pretended to search for her father. She removed her mask and took her glasses from her purse. Her hands were trembling slightly and felt clammy. She was used to being alone, yet she felt suddenly panicked here amid the hullabaloo, the cheerful revelers with their well-ordered lives, and wondered how her own life would turn out. She began to fidget restlessly, afraid to allow her mind to dwell on her friend's provocative news. She knew that if her father became enmeshed in a business discussion, he would forget all about time—even about her.

She replaced her mask and was about to get up to seek refuge in the ladies' room when a tall man approached her, bent low over her hand and kissed it with a mock grace. "Good evening, My Lady," he said. "Are you leaving again? Where can you go dressed like the Wife of Bath?"

Before she could answer he said, "Come, this is my dance." The voice was rich. It chilled her to the point of paralysis. She was unable to move or answer. He pulled her to her feet abruptly and swept her out onto the dance floor. He was dressed in formal attire, a black tail coat and the incumbent eye mask. She was conscious only of her perspiring hand in his cool dry one as he swayed and moved with enormous grace across the floor. She followed automatically every step, pulling back, moving

THE PLEASURE DOME

forward, her body curving into his. Her eyes sought a means of escape in the crush of dancers, but there was none. The music changed to a sensuous waltz, whose name she struggled to remember . . . She caught the glint of green eyes through the slits in the mask—staring at her, smiling—smiling, golden-flecked green eyes. She wanted to say something, but she could not find her voice.

The music sizzled, spiraled and then suddenly stopped and in the whirl of crowd and confusion she found herself looking up suddenly into the friendly horn-rimmed glasses of David Goldmark.

"Hope you don't mind my cutting in. That ox of an uncle of mine was giving you quite a workout. You two looked wonderful together, whirling around the floor, like a pair of animals in heat."

She was confounded by his statement.

He waved it away with his hand and said "Oh, darling, don't look so shocked! I imagine that's the way that sort of man usually makes a woman feel." Still she seemed unable to speak and he led her deftly into a swingy foxtrot. "I've got a special dispensation from all this because of these," he said pointing to his glasses.

She asked to sit down and they returned to her table. The excitement was still with her and she was plagued by an acute shortness of breath. She thought she must appear disheveled, wild.

"Can I get you a drink from the bar?" he asked.

"No, no," she was afraid to go out to the bar. She was sure that's where Harlan must have gone.

"Well, let's go over to my table. We have everything all set up there for drinking. You can have your choice." David looked at her approvingly. "You are indeed a toothsome wench!"

Her hair felt damp beneath the confines of the headdress, strands spilled out here and there, but her lovely golden eyes shone with a strange radiance, an inner excitement.

"Tell me, David, how have you been? You were excused from the service because of your eyesight, I imagine, and, of course, a college exemption too."

His face colored violently and he blinked behind his spectacles. "Well, don't let these fool you," he said tapping his glasses. "I wouldn't want you to think I *wasn't* a wolf in sheep's clothing."

"Oh, I don't know, I think you manage to look quite lewd behind your spectacles."

He seemed satisfied.

"Congratulations must be in order on your graduation."

"Oh, yes, thank you," he murmured and changed the subject easily. "Why don't you come and sit with us? Don't let the Goldmarks intimidate you, we're really not such a bad lot when you get to know us. Your father is there already." He said this as if that were expected to seal the bargain.

Alex was delighted to see she had capitulated after all and had done so at David's behest.

Laina sat uncomfortably between David and Matthew. She watched Vivian out of the corner of her eye, looking away quickly when their eyes met. Jessie took her hand in his and told her how beautiful she had grown. She spoke to Vivian occasionally and seemed surprised to learn that she had two children, the elder almost five years old.

David began talking to her quietly about his music, his ambition to compose and write for Broadway. "This is the first summer in years I haven't gone to work in summer stock. That's where I really learned about production, and staging and music."

She looked surprised. "Aren't you planning to take over here sooner or later? You are the *only* son."

"I'm not sure my father sees it just that way," he said, his smile an enigma. "I don't think I'm cut out for this sort of life—or maybe what I'm really saying is that I'm *too* well suited to it. I'm probably a sybarite like my mother, only I'd prefer to fight it. These lotus eaters would probably be my undoing."

"And mine," she answered laughing.

"What do *you* plan to do next?" he asked.

She seemed confused as always when faced with questions about her future. She had been too consumed by the past to contemplate the future. She knew her father's plans for her were to get married—and she had grown accustomed to letting him have his way, particularly as she was uncertain as to what her own way was. "Well, I've got another semester more after this one and then... I don't know yet, David. I haven't really thought about it. Perhaps graduate school, I don't know."

"I'm working on a score now that I think has all the makings of a hit—awfully good. Broadway's my goal, but I'm fully prepared to make the necessary stops along the way if I have to—Grossinger's, summer stock, etc. Maybe my dad can get me a shot at one of those summer deals.... I'd like to play some of my music for you, Laina, see what you think of it."

She smiled her pleasure. "Still write poetry like you used to do?" he asked.

"Yes, as a matter of fact I wrote a couple of volumes as my senior English thesis."

"Well, let's see them sometime. Maybe I can set them to music!"

They both laughed. "Listen, next weekend is Singles' Weekend here at the hotel. One of my uncle's vulgar ideas to make us rich."

The way he said "uncle" made her uncomfortable.

"Let's go somewhere, have a shore dinner maybe, let some fresh air into our diets. The cuisine á la Goldmark is plentiful but *repetitious*, you must admit." He laughed and patted his flat stomach. "And I mean that *literally*." He pretended to belch politely behind his hand.

"No, really," he said, "lobsters are lovely in midsummer."

Craig Rosensweig passed by and said "Down, boy" and rumpled his hair in a gesture of camaraderie.

"Ah, young Lochinvar come out of the west," David said, then murmured, "Central Park West, that is."

"David, you're incorrigible," Laina said, but she was obviously enjoying herself.

"Well, is it yes or no, about next Saturday night? You know if you stay in these joints long enough, the real world starts to look weird. I should think you'd be glad to get away from this place once in a while."

"I just don't like leaving my father alone."

"Did you ever stop to think that he could use some time to himself?" She had always considered his working hours his time to himself. She reconsidered.

"I'd love to," she said.

"Good, then that's settled." He pulled her to her feet and ran out with her to the dance floor.

CHAPTER 17

The return to Broadbeach was not merely a business adjustment for Harlan. It also marked the first time since his marriage that he would return to his hometown. He had virtually washed his hands of all of them, with perhaps the exception of Janine. Although he had been excited by the prospect of his opening summer at the Broadbeach Club, he dreaded the return to the desolate town of his boyhood. Memories of a lesser day.

He had not seen his father for years, his mother only once in the three years since his return from overseas, and that was only recently. When they were still living in Massachusetts, she had expressed a desire to meet his wife. James had not. She asked if they could meet on the outside somewhere. Harlan invited her up to their home, but when she seemed terrified, and ultimately had to decline, he knew it was because of *him*. Vivian was hurt more for her husband than for herself.

As for himself, he set a great deal of store by his marriage, in his relationship with his wife, and he felt bereft by the loss of his mother, his sister Janine. Deep within him was the need to be loved by the women in his life. He had no consciousness of it, but he was perhaps seeking in women his loss of identity with the church—*Mother* Church.

It wasn't even that Harlan didn't believe in God. He just wasn't sure.

JUDITH LIEDERMAN

* * *

Harlan sat with his long legs stretched out in front of him, his hands in his pockets in a relaxed style. He was listening to himself being immortalized, at least that's what Martin Blackman, the celebrated PR man, called it. Harlan glanced occasionally at his father-in-law and tried to assess the expression on his face, but he looked deceptively bland as he puffed his expensive Cuban cigar. When they were at the Gardens, he had them flown over weekly from Havana. Matthew sipped uneasily at his coffee while Blackman did most of the talking. He leaned back in his chair and pointed a pencil like a weapon directly at Harlan.

"We'll make you into a legend, guests will come here if only to meet you, to see what you look like. Maybe we'll even play up the limp," he said, wiping his forehead with a large initialed handkerchief. "You know, the war record, that sort of thing. Besides, women find cripples romantic. Look at the poet Byron."

Harlan threw his head back and roared with laughter.

"Well, now," Jessie said carefully, "I would hardly call Chase here a cripple or a poet. I don't exactly want to make a three-ring circus out of this, or put him on display like some sort of oddity."

"Entity," Blackman said grandly and with an extravagant arm gesture. Harlan wondered why they kept lapsing into conversation about him as if he weren't there. "Entity," the PR man's voice thundered through the small office and he pounded the desk for emphasis. We'll create a somebody out of nobody. Harlan could see the unsaid words hanging in the air like smoke clouds. He did not really care. It was a heady feeling anyway. The

THE PLEASURE DOME

thought of being the focus of all those ads, all that attention, his picture in the newspaper almost daily. It would cost a barrel, he thought. They couldn't have afforded it if it were not for Alex Eastman, and in a sense Eastman only came in with the money because of him. So it was all quite fair, yes, eminently fair, he decided.

"And I like his idea for a trademark too, uniting the Goldmark Hotels, 'The Golden Mark of Excellence'—a shiny bar of gold—a gold seal at the bottom of every ad, very good," Blackman clucked, "very good indeed." He nodded at Harlan.

"It can be our seal, our coat-of-arms, you might say, on our stationery, on our matches, on our towels, on everything!"

Jessie smiled and looked approvingly at his son-in-law. Harlan thought if Jessie could read his mind he would not really be smiling. His thoughts had automatically moved to Laina. If it had not been for Alex, he might have forgotten her, until he saw her again, and then the reality of what he had done hit him. Not that he considered virginity a commodity. It wasn't that so much, he argued with himself, but the strange position he found himself in now and the way he felt when he held her in his arms at the masquerade a few weeks ago—that strong sweet urgent pull, a subtler, more cunning sensation than he usually enjoyed with women. And the way her father talked about her—no, canonized her was more like it. Perhaps Eastman was just lonely. He could understand that. Only Vivian and the kids had begun to cure that gnawing illness for him. He was certain he loved Vivian. His thoughts about Laina had nothing to do with his relationship with his wife or children. Vivian had given birth to another son last winter. He had been faithful to her right along, since his return from the service. He could not count those occasional drunken orgies during the war—nurses, faceless native girls. . . .

"Hey, Chase, are you still with us?" Blackman called.

Harlan straightened up in his chair. "I was just contemplating my new image—limping through the lobbies of once and future Goldmark hotels, trailing my medals like clouds of glory."

The PR man laughed uncertainly. Matthew's smile was remote. They talked a little more generally now, the price of entertainment, advertising, the general budget, the difficulty in obtaining produce. One of the secretaries came in with a platter of warm danish pastry, prune and apricot miniatures, freshly baked in their kitchens. As the girl walked out Harlan stared at her shapely legs, and was brought back to his reverie. He thought he had been in fact rather an exemplary husband, perhaps only because he had been so preoccupied with business, with plans and schemes. His need to win, to overpower, was channeled now into more fairly balanced tournaments. And Vivian, in any case, satisfied his needs . . . but still at times he was sorely tempted. The women, always the women with their intimate complaints. Only this afternoon after lunch the lovely young Mrs. Wilde had approached him with a problem. "Well, you see, Mr. Chase, my husband and I cannot sleep in a double bed, it's simply too uncomfortable. He's practically on top of me all night, er—I mean—" A blush seeped through her tan. "We would like our beds changed to singles, please!" Comments like that made his imagination run wild, but he had no intention of letting his appetites run away with him. If only because of Matthew. If Matthew ever dreamed that he was dallying with the guests, his credibility with Jessie would slip to naught.

THE PLEASURE DOME

The meeting seemed to be grinding down to a halt now. Irv Maslow, the Goldmarks' lawyer, sauntered in, helped himself to a generous amount of danish and sat in a chair near Matthew, who had said very little throughout the entire meeting. "What's Faye doing now?" he asked Matt with his mouth full.

"Oh, I don't know, Irv. I don't keep tabs on her. Why?"

"My wife was looking for her, wanted to play canasta or Mah-Jongg or something. I don't know, couldn't seem to find her anywhere."

Matthew shrugged, brushed his hair back from his eyes with a weary gesture and continued talking to Blackman. Matthew knew when he was being needled.

Harlan got up to stretch his legs and leaned against the big windows with their view of sand and sea. He missed a little his life of former anarchy, felt a prisoner of his new affluence.

He noticed Orlando Ortiz, the supplies steward, hurrying down the gravel driveway toward the parking lot. For some fifteen years, through wars and rationing, Ortiz was a fixture at the Goldmarks'. He was Matthew's man. Harlan was about to turn away from the window when the car with Ortiz at the wheel passed almost under his window. It was a dazzling, new, red Cadillac convertible. Harlan did a double take. It took money to buy a car like that.

CHAPTER 18

Harlan determined to familiarize himself with every aspect of the business. Even the purchase of supplies bore his careful scrutiny, though it had always been Matthew's domain. He spent long hours poring over the bills of lading in Ortiz's office in the pantry, late at night, long after Ortiz and the night porter had gone home. He was confused by certain inclusions, annoyed by certain omissions. But he could not discuss it with Matthew just yet. He wasn't ready, and even if he was, he did not expect him to take kindly to his suspicions.

Instead he came into the kitchen office after lunch one day and began talking with Ortiz. "How goes it, Ortiz?" he said, rubbing the man's shoulder convivially. Ortiz wore a large golden cross around his neck that was encrusted with rubies and sapphires. It gleamed richly through the dark hair that matted his chest. For a moment Harlan was frozen in his tracks by its opulence. "Still having trouble getting sugar and coffee?" Certain commodities were still hard to come by.

"No, Mr. Chase, as a matter of fact, everything is beautiful," he said, smiling. He had a charming Cuban accent. He was an attractive man with early signs of gray in his rich black hair.

"Good, good, that's what I like to hear. I like your choice of words, *hermoso*," Harlan said, rolling the Spanish around his tongue. "'Beautiful' is a very optimistic word in my vocabulary."

THE PLEASURE DOME

They bantered a bit about the economy, Harry Truman, the weather, the new hotels that were springing up everywhere.

Ortiz's conversation began to grow stilted and wooden. He was eyeing Harlan warily.

"By the way, Ortiz, I noticed you've had extremely heavy deliveries of ketchup and condiments in general, lately; how come?" The two men were still standing. Ortiz thrust his hands deep in his trouser pockets as if searching for loose change. He looked bland and shrugged his shoulders.

"Who knows? Some months guests spill more than other months—more waste than usual, bottles go up to room service and don't come down again."

"Yes," Harlan replied, "but that's all incidental. I'm talking about almost double shipments, almost double every month."

"Well, it can't be that bad, Mr. Chase, or I'm sure Mr. Matthew would have checked into it."

"Mr. Matthew," Harlan said, his voice rising only slightly, "has been busy with other problems, and *I'm* checking into it. If the books are right and the bills we've been getting from Prexy Condiment are in order, it's that bad alright."

Ortiz contemplated his alligator shoes.

For a moment neither spoke. Then Harlan asked, "Well, why don't you call Prexy? Look into it for me, will you? Let me know what they say."

"Yes, Mr. Chase, I'll do that."

Harlan needed a little more time.

He decided to talk to Matt before Ortiz did. Harlan made no accusations. He only recounted the situation as it stood at present and asked about Ortiz, his background, his record.

"What the hell?" Matthew said. "It could happen,

couldn't it? I mean, we could use more of the damn stuff some months than others; after all, the summer season is our only one here and Ortiz knows how busy we get. Maybe he wants to be sure there's enough." Matthew scrupulously avoided Harlan's incredulous stare. "It's not like him to overpurchase; he goes back with me a long way."

"Doesn't anyone check his books regularly, like you or the accountant?" Harlan interrupted.

"Yes, I check but I'm busy. You must know this is our first season back here in six years. Things are not exactly in their right cubbyholes just yet." Matthew was growing furious at having to defend himself to Harlan.

"You've been very pressured, Matt, I know, so do you mind if I help you put them back—in the right cubbyholes, that is?"

"Go right ahead," he said magnaminously, "but just make sure you pay attention to your part of this business."

"I like to think that all parts of this business merit my attention; that's the way I learn," Harlan said.

Two weeks later, Harlan said to Matthew over lunch, "I think Ortiz is stealing ketchup off the shelves."

Matthew was less benign now. "What do you mean you 'think'? You've got to do more than 'think' when you make an accusation like that." Matthew immediately sensed the implied criticism and rose to his own defense.

"I did."

"You did what?" Matthew growled.

"I checked carefully, the books, the bills, Prexy."

"You mean he's selling off?" Matthew asked, genuinely astounded.

"Yes." There was a pained silence.

"Who? What?" Matthew asked, his gray eyes filled with disappointment.

Harlan was not enjoying this. He did not wish to continue to press his brother-in-law's Achilles' heel, and yet certain things had to be done. "To other hotels, smaller hotels, in some cases restaurants. He sells them well below the market price."

"How long could this have been going on? Christ, he must have made a small fortune on us." Matthew shook his head in disbelief. Almost weekly his loyalties were being tested, all allegiances severed. "How did you get into this anyway?" he asked Harlan accusingly.

"I saw Ortiz driving a brand new Cadillac convertible. Since the war they're not easy to come by, and they don't come cheap."

"That's no proof," but Matthew looked uneasy.

"Come on, Matt, the guy is hardly living within his means."

"Christ, if the old man finds out he's been stealing, maybe for years—"

"He won't find out from me, Matt, that's why I talked to you right away. But you've got to get rid of Ortiz."

Matthew knew he was damned if he did and damned if he didn't. Either way, Jessie was sure to know about it.

"I'll have to check your facts first," he mumbled and ordered a stiff drink.

On the following Monday, Ortiz walked into Jessie Goldmark's office, his face suffused with fury. He said that his son-in-law, Chase, had gotten him canned. After all those years of loyal service to the Goldmark Hotels, this was his thanks?

Jessie had heard nothing about it either from Harlan or Matthew and was taken off guard.

Ortiz proclaimed it a bum rap, terribly unjust. "Mr. Matthew should certainly know me well enough."

Jessie listened carefully and promised he would discuss it with them. He promptly called Harlan into his office, then he summoned Matthew.

"Why couldn't you have left well enough alone?" Matthew asked him as soon as they left Jessie's office. "Why did you have to rock the boat? You made me look like a goddamn fool," he said.

"I'm sorry it turned out this way, Matt, but you must see . . ."

Matthew didn't allow him to finish. "Christ, Chase, the trouble with you is you're bored here, you're looking for some excitement, you're looking to win some more medals," he said bitterly.

Perhaps Matthew *had* sensed some of the army-post flavor in his brother-in-law's attitude. Harlan had made the move from the Broadbeach to the Hibiscus easily. He was used to mobility in the service, familiar with the ways of a large organization, the marines, where he had reinforced his natural ability to get along with strangers. At least for the present, his goals were to move up through the ranks which were, here, mercifuly small, and also to enjoy what men in battle dreamed about the most, a home and a family. He was confused. The postwar world had opened up a bewildering array of possibilities. He had always chosen the path of least resistance before; perhaps this time it would pay off.

CHAPTER 19

The summer would have been a lonely one for Laina if it were not for David. Laina was enjoying the attention. She had always enjoyed male attention. It was heightened by her father's obvious approval and Caroline's combination of envy and newfound respect. David Goldmark was considered quite a catch.

Laina spent most of the week at summer school. At night she came home to the apartment on Central Park West, which suited Alex well because he did not want to take off a whole summer from business and remained in town all week. So passionately did she love the city that she did not resent it in summer, hot and deserted as it was.

She began spending many weekday evenings with David, going to band concerts in the park, eating in little outdoor restaurants. Sometimes it was Carnegie Hall, richly musty in the summer night, followed by iced tea and smoked salmon sandwiches at the Russian Tea Room. And they caught every good show on and off Broadway. She had always loved the theater and went often, even in college. That was, in fact, the one great compensation for not having gone to college elsewhere. But it was different now, infinitely more satisfying and complete. David helped her see, helped her understand the richer kernel beneath the surface of a drama or the inherent whimsy in a good musical. Often, after a particularly good performance, they'd come back to David's apartment inspired. They would sit down at the piano and try out some of their own creations, extemporaneously. David noodled at the piano, moving his head like a metronome in time to the music, stomping hard on the pedals with a peculiar intensity she found satisfying, while she supplied the lyrics, laughing and stumbling over the rhymes as they went along.

"Jesus, you know you're good. You really are good," he said to her one evening early in their relationship. "Have you ever tried to sell some of your stuff?"

"Sell? To whom," she answered. "And without music? Fat chance."

"You can sell them to me anytime." Laina was pleased. She was happy to be appreciated for something other than her appearance. He pulled her down next to him on the piano stool, rumpled her hair, and lifted her chin.

She thought he was going to kiss her but he was too shy. She said in a soft voice, "Go ahead, David, you can kiss me." She was eager to test her own reaction.

He seemed surprised, embarrassed. "Who said I want to kiss you?" and winked at her playfully. She assumed he was flirting with her, playing a cat-and-mouse game.

She had dated infrequently, finding it burdensome and confusing, but she had been deluged by male attention through most of her adolescence. When she accepted a date it was usually with quiet, introspective boys whom she thought she could control, boys who did not present a threat and with whom she didn't run the risk of letting down her carefully constructed defenses. She imposed an erratic set of rules upon herself. Good-looking men were decidedly off limits, very tall or large men were forbidden. Her school friends considered her mad to turn down some of the choicest specimens. The young men assumed it was a pose, a game she was playing at their expense, that she was being disingenuous with them because she was beautiful and spoiled, one of those hard, careless girls blessed with a wealthy daddy. They would stop calling sooner or later. She was in a strange, self-imposed bind. Underneath her layer of reserve she was wildly romantic. She believed in the extravagant sentiments of the popular songs of the day, but she had learned early that sex had the power to change your life.

With David it was different. While he was not unduly handsome, there was an untidy romanticism about his appearance that she found appealing. If she found him somewhat impersonal at times, it was, she imagined, her fault. She had been told that she encouraged men to keep their distance. His nonaggressive sexual attitudes calmed her fears. Perhaps it was due to his enormous respect for her. She needed respect. The tension she had sensed in her dates with other men was lacking here, which was all to the good. She lost some of the dread, but also some of the secret excitement she had felt for men ever since that summer before the war when she had wavered between childhood and sensuality.

She was impressed by the casual elegance of his lifestyle. He had his own English butler, whom he had collected in his travels and who served them intimate dinners in the small charming *bois de rose* dining room of his Sutton Place apartment. The apartment was a luxury that Matthew strongly disapproved at first. But Faye had insisted upon it, would have financed it personally if necessary until David got on his feet. It would be better certainly than his waking up in strange apartments in suspicious neighborhoods. Matthew tried to see the good side of the situation.

During their long talks together, David seemed to

understand Laina, to touch the deeper reaches of her soul. And he appreciated her rare and fragile talent. He was exciting, his life, his music. The fact that he might become both barrier and conduit to Harlan Chase did not even enter her mind.

When Laina did return to the Broadbeach, she tried dodging the continuous shows and galas that were a feature of the resort. Sometimes she went with her father to the more informal parties held on the Ocean Terrace or on the beach, but Saturday nights now were usually reserved for David, often *en famille*, sitting at their formidable table. Harlan rarely appeared at the shows, which Matthew complained was not good for business.

Laina politely declined most of these family invitations. She could not bear the tension of waiting for Harlan to arrive from one hotel emergency or other. When he did not, she was caught between relief and the numbing drabness of disappointment.

"I don't blame you for wanting to keep a comfortable distance between yourself and them, I try to do the same whenever I can," he said ruefully.

She assured him that wasn't the case. Actually she was fond of the family, particularly Faye and Jessie. "I'm just not crazy about country club life in general."

David looked skeptical. "Oh, I don't know, Laina, I seem to remember you before the war as a budding sybarite, just like the rest of us."

She felt vaguely defensive. "Well, perhaps I've grown up a little since then. I'm having a much better time working with you on your musical. Maybe my father could help you to get it produced off Broadway or something."

"Or my father," he said wryly, pursing his lips. "No

thanks, I think I would like to see what I can rustle up on my own first."

She could not help noticing the strained relationship between David and his father and the somewhat overly romantic aspects of the relationship with his mother. He danced constantly with her, smiling and proud as he whirled her around the periphery of the large dance floor. Faye loved it. She could smile and acknowledge everyone, and at the same time afford the guests the opportunity to view her latest Paris gown. It was her idea of being a gracious hostess.

The hotel was large and generously laid out, and since she spent much of the week in town, Laina managed to see Harlan only in glimpses. But the essence of the man was everywhere.

The hotel staff was zealous and seemed to engulf her. She heard a number of people say how much the service had improved since "that nice Mr. Chase took over," "that handsome Mr. Chase," or "that charming Mr. Chase." His name hung about the place like a magic vapor.

She returned on the commuter train one Friday. It was near the end of August, hot and sticky, and she still wore her city clothes. She was hurrying down the boardwalk toward her suite, anxious for a shower. She had just passed her old cabana and rushed ahead down the planks, when she saw *them* up ahead.

Their backs were silhouetted against the sun. They were all in bathing suits. It was a family coming from a late swim, basking in the pleasure of just being together, alive and loved and loving. It showed in the way the father walked with his young son perched on his shoulders, the smaller boy in the cradle of his arm. His free arm was draped casually about his wife's shoulders. It was empty and silent at the beach except for the seagulls' occasional squawk. She saw the man incline his head, move his arm to bring his wife closer into his body; then he tilted her face and bent to kiss her, still walking their slow unbroken pace. It was Harlan.

Laina panicked. For the first time since that crazy night long ago she saw him as something other than her most intimate fantasy—saw him in context, in relation to his universe. She felt a lump in her throat that was painful and threatened to choke her.

CHAPTER 20

The following Monday Laina didn't drive into town with her father. Instead, she pleaded a headache. She said she wanted to take it easy, stay away from the furnace of the city. Lush thoughts nipped at her senses.

Their suite on the ocean was cool and pleasant enough but she felt restless and uneasy. She tried hard to think about David Goldmark and how much she had grown to like him, perhaps even love him. Thinking of David, she began to think about the musical they had drifted into together, "their sweet collaboration," he called it. She didn't seriously believe it would come to anything. David's music was strong and lyrical; it satisfied her words beautifully. Her lyrics seemed to enhance his score, but she wondered if perhaps the story was too heavy for musical comedy. It was to be an allegory of sorts. The lure of money and success versus the life on a farm, a sort of popularized version of the Kurt Weill opera *Mahagonny*. A haunting minor key theme ran through the music, changing octaves in a restless and tantalizing chase. She couldn't stop humming it; it inundated her senses.

Her eye caught the brand new television set that had been sitting forlornly on the floor of their living room for days. Alex had asked her to arrange to have it installed as soon as possible. The trouble was nobody knew exactly how to go about it. Television was still a new and mysterious invention and the hotel was not at all prepared for reception. Alex had insisted she arrange for it with housekeeping or engineering. He was anxious to have it for the balance of the summer, as he usually took off the last couple of weeks and stayed at the hotel. The unit, a ten-inch set, luxurious for that time, would be complicated to install, but Matthew had assured him he could leave it in the suite for the following summer. Laina got nowhere with the housekeeper and the engineer told her it would need a special TV installer. There was, of course, no such exotic personage in this small seaside town.

"Speak to Harlan Chase," he said. "That's the only way, I suppose." The prospect threw her into a strange inertia, from which she barely emerged until Alex returned and complained.

"Laina, what were you so busy with that you couldn't get this done for me? I need this set for business reasons. Is it your studies? Were you daydreaming again, writing poetry?"

In a way it was daydreaming, she supposed.

"I'll call up Matt or Chase now and get it done myself," he had said wearily.

"No, no," she almost screamed, "I'll do it tomorrow, I promise." She could not believe it was her own voice. "I want to, let me do it," she begged in a way that caused Alex to look at her curiously.

The next day she had planned to finish her studies and work on some new lyrics for David, but she sat around again in an agony of indecision, roaming the suite, staring out of the window at the ocean.

Finally at about four in the afternoon, she began to dress. She dressed carefully, and brushed her hair absently for a half-hour. Then, no sooner had she finished carefully arranging it, she decided it was unbecoming. She removed the barrettes and let it tumble down helter-skelter to her shoulders.

She sat down on the sofa uncertainly, then jumped up again and looked in the mirror. She thought she looked pale and gaunt and applied more rouge and a little more lipstick. Her hand trembled slightly and smeared her lipstick. She had to clean it off with a tissue and reapply it. . . .

The sign on the door said "Executive Offices." She knocked and decided that he was probably gone for the day; it was almost five o'clock. A woman's voice called to her to come in. An attractive girl looked up from the switchboard desk and asked her if she wanted someone in particular. The question took her off guard and for a moment she couldn't think of what it was she wanted. "To see Mr. Chase," she said in a rather penitent voice.

"Who shall I say is waiting?"

"Laina Eastman."

At the mention of her name the girl smiled politely and said, "Oh, good afternoon, Miss Eastman. I'll let him know immediately."

When she came out of the office she said, "You can go in, in a moment. He's just finishing up on long distance." She sat down at her desk and began gathering up her things as if preparing to leave. She fixed her hair and applied lipstick, eyeing Laina through her compact mirror.

In another moment she saw Harlan filling up the narrow doorway to his office. He greeted her formally, but not without warmth. As she followed him into his office she thought she heard the girl let herself out. His office was small but comfortable. Her eyes digested the myriad books, the record player in the corner, the neatly stacked record albums, mostly opera, many she had never heard of. She made no comment; instead she looked away.

He leaned back in his desk chair and looked at her. She met his gaze but could not sustain it. He had grown handsomer with the years, his eyes more penetrating, his expression compassionate. "Haven't seen much of you this summer, Laina."

"I've spent most of it in the city."

"Hot, wasn't it?" he said, "but then that is the price you pay, I suppose, for avoiding me all summer." Having unburdened himself, he appeared more relaxed. "Well, now that you've found me, what can I do for you?" He looked down at his desk, pretending not to notice how much more beautiful she had become. She sensed his pretense and felt relieved to let it go.

"Do you mind if we have a little music in the background while we talk?"

He jumped up and chose a record from the stacked albums. He slipped one deftly on the phonograph and kept the volume on low. "Will you have a drink?"

"This will only take a moment," she said. "Let me tell you the problem." She had no intention of letting this digress into a social hour, but somehow as she said it, she felt narrow and spinsterish, her old wound blanched into insignificance before his easy lassitude.

He poured a drink into a glass and drank it neat, quickly, as if in a hurry to unfold.

She stated the situation briefly, anxious to get it over with.

When she finished he looked at his watch and said, "Unfortunately it is too late for me to contact the man you need, but I will do it first thing in the morning; I'll try him at home tonight." When he said at home, she imagined his hotel suite, overcrowded with dogs and children and Vivian.

"Your father should have told me about this immediately, he knows I would do anything to please him; he only has to ask." She colored violently.

"He's been busy."

"I'm very fond of Alex, you know," he said evenly. "We have become great friends. In fact, I expect him at my apartment in an hour or so."

She looked at him levelly now, and he returned her gaze defiantly, as if nothing she had to say could possibly affect him.

She got to her feet and prepared to leave. She said, "Good-bye, and thank you," and went to the door.

As she got to the outer door he was close behind her and closed it firmly but quietly, blocking her exit. He rested his arm against the wall, imprisoning her there, as if awaiting her surrender.

"I can't let you go like this, I've wanted to talk to you for so long."

"Let me leave, please."

He touched her throat with his fingers—she stood rigid like a child awaiting a spoonful of medicine. "Why do you hate me so?" he murmured.

She did not try to reopen the door. "What does it matter? You have everything you could possibly want."

"I don't really know," he said, caressing her face with his hands. "But it does matter to me, you are somehow part of me."

"It's that Catholic conscience of yours."

"I have none," he said, still close to her, his mouth not quite brushing her lips.

"Let me go. This isn't how I want to be. Let me go on with my life." She spoke barely above a whisper. "You changed me, I became a different person after I . . . I *knew* you."

"How archaic you sound—for such a child."

"My age never presented a barrier to you before," she said, trying to regain her equilibrium.

He pinioned her against the door. "After all these years, you come to me as if in mourning, wearing black, ecclesiastic black! A fitting attire for a nun, but not for you."

He unbuttoned the top of her dress and seemed oddly startled by the exposed deep white slit in contrast to the black linen of her dress. She leaned against the door and made no further effort to stop him. She closed her eyes for a moment, and then flung the door wide open and walked out, her fingers trembling on the buttons.

She thought she heard him say, "What are you going to do?" as she walked down the long corridor toward the elevators.

Upstairs in his own apartment, Harlan tried to regain his easy jocularity and rolled on the floor with Gerald, the baby. Lately he went from one activity to another, business, recreation, children's hour, with a growing intensity. He felt compelled to keep busy, to keep his mind occupied.

He wondered even now what had possessed him to touch her, to dare to lay hands upon her body unbidden, as if it were *his* property. He wondered if anyone else had touched her. She was inviolable, gift-wrapped for some undeserving man. He was sustained by the inherent irony in all this. She obviously hated him. Shrank from him. Yet when he drew her close, for that brief instant, her body seemed pliable, yielding. Conflicting signals emanated from her. Once before their signals had gotten badly tangled.

In the living room were hydrangeas in a tall vase, graded from tenderest pink to savage blue. Vivian had discovered them in a secret corner of the grounds and had made them her private cache. Nearby on the same table, a half-filled baby bottle with a badly chewed nipple lay next to a cup and saucer of hotel china. On the floor was a playpen with a broken peg, in a corner Steven's tricycle. Their four-room suite was a mélange of commercial furniture plus a smattering of Clara's precious if overbearing antiques. Here and there Vivian had added a fresh touch, a Maguire chair, of reed and cane, a few pillows in tart citrus hues, as if in protest, to lighten the effect and bring the beach inside. She needn't have worried, her children had already taken care of that. The furniture and floor were gritty with sand. Everywhere were signs of easy domesticity that were a tribute to Vivian's knack for creating a climate of permanence out of transiency.

Still he enjoyed his sons. The children were enormously satisfying, and so was Vivian. In fact, never had the term "married man" been more gracefully worn by less likely a candidate.

Today his mind was more than sufficiently occupied. Jessie had called a meeting to discuss long-range plans. An "idea conference," he had called it when he summoned Harlan and Vivian. All principals were to be present.

Harlan had suggested the meeting be informal, at his apartment, "over cocktails and hors d'oeuvres," he said. At first his father-in-law had rejected the idea of alcohol being served, but later he relented. "Perhaps it would be better if we all felt completely relaxed. A few drinks might bring everything to the surface, the good and the bad."

Harlan had formulated his proposals for this occasion, and now was relaxed. He would have preferred to air them alone to Jessie, but any time he had approached him, Jessie had put him off with "Save it for the meeting," Jessie's concession to fair play.

Harlan was playing now with Gerald. He butted his head like a gentle charging bull into his son's tiny chest, evoking wild peals of laughter with every fresh assault. Steven, serious and darkly handsome, sat on the sofa beside his mother and looked skeptical. He still hadn't decided if he loved or hated, welcomed or resented, this latest addition to their family.

Harlan jumped up carrying the baby high in the air with one hand like a balloon and brought him down on his lap in a wriggling heap as he collapsed on the sofa.

"Darling, I was just thinking," Vivian said, "perhaps you could wait with that part about going public. That seems to be quite far off and . . ."

"Oh, you're afraid Matthew won't like it, will be *offended* by it. You're right, he *will* be offended by it, and damn it, that's his trouble, he sees everything as a personal threat, instead of a joint endeavor. Matthew stopped growing somewhere in his adolescence, and he doesn't care to get any older."

"Who does?" she asked, her clear dark eyes resting on his face. "He's got enough to contend with. Don't make this a contest."

"Viv, it's not our problem his wife can't keep her legs together or that his son prefers boys. There's too much at stake here."

She reached over and quieted him with her hand. "Someone will hear you."

"Who? Certainly not your brother, he's always late."

It was seven-thirty. Alex Eastman, tanned and narrowly tailored in a sky blue Italian silk suit, relaxed with soda and lime. He was fond of saying he never touched liquor. Harlan, his mouth full of hors d'oeuvres, laughed warmly at one of Alex's risqué jokes. They were all there, relaxing and trading stories when Matthew arrived, having been caught in traffic and somewhat befogged by liquor, his face florid with frustration and chagrin, and perspiring profusely.

"I'm sorry . . . I . . . car trouble," he blurted out.

"You're an hour late," Jessie said testily. "Let's start kicking things around a bit."

Matthew, in his present state, hoped it would not be him. He took a chair across the room from where Alex and Harlan sat together on the sofa. They certainly had become big friends. Matthew envied Harlan his knack for catching and holding onto relationships.

"So what have I missed?" He was unmindful of his lack of subtlety.

"Well, actually what you missed," Jessie answered, "were some rather arresting ideas that Harlan and Alex have been considering." *Working on*, more likely, Matthew supposed. "But let us hear your feelings about the hotels and their future, Matt," Jessie said.

"Well, I have been giving it a great deal of thought. Anything highly innovative would take some money." He flicked a glance at Harlan. "Since the war people want to stay at home—home, after all, is what they fought for—and a television is what's going to keep them there. We've got to drag them away from it if possible, by offering them bigger and better entertainment. After all, ours will be live. So I figure on adding onto the Hibiscus. It would be a recreation wing, a g-glass d-domed night club with g-game rooms."

"Game rooms," Alex said, "by that I hope you mean 'gaming.'"

"Gambling is illegal in Florida, you know that Alex," Matthew answered.

Alex smiled enigmatically.

"Go on, son," Jessie encouraged warmly.

"Then, too, I want to build a brand new and separate kosher dining room in both hotels. A lot of the older guests are not satisfied with just the back of the regular dining room. There are, of course, m-many, m-more suggestions."

Harlan interrupted. "The old kosher people will always come back, no matter what. They are rooted in custom. But they're old and their old ways are dying with them. Do you think it's wise to pour money into an area of business that's becoming obsolete?"

"This hotel has always catered to its old people; they are a solid and loyal clientele; they are the ones who *have* the money to spend here. Besides," Matthew said in an irritated voice, "who told *you* that keeping kosher was on its way out? I haven't heard about it yet."

Harlan smiled tolerantly at the innuendo. "We're going to have to keep raising money, big money to keep up with the trends. Air travel, the Caribbean, even Europe, what with the new luxury liners, are all big competition for us."

"So what is your point, Chase?"

"My point is we need to grow and expand so that eventually we can go public, or take over a small public company. That is the only way we can ever gain the kind of equity we need here and have the liquidity that stock provides."

Matthew was livid. "That is not the kind of business we are in, not the sort of hotels we run. We leave that sort of thing to the Hiltons of this world. We are a family business."

"That's what you are *now*," Eastman interrupted, "but we are talking about what we can become."

"What we can become is poor if we start screwing around in water over our heads."

"Why can't we learn new ways?" his father said quickly.

Matthew considered his father disloyal. Before he could answer, Harlan said, "These changes cannot take place overnight. First we must expand a little, perhaps build a hotel, a more modern type of resort, here or, better still, in Palm Beach. They could use a nonsectarian hotel there."

"Ha!" Matthew laughed. "I'd like to see that. Jews in Palm Beach."

"Why not?" Jessie asked. "Matt, suppose I had said that to *you* when you came to me with these two places?"

"Where is all this kind of money supposed to come from?" Matthew asked, deflecting the question.

"Eventually it will come from public financing. For the time being, Alex has agreed to finance it," Harlan said, "at least to guarantee another loan at the bank. We can't afford to go much further into hock at the banks, you know, Matt. Then, too, there are special loans now for veterans. I think I could arrange to get us a favorable deal."

"Chicken feed," Matthew said. "Why would Eastman do this for us, stick his neck out for a paltry twenty-five percent?" He looked at Alex suspiciously.

"*If* I were to do it," Alex said levelly, "it would be only because I think it would be a good business deal and I want to diversify. I've been wanting to for some time now, if only because of the advent of television. In fact, it is *my* business that will suffer the most if it really takes hold. Do you know how many bands have broken up? Hundreds. They can't get bookings. As I see it, entertainment and recreation are going to become package deals!"

"Package deals, glib *Wall Street Journal* phrases," Matthew said. He felt himself being dragged into unfamiliar territory.

"Well, Matt, it seems to me that you have to ask yourself how enlarging and remodeling what we already own will move us along. We may be throwing good money after bad."

"Good money after bad," Matthew's voice cracked, "everything we've done here has been bad? What's bad?" he shrieked. "Paying close attention to detail, offering the fullest and most abundant kitchen in the history of the resort business, providing blockbuster shows, top entertainment? We can do this *because* we're small."

"We could do it even if we were larger. You would be able to afford top management, top entertainment."

Matthew looked frazzled and worn. He caught his sister's eye. She had been silent throughout; now she looked with concern at him. "I don't want to relegate management. I haven't liked doing it with Chase here, quite frankly." He shrugged his shoulders.

Jessie said, "Well, don't fret, Matthew, that wasn't all your doing. I'm still alive. I still have something to say here."

"Oh, Father, I didn't mean . . ." He dabbed his forehead with a trembling hand but persisted. "I won't allow Chase to come in here and change all of our policies, our traditions, which are what people come back looking for year after year. Tradition is soothing to them in these

THE PLEASURE DOME

unsettled times. If you're going to remain here and work for us, for me, Harlan, you'll have to try to get in step with *our* ways. We have experience on our side, we shouldn't have to get in step with *you*. Your ideas are as yet unproved."

"I have never allowed myself to be dictated to and I don't intend to start now," Harlan said with conviction.

Matthew saw a faint smile of approval on his father's lips, which made him angry. "Well, as everyone else present has twenty-five percent or more interest in the corporation and you are only our employee, it seems to me *we* will dictate policy. If you are unhappy here, you are not forced to stay."

"Matthew, Matthew," Vivian said, "my twenty-five percent is Harlan's too. It is the same thing. We all appreciate what you've done for us, but we appreciate what Harlan has been trying to do also. The guests love him." Matthew looked wounded and Vivian relented, "Just as they love you."

"Well, these are, after all, only ideas," Jessie said with a grim smile. "Random thoughts on what direction to take—a glimpse of a future I won't be here to enjoy."

And at that moment Matthew had a strange presentiment—this had probably been a test of sorts, a trial for some unformed plan that would bear his father's manipulative stamp, insure his immortality. Jessie was indignant about age and impending death. Matthew realized he hadn't explained his architectural plans and financing suggestions. He was overpowered by his father's determination, his brother-in-law's youth and Alex Eastman's money.

CHAPTER 21

Two weeks later Jessie was dead of a stroke. Matthew would remember only that he alone had held his father in his arms and that his last words were to him.

They had been sitting in the old office near the tennis courts, the one where Jessie had spent more than a decade. It was the same small office where Jessie had felt so defeated two years earlier, before they had begun rebuilding, recouping, reorganizing. Before Harlan Chase.

They had been talking, father and son, about the war, about mama, about David. Jessie had even agreed reluctantly that David must stay in the world of music and theater, that he would never be able to cope in their business. Matthew was comfortable with his father for the first time in many years—as long as they stayed away from the subjects of business and money. And then suddenly Jessie fell forward on his desk. With a powerful effort the old man tried to move his lips to form words as if of the utmost urgency.

"Talk to me, Father. Oh, talk to me," Matthew cried. Nothing ever changes, he thought sadly! They had never been able to communicate in life; why should it be any different now? Jessie's eyes closed, his lips still, everything quiet in death. Gone. Vanished forever the boyhood dreams of running away with his father . . . Matthew put his head on his father's chest and wept with sobs that wracked his whole body and the frail lifeless body of the old man in his lap.

A few days later, after the funeral, only the immediate family gathered in the executive offices. Irv Maslow read the will. Faye looked solemn in black. Vivian sat between her husband and her brother, looking even thinner than usual.

In his own personal bank account there had been some three-quarters of a million dollars in cash, stocks and bonds, all of which he left to the Federation of Jewish Philanthropies, a part of which was to be used expressly for persons displaced by the Holocaust. The rest, his equity in the hotels, was simple and intact as expected, except for the allocation of the stock. Alex Eastman had already purchased the agreed-upon twenty-five percent. The rest was evenly divided between the children—Matthew and Vivian—and Harlan Chase. At first it did not sink in, then Faye looked at Harlan, amazed, to gauge his reaction. But he continued looking straight ahead at Irv Maslow, expressionless, as if Maslow were the oracle at Delphi. Vivian looked immediately at her brother, whose face was white.

Before Maslow finished reading the minor bequests, Matthew interrupted. He stood and in a barely audible voice he said, "This isn't possible, he has given the hotel away to a stranger."

Maslow looked politely perplexed. "What do you mean, Matt? You are *all* equal, except for Eastman, the outside investor."

Matthew took his seat again heavily, as if his legs could not sustain the weight of his own body. "No, no, that is not the way it is," he cried. "My sister and her husband are as one, a solid fifty percent and Eastman is a hundred percent behind him!" Matthew had lost all sense of propriety now. He didn't care. "Why didn't he at least leave it in Vivian's name? Why?" Perhaps Jessie had been trying to explain it—to ask for his forgiveness, his understanding, when he died.

Faye touched his arm, a futile effort to restrain him. He threw her hand off. "This was my father's parting lesson to me, retaliation against me because—because I don't know why—because I loved him too well, because he disapproved of my wife, my son. I couldn't satisfy that man." Tears stood sentry on his lashes but he fought their release. Matthew jumped up and walked rapidly out of the room. The women sat with downcast eyes, embarrassed to look at one another.

Outside Harlan put a hand on Matthew's shoulder to stay his rapid pace.

"Matt," he said awkwardly, "Fathers—well, all fathers resent their sons' youth, their opportunity; it extinguishes them somehow. It's a kind of jealousy. It's human, I suppose, but it's not personal."

Matthew removed his brother-in-law's hand from his shoulder as if brushing off dandruff and walked quickly away.

As the women rose to leave, Irv Maslow asked Vivian to remain behind for a moment. Faye looked perplexed, then resolutely gathered herself together and walked out quickly without a backward glance.

Vivian looked at the lawyer, startled, and doelike. He handed her a large white envelope. "Your father wanted you to have this—I do not know what it contains," he said, somewhat agitated by having been excluded from a confidence. He pressed her arm and said, "Once again, you know how sorry we are. We will all miss him," and he was gone.

She sat down in an armchair across from her father's desk and recognized with fresh shock the familiar handwriting.

Dearest Daughter,

I am writing to you in order to explain my actions concerning what you and Matthew may consider my unusual bequest to your husband.

I am not certain that I have done the cleverest thing. Only time will tell that. I did not do it to be clever, but to be practical.

First there was the plain cold business reality— Matthew, dedicated and clever as he is, is, after all, a rich man's son and as such his horizons may not be as broad as someone who grew up wanting. Frustration can be a very powerful incentive. Harlan seems to have his finger on the pulse of the postwar business climate. He is ambitious and fired with enthusiasm. He can breathe new life into this business— perhaps Matthew will catch his sparks—and with his own shares he will maintain an abiding interest. I want to see this business grow into something broader and more comprehensive—a legacy for my grandchildren, great-grandchildren. There is enough for everyone. There can be more. I saw the potential. Harlan sees it too.

Then there is the question of integration. Our hotels are becoming too ingrown. Matthew would prefer to keep them only for our own people. We have just witnessed what must surely be the central greatest tragedy of modern times, the systematic annihilation of a people because they were different. It is unique in the history of mankind but it is mankind's war. There but for the grace of God go I. Historically, our people were forced into isolation, banding together out of fear and rejection. I believe the war has changed all that, has opened the way for one world through mutual understanding. Harlan will open our doors to the world. There have never been *shtetls* in America—those in Europe are all gone. Perhaps if people can play together, they can work together. I suppose you and Matthew thought me cold, uninvolved concerning the war, the Holocaust. For a while, American Jews, like their more unfortunate brothers in Germany, eager to assimilate culturally, felt unable to fight a purely Jewish battle or perhaps there was nothing they could do. This failure sealed the fate of European Jewry. But the massacre brought my Jewishness to the surface and suddenly I became a Jew and looked at life with Jewish eyes.

Last but hardly least, there are the emotional reasons—I like that big goy of yours. For some reasons he got to me. Perhaps in the same way he won you and Alex Eastman over, with a certain nervy ingenuousness. But I never want him to remain tied to you for your money, or for a job. You would not be happy with him that way. You are too proud. And he would only grow to resent you for it. This way you will be bound together only as long as love lasts. It is up to a woman to make certain it does. And this way you will not grow too complacent. Trust me, I love both my children very much.

Father

The voice from the grave was unchanged. She sat there allowing her mind to adjust. In her head rang his words, "I want, I want"—reaching out—stage managing from the grave—he loved us both—but had faith in neither, she thought sadly. For a moment she considered showing the letter to Matthew—thought it might somehow mitigate the pain, liberate him from the past, but instead she tore it up into tiny pieces.

Faye hurried directly to the apartment to find Matthew, who was sitting on the sofa, staring straight ahead.

"Matt, it really isn't a terribly serious matter. There is enough, more than enough money to go around," she said. He looked at her in disbelief.

"God, it's not the money. You don't think it's the money, do you? I'll be working for some stranger, an Irish Catholic stranger at that."

"Why, Matthew? You are all equal partners and you are still president."

"Oh, Faye, stop placating me as if I were some sort of fool. What's in a title—president?" he said with a deprecating gesture of his hand. "So he is executive vice-president. I must defer all decisions to him and when there is a disagreement in policy—what then, eh? Tell me, what then?"

"Well, I suppose there will be a vote."

"And?" he said, looking at her amazed. "I told you in there just a few minutes ago if we must put an issue to a vote then I'm finished. Vivian is thoroughly mesmerized by him."

"Why do you assume that he wants to squeeze you out? That you are not needed here? He needs you, he learns from you, and what's more you need him. The total responsibility for carrying and running these places has been killing you. I have seen it, even if you haven't. He's young and strong, let him do the legwork, run the length and breadth of this place everyday. You will be the guiding genius in the background."

Faye saw her husband fitting into Jessie's place behind the scenes. She knew Matthew had always preferred that, yet he was reacting badly now.

"The problem is I really don't know where to go from here and he knows it," Matthew said in a tired voice. "The real problem is I'm scared and he's not, and he sees it."

She held onto her husband's arm tightly. "I'm scared too, Matt," she said. "And I *don't* have the responsibility for these places—the work, this kind of business wraps you in a warm safe cocoon. It's as if the battle rages on out there for everyone else but you. You're immune somehow, you're different. You think these pink stucco walls will protect you, hide you, succor you. But now you must either emerge from behind these walls and work it out or seal yourself up inside them like the cask of Amontillado."

"Why should I have to compete for what is mine?"

"Nothing, no one, can be irrevocably possessed," she answered with a note of sadness he did not wish to recognize.

CHAPTER 22

In the fall Laina became engaged to David. If she was not madly in love, neither was she terribly disappointed, for she didn't really believe that she deserved love. Marriage seemed the safest refuge. Unlike the people around her, she had a maturity that accepted the fact that immediate gratification was not necessarily the answer to ultimate happiness. There were other needs, she convinced herself—to be understood, to be appreciated, encouraged, and then, too, there was companionship. And she realized that she must escape the obsessive scrutiny of her father.

So she put David's impressive pear-shaped diamond engagement ring on her finger (paid for by his parents) and exhaled her youth.

Occasionally during the summer they had satisfied the families and the hotel guests who whispered and gossiped about the "owner's son and that beautiful Eastman girl," by appearing dutifully at the family table for club galas. Other times they took seats at the Rosensweig table where the gilded youth held forth.

They held hands and looked happy and glamorous; it was expected of them. Faye had a new attention-getting device now—her son's beautiful future wife. Matthew seemed confused and pleased. Faye said, "You see, I told you it was a phase, it just takes the right girl, that's all." Matthew looked skeptical.

Laina thought that David, with his easy charm, his sure direction at least in regard to music, would take her hand and lead her down the path of the secret garden that was herself, and she would find out who she was and what she really wanted. Perhaps he was hoping she could do the same thing for him.

At times she wondered why David seemed to have so few friends of his own age. He enjoyed hanging around with the show people at the hotel and seemed to hit it off with Russell Drake, who had a dazzling, if somewhat specious, charm. She felt a kinship. We are both loners, she told herself.

David knew there was something strange about the way she accepted his proposal. There had been nothing between them. The night he proposed, they were driving back from seeing a show in Greenwich Village. David had been pensive all evening. There had been a female impersonator in the show who had been very good, but the harsh outlines of physiognomy—jaw and chin—created a macabre illusion. Laina assumed the show embarrassed him. When they got into the car he took her in his arms and kissed her hand, but she had the feeling that it was less in passion than in desperation.

"I want you to love me," he said earnestly, like a teacher exhorting a pupil. She had to admit to herself that she was drawn to him because he provided a certain protection while requiring little commitment, so that she could still keep a part of herself free, keep a door open. She had been thrashing around looking for a loophole and she had found it in David Goldmark. She was appalled by her own selfishness; she owed David so much more than this.

CHAPTER 23

Harlan somehow managed to combine being an extended guest while working demonlike. Being in a position of command, being waited on hand and foot, was still a new experience for him, so while the majority of the family and steady clientele took it for granted, it was difficult for him not to let it go to his head. That was part of his charm, mixing the innocence with the experience. He was beginning to find it almost too easy to implement his own way. He was finding it less and less necessary to ask Matthew's permission for his latest innovations.

Matthew would have to face the fact that the business had gotten away from him, or was taken away—or given away. He was not quite certain which, since any one of them implied negligence on his part. Much the same thing could be said about his wife. She had moved further away from him in the last few years. Shifting gears in midlife was not an easy process for Matthew. Harlan was inundating Matthew with changes that, good or bad, he abhorred largely because they were *new*. But the hotels were making money hand over fist. Recently Harlan had begun accepting convention business off-season at both hotels. Matthew argued that conventions would downgrade the quality of their business. Harlan explained that not only would they make money by doing so, but that it would in no way corrupt their usual clientele. They also decided to keep the Broadbeach open for the month of

September. They would cater to the older people for the Jewish holidays. They would be able to extend their vacations and remain at the seashore during Indian summer. The weeks before and after the holidays would be for convention business. Alex had arranged to get a famous cantor and rabbi for these solemn holidays and before the big Labor Day weekend had even begun, the hotel was solidly booked up for the month of September.

Recently Harlan had become obsessed with buying a new yacht to replace the hundred-footer that they had sold shortly before the war. In those days, the family had kept the boat for their own pleasure, to invite guests aboard for private yachting parties. The boat had been permanently staffed with a French chef and crew who turned out gourmet miracles in contrast to the more commercial Jewish-style cuisine at the hotel.

Harlan confided his plans briefly to Alex. He wasn't certain yet whether the hotels would or could finance it. There existed the possibility that Alex would underwrite the loan. Together they went to the marina in Bridgehampton, not far from the hotel, to get ideas and prices. Before the war many of the hotel guests had pulled their magnificent yachts into these slips, stayed a few weeks at the Broadbeach then sailed to other resorts along the coast.

October at the boat basin was raw and windy, the sky a mix of slate and blue. The slips were still full because the yachts remained here until the cold weather chased them to balmier climates of Palm Beach and the Bahamas.

The boatmaster Jay Ormsby knew where to find distress sales, and who was selling what almost anywhere on the East Coast.

They boarded a hundred-and-twenty-footer, custom

built and exquisitely appointed. The woods gleamed and the rooms smelled faintly of salt and leather and lemon oil.

Later, driving home, he told Alex that he did not think the boat was big enough. Alex looked at him amazed. "Any larger and it loses its charm, its quality and would be prohibitive to maintain."

"No, it will cost nothing to maintain," Harlan said, looking straight ahead and keeping his eyes on the road. "It could be self-supporting if we made it part of the operation, a floating hotel—a gambling ship for privileged guests—sort of a gambling *club*—I'd keep a special wing for private 'family' use," he added magnanimously.

Alex was unimpressed by the last remark, but he was silent a moment, considering the whole concept. He knew plenty of gamblers, and with the right connections it could be done. It would throw off a fortune in cash, virtually pay for itself. Alex's connections were mostly Mafia. He had managed to traverse the questionable dividing line very well. As to whether Harlan, and particularly Matthew, could do the same was doubtful. His own roots were in the lower east side and though he was by nature a fastidious man, he considered nothing beneath him if it meant making "a good buck," as he liked to say. He felt vaguely uncomfortable now. He was not used to thinking about business decisions in terms of partnership.

"Christ, you know what kind of money we're discussing here? Big money," Alex said. "It will cost big dough to buy and outfit a boat like that," he said knowledgeably. "Besides, Matthew will never go for it."

"I'll worry about that, Alex."

A grin spread across Alex's face. "Geeze, you're a son

of a bitch like me, so why pretend otherwise?" Alex put an arm around the younger man's shoulder conspiratorially, a gesture of solidarity or duplicity, or both.

Harlan was not really listening. He had just decided that he would buy a boat that was fully decorated. He could always convert it later. All he really wanted at the moment was to have an expensive, impressive yacht. He had his reasons.

Laina had in effect traded off an engagement party, which Alex was pressing upon her, in favor of a large wedding. She really didn't want either.

Alex was friendly with Jack and Charlie since prohibition days, but when he told her he had arranged for an engagement party at the 21 Club—"Just the families," he said—she was furious. She had no wish to spend three tension-filled hours in Harlan's company or for that matter to be put under the further scrutiny of the family.

"Why don't you let David and me decide these things?"

"Laina, I don't understand you. It is naturally a time to celebrate and the Goldmarks must adhere to social protocol. It is their business to give parties, to be festive."

She looked at her father with a certain sadness, and then thought he never could see beyond the dollar; he made few allowances for individual needs. She was beginning to understand her mother's life and death with this man, even before the invasion of her illness. "Our engagement is nobody's business but ours."

Alex looked wounded. "But why wouldn't you want to mark it with some sort of celebration? Aren't you happy about it?" he asked, taking her hand in his. She noticed that his hands were graceful and still young. He sat down next to her on the sofa.

"Yes," she replied matter-of-factly, "very happy, Father." She felt sorry for having been so short with him. "It's just that David and I are rather private people."

"David doesn't strike me as that sort of boy, he seems quite outgoing and gregarious to me. Well then, what about the wedding?" he asked, making himself appear somehow vulnerable and at her mercy. Through the years since Seth's death, she had grown accustomed to acquiescing, indulging him. Now that she would soon be independent of him she could afford to be charitable. "You know these things have to be planned well in advance. Faye and Vivian can help you enormously!" He was encouraged further by her silence and pressed what he imagined was his advantage. "Harlan has suggested we have it at the Gardens." Her eyes took on a glazed look. "I can picture it now, in those lush tropic gardens, under the palms, the peacocks mingling with the guests." Alex drew the exotic setting with the flat of his hand.

"By the light of the moon over Miami . . ." She finished it for him. He could feel her anger.

"What is it, Laina, what is wrong?"

She got up from the sofa and stood looking out at the autumn russet glory of Central Park. "It's just that somehow, little by little, you seem to be allowing this, this interloper to preempt our lives." She spoke quickly and with mounting hysteria.

"What interloper?"

"Chase, of course. Harlan Chase. That's all you talk about lately. It seems obsessive to me." She spoke with her back to him as if she could not bear to face him. "What is it, Father? Do you imagine you are somehow making restitution to Mother by taking under your wing this Catholic upstart—this pretender? For that is clearly what he is, or is he a substitute for Seth?"

Alex leapt out of his chair and crossed the room to where she was standing. He whirled her around to face him and shook her hard. "How dare you? How dare you say such things to me?" he cried in a hoarse whisper. "It wasn't *his* fault—because—because Seth followed him into the marines; it was mine, only mine for being too busy, too preoccupied, too blind to see!"

She saw that his cheeks were wet with tears and she relented. "No, no, Father, it was no one's fault; it was wartime. Everything was so sudden, so ill-advised."

He sat down slowly, shakily, on the nearest chair. Then as if talking to himself, he said, "He is in some way my youth . . . the youth I never had."

He was talking of Harlan once again and she was annoyed. "You equate yourself with him? Well, don't bring him around me, that's all. I don't trust him, he's too lucky."

Alex was looking down at the floor and suddenly his head shot up. His eyes were wide and clear, the eyes of someone who had suddenly seen the light. "Why do you fear him so Laina?"

She looked at her father and said in a voice that was flat and unequivocal, "Why do you *not?*"

CHAPTER 24

The second week in January was chosen for the wedding. The hotel in Miami would be quiet after the holiday throng had departed and would be, in a certain sense, returned to the bosom of the family. It would be shortly after Laina's graduation. Laina and Faye agreed on having the wedding in the tropic gardens and for the occasion Faye decided to supplant the peacocks with flamingos because of their gorgeous pastel plumage, which she decided should be the color key for the whole affair. The bridesmaids would wear the palest, pearly shades of peach, and she herself would be resplendent in the true flamingo shade to match the exotic birds' plumage. It was to be a five o'clock wedding, the time that the orange sun began to dip behind the palm trees, turning them a stony-green.

For weeks the entire staff bustled, polished, recovered, refreshed, renewed and revamped. A special crew of gardeners was hired to prune and augment the already abundant gardens. For days in advance the kitchen staff shopped, cooked and gossiped.

Matthew was pleased and bewildered by the whole proceedings. It called for a reevaluation of his thinking about his son and this was hard for him to accept. Perhaps David had only been experimenting in his adolescent years and he had misjudged him all around. Perhaps his work, his music, this lovely young girl, had succeeded in providing the stability he needed where the parents had failed. Perhaps Faye had been right after all. Matthew was always ready to accept Faye's ultimate rightness in most things, for at fifty years old, he was still in thrall to a physical dependency that had not dimmed with the years.

David insisted that the honeymoon was solely the groom's province, and as such he wished to keep it a great surprise. In fact the only thing he would reveal, and that was with reluctance, was that they were going to a warm and tropic climate. "And only because the trousseau had to be taken into consideration," he said. He was thoughtful and considerate of the tremendous trifles that concerned a woman. Most men would probably never have understood . . .

When the wedding day arrived, the various ponds in the gardens were afloat with giant white orchids. As the guests waited patiently for the ceremony to start they were regaled by the melting voice of Russell Drake, who flew down for the occasion. Caroline Segall and Madelyne Maslow, Jean's daughter, led the procession, followed by four of Laina's high school and college friends. There was a breathless hush as the bride descended the flower-bordered aisle on the arm of her father. She was resplendent in an antebellum gown of heavy eggshell satin. Her small waist was cinched in, according to the latest Paris fashion, and appeared tiny above the great expanse of skirt puffed up by crinolines. The jewel-necked bodice thrust her breasts high and made them look large and seductive, especially beneath the coquetry of Alençon lace that rose from above the breasts to cover shoulders, throat and sleeves. She never looked more beautiful. When it was over, David stamped on the glass in the ancient tradition. There was a hoarse cry of "*mazel tov*" from someone in the audience, and they were man and wife. For one brief moment Laina felt as though her future had passed. Then they were swallowed up in the enormous reception, so that they barely touched for the balance of the evening.

Two of Matthew's famous hotel orchestras alternated— Joe Styles and the immensely popular Latin band of Tito Puente. The waiters circulated feverishly with drinks and hors d'oeuvres. Immediately after the ceremony, Matthew, who had been feeling extremely magnanimous toward his son lately, presented the young couple with a very special wedding gift. One that he had been collaborating on with Alex Eastman for some time. It was a check for five thousand dollars enclosed in an invitation to a theatrical investors' audition. On the bottom of the invitation was listed the names of all those who had accepted. They formed an impressive list. Above these names Matthew had added his own and written, "I have taken the liberty of being your first, although modest, patron. Good luck, son." He would have preferred to have given him more, a larger check, but he couldn't afford it. Matthew in his heart wished to improve on his own father-son relationship if he possibly could.

David was deeply touched by the thoughtfulness of the gift and embraced his father warmly. Alex, not meaning to upstage Matthew, gave them a ten-thousand-dollar check, suggesting that they use it for whatever they liked. Russell Drake had agreed to sing the leading songs at the audition, which in itself would lend weight to the occasion. That was Russell's wedding gift, that and the promise to bring along a couple of producers who might be interested.

David and Laina danced the first dance together, to a lovely ballad from David's new score called "Such Is

Love." Laina held the voluminous gown adroitly over her arm the way the saleslady at Bergdorf's had demonstrated; its graceful sway as she moved in the gathering dusk was a memorable sight. At that moment she felt completely happy. David had invited some of the Broadbeach crowd from the old days—the Rosensweig brothers, Jay Sachs, and much to Caroline's distress, Babs Singer because she was spending the month at the hotel with her parents. She looked only a little less lovely than the bride. Laina noted briefly and without much interest that David had invited no college friends to the wedding. When she questioned him about it at the time they were composing the guest list, he waved it away with his usual nonchalance. "You know Yale men, no basic substance, hence no basic attachments," and he laughed.

Faye, who rarely ever missed a dance on any occasion, danced the first with Matthew, who looked tanned and distinguished, and the rest with Russell Drake who held her tightly, his hand intricately woven through the back of her straps.

Laina circulated graciously among the guests. She noticed that David had been drinking considerably. Although it was *only* champagne, she rationalized, he was growing increasingly boisterous at the table of young people where he had been sitting. The champagne had now been replaced by scotch. She whispered something in his ear and he brandished his glass and said, "Oh, come on, Lainie, join us, let's have some fun. Don't break up the party just yet."

Her senses were in turmoil between apprehension and pleasurable excitement. She was anxious to get upstairs to the bridal suite, to be alone with her new husband. Yet she was glad of the hiatus. She wanted to have this time to herself to carefully attend to her toilette, to appear dazzling in her wedding night finery when David appeared.

She began to disrobe slowly before the mirror, standing in her chemise and stays as the gown billowed out around her feet; she felt like a latter-day Scarlett O'Hara. She removed her bra, her heavy breasts tumbled down in a torrent and she was overcome with anxiety. How could she appear before him with such large breasts? David had never touched her breasts; perhaps he would not like them. She sensed that David would expect her to be a perfect beauty. Should she wear a brassiere to bed? Then she realized that would never do beneath the delicate white wisp of a nightgown she had chosen.

For a moment she was lost in thought, remembering her mother urging her to wear a good secure bra when she was just thirteen. All the other girls were easing gently into training bras while her mother was trying to harness her like an unwilling pony. But she had put off wearing it for as long as possible; somehow she had felt the need to prolong her childhood. She bathed and stood in front of her full-length mirror and rubbed a perfumed oil all over her body and into the hidden crevices. She cupped her breasts in her hands for a moment, the better to examine her firm stomach. Then she slipped into the gown and felt the delicious slither of satin against her skin.

She brushed her hair until it shone a molten gold and was about to slip into the lacy peignoir when she heard a sharp knock at the door. She threw the peignoir hurriedly across her shoulders.

Harlan strode through the door wordlessly with David's limp body draped over his shoulder, like some exotic quarry, and deposited the unconscious body on the large double bed in the bedroom. Laina stood frozen in the living room near the door. "Well, there's your bridegroom," he said smiling slightly, "but I'm afraid he won't do you much good tonight."

"Is he alright? What—what happened?"

"Of course he's alright, he'll sleep it off. I removed his jacket and shoes for you, but I'm afraid you will have to do the rest," he said with a sly emphasis. "He's just had too much to drink, that's all. I suppose if I were he, I'd celebrate too," he said in a more intimate voice, walking over to where she stood clutching the negligee desperately across her breasts. She felt suddenly foolish in her *bridal* white. He took the robe and threw it on the sofa. Then he went to gather her into his arms. She could smell his sharp clean scent. "I haven't yet kissed the bride."

"Will you please leave here at once?" she said. She twisted away from him so that his mouth was pressed against her hair.

"Your hair smells of orange blossoms and honeysuckle. You are indeed a bride from the top of your head to—ah wait, let me look at you." She folded her arms across her breasts, as if hiding them. "The wearing of white should be only for me, it is really my prerogative," he said.

"You have no prerogatives. Why can't you understand that? You are living this lofty life on my father's charity. One word from me and it could all come crashing down around you."

He would not ask her why she had not told her father about him. He suspected it was for the same reasons he did not toss in her face what he knew about her new husband. The knowledge of either could cut them off from one another—separate them—disperse them to God knows where . . .

He pretended not to hear. He still had his hand on her hair. Trancelike he said, "You worshipped me once."

"I was a fanciful child then."

"I took advantage of that childish love—and I've suffered for it since."

"It is not apparent," she said, moving away from him. "Now, will you leave here and let me tend to my husband, please?" He felt the desire to punish her. "Before he *is* technically your husband, do one small thing for me please... let your straps down... let me see your breasts once again."

"You are mad," she said, moving farther away from him so that a large coffee table was now between them.

"Do it and I will leave immediately, I promise you." His eyes caught hers and held them in the same strange way that had always affected her so in the past, cold and green and compelling.

Her eyes still on his face, she raised her fingers to her shoulders and slowly lowered the tiny straps. She stood bare to the waist.

He dropped his eyes from her face to her breasts, resplendent now with their large area of peach-colored nipple. There was silence. He closed his eyes for a moment as if to commit the image to memory. When he opened them again she was putting on her robe. His voice was low and husky. "When I see you like that next, it will be because *you* want it that way. It is *you* who will come to me next time. You will see." He spoke with an assurance that suggested some mysterious privy knowledge, and it made her uncomfortable. He was almost out the door when he said, "Oh, by the way, I would tell you to have a nice trip but I thought I'd save it for when I see you tomorrow morning down at the boat. I have given your husband my yacht for the honeymoon. I hope you'll find everything to your satisfaction."

So that was the surprise, Harlan's new yacht. She wanted to cry out, to rake his face with her nails until she drew blood, to run tattling to her father. But in life you rarely got a second chance. It was too late now. She understood that.

She was trembling uncontrollably and she felt terribly cold in the thin gown. She opened the door to their bedroom. David was sprawled across both beds completely unconscious. She lay in a tight ball at the edge of the bed and stared up at the ceiling and listened to the percussive sound of her heart.

CHAPTER 25

And so Laina "was sailing on the sea of matrimony," as her father would say, and had been honeymooning some three days aboard the luxurious yacht, heading for the Caribbean. She found herself alone with her new husband and sixteen crew members carefully chosen by Chase. The two-hundred-foot cruiser, underwritten by her father, was originally christened *The Sea Chase* but had been temporarily renamed *Laina's Song* for all intents and purposes. Harlan did not know that it was considered unlucky to change the name of a ship.

She was astonished by the elegance and good taste that engulfed her everywhere she looked. The main sitting room or salon was opulent but tasteful. Bronze-colored mirrors lined one side of the room to increase the appearance of width. The colors, soft apricots and tans, were her colors, she realized. Perhaps Harlan had thought so too.

Everywhere were matchbooks, napkins, glasses with *Laina's Song* embossed in raised gilt letters. But there remained a curious absence of anything pertaining to the fact that they were, after all, a honeymoon couple—Mr. and Mrs. David Goldmark.

David was delighted; this was, in all fairness, the sort of thing that appealed to him, the perfectly executed grand gesture. He considered it very cavalier of his uncle—he was impressed, such attention to detail was

213

flattering. Laina secretly thought that rattling around alone in the immense space was depressing.

They had just finished dinner and were sitting in the salon where a trio had appeared mysteriously and were playing prewar love songs.

The dinner had been delicious, served by two waiters who hovered over them solicitously. To start there was a mousse of whitefish and salmon in a delicate béchamel sauce, then a choice of boned duckling with cherries and strawberries or freshly caught pompano almandine, or both. David had ordered a Chateau Lafitte Rothschild for the first course and a slightly milder white Bordeaux for the entrée, both of which he rolled lovingly on the back of his tongue at the first sip.

Dessert was flaming baked Alaska, a delicate pink-and-white confection complete with a bride and groom atop. Laina, fearful that the tiny couple might be consumed by flames, did not know whether to laugh or cry, they looked so helpless and vulnerable atop their meringue Mont Blanc.

David noticed that she had barely touched her food. "A touch of *mal de mer*, my sweet?" He patted her hand reassuringly but the gesture irritated her. It seemed to her fussy and pretentious, rather like a maiden aunt.

They had been almost completely alone for the past two days. They'd basked in the sun, swam in the pool, played quoits, cards and Monopoly. They had even spent a few hours each afternoon at the piano in the playroom, working on some new songs. But instead of feeling refreshed and rested, Laina felt tired and restless; she had not been sleeping. The night before, their first night out, she had come into the salon and David was playing the piano all alone. He pleaded seasickness when she reminded him of the hour and that it was time to come to

THE PLEASURE DOME

bed. He said he felt better working at the piano, he could not think lying down. They kissed good-night then, warmly, and she went to their bedroom alone, somehow relieved. She was still wide awake reading an hour later.

She looked at her watch. It was almost midnight. She went to get him. She sat down beside him on the piano stool. "David, do you realize we've been married almost three days and we haven't yet, well, I mean we aren't, really."

"Aren't really what?" he asked coolly, leaning forward to change a note on his music sheet.

"Married," she replied in a low voice.

David looked at her and began to laugh. His laugh seemed tinny and loud and rang with hysteria in the large silent chamber. "Laina, is that what's troubling you, my dearest, you are a conventional girl at that!"

She searched his face to see if he was clowning as always, but she couldn't read his expression.

"Well, come along then," he said resolutely, "let's go to bed." He took her hand and led her across the grand salon, not making a sound on the carpet, then out into the wide handsome corridors.

Their heels clicked smartly on the highly polished parquet as he sped along relentlessly. She was breathless when they arrived at the door of their bedroom suite.

"What is the rush?" she asked, perplexed.

"Why put off for tomorrow what you can do today?" he said. "Your wish is my command." His attitude struck her as strangely sardonic.

"But it must be your wish, too." Her own voice sounded choked and thick.

"This is no time for semantics, my dear."

Let's just get it over with, she wanted to say, but thought she was being unfair. He was being extremely considerate of her innocence, giving her time to adjust to him, the newness, and here she was making him feel foolish. Yes, she was being unfair, oversensitive because of her own conflicts.

David began undressing immediately. She slipped into the bathroom to undress. She emerged wearing her bridal negligee over her naked body. She approached the bed shyly where he stood smoking a cigarette, something she had never seen him do before. She noticed that his hand trembled slightly. She wondered if it was excitement. He immediately extinguished his cigarette.

"Let me look at you, darling. What a lovely peignoir," he said. She waited for him to go on, to make some more intimate comment. But he said nothing more, and took her into his arms and held her tightly. She held his young strong body against hers, warm and satin smooth as her own.

Together, on the great bed, he stroked her breasts, her belly, her thighs. He whispered how beautiful her skin felt beneath his fingers. They kissed and he pressed the length of his body against hers, but she was disappointed at not feeling his own hardness, his own urgency.

He whispered something to her and guided her head toward his stomach. She kissed his stomach. He gently pushed her head further down to his thighs. He whispered to her again, "Please, Laina, please—don't be afraid." Still she resisted. She took his limp penis into her mouth. Her delicate body lay across his like a loincloth. She felt him grow suddenly live in her mouth. He moaned and tried to guide her. He pulled her up suddenly and rolled her underneath him and entered her, with difficulty. In his arms her body was light and dispassionate as a wraith. A few moments of uneasy grappling, and it was over. She moved slightly away from him and felt somehow wasted. She made no comment. She thought that probably her husband was as inexperienced as herself, and that they would learn together. After all, one of the reasons that she had been drawn to David was that she felt comfortable with him, he didn't overwhelm her with his sexuality. He fell asleep almost at once, his arm still curved around her body. She lay there and thought perversely of Harlan Chase, and wondered if this was what marriage was all about, lying in one man's arms and longing for someone else.

David Goldmark remembered his childhood as a time of enormous precision. His mother had handed him to German nurses almost from the moment of his birth, and everything around him had been superbly organized and departmentalized. Afternoons, until he was old enough for school, he had a three o'clock nap, four o'clock play period, and a five o'clock hour alone with his mother. His mother was adoring, his father a shadowy figure he encountered between five-thirty and six in the evening. His nurse loomed larger than life. When he approached his teens, his mother emerged from the shadows to engulf him in an excess of pampering.

To his peers at college, even to Laina, he sometimes described himself as weak, but it was too harsh an assessment. He needed authority and direction in his life, he had learned to depend upon it and he was probably on his way toward finding it at Yale. His father was terribly preoccupied with the hotel business and always rather distant anyway; his mother was enmeshed in her social vortex and had a tendency to value *things* more than people. So his needs were terribly unfulfilled when he began college and discovered that in addition to this inner turmoil he might also be homosexual.

The real disappointment was the lost opportunity to study at the Yale drama school. He had hoped to get in on the new Yale repertory program after graduation. Sometimes when searching his soul, he thought it was only a phase, only his genuine humanism, his artistic temperament. He made many excuses, none of them really satisfactory. He was painfully anxious to keep it a secret, to make every effort to play it down, even to reject it. It was simply not acceptable in that family and in those times. Then too, David wanted a child, a family. David Goldmark wanted it all.

Apartments were scarce then, and they agreed to stay in David's Sutton Place apartment, which Laina would redecorate to her taste. Matthew generously offered an apartment at the Broadbeach for summers, which they both declined with alacrity.

Laina felt stronger than when she was only her father's daughter. Now she was endorsed, insured, invulnerable. She might, if she wished, assume her rightful place among the melancholy ranks of young matrons who thronged upper Madison Avenue, pushing prams and complaining in the playgrounds on the maid's day off about the paucity of good domestic help, and their husbands' infidelities, an existence most of her friends aspired to. She did not.

CHAPTER 26

Caroline Segall's mother, Tash—short for Natasha—said, "The trouble with Faye is she's overexposed!" She spoke of her as if she were a clouded negative. "She should keep something of herself as a secret, if only to create some mystery." She picked a jack of clubs, discarded it, and picked up an ace. "I can't say retain, because she never really had any to retain. Mystery, that is the key," she murmured as she deftly arranged her fan of cards.

"Is that the key to your success, dear?" Jean Maslow asked waspishly. Jean, the hotel attorney's wife, was a good friend of Faye's. Faye was in fact immensely popular with the guests in general. Caroline, who was called in hurriedly to fill in for the absent Faye, thought that Tash resented Faye because they were so much alike. Both suffered from the same disease, terminal boredom. What Caroline didn't know, which was probably closer to the truth, was that Tash was still smarting from a sharp lecture Matthew had delivered her on the subject of keeping her latest young escort in her room at the hotel. "This is a family hotel," Matthew had said. "We don't allow gigolos here, particularly when your husband pays the bill."

"Oh, balls," thundered Mrs. Van Danziger, to no one in particular. Mrs. Van Danziger made up the regular fourth at these daily canasta games. (The "Van" they suspected had been added on.) A stocky woman in her

219

late forties, she wore her rouge high up on her cheeks like a Kewpie doll. "A cuckoo," they all said among themselves. But she was a good player, and could afford to be a good loser. They played for one-twentieth of a point—considered by them a steep game. She reached forward and chose a card reluctantly from the pile. Her wrist glittered in the tropical sun. She wore a gold-and diamond-bracelet over her glove. Mrs. Van Danziger *always* wore gloves. Nobody was exactly certain why. Perhaps to prevent freckling or to hide it; she might have been a natural redhead once, her skin was so milky. During the day it was short white gloves, but at night they climbed to her elbows or even on occasion to her shoulders, dyed to match her evening gowns which were inevitably shades of pink.

"Where did you say Faye was?" Tash said, still engrossed in her hand.

"I didn't say, because I really don't know," Jean said. "She doesn't check in with me."

It was a scorching day and sweat stood out on their well-oiled faces.

"I hear the wedding was fantastic," Mrs. Van Danziger said, and pursed her lips disapprovingly.

"It was truly beautiful," Jean said.

"*I* wouldn't know; *I* wasn't invited." Mrs. Van Danziger drummed white-gloved fingers on the card table. "Evidently *I'm* not a privileged guest. I don't mind telling you I'm considering not returning here next winter." Her voice was shrill with offense.

"I wonder who fixed up David Goldmark's marriage," Tash said, her face tense.

"Those two seem an unlikely pair."

"Oh Mother, they've known each other since they were kids—from before the war, you know that."

Caroline wondered if the game would go on forever. She was anxious to quit; the women were getting on her nerves.

"He's a bit of an oddball that kid, don't you think?" Tash said. Caroline was silent. She had faint misgivings. But she was a little envious.

"Oh, a bit formal perhaps, but it's probably due to his prep school background, and then again Yale, you know, his father's alma mater," Jean said, feeling somehow like devil's advocate instead of the advocate's wife.

Tash looked skeptical, as if they were poor excuses. Tash Segall liked to create the illusion of being the Duchess of Omnium. "Hmf! Still, I'd like to know what Faye is doing right now," Tash said, applying a towel daintily to the perspiration above her lip and then under her arms.

What Faye was "doing right now," as Tash had put it, was spending the day in neighboring Palm Beach, ostensibly to do a little shopping, have lunch and visit some friends.

Russell Drake had rented a small but charming cottage in Palm Beach for the season. "Cottage" was the generic term given to almost any or all vacation homes in Palm Beach at that time. Even Mrs. Merriweather Post's sprawling estate Maralago that ran for one hundred and seventy-five miles along the choicest strip of oceanfront was called a cottage. However, the house that Drake had rented on Coconut Way belonged to an important Washington socialite who had decided to bypass "The Beach" until it was properly cleaned up after the previous year's devastating hurricane. It was not usual to rent in season then, and certainly not to Jews or show people. As Drake was both, he paid twice what it was worth. The house boasted a small pool and essential privacy. His schedule of engagements for personal appearances and recordings was a heavy one, but for now they centered around the eastern seaboard cities. He was not keen on going back to Hollywood. His tangled personal life during his brief period there had left him with bitter memories.

Late in the afternoon Faye and Russell were bobbing around the pool like children. Faye appeared young, almost tender in her nakedness. The water's buoyancy made her body look even firmer. Certainly she did not look some ten years older than her companion. Faye was forty-one, but could get away with it. Her refusal to bow to the inevitable was at the root of her personality. Faye had no intention of growing old gracefully or disgracefully.

Russell swam up behind her and embraced her, assured of his welcome. He touched her breasts possessively and she could feel the hot length of his erection in the icy water. It made her shiver deliciously. He kissed the nape of her neck, bared beneath the heavy pile of pinned-up hair.

"Bend over a little, baby."

"Really, Russ," she said, demurring with a laugh and playfully splashing him. But a man used to being indulged by women was not so easily deterred. She floated gently into his arms.

"Come on, Faye, don't be conventional, what's the difference if it's here or on a bed? Pretend it's the shower. It's just like being together in the shower, remember?" He turned her around gently so that her arms rested on the pool's ledge. He held onto her waist tightly from behind. Her thighs parted easily, and she took him in. The only weight she was conscious of was inside her body; outside they floated light as a feather. He pushed himself up high inside of her and she made a guttural

THE PLEASURE DOME

sound of intense pleasure. His hands freely caressed her breasts and her belly, and he touched her below lightly but deftly. When she cried out hoarsely, her wildness drove him to the edge and he cried out too. They held onto each other limply, floating, bobbing, like lifeless rubber dolls.

"Fantastic, that's all I can say," he breathed enthusiastically, "really fantastic."

That's all I can say struck her as the unvarnished truth. Russell's frame of reference was somewhat limited. She didn't much care for being graded on her performance, either, and didn't see in any case how one could be particularly inventive in the water without drowning. Postcoital *tristesse* had set in.

"Well, there's nothing like dealing with an old established firm," she said, laughing but ever conscious of the age difference. He heaved himself out of the pool and she noted his long smooth body with satisfaction.

As he dried himself with a towel he said, "That was only an hors d'oeuvre, honey, I was just preparing you for the main event, trying to teach you to lose some of your inhibitions." Faye thought to herself that she had lost them long ago. Perhaps Christian women were more relaxed about sex, even Catholic girls enjoyed now but paid later. She was flattered to think that no sooner had he finished making love to her than he was planning their next encounter. Ah, the advantages of having a young lover—and then, too, his Hollywood experiences were titillating. What the gossip columnists hadn't told her he'd filled in. She had little doubt that he'd embroidered here and there, but still . . . With Faye, most of her life was mind over matter, and what mattered to her the most was to have a good time. Her courage had long ago been sapped by the mind-dulling routine of resort hotel life, her natural hedonism reinforced by the desultory lifestyle she led. It was hard to grow old before you had even grown up. For her the fountain of youth was the semblance of youth. She looked in the mirror on the day of the wedding and had actually cried out loud, "But I was only nineteen yesterday!" There was never any doubt in her mind that she had married too young, and if she bore Matthew any resentment at all, it was for that fact only—that and the birth of a baby a year later.

They went into the enclosed portion of the house and sat muffled in terry cloth robes sipping screwdrivers in tall frosted glasses. Faye only drove down on certain Thursdays, when Russell's houseman was off. She rarely stayed through dinner. Russ stirred his drink thoughtfully with a pineapple stick.

"Faye, I'm having a little cocktail party tonight and I want you to stay; you'll meet some interesting people." She was offended; why had he invited people down on her day? He knew she couldn't or wouldn't stay around for it.

"This is *our* day, Russ, why?"

"Why? First because it was unavoidable, sweetheart, and secondly because I particularly wanted you to be here, it wouldn't be half as much fun without you, believe me." She was not really in a party mood, nor did she think it was a very smart idea.

"Russ, you know I can't meet your friends, I mean you never know—"

"I *guarantee* that these people have never so much as heard of Goldmark Enterprises; as far as they're concerned, a gold mark was a good grade in public school."

Faye laughed. "Who *are* these people, Russ?" She was growing apprehensive.

THE PLEASURE DOME

"Nobodies really, don't fret, darling, just sort of an open house, I suppose."

At five-thirty they started drifting in, girls, girls, girls. Some were escorted, most were not. She knew she should leave, should have done so hours ago, but she was ambivalent about leaving: She was afraid that it would appear that she had run away, bested by their youth; besides, she hesitated to leave Russell completely to the elements. She imagined she might be in love with him. In the few extramarital affairs she had had (despite torrid rumors, there had been very few), this was the first time she had felt emotionally involved. She thought, so I have a crush on Russell Drake, so do a million other women.

She was about to leave when a handsome couple came in. Russ introduced them as Quentin Davies and Jasper Whitman. Quentin was a famous model, and Jasper a celebrated photographer. Faye did not recognize her, and thought that if she had seen that face anywhere she would not have forgotten it. Faye had never seen anyone quite like her. She was a brunette with pure alabaster skin, and large gray eyes, a Hedy Lamarr type. Her heart-shaped face with its cleft chin was almost too sweet to resent. Jasper Whitman was a ruggedly handsome man with a fleshy, sensuous face, a face burning with curiosity and humor. Faye was immediately drawn to them in a perverse sort of way. She judged him to be close to her own age, although Quentin couldn't have been more than twenty-five.

Their relationship appeared tenuous, one minute they acted warm and possessive and the next detached and impersonal. After Russell introduced them, the four of them stood talking. Quentin rolled the glass seductively between her fingers and it clicked musically against her rings. She spoke little, and seemed to be sizing up Faye. She was dressed in black toreador pants and a high-necked black jersey. A ribbon of red satin at her waist was meant to join the two parts, but instead bisected her body like a scarlet slash. Faye felt prim and overdressed in her purple linen sheath, even though it was tight and showed off her figure to advantage.

As the party waned, the four of them sat together, drowsing around the coffee table. The all-afternoon drinking was beginning to get to Faye. Quentin stretched and put her head on Jasper's broad shoulder. He kissed her ear and slid his hands down to her breasts. This seemed to excite Russell, and Faye caught the sparks. Whitman passed around some marijuana.

"Here, try one of these," he said to Faye, "I guarantee you'll relax."

Faye smiled knowingly. She had only begun smoking marijuana since she met Drake. They leaned back, sending clouds of green yeasty smoke up to the ceiling. Drowsing, Faye wondered if Quentin had been swimming because her long legs were bare beneath the black jersey. She wondered when she had changed to a swimsuit. Faye and Russell were seated on the sofa, the other couple on a love seat opposite. Quentin took a drag of her cigarette, put her head back on Jasper's shoulder and put her legs up on the coffee table. She let her thighs fall open slightly to reveal that she had nothing on underneath. Faye was at first shocked but determined not to let on. Quentin stared at her provocatively under half-closed lids, rolling her head slightly from side to side. Faye noticed that Russell was growing excited. Quentin obliged by slightly parting her legs and leaving them that way. Jasper put his hand up under her sweater and caressed her breasts, bare beneath. Faye said something about leaving again, but seemed rooted to the sofa, overcome by a sweet erotic lassitude. Russell put his hand under her dress, gently massaged her thighs, and put his fingers inside her bikini panties. She was conscious of their eyes on her, and was torn between embarrassment and arousal. Sitting across from them, Faye couldn't help but notice that Jasper Whitman was ready—very ready. His trousers were straining.

Quentin got up languidly and said, "Jass and I are gonna take a nap." She yawned and stretched provocatively. "Anyone want to join us?"

Jasper Whitman leaned over to Faye. "C'mon, Faye, you won't be sorry, I promise you." Faye began to demur when Russell got up, rotating his hand gently on Quentin's behind.

"You better, baby, 'cause I'm going with or without you." Faye looked at Quentin and was at an impasse. She secretly believed that nothing could compensate for irresistible youth and beauty, but she wanted to compete; she really wasn't bed weary, but she *was* bed wise. Faye rose, slowly, with some reluctance, and followed Russ.

The king-size bed was big enough for four or more. Faye was conscious of a lot of arms and legs in the process of disrobing. She couldn't seem to make her fingers work, to unbutton her dress. Russell obliged by doing it for her. In a moment her linen dress was a purple pool at her feet. She was the last one to come to bed and she felt their appraising stares. Even Quentin looked appreciative.

Lavender dusk descended, throwing the room into thankful shadow. That was how she was to remember the incident in years to come—a kaleidoscope of moving, urgent shadows, something she hadn't really wanted.

Until then her romantic life had been casual, but not evil.

It was late. She had a two-hour drive back to Miami. In the old-fashioned clinical bathroom she repaired her makeup in a desilvered glass. Her skin appeared slack like melting candle wax. She drove the lipstick savagely, as if committing a murder.

CHAPTER 27

Caroline sat weeping over an old wound in a corner of the lobby. Craig Rosensweig strode away angry and frustrated at her refusal to agree to a request she could not possibly honor. Laina, stopping over briefly in Miami after her honeymoon trip, walked rapidly through the lobby, her high heels clicking with authority on the polished marble floor. She stopped abruptly when she spied her friend huddled miserably in a deep armchair printed with large green palmetto leaves.

Laina sat down beside her on the same chair. Mutely Caroline groped for a tissue and made a successful effort at recovery.

"Did you have a nice trip?" she inquired.

"Yes, it was lovely," Laina shifted the subject easily. "But what's been going on here in my absence, for God's sake? Can't I leave you alone even to get married?" At the word "married," Caroline's eyes clouded over with a gray rain.

"I just passed Craig in the front lobby, he was walking so fast I don't think he noticed me. I suppose it has to do with him again, doesn't it?" Laina said, voicing her disapproval in matronly tones. A bellman passed by paging a Mr. Drinkwater—Caroline looked down as if searching for something on the floor. She didn't want to become a subject of gossip. The *help* thrived on gossiping about the guests.

She slowly began to recount the rather remarkable conversation that had just taken place, the latest installment in her unhappy saga.

"Craig called me up and asked me to meet him for a drink in the lobby. He says, 'Caroline, how long have we known each other? God, from way before the war. We were practically kids together. Childhood sweethearts, you might say.'" She stopped for a moment, chastened by having even been relegated to that lofty position. She gave a joyless laugh. "I felt certain that he was about to—well, what would *you* think, Lainie? I mean wouldn't you think he was about to propose?"

Laina nodded, feeling apprehensive.

Caroline went on. "'Well,' he says, 'when a man has the good fortune of knowing such a girl as yourself, he rises to the occasion—and—hopes she will do the same, do a wonderful charitable act and perhaps save his worthless life.'"

Laina was wary of such uncharacteristic humility from this usually arrogant source.

"Luckily I controlled myself. Then he says, 'And speak to my parents for me. They like you.' There was a silence while I tried to digest this information and I thought he probably meant speak to *my* parents about our getting married. So I said gently, never taking my eyes from his face. 'About what, Craig?' 'Oh, well, you know my folks,' he says, 'set in their ways unable to give an inch in this thing . . .' By now I'm wild with curiosity. 'What thing, Craig, for God's sake?' 'Why, the relationship between Babs Singer and myself—of course,' he said, as if there could not possibly be any other major issue in his life."

Laina watched her friend visibly fold like a moth's wings, crumple at its telling.

"'Perhaps if you spoke up for her, told them she was,

well, okay—you know—that you thought her bright and talented,'" Caroline droned on in her husky monotone. Laina, of course, was familiar with the rest of the story. The Rosensweigs looked upon the Singers as blatantly nouveau riche since they made their fortune in rags. And then not quite *riche* enough. Not only did they suspect that the rag business had its early roots on a lower east side pushcart, but they didn't approve of Babs either. They considered her "fast." She was too slick, too done up, wore too much makeup. The fact that she hadn't gone on to college, but had chosen to work for her father, coupled with her questionable reputation, conspired to disqualify her completely.

Although the four Rosensweig bachelors, all well above six feet, presented a somewhat terrifying armada when displeased and an almost equally impressive one when pleased, they were reduced to diffident schoolboys before their parents. Respect for parents was the keynote in their training. However, the lure of money was a contributing factor to their obedience. They were crazy about money, and all worked for their father in his vast complex of woolen mills. Laina was about to comment that she could not see why Caroline would want him in the first place, but stopped short because she knew the inherent loneliness of her friend's life.

"I want him with all my heart, Laina."

Laina, hearing this, began to listen differently.

Caroline had by now regained her equilibrium somewhat. "Can you imagine that, Laina, asking me to plead for Babs with his parents?"

"So you told him no, and he strode off furious?"

"Yes, exactly. What should I have done, said *yes?*" She shrieked, causing Laina to wince involuntarily. She had just returned from twelve intensely quiet days—

"Yes, I think perhaps you *should* have told him yes—I think in pleading his case you would be unconsciously winning your own—you know they will never agree to his marrying Babs—but how they will admire you and, how close he will feel toward you for doing him the favor."

"Yes, big deal! So he'll probably come up with one of those wholesale woolen coats from Ben Reig or something."

"Or he could wake up and realize it's you he's loved right along and not Babs at all, if you handle it with enough diplomacy."

Caroline looked up surprised, studied her friend with new respect. "Only two weeks married and already you have become the wise. I'm listening to you as if you were an oracle. David must be doing marvelous things to you!" she said with a lascivious smile, "which brings me to that most important of all topics, your honeymoon. How was it, for God's sake?"

Laina shifted uncomfortably in the double armchair. She stood up.

"Hey, where are you going? Don't run away just when we are about to change the subject." Laina sat down again in the small chair opposite Caroline; from here she had a broad view of the hotel lobby and suddenly appeared edgy.

"Well, let me look at you—of course, you are still beautiful, damn it. But you don't look so awfully well at that," Caroline said slowly. "I mean you seem pale through your tan. Of course I know what that's from." Caroline winked and said, "So Mrs. Virgin, you've lost your title at last—c'mon, tell all." She seemed to have completely regained her good humor.

"We had a *lovely* trip, very luxurious. The ship is really quite beautiful—"

"The ship. Whose ship?"

"Harlan Chase's. Yes, didn't you know Harlan lent us his yacht for the honeymoon? It was a surprise—"

"Well, it certainly was," Caroline breathed meaning into the lines.

They were silenced for a moment. Laina felt Caroline was carefully mulling over the information, or just feeling pure envy or joy—or curiosity—or all of those emotions.

"Harlan must be some in-law to reckon with," Caroline said dryly. "Anyway if you don't care to discuss your honeymoon with me it probably was nothing to rave about."

"Please, Caroline, I didn't say that. Everything was really quite lovely—"

Caroline was not satisfied by her pallid denial. She leaned back in her chair now as if it were a throne, her own recent defeat already buried. "You know, my dear, if you want to make a marriage work you'll have to learn how to please a man in bed—"

Laina looked at her quizzically and thought at this moment how much Caroline resembled her mother. "Even my doctor says . . ." Caroline frequently endorsed doctors. ". . . in the beginning you must tell a man what pleases you, guide him if necessary—and if that doesn't work, then for God's sake fake it!—you know—you're not a bad actress, a little overly romantic perhaps, but that's to your advantage here. You must learn to simulate orgasm, if nothing else," she said with finality and tugged thoughtfully on a dainty gold earring. "They never know the difference anyway."

Laina, smiling tolerantly, asked, "Did your doctor tell you that also?"

"No—" Caroline shook her head. "My mother did." Like her mother, Caroline really did not care very much for men.

Laina told her about the forthcoming backers' audition and their musical.

"Christ, all this and heaven too," she said. "David Goldmark and a ready-made career for you to step right into."

Laina was not flattered but recognized her advantage. "I'm not ungrateful, Caroline, and I do very much want a career. I love David's music. He's very talented."

"I hope he doesn't resent your having a career, sharing his success."

"Why should he?"

"Well, look, Laina, women are just not programmed to have a sense of self today. Certainly not Jewish women. Their lives are *Kirche, Küchen, Kinder,* even the upper classes. Mothers first. Wives second. Careers? Running to doctors with their children becomes their careers. That's the *only* place that my mother qualifies as a Jewish mother. Look at her, exquisitely conscious of her body, every ache and pain duly recorded like a cash register ringing up sales."

That was Tash all right. Laina smiled knowingly. "That's only because she's unhappy," she said.

"Aren't most people?" Caroline replied in tones of carefully cultivated fatigue. "What about you, Laina? Are you happy?"

"I really don't know yet, Caroline. My life is just beginning. I'd like to sketch it carefully, beautifully, without too many erasures, but who knows? Human emotions are interdependent."

"If I didn't have such a tangle of emotional problems I know I could get down to the business of writing," Caroline said wistfully. "But you've got to have a perfectly clear head to write—you've got to put your life in order first and gain some perspective. I have nothing much to look back on yet." Caroline wanted to be all the women her mother was not.

"But a great deal to look forward to," Laina said generously. "You'll put it all in a novel someday, Caroline. I'm sure when you're comfortably ensconced as Mrs. Rosensweig, you'll be able to free your mind from all this minutiae so that you can write. Writing can be a blessed catharsis."

"Oh, Laina, don't tease me. He's in love with someone else."

"Perhaps he only thinks he is," Laina said, her natural kindness coming to the fore.

CHAPTER 28

Laina was not the only one who had to adjust to the marriage. Faye had to accustom herself to losing her best dance partner, Matthew had to force himself to believe in the mysterious healing power of love, and Alex Eastman, baffled by his new son-in-law, had to get used to David calling his mother "Faye" in that special and rather exquisite manner, which he tried to assure himself was a result of overbreeding.

In David's apartment overlooking the East River with its view of tough urban beauty and the gossamer bridges, she was content. She was happiest when she was working, preparing for the investors' audition that would take place in late spring. They rented a small studio in Carnegie Hall, their "office." At night they took turns cooking gourmet specialties from different countries, recipes David had culled from *Town and Country* or *Gourmet* magazine. When they worked late and were too tired to prepare a meal, they dropped in next door to the Russian Tea Room. Ensconced in the soft red leather booths, sometimes sitting for hours, dreaming over their steaming tea, they would invariably meet people from show business who would in turn introduce them to someone else from the Broadway scene, musicians, writers, actors and directors. David always had with him an extra audition invitation for anyone who showed even the slightest interest. If they could raise enough money

THE PLEASURE DOME

he might even open on Broadway instead of the Village as expected.

Russell Drake came to the studio to rehearse the songs for the show. He loved the score and sang it gracefully and with style, suggesting flourishes here and there. He also suggested they call in a playwright. The book was ponderous, he said, rambling. It needed work.

"It's mostly the music and lyrics that are important for the audition," David argued defensively. "We'll only have to do a few scenes for the backers, and we can tighten those up ourselves. After we raise some money we can invest in a good writer." Russell looked skeptical, reminded them that they had very little time. "For the moment the idea is to make what we have look sensational!" David said. "The audience must leave the audition humming the tunes—"

"And signing checks," Russell added. Russell warned them darkly that backers didn't part with money readily, even if "the fathers" were well-known.

"A Broadway musical has to be one of the highest-risk investments there is," Alex cautioned the eager young couple. "You would be best to plan on an off-Broadway production, in any case. Less money, less risk involved. The small theaters downtown are a better showcase for introducing a new talent and a small show." There was always the hope that it would succeed and move onto Broadway. "Even if it's a hit off Broadway, it's rarely profitable," Alex pointed out, unwilling to shelter them from the vicissitudes of life in the theater.

When Laina was not writing lyrics and working, she was redecorating the apartment. Determined to keep busy, she had rejected the idea of hiring an interior decorator. She had let David's houseman go, pleading the need for privacy. David agreed with great reluctance.

They could make do with a day lady a couple of times a week, she said. Without knowing exactly why, she was cleaning the slate, extinguishing David's past life—"beginning on a fresh page," she said. David looked at her curiously. She asked few questions about his past. Was she uncommunicative or just disinterested, he wondered bitterly. Maybe she was afraid to probe, which might have been closer to the truth. Their old secrets would bind them as surely as they would pull them apart.

Running around in the decorators' mart, standing between the tall racks of fabric, great slices of delicious color, celery, kumquat, mandarin, she felt satisfied and complete. Her life had become a feast of the senses, filled with words and music, color and design. Under David's careful instruction, even the preparation of meals had the excitement of artistic creation.

At first when she found herself alone in the apartment she wandered about trying to guess the secrets of the man she married. Amid David's few possessions and library still filled with childhood books, she learned little. The complete works of George Eliot, the Hardy boys series, high school and college textbooks, numerous books on music and an elegantly bound series of *The Lives of the Composers*. There was also a blue-and-gold leather bound copy containing the works of Oscar Wilde with an inscription inside that read: "Lo! With a little rod, I did but touch the honey of romance and must I lose a soul's inheritance?" Beneath were only the printed initials "J.G." Curiosity rankled, outweighed her own feelings of culpability. The fact that she had not one positive, concrete memento from her own past rankled even more. The apartment had a light smell of books and leather and furniture polish, and the faint residue of Vitalis lotion—male prerogatives had yet to yield to female. Sometimes

THE PLEASURE DOME

she would look at her clothes in the closets to make certain she was really there, had moved from her father's house. Among her fragrant clothes hung Seth's old swim jacket with the AAU insignia on the sleeve, still baggy and shapeless from innumerable drenchings.

The one thing she seemed most unwilling to do since her marriage was be alone. On evenings when she returned from her decorating chores, the walls of the half-empty apartment seemed to close in on her. She felt restless and jittery until the time came to go into the kitchen and start preparations for dinner. At first she liked to switch on the radio while she cut and sliced and marinated, but the romantic music that infused the airwaves with their message of loving and losing made her feel somehow unloved and lost. She kept thinking of something she had once heard her father say regarding her mother—"Your mother was a disappointed romantic"—*in other words, a loser*. Laina wondered how much she was like her mother.

Often David did not come home from the studio until seven or eight in the evening. Waiting for something to baste or boil, she would pick up a novel and try to concentrate. But she kept rereading a passage about a young married couple. *"She rushed home to make her husband dinner. But when he got home he didn't want dinner, just to make love."* She really didn't see why this prosaic passage should speak to her so strongly, but she read it over and over again and was inundated by an indescribable melancholy.

CHAPTER 29

The backers' audition was held in a large oak-paneled room of the 21 Club. It was an uncanny success. The strength of the pitch to the backers lay partially in the fact of its timeliness. The government had promised that the GI loan would provide a small patch of America for every veteran, they would all own their own dream house in the country. But the play picked up where the government left off, following the fortunes of a young newlywed veteran and his wife, their problems of personal and economic readjustment. It was a simple but bittersweet story. Of course, the personal attractiveness and charm of the young couple certainly helped, but the immediate impact was the music. "Music that was subtle yet commercial. Music that was delightfully singable," Russell Drake said when introducing the program, called *Out of Tune*. His presence in itself was an endorsement.

Laina was asked by various potential backers if she herself might play the female lead. Wouldn't it be charming if the lyricist was also the star? These compliments she deflected, unwilling to steal the spotlight from her husband, whom she imagined would soon be lionized by those women who were only too happy to attach themselves to a future celebrity; composers always had had a fatal fascination for women. There were only a few women at the audition, a smattering of wives—Vivian, Faye, and Fair Osborne.

Fair was a playwright who had some recent success with a Broadway farce, and a couple of serious off-Broadway plays. Russell had taken David at his word. Here was a "hot writer," he said. She had come to the audition to decide if it were worth her while to work on David's straying book. It was, but she made it clear in advance that she would not come cheap. A handsome woman in her early thirties, Fair hung on David's every note and draped herself provocatively around the piano as he, together with another pianist, played the songs. The pianos were set up back to back and the hired pianist, glared sourly at Fair, who stood as if on guard, turning pages for David and dropping cigarette ashes onto the keys of the adjacent piano. Laina, watching from her front row seat wondered if Fair Osborne might not be misplaced among this band of "angels." She had never been married, but was reputed to have had innumerable love affairs with members of both sexes. She was provocatively named because she was so fair in an esthetic sense and so dark physically, with Indianlike black hair, olive complexion and long dark eyes fringed with sooty lashes.

After the performance the guests dined lavishly on a late supper of the celebrated "21" burgers and chicken hash, green salad and small *coupe marrons* for dessert. This was accompanied by magnums of Dom Perignon, courtesy of Goldmark Enterprises.

Harlan was conspicuous by his absence. He was in Palm Beach overseeing the rehabilitation of the new Palm Gardens Hotel there. Laina was blessedly relieved. She preferred to have the evening unencumbered by emotional turmoil—it belonged to her and David. Furthermore, she realized she would have disliked introducing Harlan to Fair Osborne. Entertaining such thoughts had the effect of making her conscious of the physical urge that marriage had awakened in her—and not yet fullfilled. It also reminded her uncomfortably of the power Harlan Chase exerted over her, always hovering in the background of her life, casting cold and ominous shadows.

They would need in the vicinity of one hundred thousand dollars to produce it off Broadway. By the end of the evening some thirty backers had pledged from two to ten thousand dollars apiece, almost meeting the proposed figure.

Now the real work would begin—reducing the size of the cast and reworking their ideas. David closeted himself with his accountants, figuring and refiguring budgets, knocking down production costs. He learned with dismay that he must cut out some of the large production numbers and extravagant scenery. These realities both disappointed and secretly pleased him. His music would be exposed in the raw, introduced to the public without frills, put to the true test.

He began to spend long hours with Fair Osborne while Laina waited home alone. Pangs of jealousy and resentment conflicted with a new respect for David. She entertained numerous sexual fantasies, and in doing so, whipped herself into desire.

Alex encouraged the band leaders at his ballrooms to play songs from the show, and the ballad "Such Is Love" was recorded by Charlie Barnett and Benny Goodman's band well before the opening, giving the show fine advance publicity. Ever since the war, a song really needed to be endorsed by a big-name vocalist. Big bands were no longer prestigious, were in fact growing more obsolete each year. Russell Drake offered to introduce all of David's songs to the public and make the first album of all Goldmark hits, provided that David would give him

THE PLEASURE DOME

the lead in the show. Drake had been trying to get into a Broadway musical for years but couldn't make any headway. His agent said it would be a comedown for him to do an off-Broadway show. Drake felt it was at least a start, and besides, it would be an excellent drawing card for Laina and David. In a year when Rodgers and Hammerstein had just closed *Oklahoma!* after a five-year run and were about to open with *South Pacific* starring Mary Martin, they would need all the help they could get.

CHAPTER 30

More than once Harlan asked himself what he was doing in this business, a failed Irish Catholic, among all these Jews, a stranger in their paradise.

Matthew secretly considered the exorbitant expenditure for the yacht a classic example of Harlan's excessive behavior. In fact he considered Harlan's whole manner rather self-indulgent and flamboyant. His casual style of dress, even his car, a white Lincoln Continental convertible, embarrassed him. Harlan's passions had always run to excess. Before, when there had been no outlet for them they simmered deep inside, coming to the surface in erratic ways. Now he channeled his excesses constructively. In his pursuit of power and style he was growing adept at escaping his own identity.

Harlan had succeeded in getting Matthew to go along on the purchase of the old Hotel Whitmore in Atlantic City. He had sold him on the basis of ego, really. He had pointed out to Matthew that it was the same proven formula: buying an old hotel at a distress price, refurbishing and building it up again until it was strong and healthy, then selling it off at a profit. But he was forced to move slowly with Matthew, who couldn't see the wisdom in planning that far ahead. For Matthew, change was trauma. A smaller but more elegant hotel in Palm Beach went along with the package. It was called the Pink Sands. Matthew immediately renamed it the Palm

THE PLEASURE DOME

Gardens, "another Goldmark of Excellence," the ads would proclaim.

They had agreed to retain the management of both hotels, with Harlan in charge of the Atlantic City hotel and Matthew to oversee the one in Palm Beach. Only the Hibiscus Gardens and the Broadbeach would have their resident management. Matthew's fear was that management would cease to be personal and would grow diffuse and remote with an absentee arrangement. He also suspected that Harlan wanted to get a foothold on the postwar building boom in Florida and build one of those white-and-marble edifices that were already springing up all over the beach. Harlan explained patiently to Matthew that the business climate was changing. Hotels offering long residential vacations like the Broadbeach or the Gardens were on the way out; people were taking shorter vacations. The big money would be in conventions.

Harlan was sensitive to the changing entertainment habits of postwar America. For some time he had his eye on a small public company of the American Stock Exchange. The Nash Company comprised a sprinkling of movie theaters, a few East Coast hotels and a fairly large resort hotel on the west coast. Movie theater attendance had dropped considerably due to the advent of television, and the company's management was stagnant. The price of the stock was selling far below what Harlan and Alex estimated it to be worth. Harlan felt that one of the advantages of being rich was in being able to grow richer, having enough cash to buy on the bottom and sell on the top, to grab up a good deal whenever it came along. That was how the rich got richer, always having cash in depressed times. They could afford to take a chance, run a risk, instead of having to squirrel it away. "When everyone else is selling, buy," he would often say.

Stock would provide the liquidity he was looking for—stock and the cash he hoped to generate by converting the yacht into a gambling ship.

Harlan and Alex began quietly buying up shares in the Nash Company. Harlan had no wish to keep his intentions secret or even to squeeze Matthew out. His ultimate goal was to take their hotels public. There would be more than enough shares for everyone.

There was only one problem with the heavy buying of shares in the Nash Company, it was driving up the price of stock considerably. But Harlan had a plan, a unique plan, whereby they could take their company public and still retain operating control of the Goldmark Hotels.

Matthew, fearful that the hotels would lose their personal quality, said they could go ahead and buy all the stock they wanted. Family hotel management was his specialty. Matthew believed that all they had to sell was the Goldmark name, that if their hotels lost prestige or anything happened to Matt, the business would be finished.

"Family hotel management is a heavy burden," Harlan said. "Before the war a name meant a lot in this business, but now many larger names eclipse ours. We have to protect ourselves with more than sentiment. Going public is a way to grow without having to finance it ourselves. Surely you know we couldn't get this sort of financing otherwise, not if we begged, borrowed or stole. It is a brilliant plan!"

"No one can ever accuse you of modesty," Matthew answered ruefully. "We were happy with what we had before you came along. It was enough, it was ours, it was controllable."

"Matt, you really don't want the business to grow. That's it, isn't it? You are afraid somehow."

THE PLEASURE DOME

"I am not greedy. I only want things the way they were before you came along."

Harlan had been brought up to believe that Jews were *too* smart about money. They could never prove it by Matthew, he thought.

Like many people who did not wish to grow, Matthew preferred the past to the future. If he could, he would begin all over again, have a better relationship with his father, relive those passionate, carefree days with Faye, restructure this business, raise his son properly. He would relive those years when his hopes were high. Harlan, who had no past, at least none that he cared to remember, was like a bucking stallion at the starting gate.

CHAPTER 31

In his open Lincoln convertible, he turned his already well-tanned face upward to the sun now and again to refresh his suntan. Clouds, like amorphous messengers, scurried across a blue summer sky.

He pulled up to a pair of stanchions that bore a white signpost in the shape of a horse's head. On it were painted in black letters "W.E. Nash." He was not surprised. It was just the way Clyde Bostwick, his attorney, had described it—Clyde Bostwick had not prepared him for much else. He had in fact told him very little, because he knew very little about the company. Bostwick only knew Bill Nash's attorney and all he had done was to arrange this meeting.

Harlan had recently hired him—his own objectives seemed to be drifting away from his brother-in-law's. He had originally planned to bring Bostwick along today but changed his mind at the last moment. He had also planned to invite Alex, but something told him that he must take this sortie completely alone.

Harlan drove for a good five minutes up a heavily wooded, narrow road, past overgrown fields dotted here and there with small white wooden rails for jumping practice, until he reached the circular driveway. He pulled up slowly, then got out and locked the car.

After the Negro butler let him in, he was made to wait in the hallway, which was simple but handsomely appointed. Gazing into the large bright living room, he was startled to see, instead of the usual family portrait, a large stuffed horse's head.

"Ah, I see you are admiring Spartacus."

Harlan turned around. "Mr. Nash?"

"Yes," he said, though he seemed uncertain. He appeared to be in his late sixties, a tall man with a fringe of hair that circled his balding head, a red face and bright blue eyes. His mouth was small and pouty. "Where is Clyde Bostwick?" he demanded rudely. He had a nasal, unpleasant voice. They were still standing in the white entry rotunda.

"Something came up at the last minute and he couldn't make it. I hope you don't mind that I came alone." Harlan wondered if he would be asked to sit down.

Nash looked at Harlan suspiciously, beginning at the top of his head and taking in the casual elegance of his clothes. He was himself dressed in knickers and a mohair cardigan sweater. He suddenly turned and walked into the living room without even a backward glance at his guest, the cleats on his golf shoes making an enormous clatter on the marble floors. He finally indicated the sofa with an imperious wave of his hand and Harlan was at last seated. Nash went over to the closet bar and ladled ice cubes into a glass.

Harlan took the initiative and said, "Er—Mr. Nash, do you know you are still wearing your golf shoes?"

"Always do," he replied as he dropped cubes daintily in a glass with silver tongs.

"Well, I mean it will scratch up these handsome floors, won't it?"

"I daresay," he replied. Harlan thought to break the ice with humor.

"And send you sliding on your behind across the marble."

"Oh yes, happens all the time," he said, quite seriously.

Harlan was confused. "Well then, why do you wear them indoors?"

"Oh, that's simple, I like to hear the click-click on the marble, it's a comforting sound, an affluent sound, don't you think?" He cocked his head on the side as if listening for it. "Other kids had taps on their shoes when I was a kid, but I didn't have any, couldn't afford shoes then—so," he said, as if that settled the matter and finally sat down with his drink. Harlan looked at the drink longingly, amazed at the rudeness.

"Er—would you mind if I fix myself a drink too?" Harlan asked politely. "You know, it's about that time of day."

"Oh? What time is that?" Nash said pleasantly. Harlan wondered if he was behaving this way for some Machiavellian reasons of his own or was simply absentminded. He tended to believe the latter. "Oh, help yourself," he said and waved a hand in the direction of the bar. "So I was saying," Nash continued calling to him in a loud voice from across the vast room, "that horse you see up there, Spartacus, well he died right after he won the Preakness back in '38. I stuffed him. Damn good job if you ask me." He spit a piece of ice into his drink.

Harlan stared at the horse, fascinated. He wondered how to get Nash on the right conversational track. Perhaps he had made a mistake in not bringing Bostwick along, if only as an interpreter. "Well, I suppose you know why I'm here," he said, forging ahead.

"No, no, I really don't."

"Well, you just asked me where Clyde Bostwick was, so obviously you expected us." Harlan's voice was strong. "He had, I thought, prepared you for this visit."

"Well, I expected Bostwick, that's true, but *you?*" he said rudely, shaking his head.

Harlan put his glass down on the coffee table. He wanted the stock badly, but being treated like this was ridiculous.

"Now, see here, Mr. Nash," he began. At that moment the front door opened and he turned to see another man approaching.

"Oh, Mr. Chase, I recognize you from all your pictures in the newspapers and magazines. Nice going," he murmured with seeming appreciation. Harlan was uncertain at this point of how to accept that "nice going."

"Dale Connors is my name, and besides being old Nash here's attorney, I am also the second largest stockholder in our little company." He said all this in a declaratory style. He was a healthy-looking man of indeterminate age, older probably than himself, Harlan guessed. "Sorry I'm late." He went to the bar, fixed himself a drink and went over to Bill Nash, patting him briskly between the shoulder blades in greeting and sat down across the coffee table from Harlan.

"So fill me in, what have I missed?" There was a small empty silence in answer. Harlan breathed a sigh of relief and sat back. He didn't see how he could have possibly continued with Nash unassisted.

"I've come here to offer to buy as many shares in Nashco as you are willing to sell me."

"What?" Connors asked, looking down into his drink. "Why?" Harlan repeated the question.

"I already own a sizable portion of your company and if we continue, that is, if my partner and myself continue, we will own enough shares to be your partners. We would like to buy the controlling interest."

"Why?" Connors asked again.

The blank stares of the two men and the monosyllabic "why's" were beginning to get to Harlan. "Why do I want to buy into your company? I'll tell you why." Their idiocy was catching. "First of all I need a vehicle, a shell to take my own company public. You're sitting there with a nice cash position and you're not doing anything with it. Until we started buying, your stock was doing nothing, just sitting and stagnating."

Nash gave a loud guffaw. "Good little company though, you gotta admit that," he said. He was seated so far away from them that his voice echoed in the cavernous high-ceilinged room.

Harlan guessed that this was his way of disavowing the matter, of leaving it all up to Connors. "Yes, it's got potential," he agreed, "but it needs time and attention . . . Eventually I'd like to see our own hotels thrown into the pot; then you'd have a company to reckon with—a recreation complex with enormous growth potential."

"Well, buy then, Chase, by all means buy away," Nash boomed from his distant chair. "What have you come here for, my permission?"

"No, sir, I came here to make you an offer for your shares and to give you a chance to participate in—"

"What's wrong with buying from a broker like everyone else, like you've been doin' right along?" Nash asked.

"We've bought a lot, it's driving the price up prohibitively, which I needn't remind you has been to *your* benefit."

"And if we don't care to sell, that is, become partners with you, as you put it?"

"Well then, we'd just have to stop, sell everything we bought, and try to buy another company," Harlan said,

THE PLEASURE DOME

allowing a note of sadness to creep into his voice. "You, of course, realize what that would do to the price of your stock."

They were silent, assessing their position.

"However, if you would care to make some ready cash without disturbing the market, which is at an all-time high, I think you'll do very well. You need help. Your management has been inactive of late, to say the least." Harlan looked at Nash. "I, that is, we, can help activate it for you."

"Goldmark?" Nash boomed. "What kind of name is that?"

Connors ignored the question and continued with the business discussion, addressing himself exclusively now to Harlan. "Please try to understand that I have tried to keep the company growing in these last few years. The movie theaters are doing very well, but as you can see—" He paused momentarily and then continued, having evidently decided upon full disclosure. "There are reasons why the management of this company has not been easy," he said, sliding his eyes in the direction of Nash. "Bill and I would consider selling our shares to you, that is provided you are willing to pay full market price."

"Well, no matter what price we decide on, it's a good deal for you," Harlan said. "You couldn't sell a large block like you've got without driving the stock way down."

"Well then, I would not sell it, that's all," Connors countered.

"I had in mind something like ten dollars a share," Harlan said.

"Two dollars below market price—I don't know, I doubt it, but let me think about it a little, will you?"

Harlan was prepared to pay twelve, but said nothing

for the moment. Then he jumped up, restless, anxious to leave. He'd made his proposition and knew it was a good one; let them chew on it for a while.

"Whoa, where you going in such a hurry?" Connors seemed worried.

"I've been here a long time, it seems. I really have to go now."

As he neared the door, Connors caught up with him.

"I've gone this long without selling my stock. What makes you think I'd want to liquidate a large block now?" Connors asked.

"Greed, Connors. You can usually count on it. And I'm offering you top dollar." Harlan lowered his voice slightly. "Who knows where this company is headed—"

"Speak up," Nash called from across the room where he remained stubbornly rooted. Harlan threw a glance at Nash, who seemed slumped in a sort of reverie.

"Perhaps if you came over here you might hear me better."

"Goldmark?" he continued, looking straight ahead while the other two men hesitated in the foyer near the front door. "What will we call the company? Goldnash?" he asked and gave a dry laugh. Connors looked embarrassed.

Harlan had the distinct impression that Connors was not so much lawyer as *keeper*. Nash rose unsteadily to his feet and was coming toward them. Harlan wondered if Nash was going to see him out.

"Well, let's discuss this with Clyde," Connors said when Nash appeared.

"Yes. Hey, how come you ain't got a smart Jewish lawyer, eh, Chase? I mean bein' in there with all those Jews—" He stopped as Chase reddened and lunged at him.

THE PLEASURE DOME

Connors intervened and held them apart.

"He's a sick old man, Chase, he doesn't know what he's saying," he said softly.

"Well, what the hell, boy," Nash persisted, "you're one of us, ain't ya? A nice clean Christian boy." Harlan pulled the front door open and walked to his car. He only wanted to get out of here as fast as he possibly could. He feared that if he remained a moment longer he might say something or do something harmful to the old man. Thank God he hadn't brought Alex along. He would never have gone for the deal after this. But Harlan was not going to let this stand in his way. He knew what he had to do. He could never be partners with these people. He would have to buy them out or at least get the controlling interest and run the company himself.

CHAPTER 32

"OUT OF TUNE, IN PERFECT HARMONY," the headline read in the *New York Times*. "Some of the most elegant, sweetly subtle and haunting melodies to have graced a stage since Jerome Kern," Brooks Atkinson wrote of David Goldmark's score. "The lyrics bow gracefully to the music and are clever and catchy. I went out humming the tunes." Other critics heartily agreed, although it was hardly necessary. If Brooks Atkinson approved, it was a hit and they knew it. They were also aware of the imperfections and planned to improve on these during the run of the show.

They began receiving much unsolicited publicity. The goings and comings of the young couple responsible for this new success were carefully recorded by the press. Popular magazines gushed over the fact that they were so young, that they were newlyweds, that she was beautiful and he was handsome. "A gifted and handsome young couple," it said in *Look* magazine above a large photograph of them smiling like film stars. They were seen holding hands at the Stork Club, dining with a group of theater people at Sardi's, or attending a party given in their honor by some prominent philanthropist or social hostess anxious to be first to claim this delightful young couple.

The show opened at the Theatre de Lys on Christopher Street a couple of weeks before the New Year of 1949.

THE PLEASURE DOME

The theater's perfect size, fine acoustics, and charming ambiance made it a great favorite among producers. They considered themselves lucky to get it. Many little musical gems had been born and raised here, before venturing out to the wilder shores of Broadway. Even the record cold and snow did not keep audiences away.

While Russell Drake received a share of good reviews, his acting left much to be desired. Laina had not wanted Russell for the part. She preferred an unknown with a less damaged reputation. A certain innocence was part of the charm of the role and Russell's brash Hollywood image did not fit the lyrics or Laina's personal tastes. She was afraid the audience wouldn't find him believable. Besides, she didn't care for Russell Drake in general, and he knew it.

She also held him responsible for the introduction of Fair Osborne into their little company, and imagined that he had chosen her with some malice aforethought. Whenever she was called in to collaborate, Fair addressed herself almost exclusively to David, virtually ignoring the female half of the team.

"The show is as beautifully unified as it is because we worked on it together every step of the way," Laina reminded David after one of those sessions with Fair.

It was not unusual for a composer to write all the music first, then shop for a lyricist to fit the words to his score. But David and Laina, like Rodgers and Hammerstein, had written the two components together as a unit and that was a large part of the secret of their success.

Still, since David was also director, he worked long hours with rehearsals, costume changes and last-minute script changes, which he continued to do with Fair at the theater or at the studio. Jealousy was completely new to Laina. She had never *belonged* to anyone except perhaps her father, and that was different. Marriage was voluntary bondage and as such carried with it a certain sexual power that was awesome, even beautiful. The thought that David might be defiling it only made it easier for her to rationalize her own secret dreams. Does he know what is in my heart, what I dream? she would ask herself. She wished he knew her secrets, wished at those moments to invest *him* with secrets that would mitigate hers.

When David came home a week before the opening and announced that Fair Osborne had asked for a percentage of the show and program credits Laina flew into a rage. His attitude suggested that he might even be considering it. He didn't seem to resent the small percentage as much as the credits. The credits suggested that he was less than a playwright. Laina secretly thought that being a composer was a far greater virtue and pointed out to him that he could really handle both. "In any case," she said, "the major work is done and Fair has been well paid for it. Somehow or other you seem to have grown dependent on her."

"My dear, the only woman in the world I depend on is you and don't forget that," he said with great warmth, taking her around the waist and lifting her arm to kiss the soft underside of her elbow.

"How about your mother?" she said archly.

"Ah ha, now you sound just like a wife."

"Still," she said, somewhat mollified, "I do resent that fatuous Drake introducing you to that femme fatale."

"Darling, you are my Snow White and she my Rose Red," he said, nuzzling her neck.

III. ODYSSEY
1949-1959

CHAPTER 33

Out at the Cabanas, the sun beat down mercilessly on miles of exposed flesh, a fact which pleased Harlan, who prayed for good weather during the height of the season, when the rates skyrocketed.

At the strategically situated cabana number one, five or six men lounged in varying attitudes of relaxation. Their cabana was at the entrance to the large horseshoe of pool cabanas and afforded them the opportunity to view each of the guests as they mounted the stairs and be viewed in turn. It was usually the most in-demand cabana, although it cost an extra hundred dollars a week. In fact, all the cabanas on the first level around the pool were expensive, causing the level to be called, by some with sarcasm and others with pride, the Diamond Horseshoe.

They stood with towels rolled around their necks, hands on hips, their flaccid sunburned bellies falling and rising. Cigars quivered between their teeth when they talked, and cigarettes smoldered ominously on the card table where two of the men played a deadly game of gin for twenty cents a point.

Joe Campano roused his head languidly from the chaise to greet Alex Eastman. Campano was one of his contributions toward a more varied clientele.

"Good to see you, Joe," Alex replied with a certain sweet respect. "Where've you been keeping yourself?

Don't see you around much anymore." Alex caught himself and looked sheepish. He remembered having heard something about Campano recently having done a stretch in the penitentiary for bribery or extortion, he wasn't sure what.

"Well, I'm mostly in Vegas now. Been awful busy lately." With a limp wave of his hand, Campano said, "You know my nephew, Marc Anselmo?" He introduced a graceful young man of about thirty, with dark Italian good looks, who had been sitting inside the cabana. He rose to his feet and extended his hand, smiling.

"So what brings you to our neck of the woods? Certainly not the sun, you get plenty of that in the desert."

"Yes," Joe smiled, displaying teeth that were even and yellow like an ear of corn. "I just came back from Havana."

"Oh. Business or pleasure?"

"Christ, who goes to Havana on business? Pleasure, my boy, pleasure."

Alex noted the group and looked doubtful. He sat down hesitantly on the edge of the chaise. "Well, thanks again for coming down, giving our place a try." These characters spend big money, travel in packs, he thought. "So what do you think of this joint?" Alex, chameleonlike, was able to accommodate himself to every milieu, and now reverted to his sidewalks-of-New-York dialect.

"I don't see nothin' wrong with it," Joe said. He slapped Alex on the back and rubbed his shoulders. "So, baby, I hear you went into the hotel business, and that you're already expanding—negotiating for the old Whitmore in Atlantic City. Dance halls ain't good enough for you no more, huh?"

Alex was annoyed. These guys knew every time you

peed. "I still got all the halls. I just diversified a little, that's all."

Campano looked around appraisingly and said, "It's one hell of a place you got here, Eastman, one hell of a place."

Harlan Chase, patrolling the cabanas, passed by in almost full regalia, dressed in white linen like an East Indian rubber planter. The only concession he had made to the heat and the casualness of the area was to remove his tie. The immaculate white shirt was open at the throat and neatly tucked into white trousers. White, the symbol of purity, had become a part of his signature.

He stopped to talk to Alex. Joe Campano appraised him silently. Alex introduced them, and Campano said, "So, kid, I hear you're the fair-haired boy of this business. Your partner here says you're collecting hotels like they was baseball cards."

Harlan was about to demur when he felt a hand on his shoulder and turned to see Marc Anselmo. Gesturing somewhat awkwardly at the young man, Harlan said, "I know you from somewhere, just give me a moment—"

The boy rushed in eagerly to supply his name. "Marc Anselmo."

"Of course, from Broadbeach—the same parish. How've you been? I haven't seen you in years."

"But I recognized you," he said in a low, soft voice, "the moment I saw you."

Campano roused himself from his torpor. "Oh, so you two know each other—well, I think I'm gonna take a swim, it's hotter than a witch's pussy. How about you, Alex?" The small cabana was crowded and it was growing difficult to talk. Campano took Alex's arm and they drifted toward the pool, talking and gesticulating.

"Sooner or later your past catches up with you here at our hotels," Harlan said smiling.

"Yes." The boy fell silent. Harlan stared at him for a moment.

"What have you been doing with yourself all these years?" He did not answer immediately.

"Well," he said cautiously, "I was in the service, in Europe—the Seventh Infantry—Salerno." He did not meet Harlan's gaze.

"I see. And since—"

"Since, I work for my uncle—in Vegas." Harlan remembered the rumors that had circulated about this uncle in the old days—Mafia, capo ditutti. . . . But he'd just met him; he seemed harmless enough. He looked at Marc Anselmo and remembered him a gangly boy of eighteen hanging around outside his house, waiting for his kid sister.

"Are you married?"

"Nooo—" A drawn-out no, as though the answer were a foregone conclusion. "I'm still waiting for Janine."

Harlan, hesitated before answering. "I'm afraid you'll have a long wait."

"Why, is she married?" he asked.

"I guess you could say she's married." There was another silence in which someone dived noisily into the pool. "She's a nun—in a convent on Long Island."

Marc, digesting the information, now searched Harlan's face for verification. "You're kidding."

"No, I'm afraid not. I wouldn't kid you." The ocean rolled monotonously and exotic birds chirped in the coconut trees above.

"Harlan, can I visit her there, I mean, is it permitted?"

"I don't know. I suppose if you came with me it would

be all right—or perhaps if you said you were related—I don't know."

"When will you be back in New York?" Marc asked.

"Not for a while, I'm afraid. I'm tied to this place for the season. When will *you?*"

"Well, I usually come back to the beach every summer to see my mother and stay for a couple of weeks, but that seems a long time from now. Anyway, I'd like to have her address. Can you give it to me?"

Harlan jotted down Janine's address on a piece of paper and handed it to the boy, then rose to leave. Standing side by side the boy was about his own height. A handsome kid, he thought, with his liquid dark eyes and his saint's face.

"Marc," he said, "Go see her. I'll go with you if you want, though I admit I don't like to go there often."

"Yes. We'll be in touch, Chase. Thanks a lot."

When his uncle came back to the cabana he was alone. "Uncle, I don't think I'm going straight back to Vegas with you, I may stop off in New York and see mama for a while—I'm so near, it would seem lousy not to."

"Yeah, sure, you gotta be good to your mama, boy. You're all she's got." He rubbed his hands along the boy's back with absent-minded grace.

CHAPTER 34

Janine lay on a cot in the infirmary and felt as if all life's essences had been drained from her body, as if she were indeed the empty vessel that Mother Blanche had often spoken to her about—"Make yourself an empty vessel, my child, so that God may enter." There had never been a teacher in her life who hadn't worn a habit, who hadn't proselytized. She turned her face to the wall, a scrubbed white stucco, slightly glazed and crenelated, it reminded her of the French nougats she used to buy at the candy shop near her house. The Sea Side Sweete Shoppe—she saw it now in all its splendid detail, the cut-glass jars glittering with their gemlike contents, a kaleidoscope of colors and textures to tempt the palate, to test the will. It seemed to her now a sensuous reminder of another life. She turned away from the wall, obsessed suddenly by a craving for sweets.

Sister Petronella, the infirmary nun, fussed officiously with jars and bottles on the little white table beside the bed. A tall, stringy woman, looming up even larger in the long black habit, she had grown more masculine each year in the service of the Lord until she now resembled Father McManus, a joke the other nuns enjoyed among themselves. If she appeared to be transcending the sexes, it had not brought with it any compensations, like a sense of humor or even perspective. She had sacrificed her personal identity to the greater glory, and was left now with only a rusting scaffold of a personality, and a high intolerance of what she considered "malingerers." If only to forestall her ministrations, Janine tried to hide her secret. But when her face broke out she was immediately placed in the infirmary for observation, lest she infect the rest of the nuns. The doctor who attended the nuns had diagnosed it as an aggravated case of hives, or measles perhaps, he seemed uncertain, but Sister Petronella said that it was "just God's way of telling you it's sinful to be vain." Sister Petronella was suspicious— Sister Mary had been novitiating longer than any other nun in the convent. "After all, the service of God is not a dress you try on. If you don't like it you can't return it," she had said, complaining to the other nuns about Janine. Perhaps she sensed that Sister Mary floated unfettered in limbo somewhere between the faith and the flesh.

For the last eight years Janine had worked through the grinding daily routines with growing disillusion. She had entered the order hoping to enlarge her spiritual horizons, to learn the meaning of the universe, if indeed that was possible. She had thought to delve into the mysteries of Catholicism, but found herself instead scrubbing floors, cleaning toilets and changing lightbulbs. Religious study centered on more basic concepts, much of which she knew well from her parochial-school days. Nothing much deeper or more profound had been disseminated. Occasionally she was sent out on an assistant teaching assignment to a nearby parochial school. She looked forward to that, getting out and being with people whom she enjoyed, but she could not become a full-fledged teacher until she took her final vows. As a long-term postulant, she was relegated to doing most of the menial work about the convent, which she found depressing as well as physically exhausting. Perhaps one naturally followed the other. She knew this attitude was in itself a form of selfishness and had begun to doubt whether she was following the right vocation. She still was not equal to the challenge of giving without receiving.

There were no guarantees that she would feel any different when she took her final vows, which she was considering taking sometime soon, but she knew the Fields of Grace was among the less severe, and she could not contemplate beginning all over again. It was in this mood of transition that she had received a visitor on a Saturday afternoon two weeks before. Mother Blanche, with whom she had developed a close friendship, had called her into her office and told her she had a visitor in the parlor, her "cousin Marc," she said. Janine was about to answer that it must be a mistake. She had no cousin Marc, no male cousins at all for that matter, when the realization struck. Even then, honesty necessitated that she speak up. But she was unable to voice the denial. She had so few visitors that even if it were some sort of mistake, she was almost willing to welcome a stranger.

Janine hurried to her tiny room and extricated from behind a shelf a jagged piece of mirror. The nuns were not supposed to look at their reflections. She realized that she looked pale and thin, and pinched her cheeks to bring up the color, enjoying a little this small defection. She walked quickly, her long skirt brushing the floor with a soft sound, her face white and wimpled like a Filippo Lippi saint, the large pale eyes suddenly alive with flecks of excitement. When she arrived at the office she found herself staring wordlessly across the room at the tall figure of Marc Anselmo. After the brief shock of recognition and an awkward silence, carefully gauged by Mother Blanche, Marc asked if they might visit alone in the front parlor. The nuns were unused to young men and although it was not often done, there were no rules against it, provided, of course, that it *was* family.

He stood in the front parlor uncertainly torn between pleasure and awe or a combination of both. Italian mothers impressed upon their sons awe-inspiring respect for the cassock and the habit. To break the strained silence he said playfully, "A war has come and gone, the world has turned upside down and still I found you."

She held onto her crucifix as if for support, her knuckles were white with tension. When she saw his gaze travel to her hand, she quickly hid it in the folds of her habit.

"I still cannot believe it," he said. "I called your parents, but they would not tell me anything, only that you had moved away."

She looked alarmed. "Why should you look for me?"

He sat down heavily on the sofa. It seemed he would drown in it, fall right through it, it was so unaccustomed to his weight. "Sit down beside me, Janine," he said softly. "Sister Mary."

Seated rigidly opposite him, she smiled a little and said, "I'm a bit out of practice, please do most of the talking."

He reminisced about the past, his mother's cooking, how Janine used to love her seafood sauce over pasta, the dinners they used to have. He told her about the wonders of television. He tendered simple temptations before the more complex ones.

"Marc, why have you come—after so long?"

"So long? You forget that a four-year war intervened."

"Marc," she said reproachfully.

"I'm looking, Janine. I'm looking," he said, his dark eyes resting on her face. He really did mean to make a break. He had in fact not meant to return to his uncle after the war, after everything. But he had needed a job and with his record, it hadn't been easy. He was now accustomed to the easy living, the big money. He needed an incentive to get out, he told himself.

"Janine," he said. He pulled her toward him and held her tightly. The sound of her own name, which she hadn't heard for so long, was exciting to her. As whispered urgently by this man, even more so. He tried to kiss her lips, but she moved slowly away.

"No, please, the nuns . . ."

"I thought about you every day and every night in these years. You've made them bearable. I had thought you were probably married . . . when I learned from your brother . . . I was relieved, this, this is at least reversible." His manhood triumphing over his faith. Certainly he preferred the church to a material rival.

"I haven't said that I want to reverse it--I—I have taken vows." She pulled away quickly, full of guilt and fear.

"You had taken other vows once," he said, kissing her hand again and again.

"Please, please Marc, you must leave now. I can't . . ."

"Will you at least walk with me to the garden. I'll leave from there, I promise."

In an overgrown and hidden corner he leaned against a tree for support and drew her against him. She felt the length of his body pressing against hers, the forgotten sensation startling in its newness.

"Why, Janine? Why did you do this? Was it to punish me?"

"Of course not. I truly love the church."

"You can love the church without becoming a part of it. Then perhaps it was to punish *them*, your parents, you wanted to please them, or to—"

THE PLEASURE DOME

"I wanted them to love me as they loved Harlan," she whispered, weak with the shock of sudden comprehension.

"Thank God you understand," he said, pushing back the wimple and touching her hair. He kissed her eyelids, her mouth parted beneath his urging. His lips ran down her throat and onto her breast.

She gathered all of her strength and pulled away. "Please, I must go now."

Marc knew he had to return to Las Vegas, if only to tell his uncle of his plans. Uncle Joe had telephoned and inquired politely when he planned to return. The next time it would not be so polite. His uncle had trusted him with secrets, he was staggering under the burden of ugly secrets. He wasn't sure of what he would do yet, how he would make a living, he was not really prepared for anything.

"I will have to go back to Nevada to put my affairs in order—I might not see you for a little while, maybe not until summer . . . but—I don't want to lose you again. Then . . . then you must make arrangements to leave here, so that we can be married." He held her close. "Janine, how I've missed you."

Now, lying on the thin cot, she tried not to think about that traumatic afternoon, but she thought of little else lately. God seemed suddenly very remote and unfeeling.

Mother Blanche slipped quietly into the room and spoke in hushed tones to Sister Petronella who, with a slight offended smile, left the room. The mother superior approached the bed. She smiled and her sweet, rounded face looked genuinely concerned.

"How are you today, my child? Sister Petronella says your temperature is normal. Are you in any discomfort?"

"No, just itching."

"You have not seemed completely at ease in this last year," she said. "Is there something troubling you, my child?"

"I don't know exactly—perhaps I have been having doubts—about the future—"

"We all have doubts, sister."

"Yes, but I thought a life of work and introspection would be enough to sustain me, now I don't know—and too, I am ashamed to say it, but I find myself resenting the work—" She stopped abruptly—perhaps she was going too far. She sensed that Mother Blanche could see through her and was conducting a little charade of her own, giving Janine the opportunity to come forth, to confess.

The most painful part would be to tell her parents, to inform her mother of her decision. She would write to her, telling her only of her decision not to take her final vows, that the vocation was a mistake for her, but she would say nothing of Marc at first. That would be too much for them to accept all at once.

CHAPTER 35

When getting through the *New York Times* had become an endurance contest for Matthew, he knew something was terribly wrong. His nerves were worn electrical wires, fraying at the ends. Lately he rarely managed to read more than the obituary page, which he pored over daily. Everyone in his life had let him down in one way or another. It began with his father, proceeded to his son, his sister, even his wife, if he were to believe the rumors he frequently heard. But of course he could not. He knew only that he loved his wife and she loved him. Yes, at least he was certain of that. He was immune to the gossip, probably brought on by the sophisticated evils of television combined with the fevered imaginings of his guests. Well, the guests had always been out to get him—their disloyalty was as reliable as their appetites. Look how easily they had deserted him in favor of the more flamboyant Chase.

It was 1949 and the country was settling down into a numb and blessed peace. All about him was a mantle of beneficence. Why did it seem that only he was denied that state of grace? Such were his thoughts as he maneuvered his way through the summer city traffic.

Matthew now felt exhilarated. The bank had agreed to make another loan, which had not been easy. His personal finances were in a hopeless jumble. He sat high above the ordinary traffic in his ecclesiastic-looking maroon Rolls Royce and surveyed the city with the same appreciation with which he had first approached it some twenty years before. In Central Park there were well-starched nannies wheeling stately English prams, and private-school boys in caps and emblems playing softball. The Tavern on the Green slipped by on his left, reliable as ever behind its cloud of trees. As he steered the loosely fitted wheel with its famous floating drive, he smiled inwardly thinking of his small triumph.

The September sweetness of Central Park faded into gray-brown west-side pragmatism. As Matthew approached the jumble of square, hunkering buildings on Broadway and turned into Seventh Avenue, his mood altered somewhat with his surroundings. Why, after all, should Eastman go for it? he asked himself while looking around for a parking place. It wasn't as if Eastman needed the money. He pulled the Rolls reluctantly into a garage a block or so from the Danceland ballrooms. He tried not to park his car in ordinary garages. He didn't like the irreverent way the attendants handled the cars. Matthew extricated himself gingerly and a young black boy jumped in, eager to get his hands on the wheel. Matthew knew he felt godlike, a Joe Louis or Sugar Ray Robinson, as he whirled the car around and backed it into a roomy space.

Matthew was shocked by the noise and music at four-thirty. He had thought to enter a hushed ballroom, go to the rear where Alex's offices were, and have a long, leisurely chat. But a large sign at the entrance declared cocktail dancing from four-thirty to seven P.M. every evening except Monday. Matthew shook his head. The grass didn't grow under Alex Eastman's feet. As he walked along the edges of the dance floor, he thought he made out little Marvin Segall bouncing about in the crowd. He was dancing with a blonde girl who was at least a full head taller than he and who seemed to be enjoying their disparate adagio as much as he was.

Alex was sitting behind a paper-strewn desk in an autumn tweed suit, talking loudly on three telephones at once. He nodded a silent greeting to Matthew, who took a seat opposite him. When Alex hung up, he picked up another call and announced grandly, "No calls for a while, Bea." He leaned back in the chair, swiveling it a little devilishly. "So, my *mechuten*," he said, slipping fraternally into Yiddish, "to what do I owe this unexpected visit?"

"Oh, I was in the neighborhood, just thought I'd drop in and shoot the breeze a bit, that's all."

"It's pretty hot here for you to be in town; it must be at least fifteen degrees cooler out there at the beach."

"Yes, well, I had things to do in town," he answered defensively.

They talked about Laina and David, their burgeoning career, their publicity. Each congratulated the other on his respective child in the way that people do whose children are married to one another. On the desk was a large and lovely photograph of his daughter.

"You know, I think I saw Marvin Segall out there, dancing his heart out."

"You did," Alex said with a proprietary air. "He's here almost every afternoon for tea dancing, goes out for dinner, then often returns for the evening session. He's won many contests, in *all* categories, I might add."

"He looked happy."

"He is happy. He is at home here. It is a friendly place."

Matthew understood this. He asked stiffly, "Who's the girl?"

Alex shrugged. "I don't think it matters to him. He

usually has a different one each time, just dancing partners. You should see the steps, such intricate steps. A dance-aholic," he said, "a secret one. How he loves bouncing around to the music!" Alex tapped his feet under the desk and snapped his fingers like castanets. Matthew wished ardently for his levity, his love affair with life.

Alex pounded his desk airily as if announcing the change of subject. "Well, Matt, I hope you're out there buying the hell out of Nash Company," he said in a strong determined voice.

"I haven't bought a share, Alex, not a single share." Alex stared at him fascinated.

"But we agreed . . ."

"*I* didn't agree. You and Chase agreed." Petulance crept back into his voice.

"But why not?" Alex looked genuinely surprised.

"You *know* why not. I don't like the public concept. I consider it risky. It's bad enough that I have to answer to Chase without having to answer to God-only-knows how many strangers."

"Matt, we would have controlling interest, we would still manage it, set policy, and so forth." The way that Alex used the word "we," as if it were already an accomplished fact, made Matthew uneasy.

"What about the present management, the Nashes? I don't want to work with them, and I'm sure they don't want to work with us."

"We can probably buy them out," Alex said coolly. "Harlan's been to see the old man, an eccentric old coot I understand, but he thinks we can swing it."

"It's my father's fault," Matthew murmured. "He set it up like this and that—that *swimmer* is running with it all the way."

"What's the difference? Let him run with it, he's bound to trip one day. He's also bound to make us all rich, I mean, very rich."

"I'm satisfied with what I've got," Matthew said, "or what I had, that is."

"Matthew, I'm afraid you have lost your sense of adventure," Alex said with a certain uncharacteristic elegance, "and with it your sense of humor."

Alex's accusation rippled through his thoughts. He sighed again deeply and realized that he was suffering from a severe case of nostalgia.

"You know, when you have lost those two qualities, there is really very little left," Alex continued.

Matthew knew he was right, but somehow the loss seemed irrevocable. Not wishing to be disarmed, Matthew murmured, "How the hell he's got you so bamboozled is what I can't for the life of me figure out."

Alex sat back and smiled. "It's greed, my friend, greed, because I'm looking to double, maybe triple my investment. I am willing to be 'bamboozled.' So why don't you sit back and relax. Enjoy growing rich. Enjoy your own bamboozlement."

"No, money by itself is meaningless to me."

"That's because you've always had it—it is never meaningless to those who have just tasted its power."

Matthew leaned forward urgently. "Alex, I want to buy out your shares. I'll pay you twice as much as they're worth. You can get an appraisal." He stopped suddenly. Alex was laughing so hard that tears came to his eyes.

"You must be crazy, Matt, you must have gone completely crazy, or else you really don't understand the concept at all. What the hell would I do with a few lousy dollars when I will get at least ten times that much in real estate—the Nash Theaters and maybe even my own places here thrown in for good measure? Can't you see that if this deal works we can buy controlling interest and buy back our companies? Then we'll have the cash, our original resources, and theirs. It is an ingenious leverage deal." Alex's enthusiasm caused him to raise his voice. "But surely you know all this. No one has kept it a secret."

Matthew knew about it but refused to understand it or believe it possible. It was too new to him. "And if I don't go along with it?"

Alex sat back and shook his head slowly, suddenly serious. "I can't for the life of me see why you wouldn't."

"But if I don't," he said levelly, "if I don't wish to take every cent I own and put it into a fading old company with a few movie houses and some failed hotels?"

"Then we just go ahead and do the deal without you, and we buy *you* out," Alex said, leaning back in his swivel chair. "You can take the money and buy into a new syndicate, rebuild, or just retire, if you are so inclined."

Matthew's chest ached as though encased in iron bands. "Just like that, you and my brother-in-law put me out to pasture, sell my business out from under me." Apoplectic now, he tried to keep his trembling voice low.

"But it's not like that, Matt, not at all. You and I, we're *landsmen, mishpocheh,* we're on the same team." Alex's voice faded as Matthew rose shakily to his feet and lumbered out past the dancers, past Marvin, the whirling dervish, past the rippling rhythms of the Shep Fields' orchestra.

Driving back toward the Island he tried to sort out the shreds of their conversation, but he drew a blank. He could not understand the concept, his mind refused to allow it. All he could think of was the injustice of others, strangers, setting policy for him, forcing him into a business procedure that was contrary to his training, that risked everything he and his father had built up over the years—all to satisfy his quite mad brother-in-law. He thought perhaps he should try having a talk with Vivian, but abandoned the idea as hopeless almost immediately. If indeed they succeeded in pulling off this erratic and crazy deal, turning the resorts into a vast recreation complex, there was no guarantee that it would work, that it would be successful. There was the great no man's land of stockholders out there.

Matthew made his ascent into Eden, the ocean-swept shores of Broadbeach. He was driving close to the sandy cliffs somewhere near Bridgehampton Beach, which meant he was only twenty or so minutes from home. He was intensely tired, overcome with frustration. The car radio had given out long ago and in the silence, the blowing rushes and reeds sounded like the onset of a hurricane. The automobile seemed to be pulling against him, rearing back like a horse, as if it had a will of its own. Then it suddenly stopped dead. Sitting there in the impotent blackness, Matthew longed for the garish splendor of the Long Island Expressway. He searched for a flashlight, but there was none in the glove compartment. He had never been well organized. He strained his eyes to see if he could see any houses where he might make a call but the darkness was impenetrable. At the thought of trudging blindly in the blackness, his legs suddenly felt paralyzed. All his pent-up rage of the last year suddenly came together in one cathartic blow to the steering wheel, which he pulled at in his rage. It came off in his hands, leaving him with a curious feeling of weightlessness. Matthew opened the car door and heaved the disembodied wheel down to the ocean. He watched it twist and flip with satisfaction. Since Jessie's death he had become irritated by the symbols of affluence. They frustrated him, cold inanimate objects that didn't respond, that made him feel undervalued. He sat in the car a few minutes longer and gazed down the cliff to the beach below where the wheel lay now like a discarded children's toy—a fine treasure, he thought, for a beachcombing collector to come upon. Matthew jumped out of the car. He began to push the car toward the cliff. It rolled lightly and easily and careened wildly down the dunes, landing in a great show of pyrotechnics, a *grande feu d'artifice*, that outlavished his own celebrated annual Fourth of July display. Maroon and beautiful, it had been a model sought by collectors.

CHAPTER 36

Faye was genuinely fond of her daughter-in-law, as proud of her as she was of her son. She readily acknowledged Laina's artistic gifts and tended to defer to her in all matters of taste. She had recently asked her assistance in redecorating an old wing of the Broadbeach.

A series of old rooms in the back that were rarely occupied because of their dilapidation had come to Harlan's attention. He flatteringly suggested that Faye take charge and oversee their disposal.

"Perhaps you should also enlist the aid of your very talented daughter-in-law," he suggested. Harlan had not seen Laina all summer long and he was surprised by how much time he spent thinking about her, even longing for her. He could not remember the last time he had seen her, perhaps it was over a year ago, sometime shortly after her honeymoon trip, when she and David had stopped briefly at the hotel. After that he had received a terse, painfully polite note thanking him for the use of his yacht. He had gotten a strange ironic satisfaction out of playing the role of benefactor. He enjoyed doing things for her; it gave him a sense of power and even a certain peace.

She had kept her distance, stayed away from the hotels; he in turn seemed to disapprove her marriage, and disassociated himself almost completely from their burgeoning professional life. He had not appeared at the backers' audition, rarely discussed the show with the rest of the family, and did not even go to the opening night, claiming to be caught at the height of Miami's holiday season.

He was frankly curious to know what she felt about him, if she had thought about him at all since her marriage. Sometimes he thought she hated him, other times he even dared to think she loved him. Those questions and the mystery of what was really between her and David Goldmark kept him in a state of perpetual excitement.

Harlan had extended the season, even though it meant the hotel retained a reduced staff and fewer guests—those whose money and leisure enabled them to prolong the summer until the last ray of sun lost its strength.

Faye now, in a dress of heliotrope pink, an offshoot of her violet phase, sat lunching with Laina on the Ocean Terrace. The early autumn sunshine was glittering on the water. Laina would remember that afternoon: the domino blotches of sunlight, the dark water, the heliotrope of Faye's dress. Indian summer. Heliotrope summer. They gazed hypnotically at the ocean.

"September has always been my favorite month here," Faye said. "It is perfectly tranquil."

"Tranquility is a luxury missing from my life." Laina said, "Tempers explode about me daily—nervous producers, disappointed directors, cantankerous conductors, and oh, the actors and actresses!" Laina pretended to bury her head in her hands.

"Oh, how I envy you, it all sounds marvelous!" Faye said.

Laina cut into her delicate, golden, herb omelette thoughtfully. "I must phone David later and let him know I'm here. I just came out on the spur of the moment, right after you called this morning. He had already left. I tried him at the studio but he wasn't there."

"Try him again later, perhaps he'll join us for dinner this evening. I know the theater's dark on a Monday. It's a perfect day for you both to get away, and I really *can* use your help, darling. I simply love the way you did your apartment in town, all those wonderful melon shades. It's so . . . well, so sort of *mellow*," Faye said, groping for a provocative word.

They walked down the dark labyrinthine corridors. Faye strode with her determined gait, a bunch of keys in her hand, jingling her importance as chatelaine.

Room 106 was not as bad as Faye had described and they decided the old blue carpet could stay, dressed up, perhaps, with paler blue accents. Faye dutifully noted the suggestions in a small leather book from Mark Cross, purchased recently for this purpose. "Well, that was not very challenging, I must admit," she complained as she opened the door to room 108, which was certainly in worse condition. "Oh, yes, now you see what I mean, this is uninhabitable as it is, completely uninhabitable." She went about opening drapes, putting on lights. It was like most of the other rooms, large and square, but the bedspreads and hangings were an apple green. The carpet, fading in spots, was of a conflicting color of green that might have been grassy at its inception, but now appeared to be the color of dried hay. The wallpaper, a floral print of peach and green, was stained with rusted water spots. The bedspreads were also running out of color. Faye clapped her hands with delight. "We can do this one from scratch. What shall we begin with, Laina? Bearing in mind that it must be a pastel of one tone or another."

Faye was like a child with an expensive and difficult new toy, at once eager to begin playing with it, and a little afraid of the challenge.

Laina suggested a parrot green with yellow accents.

"Yes, yes that's it, all green and yellow like a garden." They closed the door behind them while Faye scribbled furiously on her pad, jotting down names of fabric houses Laina recommended: Jofa, Stroheim and Roman, Brunschweig and Fils. They repeated the procedure with a few more rooms in that wing. Laina grew dizzy from the bilious colors, the mustiness, the sameness. They had to turn a corridor and walk halfway down a long dark hall to get to the next group of rooms. They were in the back wing and faced a court without any view. "These will have to be done handsomely to compensate for the dismal location." She fussed with the jangle of keys once more and opened the door of room 118.

The room was lit only by a murky light on the night table, and when the two women entered, they were startled to realize that it was occupied, and worse still that they were intruding upon a couple in bed together. They would have turned on their heels and walked out immediately, but it was already too late. They had recognized the couple—stricken men, who in their hurriedly gathered tent of sheets, appeared as apparitions, or as ungainly blocks of furniture draped in sheets to avoid discoloration. David Goldmark, deathly white, stared piteously into the faces of his wife and mother, while Russell Drake hurried into a dressing gown, and quipped nervously something about "politics making strange bedfellows."

Faye took a step toward Drake and cracked her hand across his face. Then the other hand lashed out across his other cheek. She kept it up, as if his face were a mechanical punching bag, first one side and then the other in slow motion . . . rhythmic slow motion, as if her arms were heavy instruments. "You were amusing yourself with us," she said in a voice strained with her tears. Finally Drake took hold of her arms and pushed her gently out of the still partly open door.

"Laina," David called his wife's name in pain as she turned to walk out the door.

She walked slowly out of the room, leaving the door ajar, the same door they had just entered with their innocent, benign intentions. She proceeded down the hall in a trance, overwhelmed by a cloying nausea. She was thinking vaguely that Faye must be nearby but was grateful that she had dissolved somehow in the confusion. In a delirium, she walked through the musty and neglected corridors, seeing the hot pink of Faye's dress. There was something about that color, its intensity of hue—the heat of the sun on the terrace—that she would associate with this day forever.

Her mind was emptied of all contents pertaining to past or present. Only the deliquescent harmonies of *his* music, lapping and overlapping in drowning waves—a man's tapering fingers, the touch of his hands—and a sense of loss, a terrible, bottomless sense of loss.

Faye sat at her dressing table and faced the mirror squarely. Before her was a staggering array of makeup. The kidney-shaped table was laden with miniature pots, tubes and vessels. On the mirror, theatrical lights shone as if in a star's dressing room.

She stared in the mirror as if hypnotized, then slowly and laboriously began to apply her face. When she was done the face she came up with was an exaggeration.

There were two red circles on her cheeks, her eyes were too dark, and her lipstick too red. It slipped slightly over the natural outlines of her mouth. She had drawn a fool's face, but in the mirror she saw only an aging one. And her son's reflection. He had walked quietly into the room and stood with his hands at his sides. She did not turn to greet him. Instead she spoke to his reflection.

"We cannot let your father hear about this."

"No."

"The car," she said in a hollow voice, "it was an accident as I thought. It was done deliberately. Your father pushed it over that cliff deliberately," she said in measured words. "He is not well, he could not take another trauma." She rose from the dressing table and began to pace back and forth.

"Mother, for God's sake, sit down," David cried. "Why do you act as if you are personally responsible? As if it were you who had done something reprehensible? Let *me* worry about it."

"Do you worry about your father? Like hell you do." She was standing in a corner of the room, smoking a cigarette. "I have watched him coming apart before my eyes. This would be the final blow."

They were silent for a moment, looking away, unable to meet one another's eyes.

"I'm not at all sure about that."

"What do you mean?" she said.

"Well, it's just that I'm not at all sure that he really cares that much about me. No, I think it's you. It's always been you. Something you would do to him is what would finally take him apart."

Faye stared hard at her son, trying to assess how much he really knew. Could Russell have been so rotten, so dis-

THE PLEASURE DOME

loyal as to have told him? She had heard that homosexual gossip was even worse than women's, *bitchier*. But she also knew that Russell was not really a homosexual.

As if reading her mind David asked, "Why did you take your anger, your disappointment with me, out on Drake? Why did you attack him instead of me? Even as a child you always upbraided Vivian whenever there was any trouble. Can't you face it? I am human too," he said. "I am *not* above reproach."

She had not really understood him. She felt only mild relief that he did not seem to know about her and Russell Drake. She stood there facing this son of hers, this genius she had created and said piteously "Don't you see you were the only thing I had produced in all my life, its sum total? It had to be perfect." There were tears in her eyes as she spoke.

"Oh, Mother," he said, "poor little Mother." He took her in his arms.

But she drew away as if in disgust. She was partly aware that the disgust was turned back on herself. She was ashamed of her selfishness, her hostility. She wondered if it would have been the same had it been someone other than Russell Drake. She sighed and sat down woodenly at her dressing table. "What have you come here for, David?" she said in a tired voice. "What do you want me to say?"

"I have come here to say how sorry I am that you should find out in this way."

"Find out? What about Yale? What was that supposed to be if not enlightening?"

"Adolescent experimentation?" he said, trying to be amusing, echoing his mother's old theories.

"And this, this is in earnest then, I suppose?"

"No, no. God, Mother, don't ask me to explain. I'm not sure that I know the answers myself yet, but I'm trying to find out."

"Why, why him? What do you see in such a man?"

"I don't know. Perhaps his fame, his aura, his reputation. He seems to know so much." David's youth, the insularity of resort life, had left him with broad patches of innocence.

"It is specious knowledge. In reality he knows very little," she said.

"I always thought you were fond of him, and father was too, for that matter."

"And look how he rewards us," she said bitterly. It was a double-edged sword for Faye. It had cut deeper than she could bear to admit, even to herself. It implied failure on every level as a woman. "How will you go on with your marriage?" she asked.

"That's up to Laina, of course."

"That poor girl, such a shock. She appears so innocent. She never really had a chance. Oh, God! How could you be so selfish? You seemed almost relieved," she said, looking at him closely. "It is obvious you wanted to be found out early in the relationship. Why else would you come clear out here?"

"I had no idea Laina would be here today, and as you know, Russell is staying at the hotel for the week, resting between engagements," David said with a crooked smile.

"What if she tells her father? He would surely tell Chase."

"Please, Mother, that isn't her style. Laina doesn't part with secrets readily."

"How do you know just what a woman would do in such a situation? Have you a precedent for it?"

"Only recently Laina confided something to me that

THE PLEASURE DOME

she had never told anyone, and for that reason alone, I feel culpable now. Her knowledge of men has always been rooted in trauma. I've only added to the burden."

"What do you mean, son?" Faye was suddenly gentle and cajoling.

"Well, she, she almost drowned once as a teenager. Some guy came along and saved her life, pulled her back to safety, and then, then took advantage of her—"

"Took advantage of her—?"

"The rotten bastard attacked her when she was too weak to defend herself."

"When, where did this happen David?" Faye asked in a strange voice.

"On some public beach, I think, late at night. I don't know, I didn't want to further upset her by asking for details."

"I see." Faye said weakly. She remembered Matthew once saying, "Saved his daughter's life once, a drowning accident or something..."

"Oh, you don't really see, Mother—all you are interested in is the sensationalism of it. Perhaps you're right. I'm not to be trusted, I talk too much," he said bitterly. He was angry with himself for babbling like a baby. He was only barely conscious of the fact that he thought telling this might somehow exonerate him. Shift the burden of blame, or at least distribute it more evenly. He may even have enjoyed a momentary victory at denouncing Laina, reducing her to his level perhaps, marring her too perfect image. He was instantly sorry.

For the moment Faye digested the information but had not exactly received its rather obvious message. Her mind was running too far ahead on the course of her own vendetta with Russell Drake.

Through the months that followed she was sustained

only by the thought of revenge. She dreamed of a hundred different situations that would bring her sweet relief, but she had not yet devised one that would not compromise herself or any member of her family. She was like a coiled serpent, ready to strike the moment the opportunity presented itself.

When life began gradually to flow back into Laina's veins, he came in and stood penitent before her. She said dully, "I always thought men like you were easy to spot." The "like you" was meant to hurt, to imply loss of respect, to render him a pariah, a freak.

"But surely you must have guessed. I thought you might have understood, being an artist yourself. Remember, the artist's feeling is law."

"That is delightfully unreasonable Jewish thinking. If you *must* be a homosexual, it's all right as long as you're a musical genius?" she asked.

"Ah, I was afraid that sooner or later you would get around to labeling me a 'Jewish prince'—of sorts."

But Laina was not amused. "Why did you marry me?" she asked, honestly perplexed.

"Because I love you," he said simply. "I—we can still have a good life together."

"And do you love Russell too?" she cut in.

David sat down. His hands were shaking. He did not answer, but his shaggy head hung down between his knees, his hands over his ears as if protecting them from further assault.

"Why should a man like *you* get married so young? Why at all, why, David?"

"I loved you, I thought, I thought I would change. I wanted a child."

THE PLEASURE DOME

"A child?" she laughed bitterly. "You want to implicate me in your charade, to prove conclusively that you *are* what you are *not?* For God's sake, David, be true to yourself at least, if not to me." They were silent. Then she said as if thinking aloud, "I thought maybe, perhaps I even hoped, that you and Fair Osborne—but I suppose it was Russell all along."

"No, no, Laina, only recently. Working together on the show, long hours, I don't know. The terrible thing about all this is I love you, I really do." He came over to her, stood close to her as if he wanted to touch her, to hold onto her solid presence, his white hope, an island in a sea of loneliness, but she edged away from him slightly.

"Look, Laina, there are the good things, we still have our work, our music, our friends; we do have a good time together. We are a team, don't forget." He tried to smile his most charming smile, as if a pep talk would mend her life. "And what about London?" They had had an offer to take the show there. "It might be a good opportunity for the show and an even better one for us to take a holiday together. Perhaps in entirely different surroundings, a fresh viewpoint—"

"I'm not going, David. I need to be by myself for a time, to think all this out. Besides, I find ships very romantic. It would be frustrating, to say the least."

There was a long disappointed silence. "Then *you* go, Laina; an ocean voyage is just what you need. You go without me, you can talk to them better than I can. I want you to have time to think. I want you to come back to me," he said in a whisper, unsure of what reaction this might evoke. He sat down heavily on the bed beside her half-packed case.

"I suppose that would be best," she said. "I just don't

feel I have the strength for anything else at this moment."

"I'll have father's butler help you to get ready," David said.

She eyed him suspiciously. "So you can spend the free time with our young crooner I suppose?"

"No, no, that's over, I promise you. I don't want you to make up your mind immediately, while it's all so fresh, so painful. Promise me you won't decide until you've given it every chance. I do believe the sea is anodyne for almost anything except, perhaps, seasickness," he said and laughed a little. "In the meantime, I'll move into the guest room if you like." She thought he sounded relieved.

She turned around to face him now. "All right, David," she said softly, "I'll go to London next month. We'll see." She did not hold David entirely accountable. By now she had committed adultery in her heart many times. She considered rather that they were caught in a shared perdition.

CHAPTER 37

Roosevelt quickly arranged the luggage on racks in the closets. He looked around the stateroom officiously, as if searching for something more to do. "Shall I water the flowers, Mrs. Goldmark?"

Until that moment Laina had hardly taken any notice of the beautiful flowers and the basket of fruit that greeted her as she entered. The flowers, dozens of yellow daffodils, were from David with a card that read "For a bon voyage and a bon retour—My love, David." The giant steamer basket was from her father and said simply, "Good Luck, Darling—Dad." She felt a fleeting stab of guilt for refusing to allow him or anyone else to see her off, but she couldn't bear to answer questions, to make explanations or small talk. As for David, they had agreed that they would have no contact with one another during the course of this separation. Aside from the pure business aspects of the trip, it was supposed to be an opportunity for her to decide whether or not she would be able to continue with this alliance. She no longer thought of it as a marriage in the true sense of the word.

Luxury liners had recently been reinstated for passenger service. And Great Britain's *Queen Elizabeth* was certainly the reigning queen of Cunard White Star's impressive fleet, superseding even the majestic *Queen Mary*.

It was a five o'clock sailing and as such extremely gala.

Before the war there would have been streamers and handkerchiefs waving on deck. Now an orchestra played discreetly, reedy violin-threaded melodies by Kern and Gershwin, as porters ran helter-skelter, pushing Louis Vuitton steamer trunks and rawhide hat cases. Had Laina been in a different mood, she would have admitted that this was a crossing to reckon with—a passenger list the columnists promised would include many of the great names from the worlds of Broadway, politics and finance.

The door was slightly ajar, for the cabin was warm and musky with the scent of flowers. A steady din of celebration drifted through the opening. Cabin doors were thrown open against the surprising October heat and to accommodate the overflow of guests. They were spilling out into the narrow corridors of polished burl and chrome, drinking and laughing and munching on canapés black with caviar. Stewards in stiffly starched bolero jackets wove in and out among the cumbersome crowd, juggling aloft trays with magnums of champagne and platters of foie gras; now and then a large *fruit en gelée* sailed by in shimmering splendor.

The festivities only made Laina's self-imposed isolation seem more pronounced. She was grateful for Roosevelt's neutral and comforting presence.

"Is there anything more I can do for you, Mrs. Goldmark?" Roosevelt asked politely.

"No, no. Thanks for your help," she said and walked him to the door.

He wished her a wonderful trip, and as he was leaving the cabin he almost collided with a steward bearing a giant vase of flowers. It was an artful selection of roses of intricately varied hues, ranging from snowiest white to deepest magenta. There were tea roses, and a dozen of a rare gray-mauve rose of such a melancholy shade as to cause an ache of sadness at the contemplation of its beauty.

Alone now she felt frightened. Her hand trembled as she reached for the card.

> In a field by the river my love and I did stand
> And on my leaning shoulder she laid her snow-white hand
> She bid me take life easy, as the grass grows on the weirs
> But I was young and foolish, and now am full of tears.

"W.B. Yeats," in a small corner of the card, was the only signature. She sat down heavily on the edge of the bed with the card in her hand. There were tears in her eyes—not only for this, it was an apology of sorts—but for everything. The words on the card only reminded her of the chaos of her life, of all the other lives surrounding her, caught in the same web. She picked up the passenger list that lay on the coffee table and fingered it idly. It was terribly long, she threw it down unread. She hoped she knew no one aboard, and had no intention of socializing, in any case. That night she had dinner in her cabin and retired early. She slept fitfully, which she attributed to the newness of the bed and the motion of the sea.

She spent the next day leisurely drowsing on a deck chair tucked up comfortably with a new novel, *The Young Lions*, while a steward with a strong Manchester accent fussed over her, bringing her hot beef tea and delicious little scones. She felt the tension draining away; for the first time in years she felt completely relaxed.

The second night at sea was traditionally formal, and aboard the great ships then they adhered rigidly to protocol. She had considered not leaving her cabin again, but she received a special engraved invitation to join the captain's table for dinner, preceded by cocktails in his cabin. She told herself it would be extremely impolite to refuse, and then too, because of her notoriety, she did not wish to appear arrogant. However, she skipped the cocktails and joined them for dinner in the enormous main dining room.

Everyone worked hard at being charming and Captain Danvers introduced her as the "distaff side of that talented young team Eastman and Goldmark." One or two of the older women squealed their disappointment that David was not present, but Laina gathered that the rest of the table were far more interested in the more formidable celebrities present.

After dinner she allowed herself to be talked into going to the top deck for a brandy in the exclusive Queen's Grill. The Grill, entirely circled by glass, was the dining room of the elite aboard ship. A few members of the party said it was frightfully expensive. One had to know the right people to get in. Some of the elite diners were still drifting in for late dinner.

Laina was thinking of how she might gracefully leave when she looked up suddenly and saw a short distance away a tall handsome man following the captain to a table. For a split second nothing registered. And then she realized it was Harlan. At the moment of shocked recognition all she could think of was that he looked as if he had dressed in a hurry. Perhaps it was studied casualness. A strand of hair fell over his eyes, his dress shirt was opened at the throat and a string tie hung loose, in open rebellion to protocol. If he saw her, he did not acknowledge it, passing by swiftly in the crowded room, and heading for a party of people already seated and waiting for him. Her feelings were confused and contradictory—tender and possessive, outraged and suspicious. She wondered if he had seen her and what sort of game he was playing now.

She had wanted to leave before; somehow she couldn't now. She sat there for another half-hour in a paralysis of indecision while Mrs. Leclerc, one of her dinner companions, grew maudlin and sloppy drunk. The orchestra played drenchingly romantic melodies, even getting around to "Such Is Love." The orchestra leader smiled and threw his baton in her direction, obediently followed by a spotlight. She stood up in a trance. All this had been so much a part of her life with David—their plans together. Even this trip. She excused herself, pleading a headache.

In her cabin she lay down fully clothed on the cool sheets that had been turned down for the night. She closed her eyes but knew she would not sleep tonight. She was no stranger to sleepless nights, she had never slept well, not even as a child. Lying there in the rose-scented semidarkness, she asked herself a hundred questions she could not answer. The ship was beginning to pitch and roll slightly—like a cradle, rocking, rocking . . . she lost track of the time. She sat up with a jolt and looked at the small bedside clock—it was eleven forty-five. She had only been back in her cabin a little more than an hour. She rose and began to remove her dress when someone knocked.

"It is the steward, madam."

She threw a robe over her half-clothed body and went to the door. The steward stood there, bearing a small silver tray and apologies for having to disturb her at this hour, but she did not have a "Do Not Disturb" on the door. Laina took the note from the tray and tore open the envelope. *Don't make me beg this time*. In the lower left-hand corner in place of a signature, it said only, "Cabin III."

Slowly, very slowly Laina continued to undress. When she had removed all her clothes, she took a white cashmere polo coat from her closet and slipped it over her nakedness. She still wore her satin evening sandals from dinner.

When Harlan opened the door and stood momentarily towering in the doorway, still dressed in his evening shirt and formal trousers, she felt suddenly foolish and adolescent in her eager response to his summons. But as soon as he closed the door, he pulled her to him and held her tightly, murmuring into her hair. He held her so close, with such fierce desperation, that she thought for a moment she might suffocate against the hard muscles of his chest.

"You *knew* I would come, didn't you?" she said.

"Yes," he whispered softly.

They stood kissing for some minutes, wholly absorbed in the newness of it. Random kisses running wild, wild as field flowers. He put his hand inside her coat only to bring her closer to him, and was astonished to feel her bare flesh. She dropped her coat to the floor, and they fell kissing on the bed. She undid the button of his trousers. He threw them across the room, and almost at the same instant he entered her, calling her name softly again and again. He moved inside her slowly as if accustoming himself to her body, but his own wildness took over, and he came before he meant to. He raised himself on his elbows to look at her. "I love you," he said, "I suppose I always have." They held onto each other, afraid to let go, until their breathing returned to normal.

Weakly she sat up against the headboard. She buried

THE PLEASURE DOME

her lips in his hair, marveling at its softness, its richness. She traced the shadow of a cleft in his chin, which she had not remembered, and marveled at how perfect his body was, so neatly mapped. She was ashamed of the esthete in her that responded to physical beauty; she knew it to be the most imperfect of perfections. But even as she suffered these thoughts, she gathered his head close into her breasts. He took her nipples in his mouth and grew hard again. Her fantasies had so long prepared her for this that with five or six thrusts she too cried out, felt herself disintegrate. He stayed inside her, longing to give her pleasure until he could wait no longer and collapsed against her slim body, shuddering and breathless.

They lay side by side, looking upward as if searching for answers. She wished that she were a smoker. In novels people usually lit a cigarette now, to ease the tension of the return to earth.

He slept only a little, while she sat watch over him. When he awoke she asked, "Why are you here, on this ship?"

"Because you are."

"Well then, what is the pretense?"

"I have an opportunity to take over a failing hotel in London and have been planning to go over and see it and talk with them for some time."

"Yet you haven't until now."

"No."

"What will Vivian think about our being on the same crossing?"

"A coincidence."

"Didn't she know that I was going to England on this ship?"

"I don't think so, that is, until I mentioned it."

She seemed surprised. "I see, covering your tracks in advance." She hated herself for probing, for sounding suspicious and vulnerable. She looked at him and they laughed collusively. She wondered at the masculine ability at self-repossession after the frenzy of desire. She felt disadvantaged because she wanted to possess him completely, to have him for her own. In a sense he had belonged to her first, she reasoned; they had belonged to one another before there was anyone else.

"Laina, what's really happened between you and the young maestro?"

She detected a little of his old taunting manner. "What do you mean?"

"Well, for one thing, he's not here, and I am, most assuredly—in the flesh, I might add."

She ignored his irony and wondered how much he knew. He always knew everything that went on at the hotels.

"Nothing's happened, nothing at all. It's simply that he's needed at home, and one of us was needed in London. In any case I've always wanted to go abroad . . ."

He interrupted her, ignoring her excuses, "So, you know, then?" He seemed genuinely taken aback. "Didn't take him long to get around to it, did it?"

There was a brief silence while she decided whether to continue the charade with him, but knew it was hopeless. "Why didn't you tell me before?" she whispered.

"Would you have believed me then?"

"No." Her reply was barely audible.

"Confess, girl" he said, his lips to her hair, "even if you knew and you probably had suspicions, you would have married him anyway to stay near me. Say it." He held her head prisoner in his hands. "Why can't you admit it?"

"Yes, alright, yes, I suppose in a way you are part of the essence of me."

"What way?"

"I don't know. Oh, God, I don't know," she cried.

"You know—but you are ashamed. You consider me a weakness in yourself and are ashamed of it. Isn't that it? Speak to me." His voice was raised.

"What does it matter now? You are married, a husband, a father. I might ask the same question. Why did you marry Vivian?"

"Because I loved her, because . . ." He was thinking just how to phrase it. He wanted to be fair. "I needed her to give me permanence, perspective. To push me on and at the same time to rein me in."

Laina imagined that he rather enjoyed this wild stallion image of himself. She could not bear to ask the next question, the obvious one, because she knew he would answer it with perfect honesty. She let him off easily.

He jumped up then as if ending the conversation. He pulled a handsome bathrobe out of his closet. She was suddenly conscious of the fact that she had come here without any clothes other than her coat. As if reading her mind, he threw her a creamy silk pajama top.

"I am anxious to see this England, this sceptered isle," he said. "I would like to rent a car and drive all through it, stopping at little inns and stately manor houses along the way. It's a small country and should be easy to do in a couple of weeks."

The statement had the effect of at once buoying her up and deflating her. His natural enthusiasm for everything was contagious, but the last words, "a couple of weeks," carried the chill of a death sentence. He came over to her and sat down beside her gently on the bed. He was all the more desirable to her for his sudden withdrawal. He cupped her face in his hands. "My lovely lyrical Laina." She was fascinated by his long slender aristocratic fingers. "You don't hate me still, do you?" he asked.

"The strongest love is distilled in hate."

"Without that, sex would be tepid, I suppose."

"Is that how you equate love—with sex?"

"Surely you must have learned by now, either one is useless without the other."

She did not reply.

"Why can't you tell me that you love me, without fencing and parrying?"

"Yes, I love you," she said, as if coming clean. She felt the sting of salt tears and looked away quickly. "I must get back to my cabin now."

"Why? Stay here for the night. Tomorrow morning you can go to your stateroom and bring all of your things back here."

"But the stewards—the gossip."

"People will gossip no matter what. In any case I have a living room through that door," he pointed to the left of the room. "It's part of the suite. When the steward comes in with our meals, you can simply slip into the other room."

She had the feeling that he had it all rather neatly planned, but she didn't care, nor did she find the strength to demur. "Who were those people you were with tonight?"

"Hotel people, business. They know nothing of my personal life."

"But they must know you are married and traveling alone."

"As far as I know, only that I'm traveling alone." He raised her hair and nuzzled the back of her neck.

Like prying eyes, the portals spilled morning sunshine on the large bed. She stirred in his arms, but warm and sleepy with the gentle rocking of the ship, she slept again until she awoke at last. He closed her eyelids with his lips.

They spent the remaining days on ship together, inseparable. They took most of their meals in the stateroom and rarely went into the dining room. They were too weak to dress, too drunk with love, too sodden with lovemaking.

However, the last night at sea they appeared outside together and danced until dawn. She wished to be seen with him, to have the world regard them as a pair.

The following afternoon, in the shimmering haze of a late fall, they stood on the deck and watched bemused, as the white cliffs of Dover loomed into view, gathering the ship in its immaculate embrace.

"A deceptively pure introduction to a thousand years of bloodshed and oppression," Harlan said.

"*And* glorious heroism!" she added.

"Anglophile! Ach, don't mind me, it's just the Irish in me talking daft," he said affecting a brogue.

The boat train brought them into London just after dark. In the high-bodied London taxi, the driver studied them carefully in the rear-view mirror, ever on the lookout for "Yank" celebrities, but quickly decided he had turned up nothing to speak of.

Harlan had booked himself into a room at Claridge's.

Laina's original reservation had been at the Savoy in the Strand, the heart of the theater district.

Across the great harlequin blocks of marble from the elegant reception desk was a small Louis Quatorze desk, offering the weary new arrivals a true reception. Still, Laina hung back when Harlan signed the register and only relaxed when they were safely ensconced in their room. It was a charming, large room with high ceilings and blue-and-white toile draperies that matched the tile around the fireplace. The great old-fashioned bathroom was large in itself. Claridge's had played host to dignitaries throughout the decades and had been preserved in all its fading glory, immaculate and unchanged by time or wars.

They dispatched their business in the next two days, jealous of the time they spent apart. She felt depleted, insubstantial without him. She knew it was risky to become dependent on another woman's husband.

Harlan was not impressed with the business offering and doubted that they would buy the hotel, he said. He had his hands full as it was, dashing north and south in his own country. But he would consider leasing it and maintaining the present management.

They went sight-seeing with other starry-eyed American tourists, and shopped together at Fortnum & Mason, where they bought tins of Dundee cake and plum puddings wrapped in cheesecloth. At Harrods she tried on cashmeres and kilts. He crowded into the tiny dressing room with her when the saleslady's back was turned. At night she sat beside him quietly, inhaling his presence like an epicure savoring a precious brandy. Food was still scarce all over England, but restaurants made the most of it. They dined at the Connaught and gambled at the White Elephant.

THE PLEASURE DOME

"You must come to our ship if you enjoy gambling," he said, watching her childlike absorption as the roulette wheel spun giddily. "Even if you don't, you must see it," he said proudly. "It has been rechristened the *Pleasure Dome*. It's only been in operation a few months and has already taken in over a hundred thousand in cash."

Laina looked unimpressed, as she usually did about material things. It only goaded Harlan further to remind her how far he had come since the beginning.

"I begged your father-in-law to allow the hotels to finance it, but he wouldn't listen. It would have meant a lot of revenue for us. As it is, I'm glad he didn't. We borrowed against our hotel stock and own the ship outright. Christ almighty, that Matthew's stubborn. He is his own worst enemy," he said, pounding the roulette table so that the neatly stacked chips jumped in front of the man next to him. "You, young lady, will be a very rich woman one day," he said, "thanks to me."

She laughed, honestly amused. "I suppose you have done all this for our enrichment only, father's and mine, that is."

He did not reply immediately, but was discomfitted by her remark. He did not always understand his own motives, especially where this woman was concerned. He realized he wanted desperately to compensate for what he had taken from her. "Perhaps," he said quietly.

"It's that Catholic conscience of yours again."

"I told you once I don't have any," he said with cool disdain.

"So you've said, but I didn't believe it then and I certainly don't believe it now."

"Look, girl, don't invest me with virtue I don't possess. Either accept me as I am or not at all," he said.

"Is that what Vivian has done?" She wanted to tear

out her tongue for saying it, but it was uncontrollable.

"Precisely," he replied.

They hired a Daimler and drove down the wrong side of narrow country roads, dispersing terrified pedestrians, sheep and cows. Driving became an assault on the senses, an emotional checkerboard, one minute through a scene of gentle haunting beauty, then through piles of charred rubble. The ravages of the Blitz were more ominous here among the pastoral innocence than in London where the damage was more extensive. They passed ancient thatched cottages and the toylike sixteenth-century churches, one to a village. In Castle Combe on the River Bybrook they had cream tea at five and ate homemade scones, exquisite with currants. Harlan questioned the plump young proprietress about this and that, congratulating her on the homebaked specialties and roaring with delight at regional jokes and confidences easily shared. Laina envied his capacity for enjoyment.

"*Vita celebratio est,*" he cried. "Life is a celebration, and so it must be, my girl, for it is all too short. But then, I don't suppose you think about that at your age—you look down at death from Olympian heights, if indeed you notice it at all."

"When you are seventy, I will be almost sixty. You see how the years have a way of catching up?" Laina said.

They stayed overnight at a four-hundred-year-old manor house and had a hunt breakfast in the wood-beamed dining room, served in a courteous hush from a blaze of covered silver dishes. The windows of the dining room framed hillocks tender with grazing sheep. Moving north toward the lakes, Wordsworth country, they saw spread out before them great squares of kelly green and gold, fields of buttercups and daisies and velvet grass.

THE PLEASURE DOME

High above Lake Windemere, the most perfect of English lakes, they lingered for a few nights at a charming inn, where they were solicitously regarded as a honeymoon couple. From there they passed through the rolling moors of the Midlands and became hopelessly lost and stopped to ask directions a dozen times. The answers were always polite but often unintelligible, for they were unwittingly heading for Northumberland County, near the Scottish border, where accents grew furry with brogue.

At twilight they drove into the tiny hamlet of Blanchland. To Laina it would be forever associated with white—*blanch*—with the milky haze on bleached-out ancient stones and abbey of the White Monks, a thousand-year-old monastery recently converted to an inn. The Lord Crewe's Arms had been the home of a secret order of eleventh-century monks. The rooms, crudely remodeled cells, were damp and chilly, and the tiny crypt bar, that had once served as charnel house, was well named, for it was still cold and damp and smelled of decay. In the ancient monastic setting, Harlan took a perverse pleasure in lovemaking that was wild and uncontrollable enough to shock the clergy, past or present.

Driving back to London he finally asked, "What will you do now, Laina?" They had carefully avoided the subject. "You don't have to go back to him, you know. It can't possibly work. I'll fix you up a beautiful place in one of the hotels until you find an apartment or something."

"Yes," she said absently, "I suppose you would. Are you telling me to stop being his wife in order to become your mistress?"

"Oh, come now, Laina, you sound positively archaic.

Would I set up my mistress in the same hotel with my wife and children, now I ask you?"

His ingenuousness did not deter her. "Yes, I think you might if it were convenient. You are so certain of your outrageous luck."

"Oh, come now, darling, don't spoil it all at the end. It's been so perfect."

"Yes."

They flew home on separate planes. She wished only to die. She had grown used to losing love early in her life, her mother, her brother, but this was almost like an amputation. It was as if a part of her body had been rudely torn and she was left to tend it alone, raw and bleeding. She wondered if obsession might be a form of madness.

"So they want our show in London, then?" David stood nervously in their living room and caught his own reflection in the art deco mirror. His face was like a mask, drawn and sallow as parchment. "That's wonderful, what else did they say?"

"Well, they will want parts rewritten to suit an English audience, pointing up British economic problems rather than American. And they want an all-British cast. With the exception of the lead. I'm not certain."

"I see, well." David sat down somewhat chastened. "That means almost complete rewriting and a British cast. I don't know, that's a big job—breaking in a British cast—time-consuming. I'd like to take our own cast to Broadway soon. That would necessitate my being here."

"Have we gotten any bids for Broadway?"

"Well, yes. Chappell, the music publisher, will invest, and I think if this keeps up we'll be able to take it to Broadway next year with no financial strain."

"You'll want to find a small house for it; the intimacy of the de Lys was half the battle."

"Yes."

She found it difficult to meet his eyes, to see him as the same shaggy-haired romantic maestro she had married. All she could think of was homosexual graffiti, dirty jokes and run-down bars she'd passed in the Village— huddled, secret places.

"Will you take it with the same cast intact?"

David looked at her carefully. "Probably—with the exception of Drake. He has heavy commitments in Hollywood and with the recording companies." He dropped his eyes self-consciously.

She imagined this concession was for her benefit but it didn't seem to matter somehow. "So who will you get in his place?"

"Broadway is almost a year away, why worry about it now? Why do you keep saying 'you,' who will *you* get, what will *you* do? You know it's 'we.' We are a *team*, Laina. Don't you remember?"

She did not reply.

"So," he said in a stilted voice, "How was the trip? Did you enjoy it? Did you really relax?"

"Yes, it was quite an experience—the ship, England. It was all so beautiful. You must go sometime, David. You would appreciate it."

He came over to her and took her hands and kissed them. "I will go with *you* someday. We will go together." He dropped his voice to a whisper. "Laina, we have our music, success can be very satisfying, you know. We have companionship based on mutual interests. Aren't these enough?"

"No, they're not enough. I am only twenty-four. I have a long life ahead of me...."

She did not know exactly where she should go or what she should do. She could not go back to her father. She was certain of that. She felt uneasy with her father. Her mother had made her suspicious of him, and she was hesitant to show him her love, which was deep though ambivalent. Her need to be with Harlan now was so urgent that she was willing to go back to David, at least for the present, if only to use him as a convenient subterfuge. *Confess, girl, you only married him to stay near me, confess, confess,* kept running through her mind. "I will have to have time to myself, David. I'll have to take frequent trips if this is going to work," she warned. She was taking the only path open to her, one where she could be with Harlan without compromising him. She did not consider herself anymore. She had little left to lose.

CHAPTER 38

When Harlan returned to business, to his family, to earth, he was confused and dissatisfied for the first time in many years. He hadn't meant to become as deeply emotionally involved as he had. He did not realize how moved he would be by their reunion, by her acceptance and forgiveness, by her complete surrender. He wished ardently to return to his former state of emotional impoverishment, when nothing seemed to matter much or affect him—those static years before the war. At the back of his thoughts was the pervasive fear that this, more than any other single act, could threaten his future plans. And yet he never for one moment entertained the thought of not being with her again after their brief idyll in England.

He had left town when business was slow and returned to find the Florida hotels in chaos; the kitchen help in both hotels were out on strike.

Matthew had flown down to Florida a little in advance but had seemed suddenly impotent where he had once held sway with both the unions and the employees. Matthew had been drinking heavily of late and generally his thinking lacked clarity and cohesion. His judgment, once sharp and clear, was now clouded and diffused, as vividly demonstrated some months earlier when he demolished his splendid automobile. Still, he had brought in an army of scabs to fill in but had been unable to quell the riots on the picket lines that resulted. The guests were complaining about the food and general disorganization in the kitchen and dining rooms.

In the midst of this they were also preparing the *Pleasure Dome* for its gala December opening in the waters off Miami. Having recently sailed down from Long Island, it had unofficially been open for gambling, first up north, and now down south, for months.

In a sense these sudden demands were a blessing, allowing Harlan surcease from the pain of thinking about Laina and his growing awareness of the uncomfortably close situation. In fact, his greatest strain came from the burgeoning guilt he tried to deny, of which he was growing ever more conscious. He had realized his enormous treachery in regard to everyone surrounding him—Alex, Matthew, Vivian, and particularly Laina. He had often fancied that he would have his fill of her; that would finally dispel the urgency, the pain of wanting. But as the weeks passed, he was astonished to discover the powerful physical urge, the drive in him to be with her. In the midst of all the chaos, he found himself inventing ways and means to be with her more regularly. He even considered personally supervising the remodeling of the rooms at the Broadbeach Club just to be near her in Long Island. He knew none of this made sense; he was thinking wildly, irrationally.

Despite all, he was happy to see Vivian. Except for the fact that he fell into gloomy silences from time to time, which she took to be the result of business pressures, there was little change in their relationship.

He continued to enjoy his two sons, who were happy children. He and the older boy, Steven, now seven, were inseparable. He had bought him a pony for his seventh birthday and took him for a riding lesson each morning at nine. Sometimes they rode together on the beach or

THE PLEASURE DOME

Harlan, riding his own beautiful mare, put the boy on the saddle in front of him and galloped along the water's foamy edge. He scrupulously reserved the hour before dinner as the children's hour, often playing ball on the beach while the three-year-old Gerald romped recklessly in the sand. At these times, on the almost deserted beach at sundown, he thought himself the luckiest man in the world.

He told them tall stories at bedtime. The ones that Steve wanted to hear over and over again were the war stories, tales of his marine experience, of Japs and bayonets and beach landings, stories of medals and heroism.

Curled up in his arms on the sofa, Steven asked his father one evening, "What am I, Daddy?"

"What are you?" Harlan asked, his eyebrows raised quizzically. "You are my son and a brave clever boy. What would you like to be?"

"Well, I'd like to be *something*, you know, like the boys in my school. They're all *something*."

"Something like what?"

"Like Jewish, or not Jewish or something *else*. Most of the guys in my class have their things cut off. Do I, Daddy?"

"Cut off?" Harlan repeated the words, then roared with laughter. He called Vivian into the room. "Would you like us to cut it off, son?" he asked in a mock scary voice. Steven shrieked in pretended terror.

"As a matter of fact," Vivian said, "you and your brother had that done when you were little babies and couldn't even remember. The doctor just takes a tiny piece of skin off your penis."

"What's a penis?" Steven screamed, laughing and knowing.

"Ah, that's the great philosophical question," Harlan said, winking at his wife, "and one that has never been satisfactorily answered down through the ages. The only thing we know about it *for sure* is that it doesn't have a brain in its head!" Harlan laughed, warmly enjoying his joke. Vivian threw him an admonishing glance.

On the few occasions he had discussed religion with Vivian he learned that she felt strongly about raising the children as Jewish. Harlan had no objection, but thought he had better cross that bridge when he came to it. He wanted the children to be imbued with life and live it, rather than to dwell on death and the hereafter, as he had been brought up to do. He believed in the tangible, in what he could see and feel and touch.

At nights the black and tropic waters off Miami's shores were ablaze with crazy colored lights that spelled out the *Pleasure Dome* from stem to stern. The surrounding sea echoed with music from the dance band.

Matthew had been reluctantly bringing large parties of guests over to "Chase's Folly," as he secretly called the gambling ship. If he wasn't altogether pleased about being an accessory to the greening of Harlan and Alex, he was somewhat mollified by the fact that the gambling gimmick was bringing guests to the hotels in droves. Even though Matthew was disdainful of the sort of clientele they were attracting, he had to admit he liked the looks of the balance sheets lately. How much cash Harlan and Alex took home from the ship was their own secret, Matthew figured. It was undoubtedly a sizable sum. Alex felt at home with a cash business. In the days when his dance halls employed hostesses, it had been an

THE PLEASURE DOME

all-cash business—from admission fees to the tips the girls received, to the prodigious bar business. It was on this basis and the sheer wild fun of it all that Alex had gone in on the gambling to begin with. Harlan liked the obvious tax advantages too. He often said, "The wealthy are familiar with paying high taxes. They are also familiar with graceful ways to avoid them. Now I'm beginning to understand how it works."

Although years apart in age, Alex and Harlan were not so different in background or interests. Neither was opposed to working in an atmosphere of chance, one that was constantly charged by the presence of beautiful women. In a way they had similar backgrounds—ethnic, deprived and deeply religious. Both claimed to disavow conscience but were severely plagued by old guilts, and both needed constant reassurance by women as to their general worth and sexual performance. One major difference prevailed. Alex had an outlet for his doubts and fears, having become more religious with the years. Harlan did not. He believed, he said, that he alone created his own destiny.

Matthew felt reckless. He had become one of the *Pleasure Dome*'s star pigeons. Drink in hand, dressed impeccably in evening clothes, he stood alone night after night, leonine and somehow noble on his terrible quest for self-destruction, and watched unflinchingly as his fortune dribbled away. He was desperate to have large amounts of ready cash on hand. He wanted to buy Harlan out, buy into some other hotel group where he might at last be autonomous, and gather in his old clientele, those who hadn't defected to the new regime.

On this particular evening Harlan, looking somewhat tired and worn from recent battles waged with unions, his libido and his conscience, came over to Matthew, who was standing at the crap table and said quietly, "Hey, Matt, I don't want to take your money. There are much better ways to invest it with me if you choose."

Matthew was silent. He blew on the dice and rolled. The shiny red cubes looked crystalline and harmless as Christmas candy cherry charms on the bright green baize. The dice came up seven. He lost again. "Look, brother-in-law, you're bad luck. Don't stand behind me. I want you out front where I can see you at all times," Matthew said, pretending a lightness of spirit he did not feel.

Harlan was actually offended. He did not dislike his wife's brother and would have preferred that Matthew not resent him as bitterly as he did. After all, he was doing his job and doing it well, which necessitated making some enemies. It was too bad one of them had to be his wife's brother, a man to whom he owed, indirectly, his present enviable position. Harlan was not unappreciative, not unsympathetic, only unrelenting. He saw that Matthew was flushed and slightly drunk. "Will you come into my office for a moment?"

"'Won't you come into my parlor,' said the spider to the fly?"

"Please, Matt." Harlan kept his voice down. There was considerable jockeying for the position that Matthew had just vacated at the head of the table. Matthew followed behind Harlan to his office.

Harlan's offices in the hotel were typical—smallish hotel suites turned into executive offices. But here Harlan had indulged his fancies—many culled from the playgrounds of the rich where he had lived and worked during his youthful, impressionable years. The office, in

THE PLEASURE DOME

fact the entire ship, had been decorated by William Pahlman in low key, art-deco elegance. The large square room was done in red and black, a humorous though completely decorous tribute to the game of Chance.

Harlan walked over to the red lacquer chinoise secretaire that dominated the room and opened the smoke-mirrored doors, revealing a bar perfectly equipped with Baccarat-cut crystal glasses in every size and shape.

Matthew commented dryly, "Ah, a symphony in red and black. Positively diabolical. Where is the sign that reads, 'Abandon hope all ye who enter here'?"

Harlan leaned back in his rich glove-leather chair, ignoring the irony, and said, "Matthew can you afford to lose, to squander this kind of money?"

"I don't exactly know what kind of money you're talking about. I've lost count."

"That's what I was afraid of. Sixty thousand dollars in the last few weeks and God knows how much more before that."

"That's my business," Matthew said sullenly, looking into the bottom of his empty glass.

"I don't want your money this way, I'd prefer that you save it, invest it in the company with Alex, Vivvy and me—assure your future *and* your old age."

"Ah, Chase," he said, leaning his head back wearily against the armchair. "You retail like a carnival barker with an elixir."

"Where did all this money come from?" Harlan asked suspiciously.

"I borrowed against my stock in the hotels," Matthew confessed wearily.

"Christ." Harlan covered his eyes with his hands; he would try to remain calm.

"Look, I've been in hock to the banks for years. This is nothing new. What do you think I needed Eastman for in the first place? To facilitate you?"

"I'm just going to have to refuse to take your money. You can't play at the tables anymore, Matt."

Matthew didn't appreciate the sudden reversal of roles at all. All of a sudden this big Irish swim kid, this nobody, is sitting behind a fancy desk and dispensing fatherly advice and admonitions. "So when it's sixty thousand dollars in *your* favor you put a stop on me. Suppose it was in my favor, huh?"

"Jesus, Matt, there's absolutely no way to make it with you—if it wasn't for Vivvy, do you think I'd give a damn? I would let you run haywire on your own self-destructive course."

"Destruction and havoc is what you have wreaked since you muscled your way in here. I worked almost single-handedly and against great odds to organize this business and it worked." He leaned forward in his chair, and his voice cracked. "It worked just fine. Now after my father dies and I can possibly begin to see the light, you come along . . ." Groping for words, he felt his Adam's apple bobbing in his throat. ". . . And victimize me." His stutter hadn't surfaced for a long while, since his father's death.

"Those who do not see themselves as victims assume the greater risk," Harlan said coolly.

"Don't give me your half-baked platitudes. I want you to let me gamble until I at least win back something."

There was a brief silence. Harlan opened a drawer and took out a wad of bills. "Here is your sixty thousand, Matthew. I will buy you five thousand shares of Nashco at my price. You're getting a bargain, believe me. Well, what do you say?"

"I say you can go straight to hell. I don't need your charity or to be told what to do with my money."

"But it is *my* money now," Harlan said.

"Then keep it—and be damned with it."

Harlan jumped up restlessly.

Matthew continued sitting there, rolling his empty glass between his fingers, in a state of painful indecision. "In my case, five thousand shares won't get me any kind of major interest, so again I'll be subordinate to you and Alex," Matthew said bitterly. "And I can't raise enough money for much more," he said in a final note of defeat.

"At least it's a beginning," Harlan said quietly, sitting down again, "and you can keep right on buying."

"Somehow or other, everything always falls right into place for you, doesn't it?" Matthew said. It was more a fact than a question. There was no reply from Harlan. There was none needed.

"When are you going to put this so-called proposal to a vote?"

"Not for a while. These things don't happen with lightning speed, you ought to know that. But you'll have time to raise some of the money if you want to."

"Your generosity is overwhelming. Are you certain that my sister will vote her shares with you?"

Harlan looked down and smiled slightly. "As certain as one human being can ever be about another."

"I see," Matthew said, "and Alex—are you equally certain of Alex's vote?"

"He's a businessman, and a greedy one, I might add." Harlan wished that Matthew were greedier, but his ego eclipsed his greed, his ego and a strange misbegotten idealism.

Matthew leaned back in his chair and suddenly began to read aloud from a handsomely embossed plaque above

Harlan's desk. It was a stanza from the Coleridge poem:

> The shadow of the dome of pleasure floated
> midway on the waves;
> where was heard with mingled measure
> From the fountains and the caves.
> It was a miracle of rare device,
> *A sunny pleasure dome with caves of ice.*

"Do you know the lines that precede that stanza?" Matthew asked in a curious mood. "They are, I believe,

> And mid this tumult Kubla heard from far
> ancestral voices prophesizing war.

CHAPTER 39

To keep his mistress in the same place where he lived with his wife and children was tantamount to madness or, at best, a blatant desire to be found out. Harlan did not see it that way. He felt that the most obvious solution would attract the least attention.

At first they had tried other hotels, but the management invariably recognized him from business circles or trade magazines. There was no possible explanation except the obvious one. He would not consider taking Laina to a second-rate hotel, even though he might not be recognized. In those years unmarried people were not permitted to check into the same hotel room; it was felonious to get caught registering falsely as man and wife. Their individual notoriety complicated the situation further. They had tried a weekend in Atlantic City at his Whitmore Hotel on the boardwalk. But she wound up imprisoned in the room all weekend long in a miasma of salt water taffy and buttered nuts, while Harlan worked. The hotel was filled with Broadbeach families, and the staff kept tabs on every move that he made.

In the final analysis he pleaded with her to come down to Florida and stay in her father's suite at the Hibiscus Gardens. Alex used it only for a couple of weeks at the height of the season. This way, Harlan argued, they could see each other daily and be alone whenever he found a safe interval.

Laina had been working with David on lyrics for a possible new production. It was a blessing, she told Harlan. It kept her busy and involved, but it also enabled her to take advantage of the option she had sought in their very fluid agreement. She would need to get away from time to time, to think, to work, she had said.

Lying naked in his arms, she felt ashamed of her almost hysterical surrender and hoped he translated it only as love, not need. She tried to rationalize to herself that her previous record of resistance where he was concerned had given her some small degree of strength in this poorly balanced alliance.

Outside the tropical sun was occluded by smoke-gray clouds that seemed gravid with rain, unable to disgorge it. The air in the bedroom was still and moist and smelled faintly of suntan lotion and stale, ultraviolet rays. The Hibiscus Gardens was not air-conditioned. Matthew said it was part of its old world charm, a part of what the people sought here, a peaceful haven of the old guard, untouched by time.

It was two o'clock in the afternoon; they had been together since noon. "Two solid hours off the floor," he reminded her of his dereliction of duty, "and on the ceiling," he said in a more intimate voice, kissing her shoulder. "Shows how reckless you have made me. For all we know, there is a flood in the kitchen and here I am, incommunicado."

She sighed. He watched her closely to gauge her reaction, alert to the slightest dissatisfaction on her part. That she had stayed here for nearly a month was an unexpected windfall for him and he was terrified that at any moment she might change her mind and leave. He was tearing himself into pieces to give her a share of his time and attention, to keep his mind on business and still be home every evening at six for children's hour and dinner in the bosom of his family. He was a hypocrite and he knew it.

Sometimes he had dinner in the dining room. Once in a great while, Faye and Matthew joined him at the family table when they were in Miami, but they now spent most of their time in Palm Beach where Matthew had reluctantly agreed to manage the Palm Gardens.

On occasion Laina dined with them too, unable to squirm out of it when invited by Faye or Vivian, silently choking when Vivian smoothed her husband's hair in a wifely gesture, referred to him as "my husband" in her proprietary manner, or asked the table in general, as she so often did, how they liked this or that item of clothing she chose for him. More often she chattered happily in her unenlightened state about their friends, their social engagements and their children. On one such evening the orchestra played "So In Love" from *Kiss Me Kate*, and Vivian wanted to dance. He held her wispy body close as a lover and Laina tried desperately to avert her eyes, to talk to Faye, with whom conversation did not now come easy since the revelation in room 118. She watched them dancing as if through the wrong end of a telescope. They looked small and far away—she wondered if he slept with her still. To Laina, brought up in the forties amid the stern morality of wartime, husband was a sacred word, inviolate. The very word conjured powerful prerogatives, life-long allegiance and dedicated sensuality, implicating her in a treacherous bind. After the first week at the Gardens she knew she should leave and go back to David or to her father, but she could not. Instead she had relapsed into a voluptuous stupor from which the only sporadic arousal was desire.

He had slept briefly while she watched, jealous as the clock loudly ticked away their time together. She herself had not slept for weeks, maybe years. She longed for a deep, untroubled sleep, uninhabited by calamitous events and avenging phantoms.

"Will you come to the *Pleasure Dome* tonight and try your luck?" he asked teasingly as he got up and walked toward the shower.

"My *Pleasure Dome* is right here," she said, lying back against the pillows drowsily, "and I don't have to *try* my luck, I'm all too familiar with it. But I like the name, and I suppose you do see yourself as a sort of Kubla Khan in miniature."

He drew himself up to his full height, tightening the towel around his waist. "Some miniature," he said.

"Some Xanadu," she said, indicating the musty hotel room. They laughed. He came back to the bed and sat down beside her. He nuzzled her belly with his lips. He moved his lips further down her belly to her smooth white thighs. She felt herself becoming liquid, her breathing grew intensely rapid. Then he got up. "I could stay here all day and make love to you, but I also have to make a living, remember?"

"How self-important you sound."

"I am important!" he said.

She heard the shower through the glass door, just as another shower—rain—broke outside; torrential rains lashed the windows with tropic fury. She knew she would be left to her own devices for the balance of the day and night, and tomorrow and tomorrow night. She was used to loneliness. She had grown up with it.

THE PLEASURE DOME
* * *

Preparing now for the Christmas holidays, Harlan was extremely busy and preoccupied. Laina had not been with him for days. She grew tired and bored with her own lachrymose company and ventured down to the dining room one Saturday night for dinner. The Carstairs, friends of David's and hers, had insisted. Joe Carstairs wrote popular songs and had written hit tunes for Eddie Fisher and Johnny Ray. Laina looked glowing and lovely on this evening. Her conversation was witty and effervescent as she recited some of her new lyrics and told charming anecdotes about their recent production experiences.

Harlan and Vivian arrived a little later with a large party of people. Their table was at the other end of the deep porticoed dining room, visible from where Laina sat. As they grew loud and boisterous, her own conversation began to falter, to evanesce, until she realized the evening was over for her.

The following day she tried sitting at the pool area but felt chilly, not much like swimming. She recognized numerous old friends but for some reason avoided them. The sun, as always in early December, was unreliable and she felt suddenly cold. She put a beach dress over her scanty bathing suit and took the long, planked walk back to the hotel. In the lobby she meant to walk toward the elevators, but found herself instead walking in the direction of the executive offices.

The door opened easily. It was a Saturday and there were no secretaries or receptionists on duty. She walked directly into Harlan's office and enjoyed the surprised look on his face. He was on the telephone but he ended the conversation quickly. In the background the phonograph played the swelling strains of Mozart's *Abduction from the Seraglio*.

"What a pleasant surprise!"

"This seemed the simplest—the *only* way I could get to see you." She hated herself for her censorious tone, for sounding plaintive.

They sat across from one another, the large impersonal desk between them. Even an ocean would have seemed to her more easily transcended. This was not the frst time she had stopped by the office to see him, usually on one pretext or another. But this time she had none; her mood was suffused with immediacy.

"Let's have a drink," he said. This time she did not refuse. The burning liquid felt good going down, relaxing her. She could see that he looked tired and frazzled. She imagined that aside from his enormous business responsibilities lately, he might also have been called upon frequently to perform sexually, day and night, days with her, nights with his wife. Instead of being angry, she saw a strange grim humor in all this and was overcome by a sudden rush of tenderness for him. She went over to him, smoothed his hair from his eyes and said, "Poor darling, you do look tired."

"I am, I am indeed." He took another drink of the scotch. He pulled her down on his lap, his voice husky. "God, I've missed you."

"Oh, my love," she said.

His eyes were strangely bright, glittering green. She assumed by the bottle on the desk that he had been drinking for a long period of time; although not drunk, he had become feverishly sexual, treating her with an enveloping hot directness, which usually, and often against her will, had the power to create in her an

THE PLEASURE DOME

immediate, passionate response. He kissed her mouth, murmuring things, and guided her hand down to the thick hard bulge in his linen trousers. She stroked it.

"Oh, baby," he said, "what are you doing to me?" Through closed eyes he began to moan against her mouth.

Slowly he began to work her bathing suit bottoms down, and in a brief flash she remembered that other time, long ago. But it didn't seem to matter any longer. Nothing mattered now . . .

Suddenly the telephone rang, like a fire alarm in the absorbed silence, a warning signal.

By the way in which he suddenly straightened up and began patting his hair into place, a small boy caught with his fingers in the candy jar, she knew it was Vivian. He appeared to recover quickly, a fact that Laina resented. She sat up, rearranging her clothing, feeling chagrined. She had come here to collect, and she knew she would have done so, would have allowed it to happen then and there, had she not been restrained by Vivian's reprimanding ring.

She sat down again, unsteadily, on the other side of the desk where she belonged, and listened unabashedly to the conversation, something about new arrangements for taking the children somewhere; she blotted it out. It seemed to last interminably, as if he were doing penance by prolonging it. She envied the ease with which Vivian telephoned her husband at all hours, with no compunctions, while she herself froze whenever she phoned, her hand trembling, praying that he would pick it up, rather than some secretary. She envied his children their intimacy, his secretary her proximity. She knew it was time for her to leave, to go home, wherever that was.

Besides, she hadn't been feeling very well lately. She was tired and gripped by a terrible lethargy and she had a steady nagging ache in her lower back.

When she left the room he was still on the telephone. She let herself out the door, which she realized with a fresh shock, had not been locked. It was hotel policy to always keep the door of the executive office open, in order to be able to serve the guests at any and all times.

CHAPTER 40

She stepped outside and felt buoyant as the air. The city was enveloped in a sorcerer's vapor. Misty fumes blew back and forth from the rivers that ribboned the city darkly on either side. On Park Avenue in front of the doctor's building, she hailed a cab. But it was getting close to Christmas and all the cabs were occupied. Propelled by a careless, giddy joy, she began walking to her lunch appointment at Schrafft's on Fifty-seventh Street. Yet she was conscious of a painful and pervasive sense of deprivation and coaxed from her rusty memory recollections of her dead mother, so sweet as to be rapturous. She might have said she was behaving like a loose woman, leveled charges of adultery or fornication at her or washed her hands of her completely, considering her a *fallen woman*, married to one man and carrying another man's child.

At Schrafft's the room was packed with women carrying colorful shopping bags from local shops. The familiar green-and-white bags from F.A.O. Schwartz transported her with a tingling expectation. Her mind raced ahead to Davega's, where she had spent so many happy hours with her brother, browsing over swimming gear. Surely it would be a son.

Women's skirts grazed their ankles, as they obediently followed the newest dictates from Christian Dior in Paris. Caroline, herself sporting the "New Look," was already on the line. By way of greeting, she pulled Laina by the arm and said, "I've given my name to the hostess." Laina was not surprised. She knew that Caroline at the slightest provocation recited her new name, *Mrs. Craig Rosensweig*, as if it were a heraldic banner to be carried before her into the new world. Her new world was based on her marriage, and she often spoke of Craig chronologically, even historically, such as "before Craig" ("there was nothing" was usually the implication here), or like the Jewish refugees who crowded the city since the war and who measured time by only two criteria, "before the Germans" or "after the Germans." Just as "German" was their aphorism for evil, so Craig was her aphorism for good. Laina herself was in no position to scoff at obsession.

When they were finally seated, Caroline said, "You look positively radiant, Laina. What's doing?"

"Oh, nothing in particular." Laina hoped she could control her secret—keep it from bubbling to the surface of her tongue when it was already spilling over the surface of her being. "Just working on a new score. It's exciting."

"So that's it. Well, you look like the cat caught with the cream."

Laina was sorry now that she had agreed to meet Caroline on this particular day, after the doctor's appointment. She had known for weeks; going to the doctor had only been a formality. She would have preferred to have gone home and thought it all through carefully, alone; the strain of having to keep it secret, at least for a while, was painful. And yet she was not ready to share it, she could not bear to part with it. Bad enough that she had to open up for the doctor. To bare her deepest secrets to him, a stranger, for those few moments on the icy, clinical slab of table as if she were opening herself wide

THE PLEASURE DOME

enough for all the world to see inside her body, her soul.

Caroline chattered on about her new apartment, her new Dior suit, and occasionally flashed her diamond solitaire, which was considerably larger than Laina's; she never wore hers anymore. All about her were signs of the conspicuous consumption of Christmas—shopping bags bulging with treasures. Holiday finery bloomed everywhere, in the women's furs, their elaborate hats, their expensive scents. From the display shelves, red-cheeked, overstuffed Santas made false promises, their contents invariably disappointing.

She listened to Caroline with divided attention and wondered why she was so disinterested in the things that sustained other women. Perhaps Caroline or Faye was better suited to their sex than she.

Caroline had done very well for herself in the last two years. She had gone to Craig's parents to speak for Babs and had been most eloquent, but was relieved to find them unmoved, except to say how altruistic it was of Caroline to take such an interest in her friend "Barbara." She assured them she was doing it for Craig. She had gambled and it had paid off. Babs, in despair, had eloped with someone else, and Craig, on the rebound, married Caroline some months later. She seemed to have forgotten all about Laina's part in this little drama and had never thanked her. Caroline told herself that all that had gone before was immaterial, what counted was the result. But there were deep lines around her mouth that Laina had not noticed before. The waitress brought them home-style chicken salads and warm orange muffins.

Caroline hardly noticed. She seemed agitated. "Well, you've told me your news, about hatching another show; now I must tell you mine."

Laina suddenly felt faint. The cumbrous and overheated room began to close in on her. She was certain Caroline was going to tell her she was pregnant.

"Well, listen, you know that novel? The one I always spoke about writing? Well, I've written one hundred pages and it's been accepted by an agent. Gina Burnside, no less!" she cried victoriously. Caroline spoke about her writing as if she were ticking off items on a well-organized list, first, get a husband, second, get a novel published, third, have a baby.

Laina congratulated her warmly, knowing from experience that *this* was the easiest part. She wondered what Caroline could write about, sprung as she was from such thin soil.

"Well, I guess I've told you before, the novel is a family story, rather heavy on the mother-daughter relationship."

Laina didn't answer, but looked about her again at the ever-widening sea of women. The "New Look" made them look old. They looked prim and Mother Goose-like. She felt a pariah among these women, Hester Prynne among the good women of the town.

There was no question in her mind. She knew what she would have to do. She was changing. That she could even consider it told her that she was different than she might have been a month, a year, a lifetime ago.

David had been occupying the guest room of their apartment for the last four months. Except for their rather punctilious formality with one another, everything else appeared quite normal. They continued collaborating on their new score, a modernized version of *Twelfth Night*, and polishing up their current production for its Broadway debut. David had indeed replaced

Drake, and while the new lead was not as well known, he was probably better suited to the part. As to whether Russell had considered this a blow to his career was not known, but the press were told that his future commitments did not allow for a long Broadway run.

They had just returned home from a late supper with a few friends one evening after the performance. They had a lot of wine and a good spaghetti carbonara at the Italian restaurant around the corner from the theater. From their windows they watched the first uncertain powdering of December snow.

"Don't let's go to bed just yet," Laina said, handing him a glass of ruby red port. "Let's just sit here quietly and watch the snow on the water."

David came up and stood close to her. He kissed the palm of her hand. "Shall I make a fire?"

"That would be nice," she said pleasantly. Even this was a departure from her usual detached attitude when they were alone. They sat by the fire drinking port and making up zany lyrics about people they knew—there had been much salacious gossip and speculation about Delisio, the aging stage manager, who had been recently intruded upon backstage after a matinee, having one of his own with an extra. Laina sang:

Seems old Malcolm Delisio
Wasn't such an old gesio
When we found him astride that young thing . . .

"I'm stuck, c'mon David."

"Well, I don't know, the lyrics are your department, but let's see, how about this:

But time will soon tell,
If her belly doth swell
Then we'll know that he's younger than spring.

"Hey, how about that?" David said proudly. "Think you're indispensable, huh?"

David's lyrics were an unfortunate choice in her current state of mind, and brought her back rudely to reality. She forced herself to laugh. She moved closer to David and placed her cheek on his shoulder. He stroked her hair. She kissed his cheek and whispered, "David, I don't think I want to sleep in there alone tonight. I've been rattling around in that big bed of ours alone for too long."

David looked momentarily confused. "Well, by all means darling, but this is so sudden," he said, rumpling her hair playfully.

"We can't go on this way forever, it's impossible, for me, that is," she added with a tinge of acrimony.

"Well, I never dreamed that, that you would even consider—"

She grew immediately impatient with him. "Women are never entirely predictable, you know."

"So I've heard."

She began undressing the way women do when they sleep alone, hanging up—folding carefully on the right creases, tissuing off makeup, playing for time, putting off for tomorrow what she must do tonight. David undressed, displaying his white body, like Silvercup Bread. It seemed to fill her sphere of vision no matter where she fastened her eyes. He walked around unabashedly naked, attending to little odd jobs here and there as if reacquainting himself with the room before getting into bed. It was strange that she had never before perceived that he had a particularly flat-footed or clumsy walk.

In the large bed she lay close to him, her hand caressing his body until she felt him respond slightly. She forced herself to relax, to think about something—music, lyrics, water, waves washing, lapping rhythmically—to think of Harlan now would be a profanation of that love. When at last David entered her, her body was a daffodil retracting from darkness. She was acutely conscious of the fact that he was just obliging her, trying to make it all up somehow. Her insides were shut tight against invasion, making it almost impossible for him to accomplish the task she had set before him. It seemed like an eternity until he finally rolled over to his own place on the bed. Both were suffering combat fatigue. Quietly, without saying a word, he fell asleep. Only when she heard the sound of his even breathing did she relax and allow herself the luxury of thinking about the baby. She considered telling Harlan the truth, but almost immediately discarded that romantic notion as a luxury she could not afford, in favor of what would be best for the child's future. She was certain that security and parental love were the vital ingredients, all the more to be desired because she had never had it. Toward these ends she was willing to sacrifice anything.

CHAPTER 41

The new decade, the halfway mark of the century, was noted by a remarkable silence and disregard, and would be remembered in history, if at all, as the forgotten fifties, the silent generation. Spiritless words like restraint, tension, distrust, *détente*, abounded and the alphabetical jumble of NATO, SEATO, OSS, FBI, PCA, ADA, and last, but by no means least, HUAC, were bandied about blithely by radio and press.

After fighting a sad but beautifully righteous war, America was in the grip of an intense love affair with itself, and nothing or no one was going to subvert her principles or threaten her peace. Peace was translated as a split-level house in the suburbs, complete with self-defrosting refrigerator and a brand new Dodge station wagon in the two-car garage. They had fought too hard, risked too much. After Russia's explosion of the atom bomb, and the beginning of the Korean war, air raid shelters were revived and augmented against the Red Menace. Some built underground retreats, and America crawled into its television sets to hide from reality and to watch and to wait out a war of nerves.

In this climate of calumny, Faye hit upon the solution. It seemed so simple, so complete, that she could hardly believe that she had not seen it clearly before now. It was a time of neatly categorized heroes and villains, and for her Russell Drake had become a villain as surely as her mighty brother-in-law Harlan Chase.

THE PLEASURE DOME
* * *

In the outdoor garden of the Polo Lounge, Russell Drake leaned back against a palm tree and put his fingers through his hair in the boyish gesture that had thrilled women all over the world for the last decade. In the cruel white light of the California sun, without his stage makeup, he looked older than his thirty-three years. His agent, Cookie (Bill) Baum, sipped his gin and tonic thoughtfully, looking pale and perplexed. He had long ago dropped most of his other clients in favor of this veritable money machine.

"I can't understand it, Russ," he said, "it just don't figure. We were supposed to negotiate the two biggest contracts of your life out here—they were in the bag. And now, nothing, n-o-t-h-i-n-g!"

"Okay, okay, I know how to spell 'nothing.' So you've got to research it for me. You gotta go behind the scenes, get to work on it, doll," Russell said in his detached manner. "Anyway, nobody's said 'no' yet. Just wait, that's all, just wait."

Russell, whose tolerance for resort hotel life was endless, looked around appreciatively at the pink tableclothed garden, and the table of beautiful young women nearby. "And let's face it, this ain't such a bad place to wait," he said.

"Yeah, but we've been waiting for two months. We've been sitting here waiting. They don't pick up the tab at this joint." Cookie lowered his voice, "Wait'll you get the bill!"

Russell eyed a tall, handsomely dressed woman who passed the table.

"I'm not even concerned about your new record contract, although it is a beauty. It's the picture contract. You were gonna be a star, you always wanted that, Russ, didn't you?" Cookie was skinny and pale. His dun-colored hair rose in sparse, melancholy strands from a pink scalp. Frustration had solidified in white flecks around the corners of his mouth. They both fell silent.

Russell thoughtfully studied his fingernails. A gaggle of starlets paused to stare at him on the way to their table. He looked up languorously, assessed them quickly, and dropped his eyes back to his nails, his interest quickly flagging. After a while, everyone looked alike out here.

"Is there something you haven't told me that maybe I should know about? Nowadays everybody's past is catching up with them, somehow or other."

Cookie Baum looked sheepish. "Don't be sore, kid," he said.

Russell Drake looked hostile. "Who's sore? Why should I be sore?" Russell waved airily to a table of men. A producer director type waved back woodenly and went on talking frantically over plates heaped high with chopped salad. Russell wondered if there was something wrong with the teeth in the movie colony. The salads were so chopped up that they looked already chewed when they were served. The climate, the life out here, did that to you, made you lazy, unwilling or unable to face reality. He missed New York, with its insomnia and its smell of incipient rain.

It was hard for Russell to admit that he was in a way exiled out here, whether he liked it or not, at least until things cooled down a little with "The Family." He had looked forward to doing Broadway with his whole being. He had come so close, only to lose the whole thing. It rankled deep inside, but it was not his style to let it show. He wondered momentarily if a few "kicks," the passing of a dull afternoon, might possibly change the course of his

THE PLEASURE DOME

entire life. He knew he had lost out on Broadway because of the Goldmark incident—but here—how could the repercussions have possibly followed him here? He could not believe that Faye would go that far. He had confided in her from time to time, lightly, banteringly, regarding his youth, his poverty, his struggle to come up out of the Brownsville Jungle, but, Jesus, this was not the first time the possibility had occurred to him. Cookie's remark about everybody's past catching up with them brought it once again into sharp focus. Perhaps the agent noticed the trapped look on his client's usually passive face because he said, "Ah, forget it. Everybody's jumpy now since HUAC and all this shit." Russell caught Cookie's viscous gaze and dropped his eyes back to the glass table where a fly was slowly dying of boredom in the butter dish.

"Hey, Drake, I thought the one thing in life you really cared about was your career, your big, big talent?"

"What do you want me to do, kill myself?" Drake asked lugubriously. "And I was going to be a cantor." He shook his head philosophically.

"You haven't got the temperament for it."

"You mean I'm not emotional enough, huh? Well, I can twist your heart with a song, can't I? So?" Russell shrugged his cashmere shoulders. "That's all a cantor's got to do."

"Yeah—you really put your soul into a song." There was an irresolute pause. "But your life, that's different."

Russell ignored the implied criticism. "Look, I'll put some muscle on this, see what's holding things up."

"Yeah, because so far I'm in the dark, and you're not telling me anything."

"What's to tell? I had to eat, didn't I?" He lowered his voice to almost a whisper, and spoke as if from a long distance. "I did a stint with the Workers' Theatre in the Village one season in '39. I was just a green kid, it was a perfect job, the only job I could get then. I didn't know from politics, I just wanted to get on a stage, to make a buck."

"Why didn't you tell me this before?"

"I'm telling you now."

Cookie pushed his empty plate away, and knocked the pink packet of sugar three or four times against his cup to open it. Then irritably he tore off the top, and emptied the whole package into the coffee dregs with a trembling hand.

"Well, never mind. Maybe you could sing under an assumed name," he said hopefully.

CHAPTER 42

A fine golden silt of euphoria settled upon David Goldmark when Laina told him about the baby toward the end of January. He asked few questions. He was too happy. She had counted on that. She prayed that her pregnancy would not soon be visible and was repelled by her own treachery. She told David that she'd prefer to keep it secret a little longer as it was still so early. But what really pained and humiliated her was the fact that she still wished to continue her affair with Harlan, yet feared that once he found out, he would insist that she admit the child was his—and she would have to insist it was not; in either case there would be a confrontation that she was not ready to face. She doubted that he would ever leave Vivian, nor would she have wanted him to do so. Such a union, in the wake of the ensuing bitterness all around, would only produce resentment on his part. She must be circumspect and cautious. She must not allow her emotions to take over.

All of her cherished values had been undermined by this selfish, greedy passion. She did not dare yet to dignify it with the word "love," although it was the only love she had ever known. She pretended to herself that it had nothing to do with the complete sexual gratification she experienced with him. She was convinced that she could let go only with him, certain that she was inviolate during that brief, terrifying loss of control.

She continued to bury herself in her work, on the new score, on the Broadway production that had recently opened to more good reviews. Still she found time to spend frequent afternoons and evenings, even some weekends, with Harlan. The months passed this way, and she was not entirely unhappy. She rationalized that what she was doing was not immoral as long as it remained undiscovered and no one was hurt by it. She simply dismissed the fact that she shared her life with two men, neither of whom could be a complete husband to her. She was used to being torn. It was a part of life. She had been divided between her parents as far back as she could remember.

By the early spring it was difficult for her to fit into her clothes. She fought buying maternity clothes by letting out her dresses or buying new ones in larger sizes. David was anxious to tell their parents the news.

"Soon," she said. "I'm superstitious about these things." She wished to tell Harlan first. As it turned out, she didn't need to.

Harlan had to fly out to the coast to look over the Nash resort hotel in San Diego, and saw it as the perfect opportunity to be with Laina for four or five days. He knew that she and David were interested in getting their show produced as a movie, and set up an appointment for her at Twentieth Century Fox. David did not want her to go alone and thought it was important enough to warrant them both being present. She reminded him gently of their agreement, and reluctantly he gave in.

She could barely imagine California . . . Movie stars, sunburned desert wastes. But it was another first experience to share with Harlan. As a child she had rarely traveled. Her father was always too busy. He had been perfectly happy with the usual circuit, New York, Miami and Broadbeach. Who could ask for anything more?

When she got to Los Angeles, she found it a city strangely lacking in vitality. At the gracious old Bel-Air Hotel, deliberately half-hidden by its jungle of foliage, she waited for Harlan. Fireplaces burned comfortably day and night in the lobby and dining room. She was surprised by the chill of the air. Low Spanish-style buildings were joined by trellised walkways encrusted with ivy. Wandering these paths alone, she was reminded of Camp Choctaw. How strange it seemed that in all these years so much had happened, and yet nothing had really changed. *Plus ça change, plus c'est la même chose.* She was still waiting for, still dreaming of, the same flawed hero of her adolescence.

He came up from San Diego then, and brought the sun with him, white and hot and out of character for March. Officially, he was still checked into the Nash Hotel in San Diego.

In her bungalow she stood naked by the window while Harlan slept, gazing out at the riotous sunset through the plume-topped giant palms. A waiter was passing by, carrying a tray of food. She moved the drape across her body, then let it drop again. She was suddenly aware of Harlan's eyes upon her, appraising her silently from the bed.

"Why didn't you tell me?"

"Tell you what?"

"That you are to have a child."

She pulled the drapery about her and looked at him innocently.

"It is quite easy to see. I know every line of your body by heart. I have watched it changing gradually in the last few months." He was sitting up against the pillow and said in a husky voice. "If anything, it makes you lovelier than ever."

She turned to him and came over to the bed. She covered herself quickly with a satin negligee, but before she could close it, he drew her against him and gently massaged her ripe breasts.

"And you feel different inside, too, more silken. Your body is preparing itself for the rites of passage." His voice was soft and sounded far away. "Why have you kept it from me?"

"I would have told you soon enough."

"When, after the child is born?" he asked, still stroking her breasts, fascinated by the enlarged and puffed areola around the nipple, symptomatic of pregnancy. His eyes narrowed. "It must be almost five months, I would say. Is that right?"

"I forgot you were an expert on such matters." She wanted to change the subject.

"And precisely what has your husband said?"

"My husband? He is delighted."

Harlan raised quizzical eyebrows. "Delighted?" He laughed richly. "Delighted that you are to have my child?"

"That *we* are to have a child, David and I."

"Stop it. You are talking to me now, not some Broadway press agent. You know it is a lie."

"How can you be so sure?"

"Because you would have had to be with him from the moment you returned from our trip and somehow I don't see such an impassioned reunion after . . . after everything." His voice dropped. "That is, knowing him and believing, as I do, what you feel for me."

At these words, spoken so tenderly and ingenuously,

THE PLEASURE DOME

she longed to crumple against him, to cry that, of course, it was his child, that it could be no other. She fought the temptation and said instead, "Been with him? How quaint."

He remained silent, unamused. He pushed her chin up so that she was forced to meet his eyes.

"Why don't you want me to know the truth?"

"What good could it possibly do?" she said.

"I will know when the child is born."

"Not necessarily." She was aware that she was taunting him and took small pleasure in it.

"The flesh makes fools of us men, I suppose," he said with unusual humility. She sensed his resentment of the sexual hold women have over men.

The subject of Vivian was taboo between them. Harlan had decreed it. It was more convenient for him. Laina had convinced herself that it was not love that bound him and Vivian, but familiarity. At times, she broke the rule. "How come Vivian doesn't make any of these trips with you?"

"Laina, please don't." He stroked her cheek lovingly. She pulled away. "Well?"

"She would not want to leave the children," he said flatly.

What he did not say was that Vivian had fallen so completely in love with marriage and motherhood that she had forgotten about being a wife. He was disappointed. In her desire to please him, she had lost sight of the world outside. He felt vaguely that she had somehow let him down.

When Harlan went to the resort hotel in San Diego, he was extremely impressed by what he saw, not so much by the buildings, but by the vast amounts of land it encompassed. He foresaw rebuilding it into a huge complex similar to the Broadbeach, with summer homes that sprawled all around the main building. Here the climate made year-round enjoyment possible; the hotel business need not be seasonal. The homes he would build and sell would be connected to the hotel in that it would use its facilities and services.

It was a new real estate concept, one he felt certain would be successful. The hotel would need plenty of money and plenty of work; he would have to decide whether to begin by putting money in the hotel itself, in order to attract a smart new clientele, or to build first and use some of that money for the hotel. He knew he was getting ahead of himself. After the merger went through, he would worry about that. Right now the merger had to be officially approved.

When Harlan stopped by the Beverly Hills Hotel to see the man from Twentieth on business there, he ran into Russell Drake in the lobby. Drake greeted him warmly and drew him into a corner. He told him his hard luck story and asked Harlan to check into it for him, to use his influence, to put back into action his proposed contracts if possible. Harlan promised to do what he could, Russell Drake appeared so hopeless.

CHAPTER 43

When Marc Anselmo left New York at the end of August, he was in an absolute bind. Only divine intervention could get him out. He seriously doubted that there would be any of that, because he knew himself to be far out of favor with the good Lord. He was painfully conscious of the fact that by sneaking around with a nun he had desecrated the church, and even more important, demeaned the woman herself.

At first Marc had thought to tell his uncle the simple truth, though not all of it: He wanted to change his life-style, he wanted to surrender his rather elaborate existence for a simple one. He had not planned to tell him about Janine, but in the finale he had to tell the whole truth, to fall upon his mercy, what there was of it.

In the meantime, he worried that his presence would cause conflict, that it would be difficult for her to transcend from the spiritual to the real world. He had made promises in the first flush of rediscovered passion that were not within his power to fulfill. Guilt and indecision kept him in a constant state of depression.

But he could not bring himself to make the decision to tell his uncle and take his chances. He had visions of Janine giving up the church, relinquishing everything she had once loved for him, only to become a young widow, once again dressed in black. If they had a child—The possibilities were endless and too potentially volatile for him to contemplate. He wished to extricate himself from his former life gingerly, without subterfuge, but he was convinced that no one ever left the organization other than in a long pine box accompanied by a car full of roses. He knew only that he was being watched day and night and that he was probably doomed to a life for which he was ill suited and a death for which he was ill prepared.

It was not until May, after an absence of almost a year and only a few carefully worded letters, that Janine received a short note from Marc, informing her he would be there within a few weeks.

Joe Campano, made intensely jumpy by crime committee hearings, had to be in Miami to testify. To assuage his guilt, he had reluctantly agreed to let Marc "visit his mother" again. But he preferred to keep an eye on him at all times. Joe figured the boy knew all kinds of things he shouldn't. Maybe the boy even harbored bitterness about the past . . .

Janine knew she could not remain indefinitely with the sisters, suspended in her private purgatory. She did not wish to use them as a place of sanctuary, although Mother Blanche had made it quite clear that the Fields of Grace was indeed a sanctuary, if one wished to accept its succor.

She was still struggling with decisions that seemed new and strange to her when she received a telephone call from her mother that seemed to bring everything to the surface at once. She asked her to come home immediately. James Chase was dying.

Janine was, of course, granted a compassionate leave from the convent. When she arrived at her parents' home, Harlan and her sisters were already there. Her mother embraced her silently and they went into the

THE PLEASURE DOME

small bedroom where James lay, a crucifix above his head.

Janine came out alone. It had been three years since she had last seen Harlan and she was pleased to find him alone. Her sisters had gone into the kitchen to prepare something for lunch.

"Why didn't you bring Vivian?"

"She doesn't feel she belongs here at a time like this, that perhaps we want to be alone together." He looked down as he spoke and seemed uneasy.

"It doesn't matter. Go in there now and make up with father while there's still time; otherwise you'll feel guilty for years to come and God knows we all carry around enough guilt as it is."

Harlan looked at her curiously, perhaps wondering what someone as unblemished as she could have to be guilty about.

"No, no, I can't feel guilty where he's concerned, he's been too stubborn all his life. Even now. He shouldn't have been working as a night watchman those terrible hours, suffocating in a uniform in this heat. He should have retired years ago."

"He couldn't afford to, I suppose," Janine said.

"That's what I mean. I sent him checks every month. He sent them back unopened. I finally stopped sending them."

"Shh." She put her fingers to her lips. He lowered his voice.

"Did you ever receive a visit from Marc Anselmo? He said he wanted to see you; he couldn't believe it when I told him."

"Yes, yes I did."

Harlan looked at her questioningly. Her eyes were

349

veiled; she was wearing her black habit and suddenly seemed to be receding into its folds.

"I am giving up the church, Harlan. Perhaps you were right, it was not my vocation."

"So," he said slowly. "You are finally disenchanted. You got it out of your system."

Janine smiled. "In a sense you are right I suppose. I do not feel the joys of my faith anymore, only its sorrows. And I've grown to love it less there, instead of more. Marc and I are to be married soon. I have already told Mother Blanche," she said in a brave rush of breath.

Harlan looked shocked and then pleased. He took her in his arms and then kissed her. He whispered, "You will never regret it, I know."

"This is a poor time for confessions," she said, "so for the rest of the family it must come later."

"What will he do . . . for a living, Janine?"

She noticed that he spoke in the future as if the past were automatically buried. "We have thought of nothing else," she said.

"I can help."

"I don't know if it's quite that easy, but yes, yes, that would be a solution! Thank you, Harlan," she said with humility. "He will be here soon and you can talk to him." She reached up and kissed his cheek.

After her husband's death, Marjorie Chase decided to remain in the house. She owned it outright now, free and clear. "James would have wanted it that way," she said. Janine had made a momentous decision, and it was at a time when she, Marge, could use her solace and company. She saw the hand of God in this, as in all things. He had taken one loved one from the world and returned another.

So Janine returned to her small room at home, where

THE PLEASURE DOME

faded holy pictures jostled for space on the wall with idols of her adolescence—Glenn Miller, Tyrone Power. She did not know how to break the news to her mother concerning Marc. She could not even gentle her into it slowly; it had not been a conventional courtship.

Marc had spent long hours promising himself that when he saw her after so many months, he would approach her more circumspectly. He would explain only that he was working it out somehow, that it was not quite as simple as he thought it would be.

In the long grass on the beach by her home, he held her in his arms. She wore a thin, cotton shift, interim clothing she had found around the house. He promised himself that they would only talk here, but all rational plans had been washed away by the power of the moment and by the sense of urgency they shared. Time was running out mercilessly while they were both so young.

Finally, his own honor made him decide. He insisted on setting a wedding date in early fall, when he returned for his two-week summer visit with his mother. Harlan's offer had helped them crystallize their plans. He could work on the gambling boat or any number of other hotel jobs with which he was vaguely familiar. Even Marge Chase accepted, seemed to rejoice in the fact that Janine was to be married to Marc Anselmo, whom she now said she had always liked. At least her daughter had substituted one holy order for another, even if the substitute was a vast demotion.

When Joe Campano returned to Las Vegas from the subcommittee hearings, he was not at all satisfied that his appearance there, before those venerable gentlemen, had put the matter to rest. He knew better than that. The heat was on. Now the FBI would take over where the committee left off. And they would aim for the weakest link in the chain, the younger members who were more inexperienced, more idealistic. He immediately thought of his nephew Marc Anselmo. Marc had been looking to break away, to go straight—Christ, to come clean. Maybe he could even wind up on TV, talking his heart out to the committee in his new misguided purity. Joe figured his change of attitude probably had something to do with a broad. He'd have to check it out. The kid had funny tastes anyway; never hung around much with the show broads. Christ! The gorgeous tomatoes he could have had. They were crazy about him, but he didn't seen to care. He liked money all right, and easy living . . . but broads? There *had* been a young girl once, the sister of that hotel big shot, Chase, yeah, that was it. Except in those days he was no big shot, just a big Irish swim kid.

In his suite at the Gold Rush Hotel, of which he owned a sizable piece, Joe chomped on his soggy cigar and called in his mistress, Mala Marshall. Mala came immediately at his summons, obedient and kittenish. She was small and auburn-haired, with sentient blue eyes. She had started her career in the hotel's burlesque show, at least ten years ago. But Joe had plucked her from the chorus and installed her here in this apartment as his mistress, five years ago. She seemed to have a real affection for Joe, and in fact had already borne him one child (a girl) and was pregnant with another.

He pulled her down on his lap and kissed her affectionately. "Hey, look's like you're getting quite a gut there," he said, patting her stomach. "Yeah, how about that, honey? How about that?"

"Joe, have you thought about you know, what you promised. You gotta do it, Joe, for me, for the kids."

THE PLEASURE DOME

Joe Campano looked uncomfortable. He was, after all, a married man, had been for some twenty-five years or so. Beatrice, his wife, Beatrici, as he still called her, was a good woman. Together they were already grandparents of three beautiful children. She kept their nice house in Reno spotless, cooked delicious meals like her mother in the old country had taught her. It was like taking a vacation to go home on certain weekends, or sometimes even for weeks at a time—a wonderful pick-me-up from the lunacy of his Vegas life. No, he liked everything just the way it was. He didn't see why he would have to change anything now . . . so late in his life . . .

"Look, Joe," she said, "I meant what I said about leaving you, taking the kids away so that you'll never see them again."

"Mala, what are you saying? You know I'll always take care of you and the kids, you'll never have to worry."

She sat up. Her full red lips pouted and she pushed a lock of hair away from her eyes. "Joey, it's just not enough. The kids gotta be legitimate. We gotta get married, or that's it for us, and I mean it. Besides, you promised, you said when I first told you about this one, that the kids would have a father."

Joe was silent, he thought a moment, a crazy solution that had been slowly taking shape in his mind had begun to dominate his thinking. "I didn't say we'd get married, baby, I said the kids would be legitimate, and I meant it."

She looked perplexed. She jumped up from his lap and sat decorously opposite him on the large circular red velvet sofa.

"I don't gettcha, Joey."

"Well, I ain't even talked to him about it yet, so I don't know for sure, mind you, but I was thinking, my nephew is single." Joe blew a smoke ring and poked it in the air with his index finger. "You'll like the kid. In fact, he's just about your same age—thirty-two or three, I think, and a hell of a good-looking kid, a heartbreaker. In fact, that's the only trouble. I don't trust you with him...."

"Stop." She jumped up. "Stop—I must be going crazy," she said, "plain crazy!"

"Wait a minute, hold on there, Mala. What's so crazy? I didn't say it would have to last forever—just till the kid is born."

"The kid?" she shrieked. "Look, what do you think? I'm some leftover piece of baggage that nobody wants, who you can palm off on your poor relations? No, Joey, it's gonna be *you* or no one."

The psychology here was sound, and Uncle Joe Campano was for the moment quite touched. He might have abandoned the whole idea if it hadn't been for a series of events that all came together to show him the way, the only way to tie up the many loose ends.

CHAPTER 44

Harlan was going ahead with the merger. He had called a meeting to put it to a final vote the following week. It seemed only a formality now; everyone was certain of the outcome. Vivian was torn, and could not understand Matthew's stubborn and unreasoning resistance. It could only benefit him financially in the long run, and if her husband followed through according to plan, they would still have controlling interest in the hotels, plus a fortune of cash in the bargain. Vivian remembered her father's letter. This was what Jessie would have wanted also.

Matthew and Faye had spent most of the winter at the Palm Beach place. Now in May they were in Miami to help with the unexpected and unseasonal influx of guests due to the Kefauver Crime Commission hearings that had just opened to the public.

Matthew lay wide-eyed, staring up at the ceiling. It seemed to him that he hadn't slept for months, maybe longer. He knew he was terribly tired but could only sleep a few hours at a time. All night he worried that he would not be able to cope with what the next day might bring. His wife was sleeping deeply beside him. He did not know that this was the first really good night's sleep she had had in months. She had finally found the solution to her vendetta and she slept the sleep of the dead—joyless, dreamless, benumbed. After hours of tossing and turning, Matthew rose and walked into the living room and poured himself one drink and then another. He began to relax but decided that as soon as he hit the bed his heart would start pounding in anticipation of not sleeping. He went into the dressing room and foraged around in the medicine cabinet until he found the Seconals. One usually afforded him at least four hours of uninterrupted sleep, so he reasoned that two would make him sleep eight hours, give him that big sleep he craved, needed so desperately to—to—he really didn't know exactly what he needed. He had not been seeing the therapist Dr. Zabar as he had promised Faye, and had broken the last three appointments with him.

Matthew thought vaguely that the pills were working this time and assumed it was the emptiness of his stomach, or the scotch. So he took a few more: When you had a good thing, why not run with it to the end, the very end? He thought about the board of directors' meeting next week, the vote. He took a few more.

He groped his way back to the bed. He lay down and closed his eyes.

Faye usually slept until ten at least. But today at eight she awoke with a heaviness in her stomach and her heart pounding in her ears. She was perspiring profusely, and thought that she was finally in menopause. She stirred and was surprised to see Matthew beside her. She called his name and tried to roll him over. His shoulder felt icy cold through the thin cotton fabric of his pajamas.

Faye sat up quickly, her breath coming in gasps. She ran into the bathroom and saw the empty Seconal vial on the sink top. She ran back to the bed, tried shaking him, massaging his chest, his hands. Circulate the blood, she thought wildly. He was barely breathing. She put her mouth to his; she was herself gasping for air. First she called the ambulance, then she called her brother-in-law. What else could she do? She was at least glad it had happened here at the Hibiscus Gardens where there was someone to turn to for direction.

As soon as they arrived, they pumped his stomach, and while his eyes fluttered and his body twitched its displeasure, he would not return to consciousness.

In the ambulance, she and Harlan sat flanking the stretcher that bore a waxen-faced Matthew, while the orderly kept trying artificial respiration. Harlan was suddenly uncomfortable, seized by the age-old Biblical concept of Jew as victim . . .

Matthew might not have pulled through if it had not been for prompt medical attention and Faye's solicitude. After an attempted suicide, he was required by law to go to a sanitarium for rehabilitation for a given period of time. So he checked into the famous and elegant Silverwood Clinic in Maryland. Dr. Zabar had arranged it.

His vote would be solicited by proxy if necessary within three weeks, in time for the board meeting on June 21.

CHAPTER 45

Laina Goldmark was on her way out of Sloan's contemporary furniture department. It was nearly closing time. She was doing the nursery now and had come to look for a bureau and mirror. She had long ago purchased the crib, and it waited expectantly in the soldier-blue carpeted room.

As she passed through the aisles of Swedish modern furniture into Early American, she thought she saw Vivian Chase coming toward her, but without her glasses she could not be certain. She quietly turned around and for lack of anything more absorbing, studied a small Baroque wall mirror. She had not seen Vivian for many months. She had almost completely stopped going to the hotels. She decided that she must be hallucinating, her conscience perhaps. She had been with Harlan only last night. David was out of town, plugging the music for the new show.

In the mirror she saw Vivian bearing down on her relentlessly. She thought the mirror must be distorted, because Vivian's usually neat, compact body appeared swollen and shapeless.

"Laina, what a surprise."

Laina whirled around to face her.

"We haven't seen you anywhere for ages."

The royal "we," used so confidently, tunneled into her confusion. She had been with half of that "we" the night before.

THE PLEASURE DOME

Before Laina could answer, Vivian said merrily, "Will you look at the two of us? I'm nearly as big as you, and you must be almost in your seventh month, am I right?" She chattered on compulsively without waiting for answers. "I just went into my fourth and couldn't wait to get into this," she said, indicating her maternity jacket. "I was suffocating in my own clothes."

Laina thought she might faint right there amid the sea of solid sofas and reliable daybeds, swoon, as in days gone by, when it was expected of pregnant women.

"How . . . how are the children?"

"Wild, of course," she said.

"But boys will be boys. I'm hoping for a girl this time." She lowered her voice confidentially. "You know Steven, my first, was from *abandon,* the second child was due to *carelessness,* but the third was very much *planned!*" She laughed, a satisfied, secret laugh.

A salesman brushed by with some customers.

"Perhaps we are in the way here with our two bellies," Vivian said giggling conspiratorially. Laina was struck by the change in Vivian through the years. How childish women became who made marriage and children their careers, living in a vacuum of mutual over-protection. "Will you walk me into rugs?"

As rugs were on the way out, Laina agreed. "How is Matthew feeling? I haven't seen him since the hospital, though David says he's coming along nicely."

"Oh yes, Matthew will be fine, just fine," Vivian said. Her excessive cheerfulness was depressing. Laina noted Vivian's radiant face; there was no doubt that she had grown prettier with the years. She tried to keep her eyes averted from her breasts, but observed that she seemed to have developed them with this pregnancy. She colored with embarrassment at her own grudging thoughts. Why should she look upon this woman as the interloper, when it was really she? Laina felt too guilty to be abrupt and suddenly leave, but longed to find an avenue of escape.

"I suppose you can guess what I'm doing here," Vivian said, lowering her voice to suit the awesome silence created by the drowning plush of carpet.

"Nursery furniture?" Laina asked weakly. She couldn't think of anything else, anything more final or more extinguishing.

"Well, not really. I can use the boys'. They've outgrown cribs and that sort of thing. Didn't anyone tell you? We're finally getting a place of our own. We just can't stay in a hotel suite forever." She continued her harrowing soliloquy, lightly patting her small drumlike belly. "The hotels are really not the right atmosphere for growing boys. We just bought a house in Oyster Bay. Actually, it's more than a house, sort of an estate—on the water—with our own dock. But you know Harlan, he likes to do everything in a big way."

Laina, had she felt less numb, might have been wildly amused by the black humor in that last unfortunate expression. But Laina only said no, she hadn't heard. She could barely hear what Vivian was saying now. All her senses seemed to have clamped shut, the flow of life turned off like death.

"Listen, let's get together, all of us. We never see you two anymore."

Laina stumbled out into the steamy, violet dusk. As she walked listlessly up Fifth Avenue, she suddenly found herself laughing, laughing aloud in the streets, like a drunkard, unable to shake the image of the two of them stranded there in the middle of a vast desert of Bessarabian and broadloom, both made swollen and shapeless by the same seed.

CHAPTER 46

When Faye first approached Harlan with her knowledge of his affair, he only laughed—shrugged it off as nonsense, "the figment of an overactive imagination," he said, "the product of extreme idleness." After all, her life had been little more than an endless vacation. Reality had not affected her very much. His total rejection of her theory, which he said was based on hearsay and innuendo (she had no proof and he knew it), was only an extension of what he had done through the years—ignored her. She would never have admitted it, but it was probably what drove her blindly on her relentless course.

Faye considered going to Vivian but discarded the idea, in light of Vivian's condition. She had no wish to be gratuitously cruel. It would accomplish nothing and might only succeed in hurting David. Instead, she took her bizarre story straight to Alex Eastman. She could trust Eastman to be circumspect. He would never say or do anything to compromise his daughter.

For weeks in advance she reasoned with herself that it was time she did something constructive, something for her husband, her family. Until now she had been too mired in her own greedy, sensual self-absorption. Once she had fixed the decision firmly in her mind, she felt suddenly alive again. She had helped her son's marriage by removing the temptation of Russell Drake. Now she would go to the aid of her poor beleagured husband. It was time.

By the beginning of June, Alex was already at his suite at the Broadbeach Hotel. He enjoyed the preseason weeks at the beach, beating the stifling city heat, having it, vast and gorgeous, to himself, as if it were a great private estate. He was in fact enjoying his life lately. Business at the dance halls was picking up, his private life was satisfactorily uncomplicated, and he was overjoyed at the prospect of becoming a grandfather in a few months. Alex was a happy man, at least as happy as he could be. He was happiest when working with Harlan, whom he loved almost as a son, and admired—*almost* as a friend.

So Faye decided to tell Alex an old, old story. At first she talked about "this man and this girl," testing to see how much he already knew, or how much more she could learn. But he seemed bewildered, uncertain as to whether he had been told an allegory or just an ugly fairy tale dreamed up by this woman he considered a rather over-ripe sex kitten.

"Why are you telling me this?" He sidestepped the issue, his mind closed up against her words.

"Christ, Alex, I'm telling you the *true* story of what really happened that night when Harlan supposedly *saved* your daughter's life. He saved her alright! For himself!" Faye was becoming exasperated with Alex's stubborn refusal to comprehend. "He took advantage of her weakened condition and raped her—a fifteen-year-old girl, that's what he did. And because of the war, he got away with it. He was able to get himself lost in the marines, and he got away with it! And he's lived happily ever since—screwing her—you—*all* of us!" she cried in a mounting fury, overwhelmed with the feeling of their exploitation.

Alex tried to keep calm, conscious of his awkward

THE PLEASURE DOME

position in all this. He must be careful not to humiliate his daughter by believing such crazy gossip. Alex did not even believe it. He remembered Laina's bitterness and resentment against Chase over the years. He threw his hand at her in a deprecating gesture.

"It is too incredible," he shouted at her. "He's not the type. He could have had any woman he wanted."

"Perhaps *that* was the point—who knows? Then was then—and now is now."

"Precisely," Alex replied wearily. "It is better to let sleeping dogs lie, to let the past bury the past. Even if it were true, what effect could it possibly have on our lives now? What are you trying to say?"

She thought for a moment. "Only that this man in whom you've entrusted so much is hardly worthy of such blind trust."

"He is if he produces," Alex said stubbornly, pretending disinterest in anything but commerce.

But the seeds had been planted and Alex brooded strangely, sorting out his guilts. He had been so busy in his relentless pursuit of the American Dream that he had neglected the children in their most terrible time of need. After Inez, after everything, he should have been there to sustain them. Then perhaps Seth would have lived and Laina would not now be struggling against a traumatized adolescence. Bitterness crept into his heart.

"You were amusing yourself with us," he said to Harlan later, when he took this revelation to him, hoping for a firm denial. Strange, but they were the same words Faye had spoken to Russell Drake . . . "How you must be laughing at us," Alex said, nodding his head with a stoic acceptance.

"I have suffered too, Alex. Every time I see you, even more, every time I see her," Harlan replied.

"You are a crazy animal," he said with disgust. "You have colored her whole life by this one selfish act. Now she is tied to a man she does not love, *and* to one she does."

"So you know everything?"

"Enough. I have watched her hate you enough to know what was just on the other side."

"What could Faye hope to accomplish by this?" Harlan asked.

"Obviously, to discredit you so that I would not vote in favor of the merger." Alex sat down wearily. He suddenly felt old. He seemed to be talking to a distant corner of the room. "I figured I could do it right. Hand her life, happiness, security, all wrapped in white. David seemed so . . . so sensible and I knew she was frightened, though I didn't know why, needed protection. I wanted her to have everything, everything that her mother and brother would never have." His head shot up. "And now I learn this—you bastard—she was all I had left. You took advantage of us." His voice cracked between pain and anger. "There are names for men like you—and special places." His eyes looked bloodshot. Harlan came over and stood next to where he sat in his chair.

"You've got to let her go, Alex, you've got to let her make her own mistakes. She's all grown up now," he said quietly.

"No, it's *you* who've got to let her go."

Harlan rose and went to the window. The ocean rolled docilely in a steady, sleepy motion. "I have no choice, she's finished with me, I think."

"Why?"

"I don't know. She fears scandal—for the child she is expecting—and Vivian—Vivian is pregnant."

"Christ," Alex said. "How can you stand yourself?"

"Does it help if I tell you that I love her?"

Alex fixed him with a black look. "You haven't the right."

"What have rights got to do with this?"

"Was it out of love that you ruined her life?"

They both fell silent for a moment. Alex wondered if there would ever be anything else to say to Harlan Chase again.

"Why didn't you talk to Laina about this first?" Harlan asked, still gazing out of the window.

"I didn't want to further humiliate her, damage our relationship by privy knowledge. And I knew that she would not tell me the truth. I knew I would get the truth only from you. Somehow I sensed you have always wanted me to know—it makes our relationship more exciting to you—the element of risk involved."

Harlan sat down in a chair across from Alex. He leaned forward and asked, "What will you do now?"

"I don't know, you have lost credibility with me. I don't feel like entrusting you with my business—*my life.*"

"If you pull out now, it can ruin me."

"Yes, I know," Alex said. He wondered if Faye knew that if he broke with Harlan now, sold all his shares on the open market, it could drive the price down dangerously low, destroy the merger.

"And it can ruin Matthew too," Harlan said.

Alex looked up in amazement. "Matthew? I thought we were to buy him out."

Harlan shook his head. "I took some seventy-five thousand dollars he lost on my ship and bought stock for him—and since then have been buying steadily for him in his name."

Alex was disarmed by this confession of altruism from

what he considered so unlikely a source; then he saw that the gesture was not purely unselfish. It was an insurance policy of sorts, sealing off all avenues of conflict.

"You too will take a terrible bath in the stock."

"I still have my dance halls."

"They are not worth much anymore; that's why you were planning to sell them to Nash, along with our hotels, remember? Probably net us some six million dollars."

Alex looked away from the drilling green eyes. His voice wavered like an old man's. "Still, I don't want to enmesh my life with yours any longer. You remind me of everything I want to forget—money is not that important to me." He said this cautiously, as if consideration were needed.

"Come now, Alex, you're talking to me." Harlan was not a callous man. He sensed Alex's dilemma between love and money and was providing him with a way out. "Would you want to have it on your conscience that you ruined the father of your grandchild?"

Alex looked genuinely shocked. "Is that true? Did Laina tell you this?"

Harlan did not reply directly. Instead he said, "You wouldn't want to take the chance, would you?"

The most bitter frustration of Alex Eastman's life had always been choosing between love and money. The whole conversation had been a traumatic reminder of that inner turmoil. Alex covered his face with his hands and wept aloud.

The deal with Nash went through on schedule, with only Matthew and Faye against it; Harlan, Vivian and Alex voted in favor of it. Matthew considered it only a formality, a foregone conclusion, one that he had arrived

THE PLEASURE DOME

at the day his father's will was read. Jessie had set him up for failure. The strange thing about it was he didn't realize how close he had come to regaining control of his hotels. Alex had not decided until the ballot was placed before him and even then, he voted almost without will. He had to remind himself sharply that he had never before made a business decision predicated upon emotion, and he certainly couldn't afford that luxury now.

No sooner had the deal been consummated than Goldmark Enterprises gave way to Pleasure Domes, Inc. The next official act of the new corporation was to sell to Pleasure Domes a package consisting of their four resort hotels plus Alex's string of dance halls, thrown in to fatten the calf. For this, Alex, Harlan and Matthew would receive some six million dollars, a figure set by an investment banking concern, minus the assumption of the mortgages by Pleasure Domes, Inc.

Harlan would have preferred to sell the package for stock in order to circumvent the enormous tax involved, but Alex was unwilling to gamble any further. He had gone about as far as he would go with Harlan. He needed to see immediate results—to assuage his fears. His share of the deal netted him personally over two million dollars, a considerable sum for a business that had been slowly dying of attrition. Harlan felt he had repaid his debt to Alex Eastman, even the old debt.

In July Laina was delivered of an eight-pound baby boy. She named the baby Warren David, as if incorporating his imputed father's name might somehow validate him, indemnify the child against the vicissitudes of life.

CHAPTER 47

For the first time in years Harlan felt impotent. Impotent with a rage that grew out of unfamiliar frustration. He had forgotten how debilitating disappointment could be. He had grown so used to winning that he had forgotten how to handle failure. He had always feared that when his luck ran out, it would go suddenly and without warning. The recent disclosure of his past, the attendant humiliation, the problems with Matthew, his own abiding guilt, and more than anything else, Laina's rejection, particularly her refusal to let him see the child, to acknowledge it as his, threw him into a despair that sapped his very being. He had grown accustomed to turning to her for solace. In her arms nothing seemed as urgent, or as threatening. Why was it that just when he needed her she rejected him so bitterly? He blamed the child, felt a surging resentment against his own son, and yet longed to see the child, to hold it, if only once. He was, after all, a man who loved children.

He was spending more and more time out west, implementing plans that centered around the old Nash Hotel. Vivian had burrowed even deeper into domesticity with her pregnancy. He frequently invited her to accompany him on these trips, but with her heavy decorating schedule and advancing pregnancy, she always declined. The occasional promiscuity engendered by these solo trips usually left him unsatisfied and feeling strangely truculent.

He had returned from California and was leaving the 21 Club after an evening with a couple of friends from the university where he had coached immediately after the war. He did not relish the prospect of the long drive out to Oyster Bay in his present condition, a combination of travel fatigue and alcohol. Maybe he was looking for an excuse not to go home just yet. He was not certain just where he would go or what he would do. He remembered Vivian mentioning casually that David was out of town on business . . . Harlan's mind raced with thoughts of David's sort of business—probably some young boy—as he maneuvered the car almost without will to Sutton Place. It eased the way for him, reinforced the justice of his sudden whim. She was, after all, he reasoned, a whim that had become an obsession.

Laina sat quietly in a large chair in the living room, nursing her two-month-old son. It was the ten o'clock feeding and she was thoroughly absorbed in the act. The baby's tiny clenched fist translated the reciprocal satisfaction the moment brought. The upturned toes were pink and tense. She looked up suddenly when she heard the disruptive sound of a key in the lock. Harlan walked in, looking flushed and disheveled, and closed the door behind him. He was limping slightly. She looked up in amazement, but tried to stay calm for the sake of the infant.

"Ah, Madonna and child," he said, feigning a gaiety he did not feel. "How lovely."

She could see that he was slightly drunk. She forced

herself to keep her voice down. "How did you get in here? I—I don't understand."

"Very simple, my girl. I told David before he left that one afternoon Vivian might need a place in town to freshen up while she's decorating, in light of her condition, that is. He never hesitated for a moment."

She moved her hand protectively about the baby's downy head—a reflex action. Her face registered her disgust. "You are behaving like an animal, a wild animal. Have you no shame?"

"Have you?" he asked in a husky whisper.

She had tried not to think about him lately, to put him completely from her mind, but the greater the effort, the less it worked. And the baby was a persistent reminder.

He sat down opposite her and watched as she nursed the child. She was conscious of his eyes on her, enjoying the domestic scene, subdued somewhat by its timeless solemnity. They sat there opposite each other for a few more minutes in perfect silence. She felt desire welling up in her. The infant's suckling had tightened her womb, knotting it into familiar sensations that were at the moment unwelcome.

"So, I finally get to see my son and I can't even see his face, for it is buried in your breast—like father, like son." His manner was gently bantering, almost rueful.

She did not reply. She kept her eyes on the child. The baby stirred, pushing the breast away with a tiny fist, and began to cry.

"See, you are disturbing him. Please leave now. You have no right to be here."

"I have every right. He is my son. I want to be able to see him, take him places with me, be part of his life. I could be a doting uncle. That is perfectly natural."

"You want—you want. You want it all. Everything . . . for nothing," she said in a low, angry voice. "Well, you can't have it, he is my son, and I say you can't, not ever."

She took the baby from her breast and tried to button her dressing gown, but her swollen breasts did not allow it to close properly. She walked into the nursery with the baby and put him in the crib. The child fussed and cried briefly, then grew quiet. She had an uneasy feeling of anger combined with sexual excitement.

He followed her to the nursery. He looked at the sleeping baby in the crib. "He is beautiful," he said, "just like his mother." He leaned over and kissed the baby's head. She walked quietly out of the room toward the kitchen, where she began nervously fussing with the baby's dishes.

He followed her into the square, bright kitchen. Outside a siren screamed, and then there was an intense silence, punctuated only by the rattling of pots and dishes in the sink. He came up behind her, picked up her heavy hair from the back of her neck and kissed her there.

"God, how I've missed you. It must be four, or is it five months? How long are you going to punish me like this? You knew I was a married man, and what that entailed. You never even asked me to get a divorce." A strange perverse complaint that rang of damaged ego.

"And if I had, would you have? You are just as safely allied with my father as with the Goldmarks, safer, it seems." She sounded bitter. She pulled away from him, walked over to the kitchen table where she closed jars of baby food and wiped the table.

He followed her and turned her around roughly to face him. She tried to push him away but her effort was weak and unconvincing. He kissed her throat, murmured endearments against the cloth of her partly opened dressing gown.

She pushed his head away from her breasts. "No, not now. You can't," she said in a voice that was barely audible.

He passed his hands gently over her breasts and undid the buttons, so that she stood virtually naked. Only the thin, cotton fabric in back of her protected her from the chill of the metal table that was digging into her flesh. He found her mouth. She could taste the sweet acrid residue of liquor on his tongue. "God, it's been so long," he said.

She found herself holding onto him tightly, unable to control her breathing. He pressed her against the firmly rooted kitchen table, and let his hand slip over her belly, which was still rounded from the recent birth, and down to her thighs. His fingers were at once gentle and hot inside her, probing the opening to her body. He felt her readiness and unzipped his trousers. He pushed her further back against the table, lifting her up a little. He entered her without difficulty. Once inside, her body responded to him as always. They moved slightly but with a sensuous rhythm. Through the thin fabric of his shirt, the little bones at the base of his spine seemed unsheathed and infinitely delicate to her touch. They reached a climax at almost the same instant, and he stood holding her in his arms, unwilling to surrender the intimacy of a moment they both knew might be the last. She began to cry softly against the hollow of his neck, a cry that grew and shook her whole body with a terrible force.

"I'm so ashamed," she said, "so ashamed."

He stroked her hair, which was moist with tears and perspiration.

CHAPTER 48

The air in Joe's suite at the Gold Rush was fetid, not only with cigar smoke and the residual odor of alcohol, but with years of mendacity and delusion. Marc tried to clear the air. It was no easy task.

The only reason that he told Joe Campano about Janine even now was out of dire necessity. His uncle had confronted him with a strange and outrageous proposition, and his refusal to accept it had created a great deal of tension. Marc had particularly wanted harmony now, if there was ever to be such a thing in his life, because he hoped to facilitate his plans. Not that he was entirely surprised. These sort of arrangements were well-known within a crime family. But the command, for that's what his uncle's proposition really boiled down to, in spite of the careful phrasing, came at a most inopportune time for him. He had planned secretly to fly to New York to be married within the next two days. He had originally hoped to get there during August, his usual vacation time. But here it was already September and still Joe kept finding excuses for keeping him in Las Vegas.

"Look, uncle, I've got to live too. I'm entitled to a private life just like you, aren't I?"

"No, not when it threatens me, all of us."

"How the hell do you figure that?"

Joe couldn't exactly put it into words. He wasn't eloquent—just a poor country boy, with old country ways, but he knew he didn't need his nephew married to some walking rosary. "Boy," he said cajolingly, "what kind of perversity is this, that you should want to marry a nun? Of all the girls in the world?" Joe held his palms out, as if enlisting God on his side.

"She's no longer a nun, she's given up the church for me."

"Not very dedicated," Joe said, still shaking his head. "You are a strange substitute. You couldn't have found someone more wrong for you if you had tried." He went on, "And the family, the girl's family. I know the brother—I met him—he's becoming big business, powerful even. I don't want to mix our blood—our secrets, with his."

"Joe, you know me, you can trust me. You've got to let me go, you owe me for those two years in prison." No sooner did he say this than he knew it had been a mistake, a terrible, irrevocable mistake. There was an abortive silence.

Joe cast his eyes down with pristine modesty. "Gee, kid, you ought'n say things like that, not now—that's the kind of thing those boys down at the committee would give their right arms to hear. Anyway, I think you've been well taken care of through the years."

"Yeah, I know, Joe, and I appreciate it. . . ."

"But you won't show your appreciation by helping me out of a jam, eh, kid? What are families for?" In a softer, more intimate voice he said, "Leave her in the church, kid. That's where she belongs. She'll be happier, I promise you. Nothing bad can happen to her there."

For a moment Marc was deflected by his uncle's sophistry. But the guilt strengthened his resolve. He would offer her a better life than what she had known. He knew there was no use arguing. He'd have to get away somehow, but he also knew there was no way to escape them if they didn't want to let him go.

"Look, kid, it's not forever, like a real marriage. It's for a few months until she has the kid. Then . . ."

"Yeah, but Janine can't . . . She won't marry a divorced man, under such . . . such circumstances. Don't you see?" he cried.

Joe Campano saw only too well. That was precisely why he must force this issue. The matter must be put to rest permanently; otherwise, he wouldn't have a moment's peace. Joe only shook his head, in amazement at the ingratitude of young people today.

Marc might have fared better if they'd never had the conversation, for it only pointed up to Joe the necessity for haste.

The ceremony took place in the apartment, witnessed by Joe, who was best man, and four of his *boys*, the biggest he had. Their neat dark suits, appropriate for the solemn occasion, were left casually unbuttoned so that Marc could not miss the flash of heavy hardware at their waists. The bride wore a white maternity dress and a pained expression.

After the ceremony, Joe kissed the bride and the groom. "Listen, kid, like I told you, it ain't forever," he said, and went into the bedroom with the bride, locking the door noisily behind them.

Forever. Marc hadn't thought about forever. In fact, he figured he'd be lucky if they would just let him live long enough to see Janine and try to explain, if such a thing were possible. He thought of Harlan Chase now and realized his life dangled precariously somewhere between the devil and the deep blue sea.

CHAPTER 49

The next day, Janine's wedding day dawned fair and perversely hot for late October, a maverick in a week of crisp October days. She was tempted to see it as some sort of omen, but put such superstitious thoughts out of her mind, relegating them to a life already behind her.

In a lovely bridal gown of white satin, a gift from her brother, she stood restlessly awaiting the announcement of Marc's arrival from her brother-in-law, Sean, who had been standing out front for the last fifteen minutes.

The last time she had spoken to Marc on the telephone, three days ago, he had sounded nervous and guarded but she attributed that to the wedding jitters. He had promised to be in New York the night before the wedding, or at least that morning.

The ceremony was scheduled for four o'clock. Before she left for the church, she telephoned him in Las Vegas, something she had not done before. He had always called her; although she did not really expect him to be there, she felt the need to reassure herself. There was no reply. She hung up quickly, confident that he was already here, or on his way to the church.

Marge Chase engaged Father McCarthy in earnest conversation while her daughters Marie and Evelyn fussed with Janine's dress and the last touches on her hair and makeup. "You've grown too thin in the convent," Evelyn said, who was herself quite chubby.

"It must be all those mashed potatoes they served," she laughed nervously.

Harlan and Vivian stood nearby. Vivian looked shy and uncomfortable under the weight of her advancing pregnancy. Evelyn had guessed it was a girl because Vivian was carrying "so large and square." Vivian was thrilled with the prognosis and pronounced Janine next. "Things tend to go in threes, I'm certain of that. My nephew's wife, Laina, just had her first child—now me— and next you, Janine," she said, ignoring Harlan's enigmatic smile. Harlan joked warmly with his mother, pinching her cheek and hugging her warmly. The death of his father had eased the way for the display of his natural affection. He teased Father McCarthy mercilessly. Father McCarthy, looking properly surpliced and sacramental, laughed good-naturedly, keeping a wary eye on the clock. This was the first time Harlan had been inside a church since the day when he had come to say good-bye to Janine before going overseas.

"Isn't he playing it a little close?" Harlan remarked quietly to Evelyn's husband, Sean, who had grown tired of sentry duty out front. "I hope he's a little more punctual about business obligations," he murmured. Harlan was beginning to have doubts about becoming involved so deeply in his sister's life; perhaps he should have been more circumspect. In his enthusiasm to help Janine, he had neglected to carefully check Marc's background, his present occupation. He just accepted the fact that he had a good job with his uncle, who had some minor connection with the rackets. He would fix that by offering him a position in his own growing organization. Yet he was not so naive; he knew instinctively it wasn't that simple. Now he did not even know Marc's address or where to find him. If Janine knew it, she was not telling, not even now. But it would be no problem; he could easily find him through a private detective, or through Alex Eastman.

At four-thirty, Father McCarthy called Janine over to him and they talked quietly in hushed tones for a few moments. She went back and sat in a pew alone. Janine was suddenly calm with the stoicism of someone whose expectations of life have always been minimal. She fingered her wedding dress, its slippery softness eluding her grasp, like happiness.

At five, Father McCarthy announced from the pulpit to the small assemblage that he had a commitment at five-thirty that he must keep, but when they needed him again, even later that evening, he would be happy to be of service. He knew it could be explained satisfactorily. They must not worry unduly, he said.

Janine glanced once in her brother's direction. He could not meet her eyes but sat in the pew across the aisle staring straight ahead. A nerve in his cheek throbbed convulsively. Perhaps it was best this way after all. There was the nagging possibility that Janine had only reasoned herself into love with this unlikely stranger, because she was not certain where she belonged, caught as she was between two conflicting worlds. He knew she would never ask the church to take her back, although they would have, he was certain. Sitting here in church he felt a brief resurgence of the old resentment. What did she know? An innocent kid of nineteen barely out of parochial school and into the convent. It seemed necessary to her then. Their lives were so lacking in transcendent drama. It struck him that she and Marc had a great deal in common. Both had sought refuge in a system that they hoped would dramatize their colorless lives, then became disillusioned with the refuge and

THE PLEASURE DOME

sought to escape. Each had sworn oaths of different kinds, nonetheless inviolate, his sworn in blood, hers in love. Each owed loyalty to a mystic thing—Nostra Damus, Our Lady—Cosa Nostra, Our Thing. Now in the space of an hour she had become one of life's displaced persons. Perhaps she had always been.

"There must be an explanation. It cannot be Marc's fault," Harlan said to Janine, without conviction. "I will get to the bottom of this, I promise you."

Janine looked at him unflinchingly and said, "I only want to know if he is alive and well—after that, he is dead as far as I am concerned." She walked slowly out of the church, her carriage rigid and erect the way they had taught her at the convent; her mother held onto her satin-covered arm with one hand, the other clasped tightly over her rosary beads.

At home, Vivian heard Harlan vomiting in the bathroom, sick with impotent rage. For the next few days he did not go out of the house. He lay unshaven and unwashed, letting his anger build and proliferate until it was wild as elderberry root, and just as bitter.

When the telephone rang, he ignored it, instructing the staff not to disturb him for anyone but his sister or Marc Anselmo. When the call came, he pounced on the line. As soon as he heard Marc Anselmo's terrified whisper, all rational plans crumbled. He had one and only one thought in mind now—and that was to make this lowlife, this criminal, regret his action, to feel his flesh give way beneath his powerful hands. He ached with the desire.

"I must see you," Marc said urgently.

Harlan tried to make his voice sound calm, rational. He wanted to get as much information as he could. "Where are you calling from now?"

There was no reply. Then—"Will you meet me and let me explain?"

"Where?" Harlan asked, not trusting the sound of his own voice.

"At the entrance to the old boardwalk, at Orchard Street. I'll be there at ten tonight," Marc said and hung up before Harlan could have the call traced.

As he drove along the ocean road, he was momentarily calmed by the familiar slap of the waves. He had recovered his natural poise long enough to promise himself to hear the boy out. The late October air was cold and wet. The moon illuminated the deserted stretch of boardwalk with an eerie, sulphuric light.

Harlan arrived exactly at ten. He looked around and saw no one or nothing. Then he heard a door slam and saw a figure approaching. In the erratic light, the beatific face looked as pale and insubstantial as an apparition.

"Why all the cloak and dagger?" Harlan asked, anger creeping into his voice.

"When I explain you will understand." Marc moved toward the cold sand, under the eaves of the boardwalk, and beckoned for Harlan to follow, but not before he threw a powerfully beamed flashlight in the surrounding sand dunes and weeds. The sand under the boardwalk was always bitterly cold, even in summer. Harlan remembered that clearly.

The sand felt coarse and damp in his shoes. "Okay, come on, kid, that's enough stalling," he said. He pinioned the boy by his collar against a rotting wood support. "Talk fast. You better make sense," he said. He let go of Marc's collar but stood menacingly close. Marc began falteringly, but Harlan was not really listening, or perhaps only half-listening . . . until he heard the phrase "already married," then something happened—something went wrong in his brain, exploding lights that spelled death.

"You what?" Harlan whispered.

"Married. But it's not what you think."

Harlan grabbed him by his collar and slammed his head against the slanted underpinning of the boardwalk. "Married is married," he hissed. "It's irrevocable." He began punching the boy with a boxer's short, savage punches. He kept hitting him until his mouth and eyes were jellied and bloody. At first Marc tried putting his hands up before his face to ward off the blows, but soon he surrendered completely, offering no further defense, as if he wanted to be punished.

Harlan swung a left hook to the jaw and the boy fell, sprawling face down in the sand. It was merciful—the sand was cool and wet.

Breathless and weaving, Harlan stood there, legs spread apart, considering pulling the boy to his feet to continue the beating, when trembling suddenly, he realized that his anger had spent itself, and he felt only weak-kneed and cold, terribly cold. That was that. That should teach the selfish hoodlum not to play games with him or his. He staggered around, looking uncertainly for his car. He got in, expending a tremendous effort in closing the door. He thought he heard the crunch of wheels on gravel nearby. He looked down to see if he had started the car in his confusion, but he hadn't. The motor was cold. He turned on the ignition, quickly now. He had to get out of there fast, had to get away, get moving. He could have killed that kid. As he pulled out of Orchard Street, he thought he saw a black sedan slide out of the tall weeds and rushes, inching up slowly in the direction from which he had just come. He couldn't be certain, everything was so dark. His mind was a series of jagged impressions.

It was with the greatest shock and disbelief that Harlan read in the newspapers that Marc Anselmo was dead. It was with even more profound shock that Harlan Chase, society glamour boy, hotel magnate, corporate genius, polo player, husband, father, realized that he was also a murderer. Certainly it did not say so in the newspapers. It only said that Marc Anselmo, "local boy," had been found that next day under the boardwalk, beaten to death. Harlan had long ago learned to live with his own selfish acts, but this—murder—this he knew was different.

In his life, he could not deny that he had been fascinated with violence, embarrassed before love, but now he was paralyzed with self-loathing, inundated with a melancholy that threatened to destroy the framework of his whole carefully constructed life. He had continued through the years to pretend he had little or no interest in the effect his actions had on the people around him, on himself. He expunged guilt and redemption from his life. But suddenly he had to face up to the realities of his life. He had scoffed at the church, married out of faith, committed adultery, repeatedly, without confession. He had raped an innocent girl, and now had murdered. Yet he did not really believe it. Murder had not been his intention— or had it? He felt himself incapable of it. Since his affair with Laina, he thought that he had discovered a new tenderness, a diminishing of that impulse toward violence. But in the grip of a powerful passion he sometimes slipped a little into madness, he thought. In such a state, perhaps he was even capable of murder. He was not certain of anything anymore.

He had an uncontrollable urge to confess. For a time, he even considered going to Father McCarthy. But that was not satisfying enough. He would not be punished as a result of that confession. He sat silently in his study for a few more days, occasionally allowing in only the maid with a bowl of soup. He pondered his life in terms of good and evil, assessed malicious intent against the ordinary accidents of life, and came out wanting.

The story got only minimal coverage in the newspapers.

He called his mother to ask about Janine, but Janine knew nothing about it—she no longer read the newspapers. She had gone home and immediately began tearing down the pictures on the walls of her room—replacing them with holy pictures. She had put on a plain black dress and tied a black scarf about her hair, like a wimple. If she had been permitted to keep it, Marge said, Janine would have put on her habit. Her little room had become a chapel. She turned the dresser into an altar of sorts, covered it with a fine lace cloth she had made at the convent. Marjorie Chase cried on the phone about the death of Marc Anselmo, about the death of her daughter. She did not for one moment connect it with her son.

Eventually, Harlan went to see Alex at his office. He had for a long time the vague, gnawing feeling that Eastman was his nemesis—yet gradually, almost without will, he made him the repository for all his secrets. He told him the entire story.

Alex sat back in his swivel chair and assessed him, his partner, his friend, probably the father of his beloved grandson, and decided to help him.

"Chase, this is madness. You know as well as I do that you did not kill that boy—obviously Campano is involved—the mob—I don't know, but I might be able to find out something, given time."

"No, he is dead, there were no bullets. I was there. I walked away and left him like that without a second look. I did it. I will take the consequences."

"Then why have you come to me?" Alex asked quietly.

"Perhaps I feel I owe you this, so you can get your house in order. Make business arrangements predicated on my absence. Sell stock. I don't know."

Alex laughed heartily. "Ah, Chase, your melodrama is touching. I always said you missed your vocation. You could have easily done Irish theater." Still chuckling, he said, "Tell me, why are you so anxious to assume the blame? The police will only laugh at you."

"We will see," Harlan said.

"Both of us have in common a large burden of guilt— Jew and Catholic. The only difference is yours are assigned and we Jews have to drum up our own, and we can be extremely enterprising."

Harlan smiled knowingly.

Alex leaned back, made a temple of his fingers, and contemplated the situation. "Campano will surely have an airtight alibi, which, of course, means little or nothing. They get away with this sort of thing every day, you know that. Minor executions within the organization, no witnesses, et cetera." Suddenly he leaned forward urgently.

"Look, Chase, it isn't only business considerations here. There is your family, your children. Once the newspapers get hold of this, it could seriously damage your reputation. Your credibility would slip, there would be unnecessary bad publicity. Jesus, don't do anything rash, like going to the police. What's the hurry? Promise me that you will wait. I'll call you in a few days."

Having confessed, Harlan felt better. In fact, well enough to return to business, though he was considerably distracted. Each day he searched the newspapers for enlightenment, for some clue that might point to his guilt or innocence. But the story had disappeared after the first day. It seemed to him that there was an unusual silence surrounding the case. He grew restive and confused. Why would Campano want his nephew dead? Wasn't family important to them? His mind raced in dizzying convolutions. He had kept the story from Vivian for as long as possible. They had only discussed Marc's death, nothing more. He didn't want her to know. She expected to give birth at any moment.

Within a week, Alex came to Harlan's office at the Broadbeach.

"Campano says he knows nothing, nothing at all about the boy's death," Alex said, "but he's investigating. He intends to get to the bottom of this. 'After all, it *was* my nephew,' he says tearfully, 'my sister's only boy.'"

Harlan was silent—waiting for the rest.

"He knows you were there, Chase, that's the problem, and somehow he holds you responsible for the kid's death. I don't really think he wanted the boy killed, but..."

"Christ, Alex, what are you trying to say?"

"Well," Alex said, looking furtive, "he's offered you er, us, that is, a deal of sorts. He'll forget about what he knows, maybe put it down to some old feud or vendetta within the ranks, in exchange for...," Alex paused dramatically, "for the entire laundry business in all of our places—for as long as we stay in this business."

"What?" Harlan shouted. He leapt out of his chair.

"Are you altogether mad? You're talking like he's convinced you! Like you're buying his shit! Like someone's got to get me off the hook!"

Alex said quietly, "You have put us in an unenviable position, I'm afraid. What did you think we'd get from him, a signed confession? It's enough that he's told you that he knows you were there. That's the giveaway. They know, because *they* were there."

"I'm surprised he even told you that much."

"Why not? Nobody can ever prove it."

"Anymore than anyone can prove I was there."

"That's right. So let it alone. Let sleeping dogs lie, for God's sake. Obviously, that was his message to you. A warning of sorts. Let it alone. But," Alex continued, "since nobody's sure, he may try to bribe some sort of a witness to say you were there. He's threatening to do that unless you . . . well, you heard the rest."

Harlan looked skeptical.

"Look, there are, of course, benefits," Alex continued, looking away from Harlan's acute gaze.

"Like what?"

"Like protection, like financing. For big projects like real estate development—things like that," Alex mumbled.

"That's what I took the company public for," Harlan barked, "to have the credibility to make big loans—and for that you have to stay clean. Don't you understand?"

"Well, an entanglement like this isn't exactly staying clean, is it?" Alex said. "So you see what I mean."

"The only thing I see is that I'm not now, or ever, going to be his pawn. I don't want to get into their hands for the rest of my life. Before I do that, I'd rather be dead."

"You just may have that option."

THE PLEASURE DOME

He is somehow enjoying all this, Harlan thought. He saw with increasing calm what he must do.

A few weeks later, Vivian gave birth to her third child, a girl, whom they appropriately named Joy. Vivian was delighted with the baby girl, but her happiness was tempered by her husband's withdrawal from family life, and to a degree, even his business. In the agony of self-doubt, his actions suddenly appeared tentative. He seemed weighted down by an uncharacteristic melancholia. Vivian felt vaguely culpable—as if she had failed him in some mysterious way. He would not talk about it with her, and still did not confide his dilemma. She thought only that he was depressed about his sister's disappointment and that in some way it concerned a reassessment of his own values, religious and otherwise. In a certain sense, she was right. The brush with murder, the fear of not being in control of himself, frightened him. He began to think that his uncanny luck, his easily gained power, could be a terrifying weapon.

CHAPTER 50

Matthew rattled the newspaper loudly and turned to the resort section. He had been resting a great deal lately at his rarely occupied Park Avenue apartment. It was a little like suicide, he thought, to be so cut off from everything. He was ready to return to business, although it would be on a part-time basis. He had agreed to this reluctantly, if only because Harlan seemed positive about it.

"Perhaps you should have an honorary position, have a sort of advisory capacity. You won't be under so much pressure and can make some outside investments of your own. When you are stronger, you can always return in your old capacity," Harlan promised.

In the six months since the merger, Matthew realized that he might once again be called a rich man. What he still was reluctant to admit was that it was largely Harlan's doing. Matthew was satisfied but hardly appreciative. He may have suffered a temporary loss of control, but he had not lost his mind. He knew that Harlan had, in a certain sense, brought him in to buy him off. But Alex and Harlan still owned the major shares in the new company and, through the usual recommendations to the stockholders, had been reelected to the board, together with Clyde Bostwick and one or two other minor executives of Harlan's choosing. They, and they alone, set policy, ran the companies. Matthew was unempowered, he could only observe wistfully from the

THE PLEASURE DOME

sidelines. Deep down, Matthew feared that his erratic behavior had been the violent reaction of mediocrity faced with genius. His father had sensed this and that was pain enough.

During those days in the hospital, he had thought repeatedly about, longed for, the past—the long earnest conversations with his mother and father. Explaining himself. Always explaining himself. He didn't care now for the idea of being put out to pasture, but he was enjoying the leisure, the privacy, and spending more time with Faye. After all, Faye had saved his life. He really wanted to live and appreciated life more now that he had almost lost it. She had never used her leisure to advantage, to understand and appreciate the world. Perhaps now he could help her, guide her. After all, he knew a few things about art and literature, at least he did once. Anyway, he didn't exactly know where to go under the new structure, how to move. He wondered, worried if perhaps the pills, the recent years of steady drinking, had taken their toll.

Scanning the resort page, he was surprised to see that Russell Drake was singing at a small hotel in the Catskills. He had started there in the Borscht Belt, and Matthew Goldmark had singlehandedly launched his career. And now, singing in the Catskills? He was amused. Drake had been a glittering star, today he was all the way back where he started. Matthew shivered slightly. He remembered Drake's gratitude. He felt vaguely responsible for his failure now but could not locate the root of his malaise. Now it seemed even that bit of his handiwork had been destroyed. He thought about his son's music and felt better. He must remember to ask Faye what she had heard about Drake. Perhaps Harlan would know.

Harlan had tried to keep Drake's name out of the papers when he was blacklisted. But even though he had talked to certain senators of his acquaintance, he couldn't keep Drake's name out of *Red Channels*, the publication that listed every person of note suspected of communist ties, and he couldn't keep his records from slipping, or reinstate the canceled movie contract either. Whoever had turned him in had done a thorough job. Although he didn't know who had done it, he had his suspicions. He hoped to keep it from Matthew. The doctors at the sanitarium said his psyche was in delicate balance.

When all was said and done, Alex had to admire Chase. He had taken the cleverest path by going to the police. He had put an end to their threats, challenged them with unwanted publicity during the crime committee investigations, and unburdened himself, something he had needed to do for a long time. Harlan had taken his chances and won, as usual.

The police had kept him overnight for questioning, then booked him on suspicion of manslaughter. After he confessed, he was let out on his own recognizance, pending investigation.

The FBI had been keeping a close watch on Joe Campano for some time. They knew about Marc's forced marriage, and about the murder weapon, a lead pipe. Now it remained only for them to prove it.

Nevertheless, they had questioned Chase closely, making sure that neither he nor his companies were in any way connected with them. By the time his brush with organized crime had reached the media, it had generated just enough publicity to depress the stock for a while. But people came flocking to the hotels in droves, seeking a little of that mystery, that excitement.

Some weeks later, his friend and attorney Clyde Bostwick called to tell him that he was no longer under suspicion. Harlan, alone in his study in the great house in Oyster Bay, leaned his head against the back of the large chair and closed his eyes in gratitude. "Blessed Mary, Mother of God," he whispered and crossed himself. "Blessed Mary, Mother of God." There were tears in his eyes.

CHAPTER 51

Twelfth Night had opened to fine critical reviews and while it wasn't as great a commercial success as *Out of Tune*, the music was praised widely. Even while the highly stylized piece of work was in the making, David began experimenting with new material.

Since the birth of his son, he preferred to work at home. He wished to be included in every aspect of the baby's life. He was a doting father and an indulgent nurse. In fact, Nurse Andrews said, in her brogue, rich as Scottish shortbread, that she had never worked for a family where the father was "so daft for a bairn." Both parents rarely accepted travel obligations now, and when they did, they did so separately, so that one or the other was always with the baby. All of Laina's pursuits involved David, her child and her music. She made sure that she had little leisure time in which to indulge in fantasy. Perhaps her lyrics suffered a little from the rigid self-discipline and lacked her usual romantic spontaneity, but she suffered less.

When everyone else was moving to the east side, they moved to the west side. They bought a large, high-ceilinged duplex apartment in the venerable old Hotel Des Artistes, off Central Park West. The building, well named, was almost a private club. Tenants consisted largely of celebrities from the world of music, theater, and the fine arts. Laina looked upon it as her first real home.

It was endlessly spacious and the decor was both elegant and seductive. Marble floors with French tapestry throw rugs—trompe-l'oeil in the entry hall—flocked red velvet walls edged in rose silk ribbons. In the dining room there were Empire chairs, satin striped recamier benches, walls lined with nineteenth-century paintings of exotic scenes, windows swagged in heavy tasseled silk. It was as though she wished to recreate her life, shutting out the past, cushioning it against future shock. It was a world of privilege and beauty without the intrusion of reality. Equally talented and glamorous people of their acquaintance sought invitations to their dinner parties. In the lovely Café Des Artistes downstairs, where walls were adorned with lush scenes by Howard Chandler Christie, they passed their leisure hours exchanging ideas and testing theories on art, philosophy and the rapidly changing tastes of the American public. They became friendly with many of their illustrious neighbors here and gradually developed a small but chic salon of artists, writers, composers and actors. Sometimes they would receive a painting or objet d'art in appreciation for their hospitality. David and Laina had begun collecting modern art on a small, select scale. If they did not share a bedroom, they shared their lives in most other ways. And Warren was their first priority.

They had toyed with the idea of moving to the country, like the majority of other young couples in those years. But they soon discarded it, reasoning that their work necessitated being in town. The time lost in commuting would cancel out the bonus of being near grass and trees. Summers, however, would present a problem. Laina eschewed camp—"It kills individuality," she said, remembering the summer at Camp Choctaw. And neither one would consider returning to the Broadbeach. Of all the family, only Faye did not press them about the summers. She alone knew the truth, and the farther away Laina stayed from the hotels and Harlan, the better off her son and grandson would be. Faye never doubted that Warren was her true grandson; she hadn't allowed her thinking to go that far.

Instead, they began to search for a permanent summer home. Since the birth of her son, she had fallen in love with permanency. A number of their artistic friends spent their summers at Candlewood Lake in Connecticut. Laina and David had always enjoyed their visits there. It was a welcome departure from their hectic city life and the studied opulence of resort hotel life. Laina was eternally suspicious of summer. Even now she considered it an imposition, an idleness forced upon her by convention and the changing seasons. But now there was her son to consider. David and she could work here without intrusion. Besides, an epidemic of infantile paralysis was sweeping the country. She made up her mind quickly and purchased a small, choice cottage on the lake.

As the years passed, she grew to appreciate her summers at the lake, the anonymity, the blessed absence of pressure. She loved the lake, strangely colorless with its ragged fringe of deciduous trees, its swooping loons. In summer the trees were full, green; they almost filled the empty spaces in her life. On winter weekends, it was a lunar landscape, the dun-colored, bare branches arching toward the mirrored, frozen lake in supplication.

Each summer brought her closer to her son. Although he loved his mother, it was his father he openly adored.

THE PLEASURE DOME

Whether David played piano for him while he improvised little dances or let him ride piggyback, Warren was ecstatic. David even tried to teach him piano, but he would have no part of it. He couldn't sit still long enough. Once he pinned his father with his great phosphorous-green eyes and told him earnestly that he would have preferred him "to stay a football player instead of a piano player."

David roared, and later commented to Laina that Warren had the most remarkable eyes, "a combination of your golden ones and my ordinary brown, I suppose."

At first Laina was delighted with their relationship. Later she grew envious, feeling shut out of their male fraternity, which she knew to be fraudulent all around. Then she begged God to forgive her for her selfishness and ingratitude.

David had become the model family man. At the Broadbeach, the entire hotel looked forward to those rare occasions when the maestro and his lovely wife would come to the hotel with their small son. Sitting there in the great vaulted dining room, locked in the bosom of his family, he almost convinced Matthew. Matthew thought perhaps he had been too quick to condemn. Harlan, seated across the room with Vivian and his brood, looked equally familial and above reproach. He would smile politely in their direction, then gaze at Warren's small intense face or stare at Laina unabashedly, all of which Laina found intensely disquieting. On rare occasions, Warren got to spend some time with Harlan, but that was only when Laina could not avoid it. She feared he might kidnap the boy, feared the impact of his influence on him. Harlan was jealous of David's close relationship with his son. He even thought of writing Laina a letter, pleading his case, then discarded it as too dangerous.

Harlan was spending more and more time in California and globe-hopping on behalf of his vast entertainment complex. Their paths crossed less and less. To Warren, Harlan was just another shadowy family figure . . .

The years passed for Laina in neat geometric patterns, the summers at the lake being the highlights.

By the time Warren outgrew babyhood and started on the often fruitless search for friends (particularly during summers), the novelty of fatherhood began to wear off for David. He became restless and preoccupied. He began to spend more time in town, often not coming out to the lake until weekends, sometimes not even then.

The summer after Warren's fourteenth birthday, David decided suddenly to go abroad, to give a benefit performance of *Twelfth Night* in Cannes during the film festival.

"It would be great exposure," he said. "Many important international film people will view it." He invited Laina halfheartedly, but she declined. He stayed in Europe three months and rented a villa at Antibes. Warren, accustomed to his father as playmate, grew intensely lonely. There were few boys his own age at the lake, and Laina was thinking reluctantly of selling the house and buying one elsewhere. She even thought of capitulating to tradition by sending him to camp.

It was a stroke of luck for Warren when the Wendelmans, who had always lived next door, decided to sell their house; their children had outgrown it. The Gostins bought the charming house with its picture window on the lake and moved in the following summer. They had two children, Gina, seven, and Robin, a boy of twelve.

Michael Gostin owned a large and successful construction company in White Plains. He possessed a dreamlike remoteness, but Laina, accustomed to effusive men, thought him taciturn, even sullen. He was sandy-haired and large-featured with a wiry, well-disciplined body. He was not a handsome man, but there was a certain mystery about him. On the rare occasions that he smiled, his face seemed to change, suggesting quite another dimension to an otherwise passive personality. Otherwise, he stayed at a chilly distance.

Robin, his son, was inventive, mischievous, and in Warren's eyes, absolutely perfect. For one thing, he did not know the meaning of fear. On the lake he tipped canoes and lifesaved Warren, he pulled stubborn leeches from his skin without so much as wrinkling his nose and crawled under houses to capture and subdue large snakes.

If Warren saw this new friend as the coming of the Messiah, Laina saw it quite another way. "A wild, rebellious child, with ideas far too sophisticated for his age," she told David.

She tried not to think of Harlan, skipping carefully the social section of the *Times* and discouraging scraps of gossip, business or social, concerning his flamboyant exploits. She turned more and more to her work, arranging theatrical charitable events, doing radio shows and some television. They had been asked to write a little musical especially for television. Laina felt the new medium might be a gratifying challenge, but David was indifferent to the idea. In fact, he seemed indifferent to most things lately, except his son. His recent affair with a leading choreographer had just ended, and David was forced once again to confront himself and to reassess his life.

IV.
RENASCENCE
1960-1970

CHAPTER 52

Revolution came with a long, low outcry of pain that ended in death—and fallen idols. A white man was killed in Dallas, his brother barely five years later. A black man was assassinated in New York City, and another three years later in Memphis. A dime store in Greensboro became "the birthplace of a whirlwind." Rage grew in the cities and civil war was proclaimed. Youth squinted at life through eyes blinded by television and found it wanting. Their pain was eased, soothed by the new music, by the Beatles. And by drugs. Hard drugs for hard times. In 1964 America went back to war unofficially.

Looking back, Harlan would think of the sixties as a kaleidoscope of whirling, struggling images on a collision course to nowhere.

Steven Chase was twenty-two years old and in love with tales of valor and heroism his father had told him through the years. He cherished his father's medals, bowie knives, marine uniforms, and other memorabilia. Steven had distinguished himself academically and graduated with honors from Dartmouth and he planned to go into the family's business. He was tall and dark, and even though he was not quite as handsome as his father, he was equally popular with women.

Harlan did not want Steven embroiled with any *one* girl now. Instead, he wanted his son to travel the length and breadth of his empire, to learn the ropes, and eventually to work beside him. To take his place was not yet an expression with which Harlan at a vital fifty-two years was prepared to deal. He felt certain, however, that the extension of his hopes for the future lay with Steven. Steven consciously emulated his father, giving careful attention to dress. He usually wore dark suits tailored to suit his long, lean lines, and discreet silver ties. His brother Gerald faithfully wore denim, the uniform of the liberation.

Gerald, Harlan feared, was a product of the new age, already casting longing glances at the counterculture. He heartily disapproved his younger son's choice of Berkeley, and would have forbidden it absolutely, had Vivian not intruded and pleaded his cause. In any case, it was too soon to tell what Gerald would become.

In the years since Harlan had assumed the chairmanship of Pleasure Domes, Inc., he had managed to follow his original overall plan for the company pretty closely. He had renovated and refurbished hotels that were part of the original company. Then he built up their reputations by good marketing techniques and sold them for a profit, holding onto the money until something else came his way. He had also renovated the movie theaters, which also ground out a steady reliable income for the company. But since the onslaught of television, movies had suffered, and the current films of the day, many made abroad, were not doing much to raise his hopes.

Between trying to get better pictures from the distributors and running the Pleasure Dome spa complex in San Diego, he found himself spending great amounts of time in southern California. He bought a ranch in Palm Springs and figured the boys would like it, but they hardly ever came. Vivian pretended to enjoy it to please him, but secretly she didn't like it—the distance from home, the climate, its foreignness. Nor was she particularly enthusiastic about Harlan's business and social friends, finding them disingenuous and self-indulgent. Vivian was a traditional Jewish girl.

Harlan had long ago dismantled the *Pleasure Dome* and turned it into a private yacht, which he usually moored at his own dock in Oyster Bay. He was tempted to rechristen it *Laina's Song*, but thought better of it. Since the episode with Marc Anselmo, he was more subdued, even though he was worth millions of dollars. He had made himself a rich man, or as Matthew liked to say, *Matthew* had made him a rich man. But in turn, he had made Matthew rich enough to retire in luxury at sixty-five. Except Matthew didn't really want to be *forcibly* retired. He had begun looking for some hotel deals of his own, where he would run things *his* way. When he thought of the decaying grandeur of the old pink Hibiscus Gardens he could have wept.

CHAPTER 53

One warm summer afternoon David sat with Warren in the trellised garden of the lake house showing him how to play Monopoly. Warren had just turned fifteen. Laina, sitting nearby, was reading Caroline Segall's latest novel. Caroline had become quietly successful, writing family stories, filling them with children. She herself was childless. "The doctor can find no physical reason for it," she once told Laina. "It's as if Craig still withholds something of himself. He cannot completely surrender to me."

Laina did not care much for her novels. They were commercial stories that skimmed only the surface.

"Hey, I've got you now, Dad. You're bankrupt!" David had just landed on Warren's hotel on the Boardwalk.

"You're quite the entrepreneur, aren't you, son?"

"Yeah, just like my Uncle Harlan."

Laina looked up in alarm. "What do you mean, Warren?"

"Oh, nothing, Mother," Warren said, jiggling the dice and blowing on them for luck. "Everyone knows he's got lots of money."

David smiled tolerantly and rumpled his hair. "You know your old man's no slouch. I've got a few credits to my name too."

Warren, who was genuinely proud of his father, said

calmly, "I'm just lucky, I guess, the whole family's famous."

During the first few years that the Gostins lived next door, Laina and David saw little of them except in the context of being the parents of their son's friend. Beryl rarely left the house, and Michael kept very much to himself. But during the last summer, they became friendlier, meeting for drinks occasionally in one or the other's garden patios. As they drew closer, Laina was struck by the custodial attitude Michael showed his wife. He was spending more time at home with his family. Beryl Gostin might have been attractive once, pretty even, but that summer she walked with a cane and looked ravaged. Some rare dystrophic disease had attacked the muscles and had been triggered by childbirth. She had been ill since the birth of her daughter seven years ago.

One evening when they were getting into the car after a movie, Laina thought she felt Michael's hand brush across her breast. She wasn't certain until their eyes met and he held her gaze for a moment, as if transfixed. She looked over at Beryl, but she didn't appear to have noticed, secure in the tyranny of her illness. It was not the first time that Laina sensed his admiration, but she had simply put it out of her mind. Although she was only in her mid-thirties, she already felt life was passing her by. She had found herself wondering what Michael Gostin might be like in bed. It had been a long time.

The following summer Michael returned to the house without his wife—she had passed away during the winter. Laina noticed a new recklessness in Robin's behavior. The wild streak had become a coat of armor against pain.

Michael didn't go into business much that summer, devoting himself almost exclusively to his children. He had grown used to the role of nurse, it had become a part of his life. Laina thought he missed being needed. They had a cleaning lady three days a week. The rest of the time Michael and the children puttered about in a sort of dreamy chaos.

The Goldmarks' housekeeper came up from the New York apartment and stayed only part of the week at the lake. While Laina enjoyed the privacy, David gradually became uneasy with the domestic isolation. In early July David went abroad again. This time he didn't press her to come.

One afternoon they all barbecued perch for lunch. It had been caught that morning by Michael and the boys and was fresh. Gina was unimpressed, wrinkling up her nose at the smoky, fishy smell. She ran off, announcing that she had a birthday party to go to two houses down the way. Laina could not accustom herself to the complete freedom the Gostin children enjoyed, ever since they were small. She assumed it had something to do with gentiles' relaxed attitude toward children—*letting go*, something Jewish parents seemed unable to do.

After lunch Warren and Robin disappeared on one of their adventures.

A slight breeze had blown up. Laina shivered.

"Here, take this," Michael said. He put his jacket around her shoulders, letting his hands slip down her arms slightly.

"No, I think I'll go inside." She began collecting plates and dishes, busying herself with a sudden urgency. He followed her into the kitchen, closing the screen door quietly. He put down the cake plate he was carrying. It clattered sharply on the tile countertop in the suddenly silent house. The small house was not air-conditioned and the afternoon was muggy and electric with bluebottle flies. She scraped plates over the sink.

"Does one use very hot or very cold water to clean fish plates? I've always been confused about that," she said with great intensity.

He came up behind her, lifted the hair from the back of her neck, and kissed it lingeringly. She allowed him to take her again and again that listless afternoon, willing herself to match his excitement . . .

When it was all over, when the afternoon sun was beginning to set in a mauve-and-orange sky, and he lay beside her exhausted and satiated, she felt only a vague sense of being terribly alone.

At the beginning of August, David telephoned to say he had decided to spend the balance of the summer at Antibes. This time he did not press her to come. David's secret life was growing more difficult for him to conceal. Laina realized that she'd have to face the fact that as he grew older and more famous, he would become more reckless.

Warren tried to keep the disappointment out of his voice when he spoke to his father on the overseas telephone. "Dad, when are you coming home?" He was afraid his voice sounded tearful, unmanly. When he hung up, he looked away quickly from his mother's scrutinous gaze, embarrassed at having to beg.

Michael was a calm and gentle man, and Laina appreciated the virtues of his being unexceptional. It was a relief, a blessing. Until now, her relationships had been with powerful men, men that belonged to the public. She felt at last a part of real life.

During the afternoons, and sometimes in the evenings, after the children were asleep, he would come into her house, ostensibly to have coffee with her because he was lonely. She usually welcomed him—she tried to fully respond, so as to exhume the pain of the past and those dark, haunting dreams she still had about Harlan Chase. She enjoyed those lazy, sensuous afternoons, enjoyed his desire and her own gradual surrender. Soon this became the pattern for the long hot summer afternoons—those days when he didn't go to work and the children were safely out of the house on some project or adventure of theirs. In a reversal of roles, they felt like guilty children, sneaking around under the watchful, wary eyes of their parents.

"Let's go down to Rick's and look around," Robin said. It was near summer's end and Robin and Warren were running out of "adventures." Rick's was a large and diversified stationers in the town of Danbury. It was a great store, no doubt about it. Warren had been there only once before with his mother. But still he didn't think the idea was up to Robin's usual standard of inventiveness. He couldn't think of anything better, so he didn't challenge it. Robin consulted his watch.

"It should be open about another forty minutes, I reckon, unless she's closed early 'cause it's Saturday." They began walking faster in the direction of the town.

"You sure are hooked on Mark Twain," Warren grumbled. "My dad says there are better books a guy can read. Books on the composers' lives or seagoing stories

THE PLEASURE DOME

like *Moby Dick*." He trudged along beside his friend. "Is your dad a good ball player?"

"What kind of ball?"

"I dunno, all kinds, I guess."

"He's okay," Robin said. "Well, you've played baseball with him. You *know* he's good."

"Yeah," Warren was thinking of how to top that. "My dad played football in college. Did you know that?"

"That was a real long time ago," Robin said.

"Well, you gotta be pretty good, you know, to play football for a school like Yale."

"Was he first string?" Robin didn't wait for the answer, but ran ahead as he saw the neat compact buildings of the shopping area loom into view.

Rick's boasted a newspaper and magazine section with a dizzying array of publications, domestic and foreign, and even some of those shocking underground magazines with their lurid covers.

Warren drifted over to the magazine stand. He found Robin glued to a magazine. A nearby salesman was eyeing him warily. Without taking his eyes from the book, he whistled and said, "Say Warren, you always said your father was famous but I didn't know *how* famous until just now—look at this, will ya?"

Warren looked over his friend's shoulder eagerly, expecting to see both his parents smiling at some celebrity gathering. But instead he saw a colored photograph of a bleary-eyed David in swim trunks cavorting around a pool with a young boy. Each held champagne glasses in hand. The caption read in French: "*Les Amants Unie a Antibes.*" Warren's French was more than adequate. The article went on to describe "the well-known American composer"—his works, his *villa*, his lovelife. Warren did not finish reading it, but closed it quickly.

"Whaddya do that for?" Robin said sullenly. "I was counting on you to translate that for me. What's the matter with you? Aren't you gonna buy it at least, show it to your mom, for God's sake?" Warren was confused and uncertain himself about what he had just seen, but he knew for certain now his father was very different from other boys' fathers. Perhaps he had always known that.

Suddenly he didn't care if he never saw Robin again. He was glad summer was at an end. He hoped they didn't have to come back here next year. When he got outside, he didn't know where to turn or how to escape. He thought of hiding out somewhere until he was sure that Robin had left, then taking a cab home. But even as he so neatly planned his moves, he began walking back into the store. There was only one thing to do and he knew it. He would make light of it . . . nothing so terrible. After all, Robin didn't understand French.

CHAPTER 54

Warren missed a lot of school that fall. He looked peaked and couldn't keep food down. If his mother hadn't known better, she might have said he was in love. But she didn't think he had a girlfriend.

His marks were slipping, and he rarely brought friends home anymore. He just slept a lot. He had always enjoyed his father's company, but now he couldn't seem to find anything to say to him. Dr. Baskin suggested that he see a psychiatrist; perhaps they should go together, mother and son. A psychiatrist might get to the root of what was bothering the boy. Laina thought bitterly that at the "root" of it was shame, confusion and a severe sense of rejection by his father. But she had not told this to the doctor and she could see that he considered her secretive and strangely uncooperative. When she left the office, she realized the tightly rolled magazine was still in her hand. She, too, had seen the article, but hadn't been able to bring herself to show it to Larry Baskin, although he had been her family doctor for years. She thought that he probably didn't know about David, and she didn't see any reason to spread ugly gossip. It might only get back to her son. Besides, if they would have to see a psychiatrist, she would prefer to show it to him. The photo of David with Brian in Antibes had come as a shock to her, resigned as she was to the reality of David's sexual preferences.

She began to wonder if all of her circumspection

through the years was as much an effort to protect Warren as to protect herself from criticism. She suffered from the questions that she read in the eyes of anyone who knew or divined the truth, of men who insulted her with their sexual offers. "Why did you marry him? Why do you stay?" It was in Michael Gostin's voice when he called to tell her about the magazine article, which Robin had shown him reluctantly when they returned from the lake, the one she held tightly in her hand.

Alex Eastman was enjoying an old age that did not hoard or count the years. One of the luxuries of being rich, he said, was that instead of being referred to as a "senior citizen" when you reached sixty-five, you were called "elderly" and given respect.

Laina knew that Warren enjoyed his grandfather Alex much more than Matthew, who seemed silent and distracted much of the time. Warren had a distinct feeling of being in charge of him, rather than the other way around. But sometimes he patted Warren's head, which was now equal in height to his own, as if he were still a baby. No, he much preferred Alex, with his blue eyes and his tightly-curled white hair, and his chiclet smile. He was fun—and as full of life as any schoolboy.

Sometimes they played baseball in the great Sheep Meadow in Central Park. When David was in town, he would often come along and they would have a good game of catch, or even run some bases, but Alex never felt very comfortable in his presence, and was relieved when he stopped coming.

Alex wore a gray sweatsuit today, with socks rolled loosely around his bony ankles. It made Warren think of

Olive Oyl in the comic strip. A jump rope was looped around his hand. He began to jump with the light, running step of a prizefighter. For some reason Warren could not figure out, he counted by twos, "Two—four—six—eight—" expelling gusts of breath rhythmically with each number, droplets of perspiration glittering on his nose and chin. Warren counted one hundred rotations. Alex stopped but made no attempt to rest. He began to punch and jab the air, shadow boxing, weaving and ducking gracefully. He was showing his grandson how he used to box in his "youth."

"How I keep trim," he said, pounding his remarkably firm stomach. "Got to keep trim, son, got to keep moving. Frankly, swimming's the best sport, used to swim with my son Seth all the time, when he was just about your age."

"Yeah, I know, Gramps, I know." Warren felt sad whenever grandpa reminisced about his son.

"Christ, when I was only a little older than you I pounded 'em into the ropes," he said. "I ran fifty laps a day, played handball until my hands were raw, and sweated drops of blood like bullets."

The beginning of a smile began to play around Warren's mouth. "When did you find time to work?"

"Work? Why, for Chrissake, I worked day and night. Things were different in those days," he said. "Yeah, things were very different. There was so much to look forward to," he said, narrowing his eyes as if to bring into focus the smeary edges of the past "Now, hell, I spend most of my time standing up looking at the inside of a toilet bowl."

Warren burst into laughter, rich, full-fledged laughter. He loved Grandpa Alex more than anyone! Alex wrapped a towel around his neck in true jock fashion, and with his hand draped loosely across the boy's shoulders, began walking him home.

"You know, son, I was thinking. Maybe you need to spend some time with someone, well, different, somebody new, get a fresh viewpoint—someone a bit younger than myself but, er, someone who loves sports, who you could have fun with. Pal around with, sort of, I mean especially, when your dad is out of town."

"Like who, Grandpa?" he said, his newly changed voice cracking.

"Oh, I don't know, like your Uncle Harlan maybe?"

Warren was silent, as if mulling this over. "No, Grandpa, I have more fun with you than anyone else." But Alex noticed a warm color had crept into his cheeks, suffusing his face. "Besides, he's only my great-uncle, and I hardly know him."

"That doesn't mean a thing, son. I never really got to know your mother until she was just about your age. Some relationships are better when you've grown up to them. Now you're more of an equal."

CHAPTER 55

Joy Chase sat with her father by the swimming pool at their Palm Springs home and lifted her face up to the sun. It was Easter break. Harlan looked at her and thought how well she looked with a suntan. She was extremely attractive, with her intuitive dark eyes like her mother's, and her narrow, delicate face, but hardly beautiful. There was a pragmatism about her that made him feel that he was talking to an adult instead of a sixteen-year-old. She had few of the flighty ways of contemporary teenagers.

"It's good to have you here, Joy. Why don't you come out here more often?" He closed his eyes and lay back on the chaise gratefully. He loved the desert house jostled by the mountains, exotic with date palms. Palm trees still astonished him. He had never learned to take his varied environments for granted.

"Oh, I don't know, Dad, I suppose all my allegiances are in the east, my school, my friends . . ." The desert silence was deep and clear, windless and uncluttered by bird sounds. The sun shimmered mercilessly against the plum-colored San Jacinto mountains. Joy's large sunglasses didn't provide enough protection against the pure, unadulterated sun. She had to make a visor of her hand in order to see her father.

When he thought she was looking at him, he said, "Aren't I among your allegiances, baby? I used to be a priority." He was remembering how she had doted on him when she was a little child. "You resent me."

"I don't. I really don't, Dad."

"Please, it's good for us to talk. You're my only daughter. Don't you want to be a comfort to your old man in his old age?" He was grinning.

"Well, perhaps if you spent a little more time at home . . ."

"Joy, your mother understands—she, above all, understands this business. The nature of it. She knows she can come here with me, and frequently does, any time she wants to."

Joy was silent, unimpressed by his party line. She dabbed at drops of perspiration. Her shoulders were already russet-brown.

"Darling, here, why don't you put this around your shoulders. Keep you from getting a painful burn." He got up and placed a large towel around her shoulders. "Out here you never realize that you're burning, not like Florida where the humidity quickly sends you into the pool."

"Tell me, Dad," she said finally. "Don't you think she reads the papers and magazines?"

"What?"

"Oh, Daddy, don't act so perplexed. Don't you think Mother knows what goes in this business? On the yacht? The starlets, the call girls, the Hollywood goings-on? Of course, she doesn't come here much, why should she? She's uncomfortable, afraid of what she may find in the drawers."

Harlan whistled and slapped his bare thighs, still firm and tightly corded. "I'm glad to see that you don't subscribe to the new morality, darling. But you know, you kids kill me, you really do. At a time when sex and love are being devalued daily by your peers, you sit here and lecture me on morality."

"Do you think I subscribe to those values?"

THE PLEASURE DOME

"No, as a matter of fact, I don't. And you are old enough to make careful judgments. An occasional business party on the boat—a little too much to drink perhaps—that has nothing to do with my feelings for your mother." He wondered why he seemed always to be apologizing to his children. "Your mother isn't unhappy with me—she's always been happy with me. If she were dissatisfied, she would have left me long ago. Besides, none of that business, the goings-on, none of that interests me."

"She loves you still."

Harlan looked up at his daughter and said earnestly, "Well, there's your answer, girl. Do you think she'd still love me if I were such a monster?"

The strange thing was that Joy suspected that her father's words were close to the truth. She had the eerie feeling that instead of speaking for her mother she had been speaking for herself. Her mother was more secure than she was.

"Anyway, there is safety in numbers, daughter," he said, stretching out his long legs. "None of it means anything anyway. Just an old man fighting the inevitable. I have never had a mistress." *In your lifetime, anyway,* he thought, by means of rationalizing the truth. "And have only been in love once in my life," he said ruefully. "Now isn't that a wonderful tribute to your mother?"

Joy ended up laughing in spite of herself. "Oh, Dad, you are a charmer!" she said and went over and kissed his cheek. "You are just irresistible, that's all."

He didn't respond, except for a heavy, intentionless sigh. Anyway, he had no tolerance for being dictated to by his children. "Why don't you stay on here with your mother and me for the balance of your vacation? Then we'll all fly home together."

"No. No thanks, Dad, really. I've had enough. There's

really nothing for me to do here, and well, I've got friends at home—dates and things." She could hardly explain that she felt trapped here by the absence of bridges—the aridity.

"I see. Nothing serious, I hope?"

"Oh, of course not. No one goes steady anymore, Dad, like in your day, nothing so heavy . . ."

He wondered why the children today found commitment heavy. Even the commitment of plain, ordinary conversation. They were even stingy with talk. Had talk gone out of style? he wondered. He had talked to the world as a boy, talked himself in and out of loneliness, in and out of battle, in and out of love.

"Besides, I'd like you and Mother to be alone for a while. It would do her—both of you—a world of good."

Harlan scratched his head and smiled tolerantly at her officious tone. He was tired of forceful women, of the new morality. There was no longer any thrill of conquest. They made the conquests. At least, these young women did, here in this casual, sun-filled lotus land. He thought about Vivian and was glad she would be out tomorrow.

The night that Vivian arrived he made sure that none of the usual sycophants were hanging around, even told the houseman in advance that he wouldn't take calls. She hadn't been to the house in the Springs for almost a year. He wanted to be sure that she didn't stay away that long again.

They had a quiet dinner on the small patio near the pool. They talked about everything, finally getting around to the children.

"Harlan," she said, laying down her dessert spoon quietly, "I think that Steven has found out that you've been trying to keep him from the draft—pulling strings."

"Oh, you didn't tell him, did you?"

"No. No, of course not, but most of his friends have been drafted—and he's in perfect health, and still he hasn't been called."

"Well, what's his rush? The longer we wait, the less chance of his having to go, and the shorter his time over there."

"I know. But Steven doesn't see it that way. He sees it as his duty."

"This isn't like *our* war, Vivvy, this is different. Our sense of the war was palpable."

That night they made love as if they were young again, and in the morning, too, and Vivian was glad that she had not left him, would never leave him, preferring to be lonely with him than without him.

Steven called the next day and told his father that he was considering volunteering for the draft. His number would probably come up any day as it was.

They took a plane out the next morning.

Here was Steven, the son he *could* communicate with, his firstborn—born while he himself was overseas fighting for his life—Steven, who, as a baby, he had carried everywhere on his shoulder, as if to show him the world from a vantage point, now telling him he was going to senselessly risk the life he had given him.

"Why, Steven? Why? There is no point to it."

"I want to see us win this war," he said.

"But this is not even our war and nobody can possibly win it, don't you see that? There will only be losses all around."

"Why are you talking this way, Dad? All my life I considered you a hero, a champion. I never expected you to react this way."

"Perhaps you have misread me, son. What in your eyes constitutes a champion?"

"Winning and money," he said without hesitation.

"Well then, there are an awful lot of unhappy champions in the world," Harlan said, shaking his head.

"It is my duty, dad, as an American. I must do my duty as I see it. Just as you did yours."

"Oh, Christ! You can't compare the situations. First of all, I was drafted. I had no choice. Secondly, it was a war that *had* to be fought—the country was in danger. All the choices were simple then, black or white, good or evil." Harlan seemed unaware that he was shouting.

"Every age has its heroes."

"Certainly they do, but yours are contrived. This war is contrived!"

"That sort of iconoclasm is cruel, Father."

Harlan felt reduced to begging. "Well, how about the huge business I've built for you and your brother? I need you here to help me run it. To be in one place when I am in another."

"I won't he gone forever—and besides, Father, you never needed anyone, anywhere, anytime."

Harlan was silent. He thought how little this son—or any of his children—really knew him.

"You've made up your mind then. So go ahead. You're over eighteen. You don't need my permission. Go ahead—waste your time—possibly even your life. You're still so young. Do you want to risk your life?"

"Why not, Dad? You've done it all your life."

"Risk?" His voice remained steady and steely cold. "Hell, I'm no different than anyone else, Steven. Everybody takes risks. Risk is getting up in the morning, but there's no thrill to *this*, there's no run for your money, and the stakes are too high." Harlan turned away. What more was there to say?

THE PLEASURE DOME

Steven walked quietly out of the room. They heard his car pulling out of the driveway.

Vivian, trembling, rose and stood looking out of the large, leaded window of the den. "He is trying in every way he knows to be like you."

"But his ethics are wrong, his values twisted."

"Ethics usually involve imitation," she replied.

CHAPTER 56

In the late spring, while playing catch in the park, Alex dug the ball into his well-oiled mitt, and casually remarked to Warren that Harlan Chase might stop by to see him and drop off some important papers. "Perhaps we can induce him to join us in the game!"

Warren returned the ball with assurance. "That would be neat," he said warmly. He spotted Harlan approaching them from across the baseball diamond minutes before he arrived. He felt a shiver of excitement and apprehension. He sensed his mother would not approve. She was not overly fond of that side of the family. He supposed it had something to do with the business, something between his father and Harlan Chase. Alex had whispered "Of course, I think it best we don't mention this to your mother, for now anyway. She might resent it—you know how funny women are." Warren laughed, an eager pledge to their secret fraternal order.

Uncle Harlan looked youthful. His rich brown hair was only touched with gray here and there. He hit the ball hard and treated Warren like a man instead of a delicate child. Warren was enjoying the afternoon. Later Harlan suggested they all go down to his club for a swim. It was on their way home, he said.

Harlan found swim trunks in his locker that fit the boy surprisingly well. Harlan said they were his, but they belonged to Gerald. Then he equipped him with a stop watch and took the entire length of the pool in what appeared to be ten giant strokes. He cut back and forth nine or ten times in eight minutes, and rose from the pool, dripping and only barely out of breath, to instruct Warren on the need for correct breathing exercises. At fifty-four, he was desperately afraid of getting too fat, of growing old.

It was late in the day and there were only a few men in the pool, so they played a lively game of water polo. Alex seemed to have evaporated somewhere into the steamy chlorinated atmosphere but reappeared like a dutiful genie when it was time to leave.

Later in the locker room Warren thanked him enthusiastically. Harlan put his hands around the boy's smooth shoulders. He could almost feel his flesh curve into his palm. The amber gloss of his hair was Laina's hair, exquisite to his fingertips. To run his hand over it was satisfying and as close to loving her as he could get. Slowly he digested the boy's handsome face. "It was my pleasure, son, we should do it more often."

"When, sir?" Warren asked politely but with unbridled enthusiasm.

"I don't know just yet, son, let's wait and see." His eyes looked distant as green seas.

June 13, 1966
Dear Laina,

This letter is not an easy one to write and so, characteristically, I am compelled to write it. Through the years I have bowed to your wishes and have had but minimal contact with Warren. I have had no choice in the matter. Only through my relationship with your father have I been able to get any information at all about him. Because I know he has been depressed and troubled lately, I feel that he needs help, warm loving friends around him. Surely I am that, even if you permit me to be nothing else. You know that during Alex's afternoon visits with Warren I have on occasion met them by accident in the park or elsewhere, and we had wonderful times together. I don't like doing this behind your back. Your father and I are no longer as close as we used to be, I'm sorry to say, and still he encouraged these meetings. Why? It's obvious. Because he loves his grandson more than he disapproves of me. He sees that he is going through a painful adolescence and feels that he needs a male influence other than his "father," who is rarely around these days, I understand. Why do you stay with David? Are you still trying to prove a point? . . .

These words jumped at Laina from the page—they seemed so suddenly out of context. She continued reading, her legs barely sustaining her. It was difficult to turn the page, her fingers trembled, her hands were wet with perspiration.

. . . I think Warren should spend some time at my hotel in California this summer, or if you consider that too far, at least my place at Oyster Bay. The sun and water, the outdoor life will do him good. Vivian would like to have her brother's only grandson with her too, and Gerald might be good company for him. But still I might want us to be completely alone, I haven't decided that yet. Before I allow myself to think about it, I must hear from you on this. Please let me have my son, if only for a visit.

                Always,
                H.C.

He was, as always, demanding and presumptuous, she thought. What gave him the idea that he, some distant relative, could help her son? As for Alex staging those meetings, she considered his behavior treacherous. As always, she resented the strange bond between her father and *that man*. She wondered if Alex knew. It appeared that he did. Why would Harlan have told him?

She sat down and wrote a stiff, unimaginative letter that was surely written by a stranger. Someone she didn't know and didn't much like. She read it over once and tore it up. She decided to ignore the letter and the suggestion. No good could come of it. She was certain of that. Better to bury the past. She closed her eyes and wondered what his feelings for her might be now, if any. She thought probably that passion had curdled to bitterness.

Harlan and Vivian spent much of that summer in Europe, and so the question was temporarily laid to rest. But Harlan had no intention of letting it go, of surrendering his son to Laina's nameless terrors and subterfuges. Or to David, for that matter, whom he didn't consider equipped to handle Warren's entry into manhood. After all, he would be going out with girls any day now, perhaps he already was.

CHAPTER 57

Caroline and Craig Rosensweig were infrequent dinner guests at David and Laina's apartment, largely because their busy lives ran in opposite directions. Lately Laina had little patience for large elegant parties and preferred an occasional dinner with old friends. Seated in their charming burgundy-and-peach dining room, they talked pleasantly. Craig, raising his glass of carefully chosen Pouilly Fuissé, toasted the "maestro" as he insisted on calling David through the years "and his lovely accomplice." The two couples had more in common at this time than perhaps at any other time in their lives. Laina and David were concerned about Warren, and Caroline's mother, Tash, was very ill, dying a slow death from cancer. For Laina, Caroline's vivid descriptions raised specters of her own mother's death, although she had died quickly and quietly, without fanfare, a prudent death.

The first course was curry soup. When the meat course was served, a delicate and lovely pink rack of lamb, Caroline politely tasted it. The truth was that she could hardly bear to eat solid food after the harrowing weeks of sitting in her mother's hospital room, listening to her be sick, watching her drop back, yellow and exhausted against the pillow, waiting for the next bout. She sipped her wine instead.

By the time dessert was served, the four were quite loose-tongued, the men even pleasantly unruly.

After dinner Warren came in to say hello. He was polite and charming, commenting on Caroline's latest book, his large feline eyes burning in his drawn and sallow face. He retreated quickly to his room without so much as a glance at his father.

"Is he quite alright now, Laina?" Caroline asked quietly.

"Well, not *quite* alright, but he's better. He's getting there."

"It's all probably a normal part of adolescence," David said airily. "The glandular changes make young boys sulky."

Laina looked away, embarrassed by her husband and his mannerisms.

"Good thing you've both got me here to take care of you, that's all I can say." David was smiling absently.

"But we haven't," Laina said. "You are usually on the other side of the ocean."

David looked wounded. He made a gesture with his hand. "Darling, in front of our guests?"

"They're also our *old* friends."

"But here? Now? Oh, I don't think so," he said, shaking his head.

"For God's sake, stop patronizing me, David."

"Pax, pax," Craig interrupted, his hands in a papal gesture. "Before you know it, you'll start Miss Poison Pen over there on *her* pet peeve—children, or the absence of them. Sometimes I think we ought to be glad we don't have any, eh, Caroline? Something to argue about."

"We ought to be glad? Speak for yourself."

"When would you find time, for God's sake—you're so busy writing—assassinating your family in print."

"Yes, I know," she said bitterly, "instead of bringing life into the world, I'm bringing it out in paperback."

"Caroline, you are too hard on yourself. All writers write from experience," Laina said kindly.

"But mine seems to have been sadly limited, and now that mother's dying, I don't know where I'll get my next story from."

"Must each man kill the thing he loves in order to gain immortality in his art?" David asked, twirling a wine glass in his fingers, holding it up to the light. "I certainly hope not."

"David," Laina said, surprised, "That was cruel."

"Was it, darling? Well, I really didn't mean it to be." He rose suddenly and went out onto their small terrace to smoke. Craig followed him, lighting up a panatela on the way.

"Good riddance," Caroline said playfully, as she waved away the cloud of cigar smoke in her husband's wake. They were silent a moment. Caroline cunningly gauged just how candid she might be. "So he's off again, I suppose? Summer is almost here."

"You mean David?"

"Yes, can't he stay just this summer? Because of the boy—he needs a father now."

"I suppose *not*," Laina said, shrugging her shoulders.

"I see," Caroline said, slowly as if she *did* quite clearly see. Testing now, pressing her advantage still further, she asked, "Well, why can't you all go along together? The change might do Warren some good."

Laina shook her head and looked pleadingly at Caroline, begging her to drop the subject.

"Men are so damn selfish," Caroline said wearily. She had lost her nerve. The subject that hung between them was still as elusive as it had been when they were adolescents in the forties. "Why don't you leave him now—Warren is old enough," she kept her voice low.

"I seem to remember your being very enthusiastic about David when I married him."

"I wasn't really as sophisticated as I pretended. In fact I was almost as naive as you." They both smiled, remembering their tempered innocence. "You're still young. You can't go on like this forever—you can meet someone else, have a *normal* life."

"I couldn't do that to Warren; not now, not until he's better. It would be the ultimate cruelty to take his father away from him now. He would ask questions, wonder what happened suddenly, what was different now than before. Nothing *is* different, that's just it, nothing *has* really changed."

"Except you—you're different. Jesus, when is it going to be *your* time? Time to live for you?"

"I've had my time."

"Was it enough?" Caroline had switched to brandy after dinner; she was feeling reckless. "Oh, I'd love to put you in a book," Caroline said, smiling and shaking her head, her stiff curls bobbing woodenly. "I don't know if you realize it, but you've had quite a fabulous life!"

"Sounds like a eulogy."

"The strange thing is that in spite of your rather remarkable career you're still huddling beneath a man's umbrella for safety."

"I have my family to think of . . ."

"Yes, I'm no different," Caroline admitted. "I couldn't write a word until I was safely married." She sipped her brandy. Her eyes narrowed as if trying to get a picture in focus. "You know, some couples tend to get themselves into situations in which the partners are rather like brother and sister, or parent and child even. Perhaps you never really wanted to leave daddy, maybe because you had just found him. David replaced both father and brother for you."

Her life synopsized in this way, the awful truth washed over Laina, and she felt faint with comprehension. "That's absurd," Laina whispered. "Christ, Caroline, you're not going to put *that* in the book, are you? You know more about me than I do!"

"Nonsense, it's just that concentrating on someone else's worries takes my mind off my own." Caroline began to cry softly, tears splashing on her turquoise St. Laurent dress. "God, that woman is lying there in the agonies of a death that is positively medieval in its horror." She took Laina's arm and dug her fingernails deep into it. "When I wrote those things in the book—the way it hurt her—you'd think that would have been punishment enough for her, but no, now this—this final agony and humiliation."

"Why do you blame yourself for your mother's suffering?"

"I resented her—all my life I resented her—for not conforming to the accepted image of 'Mother'—the way she was in the story books—the way *other* mothers were—for not loving daddy," she said in a childlike, embarrassed voice. "Well, you know how she was," she said, blowing her nose, shifting the burden of proof. "She thought I was trying to get back at her in my books, but I swear I wasn't. I was just trying to expunge my own demons." She dabbed at her eyes and smoothed her dress, respectful of its impressive origin. The two women sat in stunned silence.

As it turned out, they stayed at the apartment in town that summer. Warren went to summer school. He needed to catch up. He would be sixteen over the summer, entering his junior year of high school in the fall and college was not far away.

CHAPTER 58

It was a house of mourning certainly, although this was by no means the usual condolence call. There had been no funeral—there would be none—until the body could be shipped back from Vietnam. The army could not tell them when or even *if* that would be. Laina and David moved self-consciously through the strangely empty house. There were a few knots of people looking drawn and tense, faces they did not recognize, concerned friends of the family, she supposed. David couldn't understand why Laina refused to bring Warren. "It is the correct thing to do, have him pay his respects," he said. She excused him on the grounds of his recent despondency. But the truth was that she feared it would appear as if now at last she was offering up her own son to Harlan as substitute for his loss. And she knew that one child could never replace another, and Harlan might somehow resent the sudden gesture. She had no wish for them to begin this very delicate relationship on the wrong foot. No, she was prepared to wait until the time was right. It had been more than six months since she had received that letter from Harlan.

Laina spotted a maid cleaning up cigarette butts in a corner of the vast dove gray and cream living room. She went over and asked for Mr. and Mrs. Chase. The maid informed her that Mrs. Chase was in her room lying down and so was Miss Joy. She thought she saw Mr. Chase go down to the basement some time ago, before it got dark.

432

"I'm going downstairs to see Harlan," she said to David. "I don't think we should overwhelm him. It is better that we see him separately. I'll go alone." It was a command. The December night was intolerant of sadness. She felt a draft of cold damp air as she descended the stairs to the basement, uncertain of what she would find there, or what she would say. At first she couldn't see anyone in the vast dark game room. But she heard the unmistakable click of billiard balls. Harlan seemed to materialize like smoke out of the hollow dimness. She could tell he had been drinking. He stood peering at her strangely, the cue stick still between his two fingers, poised for a shot.

"Well, well, what brought you here over the avalanche of years?" He leaned down heavily on the stick and squinted at the white number twelve ball, putting it neatly into the side pocket.

"I've come to see if . . . if there is anything I can do to help," she said.

He didn't reply. Just went on playing his solitary game. He could hardly see her anyway. The small light over the green baize table gave off a murky olive glow, indifferent, merciful. Nothing could be seen clearly.

He thought she had put on weight and seemed more at ease with herself. She was still beautiful. He wondered what his life might have been like had they married, asked Vivian for a divorce, given up his boys—*boys*, the word went through him like a knife. One boy had already given up his life, the other had given him up—disapproved the easy life that he and Vivian had provided. He hit the wooden ball hard with a stick that became a mallet, with heavy blows, his heart demanding release. He looked at Laina standing there in mute grief and impotence and thought of her brother Seth, all those many years ago—and now Steven. He could not ask about the boy now, her son. It was too soon. He could only think of Steven, the boy he'd brought up since babyhood, his firstborn. There was no room in his heart for another now. Not even Gerald, God help him, who sat dazed and angry in the dining room. Only Joy stayed close to her mother, comforted her. He couldn't bear to be with any of the family now. His mother had come by to see him yesterday, but only Vivian had sat with her in a queer, silent, locked-in sort of grief. Her sweet face was set for long suffering. He felt that his mother was accusing him of ruining Janine's life, of ruining his own with greed and lust for power, perhaps she even held him accountable for Steven's death. In the years since his father's death, Vivian and Marge had grown closer, even militant he thought, where he was concerned. The women in his life had all hardened their hearts against him. He was delirious with sorrow. He looked up at the step where Laina stood, still unmoving. He cried out from his reverie, "What have you done to yourself, living with him all these years? Why, why?"

She wanted to say all that was unimportant at a time like this, to diminish the past, but instead she said in an even tone, "*You* ask me this?" She was ashamed of the harsh metallic sound of her voice.

"Laina," he called out to her. He was weaving. "Do you suppose *this, everything,* is my fault?" She came over to him how, took the pool stick from his slackened fingers, and set it against the wall. He slumped against her for support. He buried his face in her long hair and cried deep anguished sobs. She put her arms around him and took careful inventory of every line and each gray hair as if to catch up with the years she had missed. She kissed his temples and pushed back the heavy damp hair from his forehead.

CHAPTER 59

Gerald Chase sat in Political Science A-202, one denim-clad leg thrust negligently into the aisle. It was the spring of his junior year. He clicked a stubby pencil restlessly against his teeth and appeared to be listening, though not exactly hearing. There was a discussion of current events—a question-and-answer period following the professor's lecture on Martin Luther King's recent proposal that the civil rights and antiwar movements merge. A tall black boy raised his hand and asked what the professor thought of King's statement that the U.S. Government was "the greatest purveyor of violence in the world."

The teacher ducked the question by calling on another student. The student, a boy of indiscriminate age, had shoulder-length hair and rumpled clothes and seemed to agree with the black leader's remark in a semidetached, uninvolved manner. He cited the latest casualty figures in Vietnam and the civilian casualty figures due to the intensive bombings. The professor seemed unimpressed. "Those facts are ugly, but they do not conclusively prove the statement. Can anyone else answer?" he said.

Gerald raised his hand. "He also counseled in favor of draft evasion—can we have some discussion on that?" he asked, unsmilingly. The class laughed. He sat down. It was terribly warm in the room, he thought. He was perspiring profusely. Everyone was talking at once.

Angry laughter. He wondered how many here in this classroom knew about his brother. He supposed no one. None of his group were in this class. While the class around him sputtered and argued in an unformed and uninformed manner, he squeezed down low in his chair and tried to conjure reasons, reasons for the senseless death of his brother. Wondered if maybe it had something to do with his parents—with God trying to tell them all something about allegiances or lack of them.

He and his brother hadn't really known who they were or exactly where they belonged in the scheme of things. He was groping for reasons—looking for answers. He wondered if he would be able to take the final exams that were coming up soon. He had not studied much lately. And he had missed a month or so in the winter, right after Steven's death. He had only returned to school for his parents' sake.

It was difficult to concentrate now, to smooth out the creases in his mind. The sleeping pills at night hadn't been working well, that is, until the daytime. Sometimes during the day he would feel his limbs jerk spasmodically as if finally clicking into place, relaxing, unfolding, just when he needed to be alert. Well, he could always take a benny—it was nothing. Everyone did it. Bennies gave him a hard nervous edge, pulled things painfully into focus, made him see things he'd never had to face before in his privileged life. Then he would light up with the others, smoke a few joints, fuzz *out* those sharp edges. He could handle it. He was sure he could handle it. He'd never resort to hard stuff like some of the guys—at least he never had yet.

The dreams were worse when he took the pills. Only the other night he dreamt that Steven and he were with their father on a glass-bottomed boat, like they used to do as children in Miami—and there suddenly, amid the exotic tropical flora, was the face of his brother, thin and mournful, looking up at them through the glass bottom. In the aqueous maze, his black hair stood up around his face like a crown of thorns. Old memories of treasure hunts, ballgames and long lazy afternoons on the beach with his father and brother brought the sting of salt tears to his nostrils.

On the front lawn bonfires burned and students seemed to be moving in great urgent waves. Gerald made his way pushing through crowds, ragged, hirsute, unwashed. Many wore their hair braided or straight to the shoulder. The young people looked strangely old and tired and unsatisfied. He pushed his way past a knot of students around a tall Christlike figure lecturing on top of an orange crate. He was dressed in black. His trousers were slit ominously to the knee so that they flapped like an Indian warrior's breeches. As he pushed past, he heard the word "millennium." Millennium had a mellifluous sound, he thought. He'd buy that—*a period of universal happiness*. When? he wondered. There was applause. A few walked away bored, shaking their heads in discord. "Doper," somebody grumbled, and shuffled off in a lopsided gait. Gerald looked straight ahead. He'd have to keep his priorities clean, not get caught up in the web of semantics—of Eastern philosophies and religions, being skimmed quickly and spewed carelessly everywhere he went. But it was tempting, gave you an excuse to drop out.

He headed purposefully for the north building. On the ground floor he opened the door of a room that bore the innocuous sign "Students for Peace." The air in the two-room suite was thick and green with smoke and smelled sour and yeasty. A few murmured greetings acknowledged him with respect. He felt better already. They hadn't accepted him at first, labeling him *rich boy* and *faggot*. But he had quelled their suspicions with his low-key militancy and family sacrifice. They believed him now somehow, he had a real stake in the movement. Gerald began to feel like the heroes of those Jewish novels his mother was always pushing into his hands—where noble young men of the Irgun, or other subversive groups, rallied to strike back, to certify that such carnage could never again take place. Yes, he thought, perhaps they would borrow the theme—update it somehow—no more Vietnams—no more martyrs like Steven Chase—Never again.

Gerald didn't come home from college that summer but wrote instead to his parents that "some of the guys and myself are considering trying a summer with Vista." A penance of sorts, Harlan supposed. "So don't worry about the bread. Might be a fine adventure and a wild change from home." His son's resentment rankled, and Harlan thrashed around, looking for reasons. He hadn't even said anything about stopping home for a visit. And he had signed it *your loving son, Gerald*. But Harlan suspected that was more as a sop to Vivian, and perhaps his conscience. When he discussed it with Vivian, she said curiously, "You have become the proverbial Jewish mother who will never let her children go."

CHAPTER 60

Laina's days were less busy than usual, for she was not working on any new lyrics. Her nights were endless and lonely, her weeks measured by the discarded *TV Guides*. David now spent almost half the year at Melodie, his villa at Antibes. She had never even seen it. She had to face the fact that her marriage to David was a failure. Their partnership was quite another thing. It was not only successful but enormously satisfying to both of them. Warren, at seventeen, understood the fine difference. But he didn't understand, or at least pretended not to understand, why the family must be separated for almost half of every year, or why there seemed to be some sort of tacit understanding that he could not visit his father.

He had driven the truth about his father so far back in his subconscious that he scarcely acknowledged it. His mother told him only that creative people needed time apart—time alone, away from family even, in order to recharge their energies—in order to survive. Because of the clumsily secret nature of the arrangements, Warren's adolescent imagination went feverishly to work. He imagined, even wanted to believe, that his father kept a woman. Perhaps an exotic Eurasian woman, or a Nubian woman, scantily clad, who jingled when she walked. Lately he had begun to think a lot about girls. His school was not coed, but he met girls at the school dances and on the bus.

David had frequently asked Laina if Warren could visit Melodie for at least a month or so, but she always refused, giving school and college preparations as the reason. But David knew why, of course, and he knew he was losing Warren. "What do you think goes on there, for God's sake? If you have a picture of bacchanalian revelries, it's simply not the case. Not at all. I work on my music, that's all."

"Then I imagine you must be quite lonely in such a big place," she said sardonically.

There was no reply.

"Well, in any case, do you honestly consider it an atmosphere for a growing boy?"

"Yes. Yes, I do, and you know I'd do my damnedest to make certain that there would be no impropriety."

She looked at him sadly. His life seemed bound in constant struggle between the traditional and the profane, between creativity and self-destruction. She looked rueful. "And what would you do with young Brian with the unpronounceable French last name, pray tell? Keep him in the dog house? Or sweep him under the rug?"

He sat down heavily and took her hand in his. "Laina, do you think I would corrupt the boy?"

"Not willingly, no, but perhaps you don't consider it corruption?"

"Laina, Laina, it's more than nineteen years since we married and still you can't accept the facts of my life."

She noticed that he had said, "since we married," but had not said, "We have been married nineteen years." Even he did not consider their life together a true marriage. Theirs indeed was a marriage of "true minds," she thought.

"Even now you are fleeing in terror from yourself,

THE PLEASURE DOME

from your son. As he gets older and wiser, you are terrified that he will discover your secrets. It is inevitable—why, already there was that awful experience with the French magazine."

"What awful experience?" He blanched. "What magazine?"

She had meant never to tell him, never to let him know, it could only further damage his relationship with Warren. But there was the need in her to punish him, to implicate *him* in her problems with Warren. Pitifully he begged her to tell him. Then he sat down shakily, his face devoid of color.

"My God, no wonder he has been so strained with me. How could you not have told me?"

"I didn't think it would help anything, and I don't even know how much of it he believes. He has never mentioned it to *me*, you understand."

"My God," he said. "Oh, my God."

She knew Harlan had been seeing Warren on rare occasions. Sometimes at the athletic club, or certain evenings for an early dinner. Warren had even asked his mother why they couldn't have him for dinner one night, "Maybe even with Aunt Vivian."

"You're really very loyal to dad," he had said, "to take the Goldmark side of the story, but aren't you carrying it a bit too far, Mother?" He seemed exasperated. "After all, that was all over years ago, and even Grandpa Alex, your own father, has stuck with Uncle Harlan. How do you think I feel when he practically invites himself to dinner here, and I have to make excuses, or just keep silent?"

Laina came close to her son and touched his shoulder. He drew back slightly. He was no longer a child, and he wanted that made quite clear. "Warren, would you like to spend some time with your Uncle Harlan for a month or so after summer school this year?"

He brightened up. His face spoke his enthusiasm, but he didn't answer, conscious of conflicting allegiances, and he didn't want to appear anxious or hungry for relationships.

"I think we can arrange something." What harm could there be in it? she thought. But even as she rationalized this way, she felt a sharp warming stab, a presentiment of disaster.

It would have been a blessed release, a catharsis, to have been able to put it all in a letter. A letter officially sanctioning their relationship, giving permission for Warren to spend the summer, or part of it, with Harlan. She would be able to finally address thoughts and doubts that had plagued her for these many years. She planned to say, "He is driven to you almost as if he sensed, as if he knew, how much you meant to me once." She would cement the father-and-son relationship immediately by reminding him of their own. There were things she was crying to share with him about the boy—about his unspoken disappointment with David, how few friends he had, and how much Harlan's friendship meant to him. But she could not do it. Behind everything lay the fear that the letter might be discovered. She would, of course, have sent it to the office and cautioned him to destroy it. Still, what if Harlan should take it in his head to show it, or parts of it to Warren, or to Vivian even, to prove some point of his, perhaps in an argument? Laina knew she was not making any sense but still could not control her fears. She knew that the correct thing to do was to invite Harlan and Vivian for dinner and then talk about their summer plans. She would include Vivian instead of shutting her out. But she remembered those dinners with them at the hotel, during those months of erotic stupor, and she could not face that either.

In the end, she and Warren together called Harlan at his office. "He would like to hear it from you," she had said to Warren.

After Harlan finished talking to Warren, he asked to speak to Laina. "Will you come down with him?" he said softly into the phone. For the moment she was completely disarmed.

"No, of course not," she said, thinking she sounded ungracious. "Warren would prefer to travel alone. The trip will give him a sense of much needed autonomy." She wondered if her sudden capitulation was misunderstood by him.

So Warren spent the month of August with Harlan at the Pleasure Dome in San Diego the summer before his senior year. He got a crash course in resort hotel management and fell in love with the business. He considered his great Uncle Harlan the perfect teacher, and generally quite wonderful. For the first summer in years, he hardly thought about his father at all.

Vivian left shortly before Warren came down. "I think it's best for Warren to have you all to himself," she said. If Harlan didn't completely understand her attitude, at least he was grateful. Warren was the ideal pupil, a veritable sponge.

Harlan knew that swimming was not exactly Warren's best sport, and tennis only slightly better. So he put him in charge of the courts and pro shop. However, his job included checking all athletic facilities, overseeing the general cleanliness of the grounds and making certain that they were kept up regularly by the various special contractors—pool cleaners, gardener, maintenance crews. He had created a sort of official groundskeeper job, to keep him outdoors in the sunshine, moving and exercising. He was forced to roam the great length and breadth of the resort daily. In a month's time, his hair had turned the soft honey color of his mother's. His green eyes were arresting against the deep tan, and the resemblance to his father had become startling. He had adopted his walk, a certain stance, and many of his mannerisms in the short space of time.

The hotel business was not all that Harlan had in mind to teach him. Warren refused to talk to Harlan about his father and was almost as reticent on the subject of girls. As for girls, Harlan quizzed him so soundly that Warren considered inventing stories to please him.

If his enthusiasm for Harlan's business was great, it was matched only by his enthusiasm for his daughter, Joy. She spent ten days with them at the hotel, but in that time Warren forgot everything but the moment. They had long soul-searching talks about everything from the weather and philosophy and politics to medicine, which she confided was her great love. She told him of her dreams of getting into medical school. She supposed her chances were next to nil in America. Her marks were excellent, she said, but of course it could not change her sex, for which Warren thanked God.

Harlan was almost painfully aware of the resemblance between himself and Warren, particularly when Joy was around. He wondered if she noticed it too. If so, she had never commented on it. He was glad they were friends; perhaps when and if Gerald ever came home, they too could become friends.

Right after Labor Day Warren went home. He kept

remembering the day before he left. They were sitting at the swimming pool, Joy's long brown legs stretched out to the sun. She had said, "You know, Warren, we were born only months apart, but I like *my* birthday month best. When I was little, I used to say 'Sep-tender' for September. And I still feel *Septender* in my heart about this month. It's so full of the promise of renewal, of ripe beginnings, a reawakening of hope, a sort of yearly renascence." He was profoundly moved by what he considered her rare combination of innocence and eloquence.

By the time summer ended, Warren had decided to apply to the Cornell School for Hotel Management and Harlan was delighted.

CHAPTER 61

Laina had developed the habit of attending social functions alone, or occasionally with Warren. She had been doing it for the last few years, since David began extending his summers abroad. She was at a benefit for the American Theatre Wing at the Helen Hayes in early fall while David was still in Antibes. The event brought out a cross section of Broadway talent. She was flattered to think that the noted conductor of the Israeli Philharmonic, Zev Elon, would conduct the overture from *Fragments*, their latest score, as his contribution. He was in New York to do a benefit program for a new university to be built in Jerusalem.

When he ascended the podium, everyone applauded. He turned toward the audience and said he understood that Miss Eastman was in the audience, would she please rise and make herself known? A spotlight sought her out and landed on her squarely. When she stood, Elon indicated her presence with his baton briefly and bowed deeply to her. He was a large, disheveled man, whose shoulders seemed constrained in the narrow confines of his tail coat, and she wondered idly if he would make it when the music reached its passionate climax before the last reprise. His entire body moved in sublime and secret motion, his straight fine hair swung like black silk in the wind. From his pictures she remembered him as having a strong face, but somehow she could not remember anything else. She found his graceful and athletic motions seductive. She could barely keep her mind on the music, although she had never heard it sound better. Semipopular music was a departure for him. He conducted classical music, though not necessarily traditional. His specialties were Schoenberg, Stravinsky and Mahler.

Later on, at the private party at the Rainbow Room, they met informally.

"I have long been an admirer of yours," he said across a tray of canapés. The waiter moved away and she felt sharply the sudden abyss between them. She met his glance and felt disturbed by his presence. He gazed at her, appraising and approving.

"You *are* beautiful," he said in his soft Israeli accent, as if surprised. "Somehow I expected a different sort of woman."

"Well," she laughed. "How do you know I'm not, a different sort of woman, I mean."

"I suppose I meant older."

"I'm that too." She realized she was flirting with him.

He cleared his throat as if preparing for an important declaration. "Mrs. Goldmark," he said, "I would very much like to talk to you about bringing *Fragments* to Jerusalem, perhaps for the twentieth anniversary independence celebration, beginning in the spring."

She wondered why he made a point of calling her Mrs. Goldmark, instead of Miss Eastman as she was known professionally. She felt momentarily let down, as if his interest in her might only be professional.

"But that is almost a year away, and many things can happen in a year."

"We are beginning to plan this now."

"Well, I do know that my son's graduation will be at

the end of May, so of course I must be here." She trailed off uncertainly. He grimaced as if to control his irritation.

"I am not thinking in terms of May particularly. The celebration will run all through the summer into the fall. You must remember that we are a country that relies heavily on tourists, American tourists," he said with a smile in his eyes.

"Will you be in town much longer?"

"Probably just through the balance of the week."

Today was already Wednesday. She hoped her disappointment didn't show. People came over and pulled him away. He smiled at her apologetically. She was very tired; her car and driver would be downstairs. She quietly got her jacket from the checkroom. Her long chiffon gown swished gently as she moved down the hall toward the elevator. At the elevator she turned quickly to see him behind her. She was surprised. She had not heard him come up.

"May I take you home?" he asked.

She was about to mention her waiting car, then thought better of it and said only, "Thank you, yes."

He was staying at the St. Regis, he said, and so if she didn't mind, he would get off first as it was close by and on her way home.

In the taxi he asked, "Have you ever been to Israel?" He pronounced it "Yisrael" in the Hebraic.

"Yes, once, but rather too briefly, in connection with our play. It was an unforgettable experience."

"I see," he said. "You bottled our local color and took it home, did you? As research?"

She colored slightly. "You make it sound so crass." There was a silence.

THE PLEASURE DOME

"You must come again," he said with a finality, "and linger a while."

In what seemed to her like a split second, they pulled up in front of his hotel. He leaned forward, gave her address to the driver, and a five-dollar bill. He kissed her hand charmingly and told her he hoped she would indeed revisit his country, and then was gone.

She felt let down. She realized that neither one of them had asked any personal questions about the other; she had never even asked him if he was married, and he hadn't asked her for her phone number. Well, she was used to theatrical people, quixotic, all of them, she thought.

At the end of the week, Zev Elon telephoned and asked if he might see her. He wished to discuss *Fragments* and the anniversary program. He asked politely if David would care to join them and she explained that he was in Europe. That was all. They met at the King Cole Bar of the St. Regis.

"Actually my husband is never here in summers, and it is unlikely that he would attend the anniversary program. He is most rigid, I'm afraid, about not having theatrical obligations after May fifteenth, when he leaves for Europe. It is his time to create and he allows nothing to interfere with it." She was conscious that she was letting him know of her availability.

"Not even you?" he asked, smiling.

She fidgeted with the matchbook. "Not even me."

"But I thought you composed together, that you are a team."

"I provide the words to fit his music."

"And what a perfect blend, and what an accommodating wife you are."

"I don't write lyrics for all of his music. Right now he is working on music that is strictly orchestral—for concert."

He never removed his eyes from her face when she spoke. His gestures were quick and nervous, but he used his eyes as a surgeon uses a scalpel, probing, penetrating. His charm lay in his intense concentration. Whomever he spoke to had the full force of his attention.

"Well, in any case I hope we will have the pleasure of *your* company at least." She knew he was maintaining protocol, perfect formality until she gave him some further signs, assurances even, that he would not be rejected. But she had forgotten how to be seductive. She wasn't even conscious of the fact that she might be, without trying. He spoke about his work, his music. She spoke little about hers, feeling unequal to his genius. Hesitantly, she asked why he had not turned to composing.

"I prefer to hear one hundred people play music the way *I* hear it. There is nothing else I aspire to." His statement was peaceful. She had known few peaceful men in her life.

"Anyway, I hope I will have the pleasure of your company. I would like to show you my country, it is exceptionally beautiful for its age," he said, smiling a little.

"Because of it."

His face, with its feral gracelessness, fascinated her. It was somehow powerfully beautiful, like the music he conducted. Wild, not always perfectly interpreted, but more powerful because of its deviations.

As they sat at the small round table, their knees touching, she felt the first sharp pull of desire since those early years with Harlan.

THE PLEASURE DOME

Delving into his past, she discovered that he had been a hero of the Irgun in the years immediately after the war. Rumanian by birth, his name had been Ellonesque. He had changed it to the more Sabra-sounding Elon. He had escaped from Auschwitz and had hidden out in forests and farm houses during the last year of the war. Later the DP camp had sent him to Israel. He was an orphan—his parents and his two older brothers had gone to the ovens. He had lived with an old Israeli couple who were childless and who were happy to take in this gangling young man with the coarse and wild look of a gypsy.

He looked somehow out of place among the insubstantial hotel furnishings, the pale peach decor. On his bureau, there was the photograph of a woman, dark, exotic, interesting.

"My wife was Arabic," he declared as if forced to confess early and get it over with. "She was killed during a raid by her own people, curiously enough. It was more than three years ago."

"I'm sorry," she said. "How terrible for you. Are there children?"

"No," he said. "Our only child, a son, died at birth."

Laina said nothing but felt intrusive here. She was conscious of the injustice. This man had given so much to his country, and it had only extracted more. She made a comment about it.

"No, they have given me much too. The opportunity to be a part of its growth and development, and the freedom to interpret my music as I wish."

The kiss was a surprise. She really hadn't expected to like it. She had forgotten the excitement of a sudden kiss that ignites like wildfire.

JUDITH LIEDERMAN

He was gentle with her, but he was also an aggressive lover. He marveled at her breasts, grew excited by them, kissed them passionately. He touched her navel with his fingertips, leaned on his elbow and discovered the richness of her body, gently probing the delicate butter-pink folds inside the downy wedge, and entering her only when she cried out for him. Her obvious enjoyment drove him to distraction, to please her further. He withdrew himself from her and while her thighs were still parted he let his lips slide down her belly to her inner thighs. His tongue caressed her liquid parts. When she moaned, he entered her again and they came together. Reality returned in slow motion. They lay beside each other quietly, waiting until their breathing returned to normal.

"Lo, my love, you are beautiful," he murmured. "I translate from the Hebrew. I knew it would be like this from the first moment I saw you. I will not be able to wait until the summer for you to come to Israel, that much is certain."

He did not speak much, and she did not encourage him, as most subjects would ultimately lead back to the realities, for now an unwelcome intrusion. But for the first time in years, she began to think seriously about divorce.

CHAPTER 62

His room in the dorm wasn't much different than the one at home, Harlan thought. No, in fact it was the same room transplanted, without the water view. He had grown up, but he'd brought his toys along. A stained paper cup held stale coffee, the chemical cream solidified on top. On the floor a tangle of sneakers, unraveling sweaters and faded jeans were tossed over a chair. Gerald's clothes blended with his roommate's. If their discarded clothes were any symbol of their lives together—they were compatible. Great friends. This was a different roommate than last year. Harlan remembered that Gerald hadn't gotten along with the last one.

"What do you want, son?"

Gerald's intense face twisted painfully, his eyes looked past his father at some unseen enemy. "I just want to be in jail with the rest of my buddies. That's all. I don't like this being singled out."

"Don't you care about graduating?" his father asked miserably. "Do you want these last three years to come to nothing?"

"No, I care, but I care about this more."

"But this can ruin your life," his father said, aghast at his son's detachment.

"Don't you care about Steven?" Gerald asked.

"Christ, what has that to do with anything now? How

will this help Steven? Will it bring him back?" Gerald, who had been sitting on the edge of his unmade bed, leaned his head against the wall and closed his eyes, as if he might shut his father out—his obtuseness. He cracked his knuckles loudly. Restless youth, drumming fingers, cracking knuckles—different youth than we knew, he thought—unpoised, unstrung. From the adjoining room Harlan could hear clearly the Beatles pulsing through the wall, singing something about *Strawberry Fields*, a plaintive ballad about the past. Nowadays youth was preoccupied with its past; in his day, it was the future.

On the wall, above his son's bed, a banner read, "God Is Dead." This was a new one. Harlan hadn't seen that one before; perhaps it was his roommate's. He hadn't imagined that Gerald thought much about God, one way or another. The children had been raised in a home without any emphasis on religion. If asked, they usually said they were Jewish. Vivian had said that children born of a Jewish mother are Jewish. But on his college application Gerald had scrupulously written half-Jewish, half-Catholic. Only Steven had been Bar Mitzvahed. After that it was as though Vivian had given up. Religion became so diluted that it was almost devoid of essence. But Vivian was proud of her Jewishness and could not be the keeper of her husband's faith, one that he neither kept, nor, she felt, ever completely let go. Perhaps each parent thought secretly that one day the children would choose for themselves. In the meantime religion had simply died of attrition in that family. Now, for the first time Harlan gave thought to the possibility that Gerald, perhaps all of his children, resented the tender no man's land of religion that their parents' union had created.

"Do you think that by violent actions you are

THE PLEASURE DOME

respecting your brother's principles? He did what he had to do, what he believed was right. He was a hero!"

"He died to have you say that. Can't you see?" Gerald said, a wild look in his glazed eyes. "Power and money were your heroes. Steven couldn't compete with that, so he had to show you he was a hero too."

Harlan looked at him, amazed. Perhaps his son was mad. Just a little mad like his Uncle Matthew, or his Aunt Janine. Money seemed to be currently *out* and sex was *in* with this generation. He had been born at the wrong time. He knew he wasn't thinking rationally himself anymore. He would try to be reasonable now—fall upon his mercy. "Don't you think your mother and I have suffered? It would be adding insult to injury to lose you too. If you are expelled, you will lose your deferment. Don't you read the newspapers? Or are you only interested in making the headlines?" Harlan sat down wearily on the roommate's bed.

"I know, Dad," he said, "I know. But I'm not going to war, I can promise you that, man."

Harlan looked confused, defeated.

Gerald closed his eyes, ran his hands through his abundant hair. "I'm sorry, Dad, but I really didn't mean for it to go off like that, it just got away from us that's all. It somehow got away," he whispered. He seemed confused, like the clothes tangled and piled in the corners of the room.

"What do you mean, just got away? What did you expect would be the result of a homemade bomb? You're lucky no one was killed. You can't go around blowing up buildings. Who do you think you are, all of you?" He was shouting.

"Hey, cool it, man, let's see what the dean has to say

first. Maybe it's not as bad as all that." He sounded toned down. "He wanted to see you alone. Maybe it's not as bad as it looks from here."

"Maybe it's worse."

In the dean's office Harlan looked uncomfortable and out of place in his elegantly tailored sports clothes, his fine custom-made linen shirt, and with his casually waving hair. Gerald had told him he looked too Hollywood to be believable. When the dean's secretary finally called him into his office, he was tired and irritable. The dean stood and shook hands across a neatly ordered desk. WASP manners, Harlan thought. Larkspur bloomed in a cut-glass vase on his desk. He remembered the quiet precision of the nun's offices at the schools of his boyhood and felt momentarily at peace.

The dean told the story of bands of demonstrating youths, marauding, burning. Harlan thought of the Ku Klux Klan stories of his youth, burning down churches, harassing Jews and Catholics. But his son was an avowed liberal, an idealist, Harlan tried to assure the dean. He called upon the shade of his dead son to spread an umbrella of mercy over this one, his last remaining legitimate son.

"He is grieving over his brother's death," Harlan said. "I—that is, we have had so many losses." He rambled, thought of his whole life in terms of loss and it just slipped out unbidden.

"I know, I know." The dean was old and tired, accustomed to appeasing over-ambitious or disappointed parents, "and for that reason alone I blocked his arrest, at the risk of losing my reputation for fairness with the other students. But he cannot stay at this school any longer. Do you understand my position, Mr. Chase? We can't have anarchy."

Harlan listened but he didn't really hear; after his initial definitive statement, everything else was blocked out. In the midst of the soft, apologetic narrative, Harlan exploded at the word "expelled."

"Expelled? But where will he go? He'll have to go to war."

The dean stopped talking. There was a sudden silence. He looked down at the discreetly polished scratches on his desk and said, "I'm sorry, Mr. Chase."

Harlan offered to make a large donation to the school in the name of his dead son.

"The Steven Chase Memorial Fund, or something like that," he said, waving a hand graciously, *noblesse oblige*.

"That is very generous. We could use the money, but of course that won't change anything. The decision has already been made."

"But what am I going to tell my wife?" Harlan asked, searching the dean's face for help.

The dean shook his head. "The only thing you can tell her is the truth." He paused a moment, seeking to ease the situation, "And that it is only a phase. It will pass, and your child will come home again." He spoke as if lecturing to multitudes.

As Harlan left the office, he realized that was what he wanted to believe, more than anything else in the world.

Harlan hadn't really expected Gerald to return with him to Oyster Bay. He had strayed too far from home.

"I'm gonna hang out here for a while, Dad, with some of my buddies—see what happens with them," he had said. He might look for a job around Berkeley, or maybe he would just head for the hills. He was not going to sit around, waiting to be drafted.

"Perhaps if you begin applying to other schools?" his

father asked falteringly, unsure of what the right side of this situation was, or even if there was one.

"What other schools are you talking about? I mean, who would take me in with this on my record, I ask you?"

Harlan dreaded confronting Vivian with the news. On his way out, he had said, "Let us know where you are, son." Then he had turned back and said, "Whatever you decide to do, I'm with you on it."

"Hey, thanks, man, that helps."

That was late November.

Except for a strange, somewhat codified New Year's telegram, postmarked Canada, they had heard nothing in months, until today.

March 14, 1968
Provence de Quebec, Canada
Dear Mom and Dad,

> Please forgive the long delay in writing, but I wanted to wait until I had concrete things to tell you—didn't want to leave you hanging again. I'm living on a farm, in a small town in Quebec. It is called "Trois Rivières." I'm learning farming from the bottom up and really love it. The Verniers have quite a lovely farm here, one that is very lucrative.

Harlan imagined that last line was for his benefit.

> They have about fifty acres of beautiful farmland here. But oh, what they could do with some modern American equipment. I tell them all the time about our advanced farm equipment, and they are incredulous. Wish my high school French were better, but I'm grateful now for two years of remedial

French I took at college (you should excuse the expression). I suppose I mostly wish my French were better because the Verniers have the most wonderful and beautiful young daughter imaginable. Her name is Nielle, small and fair, with mounds of russet hair, and she laughs a lot. She is extremely devout and pious, more so even than her parents, and is teaching me all about Catholicism. It is so fascinating, I never realized how beautiful it was, living so near to it all my life and yet so far.

Harlan stopped reading for a moment, crushed by the implication in those words. He remembered the banner above his son's bed, "God Is Dead." So Gerald resented his failed Catholicism.

Vivian put her hand gently on her husband's arm, "Read on, darling, please."

I go to Mass with Nielle every morning. It is no longer said in Latin, as you know, but she explains that she was brought up on the Latin Mass and that it was even more moving and spirited. I have all I can do to understand the ecclesiastic French. I am learning to say the catechism like a schoolchild.

"Perhaps he needs the sting of Catholic discipline," Harlan said. He read the closing lines.

I really do miss you. Please write. Perhaps you will come up here to visit one day, or God willing, when this mess is over I'll bring Nielle down to meet you.

> Your loving son,
> Gerald

JUDITH LIEDERMAN

Harlan had been standing by the window, reading the letter and leaning on his cane. His old leg wound had been acting up lately. He folded the letter and handed it to Vivian. "He sounds like a stranger." Slowly he lowered himself into a chair.

"Well, I'm glad he's safe and happy. That's all I care about," Vivian said.

As the children grew older, it seemed to him that they had exchanged roles. Vivian's once impassioned orthodoxy had given way to a laissez-faire attitude about the children, even before Steven's death. She had become rather disenchanted with her assigned position of Housekeeper of the Flame. But he found himself more and more dependent on the children. He had few friends. In the past he had no time for them, and he trusted few men and fewer women.

"He's a fugitive now, you know." Harlan remarked.

"Aren't we all?"

"Well, at least he found himself a farmer's daughter, that's in his favor."

Vivian smiled. "She's very pious, darling."

"They're the worst kind." Ruminating, he said, "Of course, if he marries her and settles in Canada, I suppose we'll never see him."

"And they say Jewish parents never let go of their children," Vivian said calmly. "You've got to stop using your children as a crutch for your old age."

"Old age! Christ, woman! I'm not old—at fifty-five. I don't look old. I can still swim fifty laps in a half-hour." He punched his stomach. "And my gut's still hard as a rock. And that isn't all, right, girl?" He winked at Vivian. "So let's hear no more talk about old age, just because of this damned wound." He threw his cane to the floor in a gesture of defiance or disgust.

Vivian was laughing. "Still," she said, undaunted by the outburst, "lean on me, Harlan, when you need to. We should turn to each other for comfort, not to them. Let them shape their own lives."

He looked at his wife with approval. She was a damn smart woman. No other woman would have been able to tolerate him. Not even Laina Eastman. Vivian's eyes, warm and brown, were smiling down at him from above his desk chair. He took her small hand and kissed the palm. A damn smart woman. He was overcome with gratitude at his good fortune.

The telephone rang shrilly. Vivian rose to answer it. When she hung up she looked at Harlan and said in a voice that was strong and calm. "The airport just called. They're bringing Steven home."

CHAPTER 63

Harlan was tired of winning. The thrill had gone out of the game, the elements of risk depleted. He had just kept upgrading the company's assets and enriching its properties. The stockholders were happy. The company had moved from the American Exchange to the big board. Still, nothing was ever perfect, he supposed, nothing as big and as glorious as success came completely easy.

He was uneasy with Alex being on the board as a major stockholder. He sensed his growing antagonism ever since he had admitted to him the whole truth about Laina, about their son. Now, if there was an opportunity to oppose him in a business deal, Alex found it. Alex had friends on the board whom he could influence. Harlan knew that Alex regretted relinquishing the hold on his dance halls, giving up his independence. But three years ago they had sold them at a surprising profit. A ten-million-dollar profit. More than three times their original value. Alex still could not, would not, admit that Harlan Chase had made him rich beyond his wildest dreams.

Harlan had often thought about selling the company. A large corporation had already made advances to him, offered him twenty dollars per share above the market price. He was tempted to take the offer, but Alex and Matthew always pulled in the opposite direction. Whichever way Harlan wanted to go, Alex wouldn't. Harlan was

THE PLEASURE DOME

paying the price for his uncanny success. He would be forced to drag these two albatrosses around his neck forever.

Nevertheless, Harlan was steadily becoming divested of responsibility. His organization ran like clockwork. He had put good people to work for him. His familial responsibility had dwindled too. Steven was gone, Gerald was on his own, and now Joy was going off to college and talking about spending the summer in Israel. So when Harlan received Warren's graduation invitation he was delighted. Maybe this child, from that impassioned union, might wind up his salvation.

Zev Elon had told Laina without apology that he had a heavily booked schedule as guest conductor, would be traveling through much of Europe on one- or two-day stands, and therefore might not be able to return to New York until early next year. He bombarded her with flowers. Everywhere he went, from each foreign city, he sent flowers. Occasionally there were letters in his elegant foreign hand. Laina was satisfied to wait for him. She was happier than she had ever been at any time in her life and began to think that life begins at forty after all.

When David returned from Europe, she asked him for a divorce. He was not surprised. He knew their marriage had always been made on borrowed time. He was grateful, he said, for its unexpected longevity. "I always thought the words and music blended beautifully," he said.

He took an apartment on Sutton Place, his "old neighborhood." They had come full circle, she on Central Park West, and he back on Sutton Place. He planned to postpone his usual departure in May until after graduation.

In January, Zev Elon returned, mostly to be with her, and they rediscovered New York. It was truly a city for lovers.

In the small Bemelman's Bar at the Hotel Carlisle, where he was staying, he proposed to her. "I love you," he said.

And I am tired of being alone. She finished the sentence for him silently.

"Of course, we would have to make Israel our home base. I don't know how you feel about that. But we would travel all over, and we could still keep your apartment in New York if you wished." He said it all in a rush, as if fearful that she might refuse before she heard the good part.

It was April, and Faye loved Miami in April. The weather was sunbathe hot, which she adored. It was a balm for the arthritis she would never admit to. Sitting in bed at her suite at the crumbling old Hibiscus Gardens, that fading bastion of civilized hospitality, she sipped the remains of the coffee on her breakfast tray and opened the morning mail. Studying the invitation to her grandson's graduation, she felt only anger toward her son for depriving her of a satisfying old age rich with relationships.

Her relationship with Warren and Laina had attenuated through the years, particularly since David had become only a part-time parent. The scene in room 118 was forever between them, her and her daughter-in-law. Faye supposed that her son felt vulnerable and superfluous with a son who was now really a grown young man. He probably didn't know exactly how to act with him, so he simply stayed away. It was sad, she thought. His work and his reputation were suffering also. In spite of the great pains he had gone to to remove his private life from the family and from public speculation, his occasional flirtations with musicians and ballet dancers were snickered at behind his back. And as for Brian Lepardieu, well, that was common gossip among the international set. She was making no excuses for him.

As for Matthew's hopes for an undisturbed retirement, he was steadily investing and losing his lately recouped fortunes. He had invested in the building of two new resort hotels, one in Atlantic City and one here in Miami Beach, but the areas were used up, rapidly sinking into obsolescence. She knew it. He *must* have known it. Matthew, the King of Marvin Gardens. Those investors who still could, pulled out, leaving the early investors holding the bag. Matthew had to sell large amounts of stock in Pleasure Domes, Inc. When Faye berated him for doing this—accused him of being reckless, he said he needed to test his ability once again before he died. Besides, he didn't care about leaving anything behind for his son. His son was a rich man. As for Faye, well there was a hefty insurance policy. Faye sighed. Her life could have turned out better, she supposed, but was not quite sure how. She rose from her bed to put Warren's invitation in her desk and mark it on her calendar, when her eyes fell on a side column of the front page of the *Miami Herald*.

SINGING STAR IN SUICIDE

Russell Drake, singing star of the early forties and fifties, jumped last night from the window of the Classic Arms Hotel.

The Classic Arms, she knew, was one of those run-down hotels on upper Broadway. The article continued.

> He was fifty-one years old, and lately had been singing only occasionally at small hotels in the Catskills. His career had been on a decline since his brush with the House Un-American Activities Committee in 1952. No subversive connections had ever been proved, but somehow he was unable to make a successful comeback, although he tried several times in the late fifties and sixties. He had been despondent over his failed career. He had been living alone.

The article continued on the obituary page, but she could not read on. She put the paper down and struggled to bring his face into focus. For a moment she thought she caught the old professional smile, lopsided and profane. If only she could remember exactly what he looked like, she knew she would feel better. She tore through the newspaper to see if there was a picture on the obituary page, but there was none. It all seemed so pointless now, so immoral. She could not even remember his face.

CHAPTER 64

The small crowded auditorium smelled of early summer and gardenias. Sitting between David and Harlan, Laina felt smothered by a lifetime with these two dissimilar men. The scene seemed bizarre. There on stage receiving a diploma was the product of her only real happiness, and her deepest shame, the most tangible evidence of a brief happiness that had come and gone in what seemed like a landslide. She felt awed by his creation and yet was tied to Harlan reluctantly, by this child.

In front of her sat Matthew, Faye and Alex. Faye's carefully lacquered and teased hair was held in place discreetly by a tiny navy-blue veil. Still attractive at sixty-one. They sat, facing the front, intent upon the action on stage, neither moving nor conversing. The three wise monkeys. She glanced at Harlan, hands folded quietly on his lap. He had calmed down through the years, subdued by tragedy and complex responsibility. His hands were strong and surprisingly youthful still. Women's hands were the giveaway of their age, but men's hands seemed immutable. She was glad that Vivian had not come. At the last moment, she had pleaded a virus. She wondered if Harlan had somehow managed that, or had Vivian herself sensed her superfluousness here at this strange reunion.

When Warren shook hands with the headmaster, David patted her hand affectionately and whispered something about his pride in Warren. She knew he wanted to assure her that this would be an amicable divorce. She had told David about Zev. He only said in his rather jocular, offhand manner, "Ah, so at last a *real* maestro, well, he's more entitled in every way."

She looked at Harlan now and wondered if he had heard about Zev also. He usually knew everything, even before it happened. This time she doubted it. She resented him for the way it had ended, the way she had learned about Vivian's pregnancy. Deep down she also resented him for not having begged her to forgive him, for having left her too alone.

Sitting beside her, Harlan was thinking about how it had ended. He had tried to prolong it until the last possible moment. They had lived their lives almost as one—until her belly grew high and hard; when he placed his hand on it, he could feel it flutter with life. Still, she had never yet admitted it was his child, though she didn't deny it either.

Now there was no mistaking it. A warm, satisfied smile played around his mouth, but he subdued it behind a polite cough. The boy standing there was so much like him as to be an embarrassment. It was *his* face, with just the right touch of her delicacy. Sitting beside her on the closely packed chairs, their thighs touching, he felt her warmth pulse through him like an electric force. For him she had always been a life force, a feeling he had never experienced until her. Even now he was ashamed of the sensation creeping up warm and slow and sweet in all his limbs, the scent of her, an ache of nostalgia. He was pleased that she had allowed him at last into Warren's life. Now, when he needed a son, when they needed each other. Much as he loved the boy who stood up there now, he could never take Steven's place. He hoped she did not think *that* . . .

THE PLEASURE DOME

* * *

After the graduation exercises, the immediate family went back to the Des Artistes. Laina's staff had prepared a beautiful celebration, and there were magnums of Dom Perignon from David's vast cellars at Melodie. The family stood around irresolutely. Some of Warren's classmates dropped in and he was busy laughing and joking with them in easy camaraderie. Laina felt gratified. Warren's marks had been excellent his senior year, and he had been accepted at the Cornell Hotel School. She felt mixed emotions; she wasn't at all certain she was in favor of Warren preparing to spend a lifetime side by side with Harlan Chase.

Alex drifted over to where the boys stood. Warren's arm dropped about his grandfather's shoulder and pulled him into the inner circle of youth. Alex told a joke about girls in hushed tones, and the boys laughed knowingly. David and even Harlan looked on in envy.

Laina was pleased by the happy relationship between her son and her father. Perhaps at last he could fill the space left vacant by Seth so long ago. She had wanted to name her son for her brother, but feared he would die young. It was *bad luck*. Now she was glad she hadn't. Warren might have lost his identity completely. He would have *become* Seth Eastman, where Alex was concerned.

Harlan found himself standing next to David in the small foyer.

"I enjoyed *Fragments* very much, David," he said politely. "You're getting closer all the time to my favorite music, opera."

"I'm trying. It's not such a major transition as one might suspect."

"Yes, well, it was a wonderful show—and timely, very

timely. Thank God for a writer who writes for his time. Artists usually prefer to go back to the past for their material." David smiled his pleasure. The two men had always kept a safe distance, each sensing the other's disapproval. Now that Harlan knew about the impending divorce, he found David much more acceptable. But it was always the same. He never knew what to talk to him about, so he just stuck to music. It was safe, orthodox conversation between two unorthodox men.

David was the first to leave, explaining unnecessarily, Laina thought, that he had to pack. He was leaving tomorrow for Cap d'Antibes.

Warren detached himself from his friends for a moment. He went over to David and shook hands stiffly. "Thanks for coming, sir," he said. "I hope you have a good trip." Words that sped him on his way. David's hand trembled slightly as he buttoned his coat.

Harlan stayed until the last. Warren had gone somewhere with the boys, perhaps to another graduation party. He did not know when he'd be home, he said.

Harlan asked if she would like to come back to the Hampshire House, where he was staying overnight. Have coffee and talk about Warren's summer.

"Yes, I'd like that," she said. She wasn't sure why or just what was in her mind, but she felt propelled by the old electric excitement. She knew they could talk right here.

Sitting on the sofa of his hotel suite, she felt reckless. She sipped brandy and listened to the deep familiar voice as if from long distance.

"I haven't even told Warren yet, but he is going to work in Israel for the summer. I am breaking ground in Jerusalem there, for the first American resort-style hotel."

"Israel?" She seemed startled.

"Is that too far away from mommy?"

"You're being sarcastic. No, it's just that, quite frankly, I had thought of spending some time there this summer." She wanted to tell him about Zev.

"So, the more, the merrier; one big happy family." He smiled suggestively, looking into her eyes with a raised brow.

"No, I think this summer belongs to Warren, unimpeded by family. He needs to feel autonomous," she said.

"Actually, I can't stay either. I just want to start Warren off. He might stay with friends of mine, at the builder's home," he said. "It will do him good to work in the sun, live simply, see the land of his forefathers—all of them," he said playfully, still not removing his eyes from her face. "Do him good to get away. My guess is you've brought him up a little too close to home."

"Too close to me, you mean?"

"Well, yes, quite frankly, I think the experience might help him grow up a bit. He's a wonderful kid, Laina, but extremely naive."

"And *you* will make a man out of him, I suppose?"

"Yes, isn't that why you sent him to me in the first place?" He looked at her with the hint of his old mocking smile.

"I didn't *send* him to you, remember? You asked for *him*."

"Look, Laina, I'm not competing with you for him. No, Alex is, perhaps. The bond between Warren and his grandfather is unique, I must admit."

"You and my father." She shook her head, smiling faintly. "The enormous enigmas."

Harlan looked uncomfortable. He flicked an imaginary

hair from his immaculate flannel trousers. He clearly wanted to change the subject. "Anyway, Warren could use a little toughening up."

"At eighteen?"

"Yes, the sooner the better. He's a man now, ready even, for love."

"I'm afraid my turn comes before his."

He looked alert and tense.

She ducked her head self-consciously. "I'm considering remarrying. He is Israeli. Zev Elon—the conductor." She said it quickly before she changed her mind.

He seemed genuinely shocked. "I—I had no idea. Warren didn't say anything."

"Well, didn't you think there would ever be another man in my life? Another relationship, I mean?" She was stumbling over the words.

"Another famous man."

"Relatively."

"You haven't said you love him."

She paused, she wanted him to realize this was well thought out, not as sudden or ill-advised and explosive as young love. "I do, though."

"Have you stopped to think what it might be like to be the wife of an Israeli? You would be servile, subordinate. I mean, you have been an independent career woman all your life."

"How little you know me," she said, smiling tolerantly. "In any case, I don't suppose marriage to Zev will be exactly an ordinary Israeli life *or* marriage, and I believe I could live among them. They are a culture-conscious people."

Characteristically, only now when he thought she might go to another man, one with whom she could have a normal physical relationship, did he admit to himself that he was still in love with her through all these years, that it had guided, colored, driven his entire life. Never, in spite of all his denials, his protests that it was *only* Vivian, did he allow the facts to invade and overtake his emotional sophistry. It was for love of Laina that he had contrived to keep Alex by his side, tied to him through business in the hopes of seeing her occasionally or getting news or information about his son. He half-sat, half-lay intimately on the sofa, very close to her.

"Why did you plan to stay here overnight rather than drive home? You knew this wouldn't be a late evening," she asked, looking directly at him.

Returning her gaze unflinchingly, he said, "Oh, I don't know, I thought maybe I'd be out late with Warren, maybe he'd even stay over here with me. But I'm glad he didn't, and that you're here instead." He stroked her face, kissed the palms of her hands, "I still want you so much."

It would be so simple, so uncontrived, and she rationalized that she owed him something. Through lean years she had derived sustenance from that remembered love.

He saw that she was wavering. He thought to seal her decision with a kiss. He leaned over to kiss her, and for a moment she let herself remember. Then she pulled away and jumped up from the sofa. She threw her coat resolutely over her arm and said, sweetly smiling, "You forgot, sir, that I am to be married."

Until that moment, she hadn't made up her mind. She was conscious that she didn't really want another man who belonged to the public. But she did. It was the only sort of man she could relate to.

Vivian had become suddenly sensitive to religion, after

Steven's death—as she grew older. She was particularly sensitive because her children had grown up without it.

Joy went to synagogue with her for the memorial service for her brother Steven. She was moved and comforted by it. She felt that she would like to go back and learn all that she didn't know about the religion. She even began studying the Old Testament.

Rabbi Meyer told her that too many children of mixed marriages were lost forever, "which is what happens when a child doesn't receive a Jewish education." He was delighted to get her back into the fold. "Judaism could die out altogether," he said. "Of course, it's not fading fast enough for some of the world." He shrugged his shoulders. "The trouble is, there's a whole new generation coming up out there who never heard of the Holocaust. The memory of the war, the six million and their lesson, is dying along with the religion, unless they teach it in the schools, and they must."

Joy saw the rabbi was perspiring profusely. He took out a handkerchief and dabbed his balding head. "They teach about the Renaissance and Reformation, the religious changes brought on by church against state. They teach about the Huguenot uprisings and other religious massacres, but the Holocaust they don't teach."

"They will, rabbi, they will," she said quietly.

"But who will be left to remember?" he said plaintively.

The rabbi's prophetic lecture did not make her feel guilty or proud, only hopeful. Since she had lost two brothers whom she loved, she needed to replace them with something of value.

She kept up with Israel's constant struggle to retain its land and grew conversant in Middle Eastern politics, with its ever-changing boundaries and shifting loyalties.

Joy's marks were exceptional and she had been accepted at the University of California in San Diego. She wanted to enroll in their school of medicine and felt that an undergraduate degree there would afford her better leverage. And because of his hotel nearby, Harlan induced her to apply. It would be nice to have his only daughter close to him.

CHAPTER 65

Harlan felt virtuous. Shepherding his flock of two to the Holy Land would put him down for posterity as a good family man. *Here lies a good father.* He hadn't told Joy or Warren that they would be travel companions to Israel. He wanted it to be a surprise. When Warren saw her at the airport, he just assumed she had come to see her father off. When he learned she was joining them and would be in Jerusalem all summer, he could hardly believe it. It was a great surprise.

They sat together on the plane and talked, or rather she talked and he listened. In school, Warren's best subject was psychology; he had an agile and inventive mind. He was quick at arriving at judgments and was invariably right. The first time he had met Joy, he knew she was different from the rest of the girls who cared only for boys and clothes and parties.

When they arrived at Lod Airport, they were met by Harlan's builder and associate, a heavy-set man called Chaim Greene. It was six o'clock in the evening and the desert was resplendent. It was the first genuine place he'd ever seen—the scenery was naturally provocative instead of manmade, yet it seemed an unlikely backdrop for the "healing hedonims" his Uncle Harlan frequently called the resort business. He thought of Jerusalem as a sobering and righteous place. He felt fortunate to be able to share this first experience with his cousin.

THE PLEASURE DOME

They pulled out of the airport in Greene's small Mercedes, only to be stopped a few yards away by strapping young men in khaki paratrooper uniforms with jauntily cocked berets and uzzi submachine guns slung over their shoulders. It was a routine identification and passport check. Instead of thinking of war and the proximity of death, Warren could only think of how romantic these dark-eyed, fierce-looking young men must appear to an American heiress. He looked at Joy out of the corner of his eye, but she seemed sunk in a private reverie.

They drove along the dusty palm-studded highway and began the climb into the Judean Hills. Warren had gone to temple sporadically with Alex on Friday nights and on the High Holy Days. He had watched and listened as his grandfather rocked and chanted and divested himself of sin, none of which he could imagine him being remotely guilty of, but nowhere in his erratic religious training was he prepared for the sensual onslaught of this land as seen for the first time.

Warren hoped Joy would stay with them for one or two nights at least this first night so far away from home, in such an exotic place. But no, she was going to her dorm at the university. Then they would continue on into the valley of Ein Harem where Chaim Greene lived.

From the car window, he watched as father and daughter walked toward the raw, new-looking dormitory, Harlan carrying Joy's one "sensible" suitcase as suggested in the brochure. She was small to begin with, and next to her father looked defenseless. He watched them until they became a tiny dot against the multicolored sunset.

"Your sister?" Greene asked gruffly from the wheel. Warren had almost forgotten he was there. He looked away self-consciously and shook his head.

"No, my cousin," he said.

"Oh, I see." He seemed relieved.

Warren felt suddenly transparent before this stranger. He assumed it was jet lag and the natural reaction to a long flight.

He worked hard during the day, hauling, hammering, pulling the desert apart. Bronzed and slender, his young body had already begun to toughen into sinew and muscle. He had only been in Israel three weeks but he felt like a part of the land, a Sabra building on the desert.

Each day black-frocked and bearded Hasidim stood in silent protest around the excavation site. Although Warren greeted them politely with "Shalom," they rarely answered but occasionally nodded, politely withdrawn. One of the other young workers, also a student, Ari Lachman, told him that they were protesting the building on this site, it was consecrated ground. A Jewish cemetery had been desecrated in order to begin building the Jerusalem Gardens Hotel. Ari shook his head and said, "It is bad luck for this place, an evil omen," and kissed the golden mezuzah he wore around his neck. But Warren was too tired and too excited to pay much attention to omens or talismans.

Each day at noon he took out his lunch of falaffel and pita, like the other young Israelis, and ate beneath the shade of a silver olive tree. He looked six thousand years downward across the Garden of Gethsemane, at the Old City and the blazing golden Dome of the Rock that held the heart of Judaism and Christianity. For the first time in his young life he felt completely at peace.

He was lonely in those first days after Harlan left. The house of Chaim Greene seemed strange, with its golden stucco color and its tiny walled-in courtyard, imparting a sense of siege, like the city itself. Mrs. Greene, a round cheerful woman, was warm and kind to him, the grandmother he had never had. He worked so long and hard each day that he had little time to brood at nights. Instead, he fell into a deep sleep from which he frequently awoke drenched in perspiration and his own semen. The days were not much better. He felt like he was running a low-grade fever and was plagued by persistent flushes and inopportune erections. He knew there was no immediate cure for his malady.

He didn't want to disturb his cousin at school, getting settled, adjusting to the language barrier, new friends, new mores. He didn't want to appear insensitive—doltish before her lofty intellectualism. He could not quite understand why a woman would want to be a doctor, but he was all the more impressed by her uniqueness. One day she would be cutting open cadavers, dissecting human organs, looking into brains and dead men's eyes, holding in her hand a beating human heart . . . just as she now held his.

When he telephoned her at the dormitory, she was out. Instead of calling her back, he decided to go out with Ari Lachman and some of the boys. They were going down to a small bar near the beach in Tel Aviv where they picked up girls. He had gone with them once before, but he had not enjoyed the experience.

The bar and restaurant was wedged in crookedly between a few other dilapidated buildings. The unlit street smelled fishy and the small crowded bar was jammed with young people. Eager, intelligent, industrious types. The women seemed completely at ease with the men. They were mostly handsome girls, dark-eyed, large-breasted, broad-shouldered girls with strong, athletic walks and swaying strides. Many came up to him at the bar without being introduced. Perhaps because he was a new face and obviously didn't speak Hebrew, although they all spoke English too.

"*Shalom*, who are you?" one asked. "An American?" As if being American was the sum total of "who."

Ari introduced them casually. He seemed to know all the girls. "Chava, this is Warren Goldmark."

"So," she said in her inflected English. "You are American, sent here by parents for the summer to learn the work ethic?"

Warren was taken aback by the incisiveness of the question. "I suppose," he answered, forcing a smile, "something like that." He was not deterred by what she said as much as the *way* she said it, sort of tough and cold. He hoped that no one here connected his name with his parents' music, although it was a common enough Jewish name. It was not that he wasn't proud of their success, but he desperately didn't want to be singled out as an American celebrity's kid. Ari didn't know. He just knew he was an American, living at the home of Chaim Greene, the wealthy builder.

The girl was sultry and handsome. She had satiny skin the color of a golden pearl. Her white teeth glittered and caught the lights when she laughed. Warren saw that she had tight buttocks and full lips.

"I suppose" ("s-o-o-p-o-s-e," she pronounced it in her soft Middle Eastern accent), "American girls have been telling you that you have marvelous green eyes," she said. "They're very suggestive."

"Of what?" he asked playfully.

She laughed. "Oh, of seas, and sighs, and sex." She made her voice an inviting whisper on the last word. Warren felt responsive in every part of his body. He had been feeling that way for weeks.

Here in this land of knowing, earthy people he was

THE PLEASURE DOME

ashamed of his intensely romantic nature. He suddenly excused himself and went to the telephone. He called the dorm again. Somebody went to call her. When she finally answered, he sounded breathless and agitated.

"Joy, it's me, Warren." Her voice sounded cool and far away. He hoped it wasn't disdain or disinterest. "How are you doing? Do you like the school?" It seemed to him he was yelling. She was noncommittal.

"Do you realize it's almost three weeks and still we haven't gotten together? Can't we make up for lost time?" He thought he sounded old-fashioned and overly eager. They settled on Thursday because she didn't have an early class Friday morning.

Alex had taught Warren how to drive and had promised him a car for a graduation present. But Harlan's graduation surprise—this trip, this summer—had superseded all else, and he hadn't even thought about what he would do about transportation here. He had been taking the black Sheruts, communal taxis, everywhere. That is, when he went anywhere.

The Greenes had two cars. When he asked if he could borrow one, Chaim immediately offered him the small jeep that he used for going to construction sites.

Driving to the campus in the open car, he felt the exuberance of the country, felt a part of the people. He hummed a wonderful number from *Fragments,* a hora of sorts. He remembered the scene from the show, young people dancing before a fire, clapping and singing. He thought about his parents' long partnership and felt sad about the divorce. But he hadn't understood his father for years. He had lost touch with him since adolescence and had not known how to behave toward him after Robin had shown him the magazine. He hoped his mother would make a new life for herself, a real life.

He had researched restaurants for almost a week, trying to find just the right spot, romantic atmosphere, good food, combinations not easily found in Israel. Money was not the problem. He got the equivalent of one hundred dollars a week and had nothing to spend it on. His mother had given him two hundred dollars before he left and it was still intact.

They went to a little restaurant inside the Jaffa Gate, in the Old City. It was a Greek restaurant called Kufkus and had an outside garden with trailing grape vines and orange blossoms. Everywhere in the desert was the smell of orange blossoms, a scent that would forever remind him of Israel. Sitting there quiet and contained, he thought Joy's face showed signs of strain.

"Why didn't you call before?" she said.

He was taken aback, pleased by her candor, her interest. "I thought I would be intruding—using our slim family connection to make a pest of myself," he said, trying to lighten the truth.

They laughed and talked about his work, "Dull routine, physical," he said self-deprecatingly. "Your father wasn't kidding when he said I should learn the work from the ground up."

"For me it's the same dull routine—biology and chemistry. But I have a nice roommate, an Israeli; she speaks perfect English, thank God, though I wouldn't mind learning Hebrew. It's so poetic. Ties this country together beautifully."

Warren looked at her silently. It didn't seem to matter to him that her medical career was a long way off or might never even come to pass.

He ordered ouzo. He had never tried it before, in fact he never had anything stronger than wine; it went down fiery and smooth. Sitting close over the spicy moussaka, their talk gradually simmered into shy looks and finger-touching. They were conscious of their blood relationship, no matter how distant. Too many new experiences were pummeling him at once. If he felt like he had been smoldering with a low-grade fever for some time, it was rising. Love seemed to suffuse his being. All of his reflexes felt liquid, liquid as her eyes. He felt suddenly alive.

"It seems so strange that we never knew each other through all these years, that is, until last summer really, and now we suddenly find each other on the other side of the world."

"*Kismet,*" she whispered in a mysterious voice.

"Sh-sh, that's an Arab expression," he said, "not very popular here, especially since the Six Day War last year."

"Anyway, what's more likely is that my father put you here to keep an eye on me," she said confidentially.

Warren looked dismayed. "He never said a word about it to me." He shook his head.

"He wouldn't, that's *not* how he works."

Warren was silent. He didn't quite understand what she was getting at. "Well, in that case I don't want to let him down. So I'll just keep an eye on you—both of them—if you don't mind."

She laughed, pressing her tongue against her front teeth so that only the tiny rosy point of it was visible.

"You're lucky that he cares about you so much."

She looked embarrassed, annoyed.

"He cares a lot about you, Warren. As a matter of fact, I'm not sure that I want to share him with you. I never even wanted to share him with my brothers," she said defiantly, as if brazening out a long kept secret. Then she laughed a little and took his hand, to disguise the sting of jealousy in her statement.

"Well, don't fret. I don't take up much of his time."

"He never had much of it to give. Only lately—only since Steven died," she said sadly, "he's had a little more time for me."

"I just came in, in the middle, so I really don't know him that well."

"We all came in, in the middle," she said with a sad smile. "He never had much time for us when we were growing up."

Warren wanted to change the subject. He felt disloyal talking about him in this way. He had grown to love and admire him almost as much as he did Alex. "What made you decide to go into medicine? I mean, it's quite a challenge for a woman," he said.

"I think I'd be good at it." She took a sip of wine and then raised an eyebrow provocatively. "Perhaps I just want to catch my father's attention."

He sensed that she was flirting with him, using her father as a competition for him. He was flattered.

"Why does it seem so strange to you for a woman to have a career? Your mother has been a career woman all of her life."

"My mother has not been happy."

"Don't you think she'd have been a lot less happy without her career?"

"Yes, I suppose so." He didn't know how they'd gotten onto the subject of his parents. He wanted to talk about her.

Driving back in the car they hardly spoke. He could hear his heartbeat in the silence. He cleared his throat and coughed a few times so that she would not hear it too. He wished for Joy's passivity, her quiet restraint. Perhaps he had been wrong. Perhaps she felt nothing for him, nothing at all. He longed to take her in his arms, hold her close, but thought he might hurt her, so intense were his feelings. He was afraid it might be considered a sin since they were cousins. He didn't know what to do. Now at last he had the autonomy he had dreamed of and didn't know what to do with it.

"Will you come up here again?" she asked as they drew near the security booth.

Warren looked confused. "You mean, will we see each other again? Of course. That is, if you want to."

"I want to."

He slowed up under a clump of yew trees and stopped the jeep. There was a sudden, clear silence. He had to test further, probe, make certain that she felt a little of his turmoil.

"It's not that you're lonely or homesick, is it?"

She was silent a moment as if carefully considering it. "I suppose I'm both."

His heart fell with her confession. In the shaft of moonlight he thought she looked wild, unearthly. She made no move to go. He was overwhelmed by her response.

"When can I see you again?" he whispered. He wanted desperately to kiss her.

"I have to study."

"But you just said . . ." He wondered if she was just being contrary with him to excite him. He reached for her, but she eluded his grasp and opened the car door and without a backward glance walked briskly up the hill to the dormitory.

He couldn't sleep well for nights—just tossing and turning and drifting in and out of lurid dreams of her, waking up peevish and tired, unfit for the demanding physical work of the day. If this was first love, which was rumored to be best, he hoped it would also be his last. He could not imagine any other love being more painful.

He called her twice at the dormitory, leaving no name or message. Each time she was out. He was suddenly terrified that there might be someone else, one of those handsome young Sabras with cocked beret and uzzi gun, or worse yet, perhaps she was just ducking his calls, had told them at the dorm, "If an American boy calls, I'm out." There were only another few weeks left to the summer and then they would be leaving for the States. Then he would be east and she would be west. Saturdays he didn't work. *Shabbat* was holy in Israel. The Arab quarter would be alive with commerce, being shut down tightly on Fridays, their holy day, but for Jews Saturday was sacrosanct. Only the temple doors stood open wide.

Two weeks had passed and Warren, in the borrowed, battered jeep, found himself driving to West Jerusalem, to Givat Ram, and Joy's dormitory. The air smelled heavy with Sabbath cooking, but his mind was not on food. He drove with a purpose, a man with a mission. All around him he saw the faces of the just; pale stubborn faces under fur-trimmed hats, returning from morning prayers, their shoulders draped in sumptuous prayer shawls, their bodies dressed in black silk tied with long tasseled cords, holiday packages, gift-wrapped for God. Passing through the commercial center, he heard Israeli music burst from the crowded cafes. *Shalom, Shalom* followed him on the wind. He thought it was good that his mother would live here. Perhaps one day he too would live among these eager, diligent people. His people.

He parked the jeep carefully and jumped down. He had to show his identification at the security gate and establish his purpose for the visit. He couldn't proceed to the dorms alone unless his name was registered. The student would have to come and meet him here, they said. He was afraid she would not come, not knowing who was there or, worse, guessing it was him. He pretended to go back and wait but suddenly remembered the path she had used that other night. It was out of the direct range of the patrol booth. He didn't know exactly where he was going or what he was doing. He went into the building he thought he had seen her go into. There was a small reception desk in the hall, but it was unattended.

He didn't even know if the dorms were coed, but he began to ascend the stairs when Joy, running down breathlessly, nearly knocked him over. She was so surprised that she tripped and fell forward for a moment into his waiting arms.

"So it's you! They called me from the gate. How did you get in here?" She seemed amazed. He noticed that she wore a cotton housedress with the sleeves pushed way up, wearing nothing underneath. She looked flushed and moist, her hair stuck in damp tendrils about her face. She looked down at herself. "I've been doing laundry, please excuse the way I look, but well, you should have let me know you were coming." He thought she looked beautiful. He was struck by the sensuality of her doing earthy domestic chores. He imagined her the young matron caught unawares, bathing the baby.

"I telephoned twice but . . ."

"You could have left a message."

They were still standing on the staircase. Students went up and down and ignored them, used to seeing intense young people absorbed in one another.

"I've come to take you for a ride, a picnic. It's a beautiful day."

She seemed paralyzed into immobility.

"God, Joy, it's just an afternoon, it's not your life I'm

asking for." He was embarrassed by his strange outburst. And he knew he was being dishonest with her, it was that too; he wanted her whole life.

When they were safely in the jeep and he had started up the snarling motor, he said, "You know the summer's practically gone, it's late August already."

She didn't reply, probably unsure of whether the statement was a threat or a challenge. He stopped the car near the entrance to the Arab quarter.

"Let's buy something for our picnic."

The ancient cobbled streets were tunnels, dark and narrow. "'And the streets will be paved with carbuncles, and all her houses shall say Hallelujah,'" he said, remembering this snippet from the Bible. The archways that housed shops were thronged with people. Whole families squatted on the dirt floors making pita bread before the eyes of the onlookers. Children squirmed and wriggled, darting dangerously in front of the broiling metal rods, precariously close to the open kiln; the parents were unruffled. In another pita stall, dusty children jumped up and down on a large soiled mattress on the floor. In jewelry stores next to the food stalls Arabs hawked *Mogen Davids*, mezuzahs in gold and silver. They bought hot couscous on pita bread and sticky Arab cakes and American soda pop. As they walked back toward the jeep he noticed she had put on a brassiere, probably when she went back briefly to her room to fix up. Her breasts were not large, but they were firm and beautifully pointed, he thought. They pointed the way out of his misery—into heaven—or hell.

The scenery on the road to Haifa was wild and desolate. He pulled the car over to the side of the road, where there was a generous open field of dried and yellowed grass. They got out and he took her hand. Yew and olive trees grew in abundance, and here and there wild mallow erupted into pink and white blossoms. Looking around her appreciatively, she said, "It feels as though you are leading me down the primrose path."

"Could I?" he asked, turning to her, hoping that a glint of humor came through in his voice.

"It reminds me of a Gothic novel. Green-eyed, handsome and mysterious distant cousin suddenly turns up and sweeps the heroine off to some sort of fate worse than death, or perhaps death itself. I think Richard Burton played it."

They found a shady spot beneath a tree. Warren spread the plastic tarpaulin that they found in the back of the jeep. She began to eat ravenously, but he wasn't hungry. He tried not to stare but couldn't help it. Drops of Pepsi Cola beaded her lower lip, making it appear ripe and juicy to his eyes, cherry-stained.

"So tell me what are you going to do with your life," she asked.

"I don't know yet." He was thinking it was too soon to tell. His life began when he met her and would probably peak now at eighteen. The short and happy life of Warren Goldmark. "I don't really know what I want to do with my life just yet, for certain, that is."

"Nothing is ever for certain," she said with her anchoring rationalism.

"You know about college in the fall and the family business," he said with a self-effacing laugh. He felt foolish and prosaic, very bourgeois. "Nothing as lofty as your plans, I'm afraid."

"Ah, the best-laid plans," she said darkly.

For some reason he felt flattered. Could that curious statement possibly relate to him—to them? Could he ever be important enough to her to change her life?

"So my father has decided you are to carry on the hotels," she said.

"And grandfather Alex too. It's what he wants."

"But what do you want?"

"When I'm working at the hotels I'm a different person. I think I could be successful at it; that's why I'm taking a business and hotel program—to find out."

"No wonder my father has made you his protegé. You even sound like him. Maybe you just want to be like him, perhaps *he's* the 'different person' you become," she said teasingly.

He wondered why she seemed to drag every conversation back to him, to Harlan. Yet there was a vital kernel of truth in what she said. Warren was basically lonely, he didn't know how to attract people to him. He would like to be like his uncle. Maybe then she would love him.

"Nowadays, to be ambitious about material achievements or sexual conquests is considered poor taste," he said.

"Are you?"

"Am I what?"

"Ambitious about sexual conquests?" she said, smiling warmly, enjoying his apparent confusion.

He leaned forward and traced his finger down her nose. "That would depend," he said softly, "on how I felt about the girl. I would not consider it ambition or conquest if I were in love."

He wanted her desperately, he even dared to let himself believe she wanted him. And he had to choose *this* girl, this cousin, the daughter of his benefactor and friend who—it appeared—he was supposed to keep an eye on. He felt insidious, the same way that Lancelot might have felt when he fell in love with Guinevere.

In the following week she had final exams and was

enormously pressured. These grades would go toward credit at the University of California, she said. He panicked that it would be time to leave and nothing would be resolved between them. Joy was going home right after exams, to get ready for California.

About a week later at dinner, Chaim Greene was talking politics with his friend Ralph Zitsky, who was a member of the Knesset.

"We're moving toward a situation like they have in South Africa," Zitsky said. "The Arabs will eventually outpopulate the Israelis. The rich Israelis are leaving Israel, and the young ones cannot make a living here, between army duty and the religious laws." Greene nodded his head and spritzed seltzer into his glass.

"Jews tend to have only as many children as they can support; there are no more expensive children in the world than Jewish children," Greene said. He had three married daughters, whose husbands he thanked God for daily.

Zitsky turned to Warren, "Well, American-Jewish children, anyway. Is that right, son?" He spoke as if Warren were representing all spoiled American children.

Chaim Greene came to his defense. "Warren here is not a typical example, I'm happy to say. He's businesslike and works hard like an Israeli." Warren was discomfitted by the remark. After all, he wasn't a Zionist and felt his loyalties being tested.

Anyway, Chaim, don't forget dinner at my home," Zitsky said. "You'll meet a great many important people there—and, of course, it will be a late evening, particularly for you. Maybe you should plan to stay overnight in Tel Aviv."

The Greenes had asked Warren many times to invite Joy for dinner but he had always found excuses to put it off, fearing they might notice something in his behavior that would give away his secret and report it to Harlan. (He didn't dare yet think—*their* secret.) And he had no wish to share her all evening with the Greenes, talking about school and probably trying to introduce her to the sons of friends of theirs. Annulling him in their innocence.

"Oh, Bella's son would be perfect for her, he's also going to be a doctor," he could hear Mrs. Greene saying as she cut pie wedges of matzobrei. "I have married off three daughters. I'm an expert by now." He shuddered. No, no, he couldn't bring her here, unless the Greenes were out of town.

He was surprised when she agreed so readily. She wanted to cook dinner, she was a good cook, she said. She took a Sherut to the house and arrived right after sundown. Warren had set the hour, "so that we will have plenty of time together before the Greenes return home."

It seemed to him then that he would always remember that moment when he threw the door open and she stood on the threshold illuminated by the savage sunset behind her, amid the golden glow of Jerusalem stone. She wore her hair pulled back and tightly wound into a chignon, highlighting the delicate planes and hollows of her face. Her olive skin was deeply tanned and the cotton batiste of her dress fell away from her body just enough to allow for the natural swing of breasts and buttocks.

He drank beer and watched her while she bustled around the unfamiliar kitchen, asking for this and that, issuing orders, assigning tasks. Finally, when she leaned over the sink chattering gaily he could stand it no more. He came up behind her and kissed her on the neck. She felt the urgency of his desire as he pressed against her buttocks. A sudden musky silence enveloped them. He whispered her name again and again.

He had learned to tread gingerly around all the complex relationships in his life. Now he didn't even think of his family, of what they would say if they knew. He was only wondering how he would get through the next year without her, when he received a letter from his mother telling him that she and Zev intended to fly to Israel over the Labor Day holidays and remain for at least a month.

"Zev has just finished concerts in London, Copenhagen and New York. I might just as well be a traveling salesman's wife, except those wives rarely go along and don't enjoy the work and the people the way I do," she wrote enthusiastically in the letter. "Of course, I'm asking you to stay on a bit so that we can at least touch hands in this relay race we are running. It will be good to see you—in *my* new world."

His mother's letter had the effect of reining him in. It was censorious without a word of censure.

From city to city across the nation, the world—she might sit behind him, watching the powerful arms and shoulders as if they had a life of their own, disembodied, self-contained. Laina considered herself fortunate that her life seemed destined to be flooded with music.

After the performances she would go backstage and watch him take his bows and walk with a springy gait from the stage, only to collapse, spent and perspiring on the wings. His dedication was pure and unadulterated. He was a subtle artist with the simple, earthy tastes of the peasant. She found the combination completely satisfying, a relief after the years of studied artifice with David.

Even the business of composing musicals was based on contrivance and artifice.

Zev Elon was a solitary man who lived mostly for his music, or had done so at least for the last four years since his wife died. If Laina had had a large, complicated family instead of only Alex and Warren, it was doubtful that he would have allowed himself the luxury of love and marriage. His itinerant life and his need for total concentration would have prohibited it. He was fifty-six years old and, except for an ancient Egyptian housekeeper, had lived alone these last four years in the exclusive Tal Bieh section of Jerusalem.

They enjoyed many mutual friends in the world of music. Zev believed in his music, his people, his religion, but he had no time for the rituals of an orthodox life. Laina hoped to return to her first love, *poetry*. Her marriage to Zev Elon would not be a terrible adjustment.

When she arrived in Israel late in August, she was overwhelmed by history and her reunion with Warren. With all the adjustments Warren had had to make in this last year and in the coming one, she was careful not to press him into staying with them or into accepting her new husband immediately. She didn't want to make him feel any more disloyal to David than she suspected he already felt. Warren would be away at college and could get to know Zev gradually. But by now Warren felt disloyal to almost everyone in his life.

When she saw him she was struck by how much he had changed in such a short time—there was a new maturity about him, an independence that she supposed was engendered by the atmosphere of this tiny country that had been a frontier for the last six thousand years.

CHAPTER 66

He tried to resign himself to a year of restless longing—waiting and longing. At college he was not particularly happy, finding the theories of business administration not nearly as exciting as their practical application. His seeming disinterest in women and his air of grave mystery, combined with his romantic good looks, made him a great favorite with the coeds, helping to give him confidence, which in turn made him appear more attractive. But it didn't seem to matter to him. Warren still thought of Joy. She was the thought he woke with and the thought he took to bed. She was the thought he invoked when he felt lonely walking from the library when everyone else moved in giddy packs, or at lunch in the mess hall where he dreamed over his coffee until the next class, with a book opened before him which he pretended to study, and saw there instead only her small face before him. He did not know exactly why he felt so close to her, needed so much to be a part of her. But she had struck a familiar chord in him; there was something about her that was the intrinsic echo of himself.

They wrote letters back and forth, he fearing that he'd lost her when she was late in replying, incredulous when she was prompt.

Close to Christmas holidays, he called her at the dormitory. He had spent weeks devising a plan so that they could be together over the holiday and then knew the moment he called that it would never work. Her parents would be coming out to the hotel for the holidays and Joy had said she would spend it in California with them. There was really nothing to do but go to the apartment in New York. He was not even sure if his mother would be there. He could not help but feel that Joy had accepted the arrangements too easily and without thinking of him. She could have said she wanted to spend some of the holiday with a friend, or some such subterfuge. He supposed she simply did not feel things as deeply as he did or was too practical to be swept away, as he was. He decided to fly out to San Diego anyway, and took a room in a small seaside hotel in La Jolla on Torry Pines Road, almost on top of the university but a long drive from the hotel. He told Laina that he wanted to visit a friend, someone he had met in San Diego; he even mentioned the name Orin Burnside for authenticity. But he said he would fly home a week or so before his vacation ended and spend it with her and Zev.

He did not know exactly what he had in mind or even how Joy would accept the unexpected intrusion, but he wasn't thinking rationally. At times he felt guilty for involving her in this questionable relationship, but he had full intentions of setting it all to rights. He would ask her to marry him.

Alone in his room in the small picturesque seaside city, he paced back and forth, undecided as to the best way to handle things. He didn't want to compromise Joy with her family and still he felt that she must share some of the responsibility—that is—if she loved him as he thought she did.

Finally the next morning he called her at their suite at the hotel. When Vivian answered, he hung up and decided to simply leave a message with the hotel operator to tell her to call this number, an old friend. He waited, pacing, flipping the television on and off, unable to concentrate.

At six-thirty that evening the phone rang. He hadn't been out of the room for two days and had forgotten to shave or eat.

She could not believe it was him. "Why don't you come and stay here at the hotel with us?" she asked.

"What good would that do? I wouldn't have a minute alone with you, we'd have to watch everything we said and did or they would simply catch on."

"Well, they're going to have to know sometime, I suppose," she said.

All he could think was *not now, not yet,* perhaps when Joy and he were older, better able to oppose them. He had no doubt in his mind that they would surely forbid it— between the fact of their youth, their first year of college, Joy's medical school ambitions, and, of course, the fact that they were cousins.

"You're allowed out of the hotel, aren't you? You're not a prisoner there, for God's sake. Meet me over here tonight." He hated the commanding tone of his voice.

She met him that night, and some afternoons and evenings too. "School friends," she would say to her curious parents. Soon they stopped asking.

He almost ran into Harlan at least two or three times. When seeing her home in a cab, as he insisted upon doing, Warren spotted him coming up to the front entrance with his familiar athletic stride. He ducked and told the cab to pull away quickly. Or once he even thought Harlan saw him in Joy's car but couldn't be certain because Harlan never mentioned it.

The fact that Joy had never had a real boyfriend before Warren created an even greater pull between them. On the day before Warren was to leave for New York, he made her promise to spend the day with him.

He moved to the famous old La Valencia Hotel on the water, where the rooms had fireplaces and spectacular views of the steely Pacific. He wanted atmosphere to strengthen his case, to bolster his dreams for the arid spells when they would be separated—and he wanted Joy to remember this, their last evening together.

It was three o'clock in the afternoon when he finally heard from her. He had waited in his room all day, afraid if he went out he might miss her call. For some reason or other she could not meet him until now. They decided to meet at the famous San Diego Zoo. It was not far from the Pleasure Dome, so Warren took a taxi. Outside, late afternoon winds pulled clouds apart in snowy dollops, the air was mild and sensuous with the sea. They spent the rest of the afternoon, or what was left of it, reverting to the children they really were, enjoying the little domestic animals in the petting area, especially provided for children. The animals' vulnerability, their deep rootless loneliness, struck a chord of sympathy in him. It was growing dark and cold and he was hardly able to wait to get back to the hotel, where he wanted to make love to Joy. But she seemed to be finding excuses to put him off.

"Let's walk on the beach for a while," she said.

"The beach? Joy, it's wintertime!"

"Where's your imagination?" she said, laughing a little. "Seasons don't set precedents; people do."

He was embarrassed by his own eagerness, caused, he imagined, by the prospect of the long separation ahead.

He agreed reluctantly, as the beach was close to his hotel. They trudged silently on the cold hard sand—holding hands loosely.

"It's interesting when you think of it, seems as if I've

spent my whole life growing up with the ocean," she said. "The nature of our business, I suppose. But it speaks to me now—I know it so well. We're on speaking terms at last."

"And what does it say?"

"To proceed with caution," she whispered with mock seriousness, and took his arm and moved in close to him.

"Joy, why are you going on this way?" He seemed uncomfortable.

"Oh, I don't know. I guess it's the endless separations ahead of us, the sneaking around. I have this terrible fear of the future—our future."

She too, was caught up in that special unhappiness of first love—its sweet anxiety.

Back at school he tried to apply himself to his studies, but memories kept getting in the way, spilling memories, flooding his thoughts, taking with them all sense and all reason.

Easter holiday proved another and even greater disappointment—she was going to spend it at their home in Palm Springs with her parents. She invited Warren, but he still held on to enough of a shred of sanity to decline. He couldn't understand why she refused to invent covering stories, construct subterfuges, not realizing as she did, that it would never have worked. It was all too close for comfort. He wished that she was a plainer girl, with an unadorned life. He wished they weren't rich and powerful, and had less mobility, less geographic options. He never knew where they might be or when they might be there. He never knew what to expect from her.

But they would have the summer to look forward to, he was certain of that. They had planned it carefully by telephone, in letters. He was going to ask Harlan if he might once again work at the San Diego hotel. Joy would be studying on the accelerated program at the college in La Jolla nearby.

When Harlan unexpectedly came up to Cornell to visit him, Warren was surprised and pleased. But he spent the first half-hour of the visit quizzing Harlan on the Easter vacation.

"Well, what is there to do in Palm Springs but bask in the sun and eat?" Harlan laughed. "Joy really only came along for us, for her mother's sake and mine. I felt she needed to rest and take it easy. She's studying too damn hard," he said not without pride. "Of course, we invited you, son, you know that."

"Yes, yes," he said, looking away. "Thank you, but I had to work, make-up work and so forth."

Harlan cleared his throat. "Which brings me to how you're doing here, far above Cayuga's waters." He seemed to be speaking unduly loudly. They were sitting in the guest vestibule of his resident house. Above his head on the cork boards were flyers reminding freshmen to investigate the fraternities. Rush would begin in the fall. Instead of asking him how his marks were, as Warren expected, Harlan asked instead, "Will you be pledging a fraternity in the fall?"

"I—I don't know, sir, I haven't decided." Pledging a fraternity. How he wished he could care about it. He wondered why it seemed that whenever he needed to throw himself into a peer situation, a normal growing experience, his life got in the way. First it was in high school and the sickening realization about his father, and now it was Joy. But it was a divine madness, sublime misery.

"Uncle, I'm glad you came so that we can discuss the

THE PLEASURE DOME

summer," he said smiling, trying to sound dégagé. "I would like to work for you again this summer, er, in connection with my work here at the school, of course. I get credit for working summers in the field."

Harlan grinned appreciatively. "Well, of course, that's what I want too. You know I'm in the midst of extensive remodeling at the Broadbeach. It could use plenty of overseeing. That old place has been a virtual gold mine," he said, smiling his satisfaction, "since the great exodus to the Hamptons began a few years ago. And then I figured working there would be nice for you, and for your mother. She doesn't get to see much of you these days, I imagine."

Warren tried to kep calm, to think clearly. "Yes, yes, but you see that's just it—too much family back there, what with my mother, her new husband and grandfathers Alex and Matthew. There are too many distractions—I want to make a success of the summer, Harlan."

Harlan sat back, beaming his approval. "Ah ha, a chip off the old block."

Warren looked up confused.

"Er, that is, like your grandfather Alex, just like him, ambitious and sharp. Well, I suppose I could find something for you at the Pleasure Dome." He closed his eyes for a moment as if giving the question hard thought. "Yes, I'm sure I could find something challenging for you there, though I myself may have to spend a good deal of my time in the east, at the Broadbeach."

Warren tried hard to look saddened by this news.

"How are you fixed for cash?"

"Oh, I'm fine, fine, thanks," he said absently, still elated over the happy turn of events. "My father sends me money every month, and so does mother, for that matter."

"Yes," Harlan said smiling sardonically. "I understand you've been sending it back to him, to your father. Don't you think you are hurting him? Sending him back his own money seems a childish punishment. Are any of us really in a position to judge another, I wonder?"

"Please, sir, I don't care to discuss my father with . . . with anyone."

"Still," he said, rising to leave, "here's some money. You'll need it for plane fare out to the coast and incidentals." He pushed a wad of bills into his hand. Before Warren could thank him he was gone. He looked down at his hand and counted two thousand dollars. He didn't need any money, but he would save it for the summer. He felt guilty about making Harlan his unwitting accomplice.

CHAPTER 67

Sitting in the glass-and-steel office of the Pleasure Dome, Warren Goldmark listened to the managing director, Harlan Chase, talking to a real estate developer about tract houses. The project seemed endless. Harlan was forever buying up land, building and borrowing from the banks to buy and build more. Whenever Harlan had critical business discussions, he liked to have Warren sit in. "Just listen and learn," he would say, "and don't be afraid to ask questions."

"I'm going to submit the architectural plans at the next meeting," Pete Dozier said. "They're beautiful, really beautiful. Should sell like crazy. We're at a great time now—costs to build are still fairly low but we make a big profit. I mean big. It's a seller's market."

"I don't want to make any undue profits here," Harlan said, looking at him levelly, "nothing untoward. I've got to be able to stand behind every vacation home I build. Not only is my personal reputation at stake, but the reputation of this hotel and my whole company. I want nothing inferior, Dozier, do you understand that? I'll go through the models bit by bit and if I discover any substituted materials or inferior piping, one—two—three—I promise you."

"Aw, come on, Chase, give me a break. There's no reason to be suspicious. You make me out to sound like a goddamn crook in front of your young nephew here."

"No, Pete, don't talk like that," Harlan said, jabbing him playfully in the stomach. "I was just coming on a little for Warren here, I suppose, just want to teach him the pitfalls—what to look for in someone not quite as scrupulous as yourself." He slung an arm around Dozier's shoulder and slowly walked him to the door. When he came back and sat down at his desk he smiled a little and said, "Hey, son, he's really okay, built the last batch and they're nice. You always have to remind them that you're on top of them, right up their ass, just so they don't get loose and sloppy. Guess you're not up to that part at Cornell yet, huh?"

"Well, we'll have real estate courses next semester."

"Yes, sure, you're about nineteen now?"

"I was just nineteen in July."

"Yes, yes, I know," Harlan said strangely ruminative. "Christ, nineteen, fantastic—what I wouldn't give to be nineteen again." When he thought about it, nineteen hadn't been very good for him; at nineteen he had been an aimless drifter. "So this ought to be an interesting summer for you, son. I'm gonna run your butt off—make you work—but you learned a lot when you were here a couple of years ago and you're gonna learn even more this summer for me," he said. "What with you here and Joy over in La Jolla." Harlan was pleased. He liked the idea of having his children near him.

Warren hoped he didn't give himself away by blushing or suddenly perspiring. He checked his hands; they were a little too tightly clenched. He unclasped them and put them behind his head, feigning nonchalance.

Warren was determined to be a success in this business. He wanted to be assured of earning a good living so that he could support Joy while she was in medical school, so that they could be married and their parents couldn't use lack of money as another argument against their marriage. He was like a lawyer, carefully constructing his case before he went into open court, perhaps into open battle.

"How's your mother doing?" Harlan asked but didn't allow him to answer. "Fine woman, a real beauty too," he said, shuffling nervously through papers on his desk.

"Yes, sir."

Harlan hadn't really recovered from the news of Laina's marriage. He never thought she'd do it, and so fast. Somehow with her married and so far away much of the time, life had lost its essence, its snap. He had been living in a kind of suspended animation for years, always thinking, hoping that somehow, someday, she would come back to him.

"What's he like—your new stepfather?"

"Oh, he's okay, I don't really know him very well yet—a quiet soft-spoken man—seems to love my mother very much. That's all that counts."

"Well, that's not hard," Harlan said graciously. "And that's a very adult attitude you have, I must say, very sensible."

Warren thought that Zev was a nice enough man, a good man really, and he had come along at just the right time in their lives—at a time when his mother was very lonely and when he, Warren, needed to be on his own. But he was tired of relationships. All his life treading around strained relationships, dark family secrets that were born of an earlier time. He wanted only to concentrate on his own, his and Joy's. Obsession made him blind and selfish, he rationalized.

At first their arrangements were awkward and stilted, often involving dinner with Harlan and Vivian, or just catching glimpses of her as he made his rounds across the vast grounds of the resort. Joy was very serious about her studies, which were growing more difficult with each month, and she didn't come to the hotel often. In a way, Warren considered this a blessing in disguise. But as the summer progressed, the young lovers fell into an easy pattern of assignation. Joy had her weekends free, and although Warren usually worked weekends, he managed to set up a slightly different schedule with his uncle, explaining that he too needed some quiet time to study, as he would be expected to turn in a term paper for credit. Warren succeeded in getting off Thursdays and every other Sunday.

Anyone could have guessed what was going on, but Harlan didn't. Perhaps because he was too close to it, or perhaps it never occurred to him—thinking of them simply as brother and sister. Perhaps he did not want to see it.

Vivian quizzed her daughter from time to time, remarking on her unmistakable radiance, and probably would have known had she seen them together a few more times. But in August Vivian and Harlan went back to their home in Oyster Bay. Harlan was needed at the Broadbeach Club, where remodeling was taking place all over, in spite of the fact that it was high season, when rates were high, and the guests were sorely complaining. Putting this kind of money into the Broadbeach, he had to apply extra care not to lose a single guest. He had hoped to be finished before the summer. If they had to stop in the middle of the job and return after the summer, there was no guarantee as to when they could continue and what the new prices would be. So Harlan and Vivian went back east for the balance of the summer.

When Harlan returned to California after Labor Day, Warren was so lost in love and its attendant fantasies that his only thought was to tell Harlan the facts so that they could get his permission to become engaged. He could not fathom going back again to the other side of the country without a commitment. And there didn't seem to be any way to work things out unless he simply told the truth. And besides, what was the harm in it? Only their ages, as far as he could see, would be the family's strongest argument against it.

Harlan had been wanting to sell the old Hibiscus Gardens for years. Miami once had the scent of coconut, frangipani and money; now it smelled of mothballs and decay. But Alex opposed it. Said they weren't offered enough money, which was true. And Vivian was against it too, for sentimental reasons, perhaps for Matthew's sake. But Harlan figured he owed it to the stockholders to do something with it; otherwise it would sink into obsolescence, already it was little more than a tax write-off.

At least these were his thoughts until recently, when he had met a large beefy-looking Texan by the name of C.P. Snow, "a cold name, a cool cookie," he told Clyde Bostwick. Snow was chairman of the board of a large conglomerate based in Houston, now eagerly acquiring eastern properties. They wanted Pleasure Domes, Inc.

In Harlan's main office in the Pleasure Dome, he said, "I admire what you've done here, suh, yes, I do. You've turned a whole lotta insignificant Jewish-type family hotels—cockolains, I believe they pronounce it," he laughed at his own humor, or the foreign-sounding word, "into big business. Yessir. And you've shown 'em that an Irishman knows a thing or three about business too."

Harlan ignored the irony and the man's bigotry. He was used to the innuendos through the years from those who resented his Jewish connection or simply didn't know about it.

Tersely he asked what the offer was.

"Well, for the whole package, mind you, the entire package, we'll give you twenty dollars a share over market price."

Harlan's face grew red—then paled—he hadn't expected anything like it. He was flattered that they wanted it that badly. He regained his composure.

"I suppose you have checked out the Hibiscus Gardens. You know it's making little or nothing?"

"I know, I know—that town has gone to the dogs—and old Jews," he murmured, smiling tolerantly. "But that's *my* problem, like I said—here's your chance to get off the hook. Take it or leave it. We'll buy you out. Controlling interest, that's what we want."

Harlan had a growing distrust of Alex Eastman. He suspected that Alex secretly believed that he may have killed Marc Anselmo, considered him capable of that kind of violence. He had always seemed bound in a web with this man that grew tighter and tighter through the years. Here at last was his chance to be rid of him, sell the company and sever this unholy alliance.

CHAPTER 68

Warren might live a long and happy life, he might even one day forget his beautiful half-sister Joy, but he would never forget the scene in Harlan's office as long as he lived. It was just retribution for this past summer of perfect and illicit happiness.

Harlan had just finished a long conference with the new head chef, and as Warren saw the tall white smokestack of a hat leave, he walked in and stood tentatively before him, not knowing how or where to begin his confession of treachery.

Harlan looked up and smiled warmly at him. "Just missed something that you could have profited from," he said, as he tinkered with his bundle of keys. He seemed bent on opening a particular drawer that wouldn't comply. Warren could see his uncle was annoyed and thought he should come back at a more auspicious time, if indeed there was one. After he opened the drawer and extracted some papers, Harlan sat erect and alert, as if to inform him that he was now ready to begin the audience. "Can you imagine, he wanted to use canned deviled ham for the canapés at the cocktail hour?" Harlan shook his head. "Matthew would have had a stroke if he were here," he said, still chuckling and shaking his head. Because Warren did not respond, he thought to bring the conversation around to him. "So when does school start this year?"

509

"In early October."

"Well, you've got a few more weeks yet." Harlan glanced at the calendar. It was September the fifth. "I suppose you'll be going home first?"

"Yes, I suppose so." Warren appeared taciturn.

"Well, what's up?" Harlan boomed loudly. Lately he had begun to talk loudly as if he thought that his voice might be fading with age, like film or flowers; that a strong voice would impart the illusion of eternal youth.

"Uncle," he began, then stopped. He would try a different tack.

Harlan looked tense. His antennae were sensitive to impending disaster.

"Well, you know how you always wanted me to go with, that is, have a girl, fall in love. Well, I have," he finished lamely.

"I don't know that I said anything about falling in love exactly, but . . . well, that's good news, I suppose. Who's the lucky girl?"

"It's . . . your daughter . . . Joy . . . We want to get engaged before I go back to college. We'd, er, wait until graduation to . . . get married. I . . . plan to buy her a ring . . . and, of course, we want your approval." He seemed prepared to run on endlessly rather than look up at Harlan's face or hear his reply, but he was stopped by the thundering silence.

The boy's words ran together in his head—like the watercolors he used as a boy at parochial school, the blues and reds running together, turning muddy brown. No, he couldn't grasp what Warren was saying. He seemed to be talking from outside the room. He knew the children were friends, but that was all for the good. He had thrown them together, but how could he have kept them apart? His head was splitting with unanswered

THE PLEASURE DOME

questions and self-accusations. It seemed he had managed his own destruction once again.

"You can't."

"Can't what?"

"Have my permission, or get married."

Warren felt the blood slowly draining from his face.

"Why can't we?"

"You can't because I say so." His voice was a mighty weapon, a thundering cannon.

"I said we'd wait until we graduate. Joy can still go to medical school while we are married and as for that cousin business, well, it's unimportant. Anyway, just look at the royal families. After all, uncle, don't you want to build a dynasty?" he said, hoping to charm him as he'd frequently seen Harlan do in the midst of crisis. But Harlan cut through his little irony.

"Yes, that's just it, look at the royal families." His voice sounded weird. Warren looked up to see if Harlan was smiling, but his face was an ashen gray. All the fine seams and tiny lines ironed in by tropical suns were suddenly visible so that he realized at last that Harlan was old, much older than his father, David.

"*Please*, uncle, this means so much to both of us, please don't force us to continue to sneak around."

"As you've been doing, under my nose," Harlan picked up his narrative in a toneless voice. His eyes had gone glassy and dead. "Well, if you both feel so strongly about it, why isn't Joy here? Why isn't my daughter here too?"

"I thought I would ask for her hand first, in the formal sense." His hopes were mounting again; he thought he could risk a little playfulness. "Sort of smooth the way for her, but she will talk with us too, if you want her to, uncle."

"No!" he shouted, "No, I don't . . ." he trailed off. Then in a strange, quieter voice he said, "And don't call me uncle. I am *not* your uncle. I am your father."

"Well, I *know* you feel fatherly toward me, and believe me, I appreciate your interest," Warren said, deflecting the statement his conscious mind had rejected.

Harlan, who had been pacing behind his desk chair for the last few minutes, came over to him and took hold of his shoulders.

"Are you purposely being obtuse, or are you really that naive, that innocent?" This was not at all the way he planned to tell him, if indeed he ever had to, but he was not thinking or behaving rationally now. He let go of him and sat down heavily at his desk.

"You and Joy are brother and sister . . . your mother and I . . . many years ago . . . we were young . . . she'd made a mistake in marrying your father . . . I mean, David . . . But she was so innocent . . . we *knew* each other before either of us were married—but she was too young." He covered his face with his hands. "Oh, Christ—I don't know—these things just happen. How does anyone know how or why, and when you try to put it all into words it sounds so damned unimportant, so cheap and it wasn't . . . I promise you, son, it wasn't at all like that." His words lay like stones on the ground, heavy, cold and filled with regret.

Warren's silence was immense and threatened to burst the walls. It seemed to Warren that his throat had shrunk and could not accommodate the back of his tongue. It was painful and he almost gagged.

"Father," he said to himself in a whisper as if trying it on. He put out a hand to touch him and as quickly hid the gesture. "I wish I could enjoy this moment. I dreamed of it, God forgive me. A year ago I would have rejoiced . . ."

Harlan was silent, looking down at his desk. Gathered tears fell onto the green blotter and were absorbed.

"No wonder I felt there was so much mystery about my life. A caul around my life, except it hasn't brought me any luck," Warren said. He spoke as if talking to himself or to some unseen presence in the far corner of the room. "So much I never understood. I never knew where the center was."

He rose quickly and went over to Harlan. In a low hoarse whisper that rasped through his throat like an angry wind he said, "What do I care what you did with my mother twenty years ago? Why should I let that ruin my life?"

Harlan wondered if obsession bred obsession, if sins ran in a family. But guilt would be an indulgence now. He thought about the boy, about himself and how passion seemed always to be accompanied by disaster.

He wanted to give him a comforting argument. You are both young, there will be others, but he saw the look in his son's eye and didn't dare.

"If you really love her as much as you say, you still have a chance to prove it. Don't tell her this, just tell her you have thought it over and decided it won't work, you are both too young, and don't want to interfere with her medical studies, you don't want to spoil her life. Or make me the culprit. Say I made you see how selfish it would be."

"You are still protecting yourself," Warren said bitterly. "She won't believe it."

"But she'll accept it. I know her pride, son, it's like her mother's. Her mother's pride would never allow what I was, or let on what she suspected, maybe even what she *knew*, about your mother and me. If you really love her, it's the only way. You'll be at school in the east, she'll be far across the country." He shrugged slightly. It seemed to Warren a brutal gesture.

"And we'll each meet someone else and forget all about it? So your son and daughter are left to cover up your mistakes—your disasters."

"It need not be a disaster, son, if you don't make it one; after all you *are* my son—act like it!"

"I am *not* your son. *My* name is Goldmark, remember? David Goldmark is my father. *He* raised me. No, you have no more sons, you've run out."

Harlan wondered if that too had been handed down. He had always hated his father—now his sons hated him. It occurred to Harlan that sons of great men were usually unhappy—diminished by their fathers' lives. Sons of actors and tycoons often wound up suicides.

He had wanted so much to make it work with this boy. He had missed his whole childhood and wanted to enjoy at least a strong adult relationship with him. Warren had accepted him so hungrily, so wholeheartedly. Harlan was well aware that almost every relationship he touched turned to ruin. Only in business was it the other way around. But money was easier to manipulate than people. And still he wasn't conscious of manipulating lives—just considered it his responsibility, his duty to his loved ones. His position demanded it.

"Warren, believe me when I tell you, this *shall* pass— passion dies, power prevails." He hated using platitudes but he wanted desperately to draw his attention away from the emotions and concentrate on the hard realities.

"That is the credo you have lived by," he said with enormous disgust. "Has it brought you any happiness? Is power enough?" Warren jumped up from his chair and walked quickly from the room, leaving the door ajar.

His children were always hurling his success at him as

if it were some sort of curse. Sinking back into his chair, he tried to answer the question his son had thrown at him. "Is power enough?" At least power had earned him the right to dictate the terms rather than be dictated to, like when he was young and poor. He didn't minimize that. His whole life passed before him like a drowning man. He knew that it was *not* enough, had never been.

Warren ran down the winding stairway that led to the main lobby. On the landing there was a huge blowup photograph of his father. It was two or three times larger than life, like the posters of Latin American dictators whose countries were papered with them. Somehow he hadn't noticed it before. He ran into the washroom on the landing and was grateful to find it empty. He was in no condition to trade small talk with the guests. He locked himself into a cubicle and sat down on the covered seat. He felt paralyzed by a humiliation that coursed through his body in sickening waves. "Oh, my God, my God—my sister, my love." His grief was pure, uncorrupted by hope. He would have died before he let his father see him weeping. Now he covered his face with his hands and the tears broke loose, and coursed down his face, soaking his lap, soaking him through and through so that he felt bathed in salt tears.

He had to admit that it would be better not to involve Joy, better to spare her this bitter humiliation, but it was not easy to bear alone. He felt so terribly alone. He felt sure that Joy would hate him if she knew.

He put his head under the cold water faucet. He had to clear his head—to think ahead, where to go, what to do next. He walked through the lobby, milling with the after-lunch crowd. Everyone looked bloated, satiated to him. The women's lips looked smeary with rouge. They all looked the same. All of them, men and women with tiny alligators on their shirts and their wrinkled Bermuda shorts and their Gucci golf bags, spiky shoes and their eternal tennis rackets, the symbols of their success. He really didn't know what he wanted to do with his life now, or even if he wanted to live it, but he only knew that he had to get away from here, from the sybaritic world of his father.

He left without seeing Joy. He planned to write her a letter telling her only of his decision to break it off. On the plane to New York he decided not to tell his mother. She had suffered enough already. Sacrificed enough of her life for him. But he became obsessed with telling David. He wrote a long confessional letter to David, extracting a promise never to tell his mother that he knew. He felt he could be trusted. No sooner did he finish the letter than he tore it up. He saw the cruelty in exposing David's entire life as a fraud. Warren didn't know what to do, or where his allegiances lay. If only he could talk to someone, to someone who knew, who understood, who cared. He thought of his grandfather, of Alex, and he realized Alex had always known.

It was late when his plane got into Kennedy Airport, about ten-thirty in the evening. He took a taxi to Central Park West. His mother probably hadn't gotten home yet from Israel. He suddenly asked the cab driver to stop at another building on the way up, instead.

Alex opened the door to the apartment himself. If he was surprised, he didn't show it. He wore his pajamas and robe, and loose-fitting scuffs on his feet. Warren didn't bother to ask if he'd awakened him because he knew his

THE PLEASURE DOME

grandfather never slept, or so he always said, but spent a great deal of time in his pajamas just in case he felt an occasional cat nap coming on. He had "to play every hunch," he said. Of course, now it was legitimate. It was night; at night he never slept.

"Come in, what a nice surprise." He took the luggage and slid it agilely down the marble-tiled foyer. "You look awful," he said and made a motion for Warren to follow him into the kitchen. Warren knew his grandfather made sojourns all night into the kitchen, making small, conservative raids on the refrigerator every few hours to while away his insomnia. Usually a little cheese or a matzoh cracker, and a cup of tea—always the cup of tea. Through the haze of his own misery he had to smile . . . No wonder he didn't sleep, he was up drinking tea all night, then going to the toilet. Warren would always remember his grandfather Alex through a mist of steaming tea. "So you'll stay here tonight." It was a command. "Your mother's still away—a few days more maybe. You look terrible."

"You said that, Grandpa."

"I know." He sloshed the tea from his cup into the saucer and drank, sucking it through a sugar cube held in his teeth. It made a dry sound like a straw broom on the grass. This style of drinking tea was recent, a grudging concession to growing old, a reversion to old country ways—what he had seen his father do.

"No wonder you don't sleep, Grandpa, you drink tea all night; the caffeine is bound to keep you awake. . . ."

"And the rest of the time I'm pissing," he said matter-of-factly, smearing a graham cracker with a thin, careful coat of farmer cheese. "Cream cheese never!" he murmured. "That stuff can kill you. So?" He looked questioningly at his grandson. Warren didn't know where to start. Alex came to his rescue. "You just came from our place out at the coast; did you enjoy the summer?"

"Yes, yes, it was a wonderful summer." The way in which he said it caused Alex to look up, to study Warren's face with his canny blue eyes.

"Ah, you fell in love, I suppose. Well, why not? You're at the right age. What kind of a girl?"

Warren looked down at the kitchen table. He made designs with the knife on the smooth surface of the cheese.

"It's Joy—Joy Chase—my *cousin* Joy." He pronounced "cousin" with bitterness.

There was a long silence. Then Alex made an unholy noise slurping tea through the sugar cube. He put the cup and saucer down.

"Well, what happened?"

"I know, that's all," Warren said. "He told me. My *father* told me."

"They should have told you before now, but your mother thought foolishly that it might never come up. She wanted to take the chance."

Warren sat back in his chair and seemed to go suddenly limp—a scarecrow.

Alex continued, "When I heard he had both of you children in Israel last summer, already I didn't like it. But he's a crazy, selfish bastard—always was. He has helped himself to pieces of me and mine all his life. He has impinged on our happiness—a dark cloud over our lives." His eyes, half-closed as he spoke, had become blue slits as if he were straining to see through the mist of the tea into the long distant past. "What are you going to do, son?"

"I don't know, Grandfather. I don't feel I can go on without her."

"You will. You must go on. You must finish college and come into the business with *me*."

"I couldn't work with him—not anymore."

"Nor I," Alex said, brushing cracker crumbs from the table carefully into his hand, "nor I. But we don't have to. I've got a plan. I've got it all worked out." His eyes looked red for lack of sleep and his white hair stood up in wild and recalcitrant tufts. "I will buy back controlling interest from him. Then I will take it private—like before —and you and I will forge ahead—together . . ."

Warren looked up at him strangely. The man was seventy years old. He seemed to take immortality for granted.

"Grandpa," he took his hand, it was cool and dry and the blue veins pushed up like bruised sinews. "I don't know just yet. Why do I have to decide now? I've got a few more years of college ahead of me—I may need to go very far away to study—away from temptation. Maybe back to Israel. I don't know."

"Doesn't matter, son, you'll come back, and claim your rightful place in this empire we have built for you."

"You said *we*; so you don't discount my father then?"

Alex sat back in the wood-slatted old kitchen chair. "Discount? Why should I discount him? Certainly not. True, he had luck all the way—always had luck," he said ruminatively, "But his genius was his ability to *control* his luck. It was his dreams, his crazy dreams that made the legend. He himself is a legend. But he has boxed himself in—or shut himself out—with his enormous lust for life. Now he is alone—he is growing tired of the business, he is considering selling out . . ."

Alex looked up, excited to catch his grandson's reaction and found him sleeping, his soft brown lashes, like folded moths' wings, resting on his cheek. Alex gently woke him and nudged him along, still half-sleeping, to the bedroom, put him to bed, covered him up fully dressed, drew the drapes, and stood looking down at the sleeping boy for a long moment.

Warren sent the letter to Joy at her home in Oyster Bay and hoped that it wouldn't fall into any other hands but hers. He made it rather brief and discouraging. He wanted her to be angry with him. It would make it easier for both of them.

My darling,
 I have returned home to the sobering realities of New York and feel I must share with you my feelings at this time. I have given it a great deal of thought. Trust me there is nothing frivolous in this decision. I believe that what we both feared was the truth. I mean by that, I think we saw the truth all along, acknowledged it and ignored it, hoping it would go away, but I suppose wishing won't make it so. You have an exciting life ahead of you—a chance to take advantage of an opportunity that ten years ago might never have been open to you, and you should be unencumbered by emotional ties in order to give it every chance for success. You seem so certain, so self-contained, regarding your future plans. I really don't know what I want to do with my life just yet.
 I don't want to ruin your life, obstruct its path with my immature and selfish passion. Forgive me, but we are both too young. Cruel as it may sound, I want you to forget all about me, and to think of me only as a loving cousin who would, of course, do anything in the world for you, should you ever need me now or in the future. You will fall in love many

times again, and each time I will grow just a little dimmer in your memory.

                Your loving cousin,
                Warren

He had difficulty forming the words in the last paragraph, they were so painful to write—*You will fall in love many times again* . . .

The letter he could not bring himself to write was to David. He realized that in a way it would be cathartic for him, a wallowing in self-pity, a foolish orgy of confession that might hurt more than it would heal. For the moment he would let it rest—only fools rush in where angels fear to tread.

"So you protected *your* daughter, but not *my* grandson," Alex Eastman said in a tired voice.

"He is also *my* son. One of them *had* to know. It is the man who must take the responsibility in the final analysis."

"How noble you've become, though it's a little late in the game."

Harlan stood by the window, looking out at the ocean. They were presently in Alex's suite at the Broadbeach. The ocean looked menacing and fierce. "What good will it do if Vivian and Joy are torn apart too?"

"And if anything happens to that boy—if this somehow ruins his life . . . I will kill you," Alex said flatly and with no attempt at drama. "I am from the old school. I believe in the Old Testament, an eye for an eye."

"I'm already twice damned—my daughter's life may be ruined and she will doubtless hold me responsible, and my son despises me and probably will not continue beside me in the business, so why create more misery?"

"As a matter of fact," Alex said, dropping his neatly placed little explosive, "Warren is anxious to write to—to David. He plans to tell him everything in a letter."

"My God, why?" Harlan turned now to face Alex. "What is this terrible need to confess among Jews? I thought that was born of Catholic training."

"Nonsense," Alex snapped. "people are people everywhere—desperate people do not fit into molds. Extreme emotions level reason. You should at least understand that. But he seems to feel he owes it to David. David has been a good father."

"I don't happen to think so . . ."

"Brought him up believing him to be his own son," Alex continued, ignoring Harlan's outbreak, "nurtured him, and he feels he repaid him by total rejection when he found out who and what he was. And then chose you over him. Now Warren has learned that he is in no position to censor anyone else, to pass judgment on another man's secret, he himself is a secret. It would be a letter of apology."

"Christ, to take away David's last illusion of himself as a man—as a father, it is cruel," Harlan said, running his fingers through his hair, his green eyes dark with anger.

"No, David will understand more now—berate himself less. It is an immensely kind and generous gesture on the boy's part . . . to absolve David of guilt."

"Warren isn't old enough to play God—and besides, the role doesn't suit him—and what good does that do for his mother, for Laina?"

"My daughter, thank God, is well out of this madness now. It doesn't matter anymore." Alex removed his jacket and placed it carefully over the back of a chair. He was perspiring profusely. "I have a proposition for you, a chance for you to sweeten your nightmares, one that might even allow you to live compatibly with yourself in your old age . . . I don't want to be associated with you any longer, I'm sure it's mutual. . . . I will match the offer from Snow and buy *you* out."

Harlan looked amazed. "But that would cost you a fortune! Why would you do it? And at your age? When you could coast into a luxurious retirement. You must be losing your marbles, after all." It's senility, he thought to himself—madness.

"That's my business. As long as I match their offer, I don't have to disclose my reasons."

Alex was obsessed with the desire to be free of Harlan Chase once and for all. But he had no wish to relinquish the company. The company kept him from stagnation, from sitting around and thinking about death. The companies represented the sum total of his life's work, and he was too old to begin again. And at the back of everything was his desire to preserve the hotels intact for his grandson. There was a long silence.

"Emotional blackmail," Harlan said, pretending to laugh.

"Yes, this time it's my turn."

"I will think about it," Harlan said.

CHAPTER 69

The party aboard the yacht promised to be a gala one. All of the Pleasure Dome's board of directors were invited, and most of the other close advisors and principals of the various hotels and theaters. C.P. Snow, his wife and a few of his associates were also present. Harlan had considered his guest list carefully for this night.

Faye was looking forward to it, but Alex had declined. It was only after Harlan told him that Snow, his rival for the stock, would be there, and promised to announce his decision on this night that Alex reconsidered. He was in no mood to celebrate, certainly not at the behest of Harlan Chase.

It was five-thirty, and in the soft evening air a singular scarlet ribbon of sunset hung by a slender thread. The ship was once again alive with a thousand colored lights. Lanterns swayed and danced in the late September night. Music from the orchestra on deck could be heard for miles around, and the cars pulling up to the dock made a constant clatter of crunching wheels and slamming doors. The air was punctuated with the sounds of women's skittish laughter and high heels clicking down the slatted runway to the yacht.

Faye remarked to Matthew that it was a little like the old days—when a ship was the *only* civilized place to hold a gala.

Harlan and Vivian, receiving on deck, looked youthful

and slender, although he was leaning heavily on his cane—the old warrior. Living here, as they did, close to the water, was not very good for the pain in his leg. He really felt much better in the desert dryness of California. The doctor advised him that a daily swim would improve the condition. He was to work up to at least fifty laps a day. The implication that it might be a slow process disquieted him. It had seemed to him that all at once he was deprived of his youth, his athletic prowess, even his impetuousness. All the things he had aspired to through the years seemed to be slipping away—the money itself had little magic.

Vivian wore a lovely simple white crepe Halston gown, dramatic against her deep summer tan. On her ears a set of matched sapphires glittered in their circlet of diamonds, and she wore a ring to match, a twenty-fifth anniversary gift from her husband. She greeted everyone warmly as if they were old friends, which most were not. In fact there were many faces she had never seen. Beautiful young women with dresses that exposed much of their breasts, handsome men in dinner jackets and black tie, here and there an occasional rebel in a suit with an open shirt carefully unbuttoned at the throat to allow for a glimpse of golden talismans nestling amidst the overgrown lawns. There were old men, young men, and some family, of course, but none of her children. Not even her nephew, her husband's favorite, Warren Goldmark. Vivian wondered why Joy hadn't come. She would have loved a party like this but instead had insisted on going back to college early, "to prepare her curriculum," she had said. Vivian told herself that Joy must have fallen in love, someone she had met at school, no doubt. That explained her urgency to get back there—but why the secret? She must remember to discuss this with Harlan.

In the main salon waiters passed endless trays of inventive hors d'oeuvres catered by the Broadbeach Club and elaborated on by Vivian. Later on there would be a sail out to the hotel. They would watch the hotel's twinkling lights from their vantage point offshore, perhaps let off some guests, take on some others from the club, those whom Harlan considered prominent.

Harlan was drinking steadily. Vivian was apprehensive. She knew his mood had been heavy for days. She felt certain it had to do with the children. He had never really gotten over Steven, *or* Gerald for that matter. He had waited restlessly for Steven's body to be returned and when it finally arrived, months later, he would not look at it. He would not remember it "mangled," he had said.

It was almost eight o'clock and still no one made a move to go to dinner. The guests didn't seem much inclined to food, just wanted to keep drinking and dancing. But the buffet was already set up in the main salon below. A handful of the older people drifted down to dinner, Alex and Matthew among them. Harlan moved with some discomfort from group to group, charming, clowning, doing his Irish jokes in brogue. He danced with a beautiful young woman holding her ridiculously close and letting his lips brush against her ear—but soon had to sit down because of the pain in his leg.

As the evening wore on, the breeze blew in scents of the city, mingled accents of sea and traffic oil. Everyone moved downstairs for the dinner at the buffet tables. Vivian chatted gaily with C.P. Snow and his wife, the third Mrs. Snow. She was a small chubby woman whose pinkish, ponderous arms were laden with diamonds.

The crowd had already begun to thin out when Harlan announced they would sail to the Broadbeach Club. It had been a balmy night, but now the air grew colder with the lateness of the hour and the approach of open sea. After dinner Snow sat back with a giant cigar and said, "How much longer are you gonna keep us in suspense, Chase? Why don't you let us know your decision?" He laughed loudly as if it was all just a friendly joke, but it was clear he was enjoying the rather childish game. Harlan felt Alex's piercing blue eyes on him from somewhere across the room. Matthew had gone down to one of the staterooms to see about Faye, who had passed out. Harlan had decided to let Alex buy him out—let Alex have it all—for whatever reasons, devious or otherwise, the old man had.

But Harlan only smiled and said, "Why can't you boys just relax and have a good time?" He was prolonging the suspense and enjoying it. "C'mon, let's all go up on deck." Mrs. Snow demurred. It was too cold, she said, her petulant doll-like face screwed up in distaste. Snow followed him up to the deck. They had dropped anchor a few miles offshore and faced the beautiful old Venetian hotel, her beckoning lights winking at them in all her faded glory, like a still saucy old whore. Harlan was clowning and cavorting with the remaining guests. He was taking bets as to his swimming time being "not much different than it was thirty years ago." Clyde Bostwick, who was by now quite drunk, goaded him on.

"It's impossible, what with your leg and all."

"It would be more impossible without it."

Everyone laughed. He began unbuttoning his collar, threw his small black tie overboard. It bobbed about comically on the water's rumpled surface, until the current carried it away. He unfastened his golden cuff links, tiny roulette wheels, and fed them to the strangely fretful waters. He tore off his shirt and strutted around in an untidy circle, punching his stomach, inviting others to do the same. "Here, feel this, a rock, I tell you, a goddamned rock." Clyde Bostwick punched dully where he was told. The air was cold now. He removed his trousers and stood in his powder-blue jockey shorts. He had taken to wearing the St. Christopher medal lately. Now he stood there, wavering a moment in his underwear and the large silver medal of his boyhood, an aging Adonis of the deep. One of the women turned suddenly scornful and prepared to disembark—the other remaining guests followed, filing into the dinghies to be taken ashore—rats deserting a sinking ship. Then Harlan spied Alex and Matthew, emerging from below deck, sauntering slowly toward the railing, just talking congenially and smoking their panatelas.

"Just time me," he cried over the confusion. "Just time me," and as if it were a last desperate gesture to recapture his waning audience, slipped overboard into the sea. Clyde saw him go, but he soon staggered to a deck chair where he passed out cold. "Just time me." The unpretentious words echoed in the keen primeval silence of the night.

He swam with his sure beautiful stroke, farther and farther out, until he lost sight of the ship. Swimming, swimming, against the tide, as he had done all his life, pressing his prodigious luck. His powerful arms and legs cut cleanly through the water. Slicing it, stroking it, exultant. His head felt suddenly clear and he felt freer than he had in years and happier too. He wanted only to keep moving, to be alone with the sea.

He had no idea how long he had been swimming or exactly where he was in relation to the ship. But his arms began to feel heavy and he had a sudden murderous pain in his leg. He tried to move it but the muscle seemed locked. He struggled to move onto his back, to float with one leg extended. The sky was devoid of stars, but there were clouds, cramped and cumulus as if in spasm. The clouds were weirdly electrified by shafts of searing-cold white moonlight, recalling that night with Laina, in some other life. Men do not as easily forget old loves as do women, he thought.

He suddenly shouted into the night—once, twice, again. His cries were faint, muted by pain and the wind. He thought how Vivian would worry. Ah, *women*. All the margins of his life had been set by women, first his mother, then the nuns, his sisters, his sweethearts, his wife, even his daughter . . . counseling, disapproving.

His leg pained him powerfully and his body felt cold all over—with an agonizing effort, he turned on his stomach. He tried using his arms slowly to conserve energy. And then the tide changed and the water began to tug and pull him swiftly out. He had to redouble his efforts to keep from being sucked under and his stomach was cramping from the cold or from the unusual exertion—he didn't know which. He found himself all at once at war with the sea. The sea that had always been his ally had now become a mighty adversary. It didn't seem to matter much. He had lived the best part of his life, and what was left seemed to be sliding slowly downhill, giving way beneath him like the heavy undertow.

He lay on his side for a moment, sidestroked the water with eager clutching gestures, but his arms gave out. He cried out again for help. He felt no pain now, but he could not move any of his limbs.

He had the feeling that, as always, it was time that was his real enemy. He was racing against time, not the sea. The words from an e. e. cummings poem he admired spoke to him clearly, as if by an unseen narrator. He thought the voice he heard might be his own. It seemed to him that he shouted the words.

> Eater of all things lovely—
> Time.
> upon whose watering lips
> the world poises a moment
> futile proud, a costly morsel
> of sweet tears, gesticulates
> and disappears.

On the deck Alex and Matthew stood at the railing, talking quietly. By now the deck was deserted. For a split second Alex's wiry old body tensed, his whole nervous frame on guard.

"Did you hear something?" Matthew said, "Christ, I thought . . ." his voice trailed off. Alex gave him a long level look. For a moment the two men seemed locked in indecision.

"I didn't hear a thing," Alex said, "Did you?"

Matthew kept his eyes glued to Alex's as if hypnotized. "No, no, nothing," he whispered.

The rumpled surface of the sea had turned suddenly dun-colored, with a calm that was more terrible than turbulence.

It had probably seemed like a lifetime to him out there in the vast blackness, but it hadn't been more than a scant quarter of an hour at most. It was a reversal of the order of things—the manner in which life itself passes by. A fragmented dream, for some glorious, for others empty, but for all as if dreamed in a single night.

CHAPTER 70

The funeral could not take place until almost a week after the drowning. The body of Harlan Chase did not wash up on the shore of the Broadbeach Hotel until a few days later. Quite fittingly, it did not wash up on Main Beach, the site of the most expensive accommodations, but on No Man's Land, that part of the property at its end, where the newer and generally less prestigious members were put out to pasture. Two of the young lifeguards, arriving at their posts at seven-thirty in the morning, found it there and didn't even know who it was. They had never met the chairman of the board, the chief executive officer of Pleasure Domes. But if they had not been new on the job, they would have recognized him. He often came down to the beach to check on the lifeguards, to touch old bases, and his was not a face one easily forgot.

The family had never gotten around to discussions about burials and plots. Harlan always said they were young, and then again who cared what happened afterwards. It was now that counted. It was the here and now that was real and palpable—the hereafter was only a hunch. Another Catholic promise, one he doubted they could keep. So Vivian was not surprised when Bostwick read to her privately the part in his will about cremation. "My only hesitation in all this," it said, "is that I will not be company for my dear wife Vivian, who I imagine will have more conservative views on this dreary subject.

Nevertheless, I must be true to myself in my fashion—so please scatter my ashes somewhere over the ocean, from whence I came, in a certain sense. Dust, thou art to dust returnest . . . ?"

Within that week *Time* magazine carried a devastatingly handsome picture of him on its cover, the way he would have liked to be remembered. The article inside was headed "The Pleasure World of the Late Harlan Chase." And *Forbes* magazine featured an article on "Harlan Chase and the Entertainment Conglomerate." He had enjoyed a great deal of publicity in his life, but nothing quite that impressive. It rankled his family that these tributes came too late. Vivian had always considered him undervalued.

It was a gray-misted, threatening sort of day, that gave itself up to recurrent bouts of warm October rain. Outside the white porticoed mansion press jostled, cameramen snapped photos of anyone who came or went, but they were strictly forbidden entry. Vivian was determined to keep this a family affair.

It had taken a great force of will for Warren to come here today, to face Joy after the letter he had written, after everything, but Vivian had specifically invited him and he wanted to be somewhere near him, somehow still a part of his life and death. He had belonged to him for such a little while. Laina drove Warren to the house at Oyster Bay, but she only dropped him off.

"I'm not going in . . . I don't belong there, I never did. It's for the immediate family," she said.

"Then I don't belong here either."

"He loved you, Warren. You belong there."

"He loved you too, Mother." For a moment their eyes met and held and then Laina leaned forward and closed the door.

THE PLEASURE DOME

"I'll see you at home later, you can always ride back with Alex." She pulled away uncertain of just where she would go, or what she would do. She sensed that Warren knew everything now. But she also knew instinctively that there was something elemental in all this that he wasn't telling. Perhaps she really didn't want to know.

Lately, even before his death—she had been dreaming of the old house at the beach, where Seth and she had been so happy before the war—before she grew up that summer. She had no set destination in her conscious mind, but she drove like someone possessed. The rain was coming down in silver-slanted sheets. She drove the car recklessly along the unprotected sandy cliffs high above the ocean, remembering her father's admonition to Seth during that summer—"drive carefully, it's dangerous terrain." A summer later it would not matter. When she finally arrived in Broadbeach, she drove with a curious absorption, up and down streets as familiar to her today as if it had only been yesterday, instead of twenty years ago.

She found herself on the street that ran alongside of the old hotel, lately closed down for the winter. Resort hotels, those repositories of secret dreams. Strange, she thought, but people would do things at hotels that they would never dream of doing anywhere else. A hotel changed people, exerted its influence, sprung into a seasonal life of its own, like certain plants or trees—only some hundred miles away from the city—but a million miles away from home.

She turned left at the hotel and drove about a block inland from the ocean. She turned her car into Old Vine Road and drove past houses that looked smaller and less impressive than she remembered. Then she saw it, looming majestically at the end of the street, large and handsome and infinitely desirable. She didn't know what she would say, it didn't matter, all that mattered now was to get inside that house once again. And she didn't even know why. She parked her car carelessly and ran out into the wet street. She stood in the pouring rain and rang the bell. It chimed a lovely off-key melody. She rang and rang, but nobody came. It seemed to her now that only the old blue-painted door stood between her and her past—where somehow the answer lay. The frustration was bitter. She had not wept once since she heard the news of his death, now she leaned against the door and sobbed, deep, painful wracking sobs, her tears mingling with the warm rain.

Suddenly the door was opened and a woman peered out through the chain latch—something they didn't have when the house belonged to them—no need. Laina told her hurriedly put-together story about having to use the phone, her car had stalled due to the weather. The woman looked hesitant; Laina stood hatless and hopeful, the rain soaking through her hair.

The woman finally slid the chain and stood back uncertainly to let her enter. Laina began immediately walking to the dining room, that idiosyncratic place where Alex always kept the telephone. The woman looked frightened. She peered at her as if she might be mad—she had let a crazy woman into the house . . .

"The telephone is in the kitchen," she said in an astonished voice. Laina looked around the kitchen lovingly, seeing Ginger there talking into the sink with her back to her, while she sat polishing her nails with expensive fifty-cent Chen Yu polish from Woolworth's. The soft aqua color of the walls was changed. Now busy flowers danced hand in hand with vegetables on a practical laminated wallpaper. She had an overpowering urge to go upstairs, but the woman was watching her closely, suspiciously. She realized she'd have to tell her the truth.

"I chose this house to telephone because I used to live here a very long time ago—when I was a girl." The woman relaxed a little, sensing at least a social equality, some small common bond with the intruder.

"Oh? When was that?" she said. She was pasty-looking and wore rollers in her hair. There was something tentative and insubstantial about her appearance.

"A very long time ago. After the beginning of the war."

"What war?" The woman looked bewildered. She was perhaps ten years younger than Laina. Laina forgot that younger people acknowledged other wars since then.

"1942," she said.

"Oh." The woman seemed relieved. "We bought it about seven years ago from Mr. Klausman." Laina didn't know who Mr. Klausman was but saw the need to reassure the woman so that she could go upstairs.

"Yes, yes, that's who we sold it to . . ."

"Would you care to see the upstairs?"

"Oh, please." As if in an old familiar dream, she sailed up the shadowed stairway propelled by an inner force. When she got upstairs she went directly to her bedroom, the only room at the right of the stairs. The glass tiles on the alcove partition still remained. Her father's decorator had installed them, the craze was art deco then—she hoped the woman wouldn't stand over her. Funny, how old houses urged you to wander through rooms papered with lost causes and furnished with outdated hopes. Laina went to the window. The fields of wild reeds and rushes had vanished and in their place there were two or three small ranch-style houses with clotheslines, flapping in the rain. Gone, too, their basketball and tennis courts—trod beneath the feet of commerce—progress could be painful.

"On a day like this I'm afraid there's nothing to see— you can't even see the ocean," the woman said. Laina looked at the beds, two stiff single beds divided by a small Hepplewhite table, a reproduction. But she saw there instead her old large double bed with its blue-and-lavender provincial print spread, and was back to that morning, waking up hot with tears and shame, choking on her own spent chances.

She thanked the woman and walked quickly down the stairs and out to her car. She was ashamed of her little charade and pretended to be trying to change the engine. She looked up and saw the woman staring curiously down at her. She started the car and pulled away quickly, creating a mighty roar on the quiet residential street. She felt better suddenly. She had no regrets, just a rich store of memory and experience that would, she hoped, help her to accept middle age with grace. She might have driven all the way to Israel if it were possible.

Vivian had enlisted the services of Rabbi Meyer for the ceremony. She had asked Father McCarthy, too, but he would not come. The rabbi's presence was mostly for her own comfort. She would have liked Father McCarthy to be there to mollify Harlan's mother and sister, and to quiet her own nagging doubts about last rites; in spite of her husband's specific request. It was the medal that bothered her. He had taken to wearing that medal again. Vivian so much wanted to do the right thing . . . She *so* much wanted him back. . . . She had counted on at least another twenty-five years together—given their parents' record of longevity. She had written to Gerald rather than telephoning. She did not want him to fly in for the funeral and add insult to injury by risking being caught and sent to jail for draft evasion. That would not have pleased his father. So Gerald would not be there, but, of course, she had her daughter Joy—although she seemed only a partial presence. Marge Chase had come, of course, and Harlan's sisters and their husbands. Alex and Matthew were there too.

The little cortege proceeded down to the dock. Vivian kept the small urn beside her all afternoon, touching it occasionally, as if for reassurance, letting her fingers slide over its cool smooth surface deftly as a sculptor. When Joy demanded to know what it was, Vivian explained reluctantly.

"I've kept some of the ashes for Steven—to bury in the plot next to Steven, so he won't be alone for so long. I think your father would forgive that small modification."

"Will that be all right, Mother? I mean, to divide up father's ashes that way? It won't cause his spirit to become, well, schizophrenic somehow, will it?" Joy asked in a strange voice.

"It's quite all right," Vivian replied firmly, but she looked perplexed. In fact she had looked that way for most of the time since that moment she came up on deck a week ago and asked where her husband was—nobody knew exactly. Someone had thought he might have gone below to sleep it off. Clyde Bostwick couldn't seem to remember much.

"Must have blacked out," he said over and over again, shaking his head apologetically. In fact the only satisfaction Vivian had been able to get at all was from Alex and Matthew, who said that the last they saw of Harlan was when they caught a glimpse of him "jumping off the deck into the water for a midnight swim." They couldn't even be certain that he hadn't come up on the other side and gone down to the cabin to change, or to sleep—anything.

"But he was such a strong swimmer," was Vivian's only comment, said in a half-whisper as if to herself, a comment that carried with it astonishment and the faint singed odor of reproof.

After the rabbi said a few words, Vivian scattered the ashes, then looked stricken by the sudden emptiness of her hand, and turning both palms out in a pitiful gesture, indicated to the family that a major chapter in their lives was irrevocably closed.

Warren kept his eyes riveted to a clutter of starlings that lined a dipping branch and looked ready to slide off in tandem, like a brace of roasted birds about to be released from the spit. They seemed unruffled, secure in their gift of flight. Warren envied their freedom. He was concentrating on the birds so that he wouldn't stare at her, at Joy. He wondered if people thought they resembled each other. He did not think so. He stared at her out of the corner of his eye, hoping to catch some feature, some expression he could recognize as his own. Something to carry with him for a lifetime, a keepsake, so that whenever he looked in the mirror he could see something of her there. This was the first time he had seen her since he left California three weeks ago, and since he sent the letter. She hardly looked at him. Her eyes were impossible to read, impenetrable and hooded with sorrow. He wondered if she would speak to him.

He walked over to where she stood. "It was a terrible accident, a terrible shock for you, for all of you." He moved his hands in a wooden gesture to include her mother, who had drifted away. He wanted to be sure not to include himself in the family circle. When she turned to face him, it was a dull look, unseeing.

"I can't imagine a life without my father in it. It will be very empty. He was at the heart of everything." She sounded so wounded that a shameful stab of jealousy shot through him. Now he was glad he had spared Joy the terrible knowledge. She might have somehow held herself responsible for his death, just as *he* did now. His emotions were terribly tangled in that awful moment. He struggled against his resentment of her singularly possessive use of "my father." Her eyes dismissed him quickly. Warren walked across the room and sat down heavily next to Alex.

"They are going to read the will now," Alex said, "then I will take you home."

Irv Maslow read the usual minor bequests first. Then the ones to Harlan's mother and sister Janine, which he said he fully expected would be turned over immediately to the Catholic church, but it was theirs to do with what they liked. The homes and the bulk of the estate, of course, would go to "my beloved wife, Vivian. The thirty percent of the stock I own in Pleasure Domes, Inc. to be evenly divided between my wife, my daughter, Joy, my son, Gerald, and my great-nephew Warren Goldmark, Matthew's grandson. Perhaps in this way I can at last render unto Caesar what is Caesar's." Harlan's sardonic words sounded awkward in Maslow's cultivated Boston cadence. "And am now returning it many times enriched to his grandson, who I hope will one day help us to carry on the name in its full tradition."

There was a powerful silence after this, and Warren, who was sitting flanked by his two grandfathers, saw a perfectly pure crystalline tear stand at attention for a moment on Matthew's cheek before sliding down phlegmatically into his lap. Alex looked straight ahead. As they walked out, Matthew took Warren's hand. "Warren, you must do what is best for you, always remember that." His hand lingered briefly, lovingly, on the boy's arm, and then he walked briskly from the room. It was a small silent exodus.

In the driveway Warren walked slowly toward the parked cars. Alex caught up with him. "You'll be leaving any day now for school, I suppose, for Cornell," his grandfather said, putting words in his mouth.

"I don't know."

"What do you mean?"

"I don't know if I'm going back there—to Cornell—to the Hotel School."

Alex looked perplexed. Then a smile suffused his face. "Yes, yes, you're right, you've had enough schooling. The school of hard knocks—experience—that's the best business training in the world. You can go right into the business...." The gravel sounded like tiny firecrackers beneath their feet. "I am president now, I will see that you are immediately put into a position of authority."

"Grandfather," Warren said quietly, but Alex didn't hear.

"You won't have to claw your way up the ladder slowly, as I did, step by agonizing step—against the tide of the thirties... a terrible depression—"

"Grandfather." He was shouting now. "That's just the point. At least you had the satisfaction of doing it yourself—I want some of that too."

"But... but I thought you were so excited about this business..."

Warren didn't reply immediately. There was really no right way to say this to Alex. "That was different—I was excited about *him*, about working with *him*, it was an excuse to be with *him*—with my father." The words *my father* were both shameful and luxurious on his tongue. "Now it doesn't seem to matter anymore."

Alex looked at his grandson with eyes that were startled and wild. "I don't think you understand. I'm seventy years old. When I die you will inherit all my shares. I am the next largest stockholder after your father. My shares together with yours—why, you could be chairman of the board of one of the world's most successful young companies before you are even twenty-five."

A faint smile played around the corners of the young man's mouth. "I don't want to be a tycoon, Grandpa, just because my father was one. Chairman of the board is not an inherited title like duke or earl."

"Where will you go? What will you do?" Alex asked tremulously.

The urge to go back to Israel was suddenly compelling. There he could live and work, a Jew among Jews. "I think I will return to Israel. Finish my education there. I started in by digging in Jerusalem, now perhaps I will continue it, but this time for a very different treasure—I would like to study archeology there."

"You would renounce everything your father and I have worked for through all these years, for a handful of dust? Escape to another world—and leave me holding all that responsibility at my age?" Alex was shouting now.

"It's what you've always wanted, Grandpa—all along that's what mattered the most to you."

Alex was silenced. They had come to where the car was parked. "But Seth," he said, "I always thought that you and I . . ." He was all of a sudden a lonely, tired, disoriented old man. Warren had the grace to ignore it.

"Look, I can't stay around here and see *her* at the

hotels from time to time, coming around with her boyfriends. She'll get married to one of them one day—a young urologist, or some other damn specialist and I'll end up catering the wedding. No, Grandpa. It's best that I go away for now—and besides, I'd like to get to know my mother better. I'm not sure that I even know her at all."

"Well, I suppose your mother *would* like that, and she has more of a claim on you certainly than either your father or I . . ." Alex spoke slowly, as if deliberating.

Warren wondered why so many people had claims on him, staked him out like a find of gold. But his mother was different. She had never placed any demands on him, and he owed her so much.

"Well, kid," Alex said, shaking his head slowly. "Life is never exactly the way we dream it, but sometimes left to its own devices, it surpasses even our wildest dreams, like your father's life, kid—like him."

His father had borrowed the name Pleasure Dome from a poet's wildest dream about an ancient Chinese emperor. Warren wondered how it might have ended if the poet had lived to finish it.

HISTORICAL ROMANCE IN THE MAKING!

SAVAGE ECSTASY (824, $3.50)
by Janelle Taylor
It was like lightning striking, the first time the Indian brave Gray Eagle looked into the eyes of the beautiful young settler Alisha. And from the moment he saw her, he knew that he must possess her—and make her his slave!

DEFIANT ECSTASY (931, $3.50)
by Janelle Taylor
When Gray Eagle returned to Fort Pierre's gates with his hundred warriors behind him, Alisha's heart skipped a beat: would Gray Eagle destroy her—or make his destiny her own?

FORBIDDEN ECSTASY (1014, $3.50)
by Janelle Taylor
Gray Eagle had promised Alisha his heart forever—nothing could keep him from her. But when Alisha woke to find her red-skinned lover gone, she felt abandoned and alone. Lost between two worlds, desperate and fearful of betrayal, Alisha hungered for the return of her FORBIDDEN ECSTASY.

RAPTURE'S BOUNTY (1002, $3.50)
by Wanda Owen
It was a rapturous dream come true: two lovers sailing alone in the endless sea. But the peaks of passion sink to the depths of despair when Elise is kidnapped by a ruthless pirate who forces her to succumb—to his every need!

PORTRAIT OF DESIRE (1003, $3.50)
by Cassie Edwards
As Nicholas's brush stroked the lines of Jennifer's full, sensuous mouth and the curves of her soft, feminine shape, he came to feel that he was touching every part of her that he painted. Soon, lips sought lips, heart sought heart, and they came together in a wild storm of passion. . . .

Available wherever paperbacks are sold, or order direct from the Publisher. Send cover price plus 50¢ per copy for mailing and handling to Zebra Books, 475 Park Avenue South, New York, N.Y. 10016. DO NOT SEND CASH.

THE BEST IN HISTORICAL ROMANCE
by Sylvie F. Sommerfield

SAVAGE RAPTURE (1085, $3.50)
Beautiful Snow Blossom waited years for the return of Cade, the handsome halfbreed who had made her a prisoner of his passion. And when Cade finally rides back into the Cheyenne camp, she vows to make him a captive of her heart!

REBEL PRIDE (1084, $3.25)
The Jemmisons and the Forresters were happy to wed their children—and by doing so, unite their plantations. But Holly Jemmison's heart cries out for the roguish Adam Gilcrest. She dare not defy her family; does she dare defy her heart?

TAMARA'S ECSTASY (998, $3.50)
Tamara knew it was foolish to give her heart to a sailor. But she was a victim of her own desire. Lost in a sea of passion, she ached for his magic touch—and would do anything for it!

DEANNA'S DESIRE (906, $3.50)
Amidst the storm of the American Revolution, Matt and Deanna meet—and fall in love. And bound by passion, they risk everything to keep that love alive!

ERIN'S ECSTASY (861, $2.50)
Englishman Gregg Cannon rescues Erin from lecherous Charles Duggan—and at once realizes he must wed and protect this beautiful child-woman. But when a dangerous voyage calls Gregg away, their love must be put to the test . . .

TAZIA'S TORMENT (750, $2.75)
When tempestuous Fantasia de Montega danced, men were hypnotized. And this was part of her secret revenge—until cruel fate tricked her into loving the man she'd vowed to kill!

RAPTURE'S ANGEL (750, $2.75)
When Angelique boarded the *Wayfarer*, she felt like a frightened child. Then Devon—with his captivating touch—reminded her that she was a woman, with a heart that longed to be won!

Available wherever paperbacks are sold, or order direct from the Publisher. Send cover price plus 50¢ per copy for mailing and handling to Zebra Books, 475 Park Avenue South, New York, N.Y. 10016. DO NOT SEND CASH.